FEAR
THE
SURVIVORS

Volume 2 of The Fear Saga

by Stephen Moss

Contents

Prologue

A man lies in a steel cell. The cell rocks gently back and forth, as though rolling on a slow, ponderous wave. The walls are inches thick. There are no windows. A small slit in the door passes fetid food and the occasional shout of abuse.

The man, like the floor around him, is covered in human feces and urine. He is chained.

There is a loud clank and the door swings open revealing a doctor who looks torn. He cannot decide between his commitment to his oaths and his hatred for the man on the floor in front of him. His emotional conflict is compounded by the vile stench emanating from the cell.

He knows he cannot sympathize with the prisoner. But nor can he let him die. Another jailor to the doctor's side opens the valve on a hose and icy sea water blasts the chained man, sending him reeling across the floor, his chains clanking as he slides into the far wall on a slick of human waste.

After a minute or so, a hundred gallons of briny baptism has returned some semblance of humanity to the small, dank space, the big drain in the corner having sucked down the disgusting remnants of the previous night's abuse.

The doctor steps in and carefully approaches the prone man. As the doctor's rubber-gloved hand touches the man's shoulder, the prisoner gently sits up. He does not say anything. His movements are careful, slow and unthreatening. He seems meek and harmless. He does not meet the doctor's eyes.

The doctor had been among the many who had been victim to the man's crime. They all had. The whole crew of the HMS *Dauntless*. They had gone to dinner oblivious and happy but then they had all slowly felt the irresistible drowsiness pulling at them. They had fallen where they sat or stood. Every man and woman aboard the powerful destroyer. All of them but one. The man who had drugged them.

When they had awoken, they had found their ship adrift. Confusion and panic had wracked the crew as they had searched their ship for signs of what had happened. Then they had discovered the changes to the firing controls. The ship's massive salvo of long-range missiles had all been launched. They did not know why. They could not know why. A billion dollars of the most advanced and lethal weaponry on Earth had been fired seemingly into space.

It had made no sense and their attempts to get answers out of the man responsible had fallen on deaf ears. No one had been able to get more than a single sentence out of him.

"It will all be explained in time."

That had been yesterday and their hot indignant fury had cooled a little overnight. There may even be some remorse at the way they had treated him, even some inkling as to the depth of their crime against him. But without confirmation of the greater conspiracy's success, the man in chains had been left with little recourse but silence. To tell these people if he had failed would only bring death down upon them.

But the doctor does not know this as he comes to check the man's vitals and feed him some vitamin supplements. Astonishingly, he seems healthy and fit. His blood pressure is good and his eyes alert, despite the beatings.

He surveys the prisoner. Looking for open wounds or signs of infection, but he is still astonishingly free of actual cuts. His bruising looks severe, and the doctor assumes his swollen nose is broken but there is nothing fatal here. Except those night-black pupils.

As the doctor grabs at the man's face to check him over, he looks into those pitch-black eyes and sees the bottomless well of hurt that this man has suffered. Not at the boots and the fists of his captors, but at their words.

"Why, John?" says the doctor once more, unceasingly surprised every time he recognizes that man he had once called a friend.

He does not expect a reply. He is surprised to hear the quick step of several brisk feet behind him. He turns to see Captain Bhade's small but imposing frame appear suddenly in the doorway. The naval doctor stands and goes to salute but something in the captain's face throws him. Emotions the doctor is not used to seeing on the stern senior officer's face. Uncertainty. Doubt. And as the captain looks down at the prisoner, something else: remorse.

Another person is trying to push past the captain and the doctor is surprised when the normally dictatorial Captain Bhade steps meekly aside and utters, "Here he is, sir."

Vice Admiral Terence Cochrane steps into the doorway and frowns in dismay. The doctor salutes again, stammering for something to say, a feeling of concern filling him at the arrival of this incredibly senior officer.

But the admiral is uninterested in what the doctor has to say and he merely turns to someone outside the cell that the doctor cannot see and says, "Dr. Danielson, it isn't pretty, but Captain Bhade assures me that our friend here is quite healthy. A fact that I am sure he knows his career depends on."

The doctor glances at the captain who inhales sharply at the stern words, but then the captain catches the doctor's eyes and his authority returns in a flash, reminding the doctor of whom *he* should be afraid.

The other man steps past the senior officers and into the cell. He is a civilian, dressed casually. He has an air of cool confidence about him. Confidence born of knowing more than anyone else. The civilian looks down at the chained man on the floor and speaks without the slightest hint of fear or concern for the prisoner's condition. His American accent stands in stark contrast to the British naval officers around him.

"Well, John, what do you say? Ready to go?"

The room pauses, the stranger's calm attitude stunning them. The doctor is about to warn them that the prisoner is in no condition to be moved when he hears a rustling behind him, and turns to the sudden apparition of the bedraggled prisoner rising smoothly to his feet.

The doctor steps back as the chains that had previously bound the traitor fall away from his wrists and ankles. The doctor had looked them over only a moment ago. They had been secure. But they fall to the floor like crumbs from a quickly forgotten meal.

The prisoner observes the look of confusion on the doctor's face and finally breaks his long silence with a sympathetic smile, "Please, Doctor, don't worry. All is not as it seems."

But then his eyes turn to the American, and his smile changes to one of genuine affection, "As for you. I can't say I like how long it took you to get here, but the fact that you have can only mean we did it."

The words hang like a question, and the American nods, smiling broadly, "We did, John, we did."

Part 1

Chapter 1: The Fallen

The dust and fine pebbles of an ancient plain crunched loudly under the thud of bare feet.

Lord Mantil ran in long, powerful strides up the side of a low ridge to gain a better vantage, wearing a shawl wrapped around his person, a shawl stolen from a shepherd's home in the first light of dawn.

Flying wild in the seat of an old but agile Pakistani F-16, Lord Mantil had done all he could to protect the pilots of the rogue B-2 bomber. They had been risking their lives to try and stop the coming plague, and even if Lord Mantil hadn't wanted to try and keep them safe just because of their bravery, he would have fought anyway, because the longer they were alive the more innocents they could save.

As dust whipped around his legs in eddies, Lord Mantil ran onward toward the peak of the ridge, his shawl cracking like a flag about him. As he ran, he considered those he had killed since he had arrived on Earth, first in the service of his alien crown, and then, after his fateful clash with the double Agent John Hunt, in defense of those whom his crown would have him wipe out in order to conquer their planet.

The desert's dry heat belied the true power of the sun on his back as he worked across the wastes toward where he knew the parachute had fallen. No human could have survived the long run or kept up his blistering pace. If the building heat and lack of water did not kill them, the bitter cold of the night would have. And now there was a fresh lethality on the plains, a plague of biblical proportions.

Dr. Martin Sobleski and Major Jack Toranssen had done their best to stop the spread of the virus dropped by the satellites to this place where the antigen had not had a chance to spread. But they had been shot down not long after Lord Mantil had lost his own plane, and he had seen only one parachute falling away from the big bomber after it exploded. He had used his powerful machine eyes to search the sky for another, but there was only one.

Whoever it was on the other end of that single parachute had fallen into the lands of a scared and enraged Iranian army, and Lord Mantil needed to try and reach any survivor before that army did.

There were few cars out here among the nomads and tribal shepherds of the plains. So he had started running, his herculean legs thrusting him forward. Within an hour, the pounding speed of his sprint had worn through his boots to the tougher skin beneath. Now he ran with the tops of his boots acting as a mockery, making comical the idea that such flimsy things as shoes could afford any protection to a killing machine such as him.

With the B-2 destroyed, the last guard against the virus had fallen, and all around were the first signs of the end of this region's story. These local villagers rarely went into the large towns. This same trait that had saved them from so many diseases in the ordinary course of life had now stopped them from being exposed to the antigen that had spread throughout the rest of the world. And though most of them did not know it yet, they were dying.

The shepherd whom Lord Mantil had taken the shawl from earlier that morning would not miss it for long. Some of his family had already begun coughing and wheezing as the virus wormed its way into their bodies. Lord Mantil had switched off his hearing and averted his eyes as he had silently stepped through the hut in the dark, gathering the cloth and shoes he would need to disguise himself as he sought his friends. He had seen six heat signatures as he had approached the hut. Two adults, four children, and one of them was already starting to burn with the first signs of fever. Within a couple of weeks they would all be cold.

- - -

Sergeant Sheba Abhadir glanced nervously at the men around him. They were rushing headlong to the crash site of a mysterious plane. Amidst reports of explosions in the air and some kind of firefight in the skies over Afghanistan, a radar blip had suddenly flared where none had been before and a huge plane had fallen from the sky, burning as it went.

Who the fight had been between was unknown. Certainly the Taliban and Al Qaeda insurgents had no warplanes to speak of. But when the fight had crossed into Iranian airspace it had become their business. Iranian fighters had been dispatched, assault troops had been loaded into helicopters. The large and powerful Iranian military had been awakened.

It had been some time after the initial reports that news had come in that there were actually two crash sites. One was apparently a European fighter, blown to pieces, and the other was something much larger. Sergeant Abhadir was among twenty men in a helicopter headed to the second site. They were five minutes out.

They came in low, circling the funnel of smoke that marked the plane's resting place like a billowing black tornado. Landing upwind, the team spilled from the helicopter, fanning out in a flood of black-booted efficiency and surrounding the wreckage. Within a moment the helicopter was airborne again, flying a wide sortie to look for other pieces of debris and report on the surroundings, the team's eyes in the air. Two more choppers were also in the air, one en route to the other crash site, one more coming in as backup to respond to any unforeseen need that might yet arise. Ground vehicles would bring more troops soon enough. This first team was here to secure the area and get an initial report to the country's panicked military, political, and religious leaders.

As the troops formed their perimeter around the plane, Sergeant Abhadir turned his focus to the plane itself. His platoon's lieutenant was staring at the big plane and speaking into his radio. But he was not a smart man and the sergeant heard him saying that the bulk of the fuselage of the plane seemed to be missing.

Not one to correct a senior officer, Sergeant Abhadir bit his tongue while the lieutenant finished his report, and then stepped up to the man.

He waited to be asked his opinion and after a moment the lieutenant turned to him, but with an order, not a question.

"Sergeant, it is clear that this is not all of the wreckage; have the helicopter search for the rest of the plane, focusing on locating the front of the fuselage. We need to find the cockpit. Meanwhile, take two men and begin searching through the remains here and see if you can find some indentifying markers or signs of what kind of plane it is."

The sergeant hesitated a moment, hoping that the officer would ask his opinion. But it was never going to happen and eventually he decided to speak up, "If I may, sir, I think I can tell you what type of plane it is right now."

The lieutenant did a double take and then his eyes narrowed into a suspicious stare, "And what, Sergeant, leads you to be able to identify the plane from its wings alone?"

"Well, sir, the wings ... are the plane. I cannot be sure, of course, but I am pretty certain that this is, for the most part, the entire plane, though some kind of explosion has clearly opened her up." The lieutenant turned his focus back on the wreckage, and a weak light started to appear somewhere deep in his dim intellect. The sergeant continued his explanation as realization dawned on the officer, "Sir, I think you'll find that this is a B-2. It would appear that someone has shot down an American stealth bomber over Iran."

- - -

The cloud of smoke was as obvious to Lord Mantil from two miles away as it was to the helicopter he could see circling above it. Focusing his vision, he could see the soldiers fanning out around the crash site and two men among them talking to each over while staring into the small crater that obscured his view of the plane's remains.

He studied the site, the direction of the wind, factoring in the altitude that the parachute had deployed. In a moment, the projected path of the plane and the parachute were overlaid onto his view of the scene as his machine mind computed the potentials. Now that he could see the plane's impact crater, he could visibly realign the estimated path of the plane as it crashed to Earth to match the reality, and thus he was able to adjust his estimation of the parachute's path accordingly.

The parachute's new trajectory dropped to a point not three miles away. Without needing to be asked, his machine mind locked on to the Iranian force's helicopter circling above and studied its widening search path, giving Lord Mantil an estimated time before the parachute was discovered.

Seven minutes. With a whir and a telltale machine thrum, the helicopter passed over Lord Mantil's head and the Agent waited, judging the moment when he was just underneath it and thus lost in their blind spot. In that instant, he broke into a run once more.

The pilot and spotter saw him standing there in his ragged garb as they approached, noting his presence on their search log as they passed overhead, dismissing him as a nomad as they continued on. Flying on their search vector, they were unaware that directly beneath them the seemingly harmless man had now accelerated into a breakneck sprint, kicking up a whirl of sand as he used their shadow to circle around the crash before arching away from them, using their shadow to head out and away from the site, searching for his friends still out there on the plains.

- - -

She had awoken to an all-body pain, emphasized and amplified by utter silence. Her body was sending her signals that her mind could not process as she tried to bring herself around. Barely conscious, she started to check herself. She was a pilot. She remembered that she had been deployed to fly a sortie with an armed payload over the Southern Atlantic.

But something had gone wrong.

Shit! Memories came to her like slaps to the face and she flinched with equal parts pain and anger. She had never gotten to the cockpit. An old colleague had been waiting for her in ambush, and she had awoken many hours later on the floor of the flight deck. The moving floor.

She had known instantly that they were airborne. She had been kidnapped, as had her flight commander. She turned her head with the effort of a weightlifter, straining with all her might to get her muscles to respond to her commands. She couldn't hear anything, but that was to be expected. They had done a high-altitude ejection at near supersonic speed and they had been trained to expect their eardrums to either blow out or at least be severely battered by the wrenching pressure change. She would know which in a few hours, but either way, deafness was going to be at least a temporary setback, possibly a permanent one.

She felt the tug of the parachute still beating in the wind and she registered that she was still attached to the ejection seat. The B-2 she had ejected from only had two seats, but there had been four people aboard, two pilots and two usurpers, so they had followed emergency procedure and double strapped themselves to the seats. It was not comfortable for the seat's primary occupant or the person strapped tightly in their lap, but those were the breaks.

She tasted sand in her mouth, blown in by the dry wind gusting over her, and realized she was thirsty. Then she registered that her captor was still strapped beneath her. He wasn't moving. She suppressed an instant urge to elbow him in the ribs and felt instead for the clips that were still holding her down. Her left arm did not respond so she focused on her right, finding and detaching the steel clasps at her waist and shoulder before reaching over with a cringe to her left side.

The movement brought a strained groan from the man under her, one forced through the bounds of unconsciousness to spill mindlessly from his cracked lips. She rolled off him, trying to be as delicate as possible, but her attempt at finesse ended with a thud on the packed dust of the plain, a shout of agony bursting from deep within her. Catching her breath as demons of pain raged inside her, she gripped the side of the ejected seat and wrestled the physical pain under control.

Lifting her head, she came face-to-face with the man who had tranquilized her and kidnapped her. His face was badly bruised, his nose broken, his lips swollen, no doubt from when her unconscious head had whipped back and forth as they fell to earth. Years of training and military fraternity overcame her anger and she set to tending to his wounds and attempting to revive him, reconciling this with her hatred of him by saying that only he had any real idea of where they were.

She did not hear the other man approach, despite the speed of his footfalls, or his screeching halt in the sand, but she felt his shadow fall across her at a primal level and instinctively swung around, her right hand grasping at the standard-issue firearm at her side … a firearm that had long since been taken by her kidnappers.

In his haste, Lord Mantil had not even factored in that there might have been others on board the B-2 he had striven to protect, and he was momentarily taken aback by her presence. But his quick-firing mind took in her uniform in a flash, assessed the situation, and was listing probable scenarios before she had completed her turn.

She stared into the black eyes of the shabby-looking man and was taken aback by the way that they surveyed her in return. She was being assessed, and not by a local farmer or nomad as his dress might suggest. This man had purpose. This man's appearance at her side was not a coincidence. He carried no weapon and made no threatening gesture. When words started to spill from his mouth, she heard nothing. After a moment he stopped talking, registering her lack of comprehension, and bent to the ground, his finger moving with swift strokes in the sand.

'friend
US Agent
we must go'

She stared back up at him, trying to assess whether to trust him, and then, leaning on her knees she wrote something in the sand as well.

'uno ab …'

He stared a moment, clearly thinking, and then nodded, bending and finishing her sentence:

'… alto'

"One over all." It was the unofficial motto of the US Air Force. A kind of Semper Fi for pilots.

The confirmation was like an elixir to her and she relaxed, almost losing her balance and he bent and wrapped his arm under her shoulders, lifting her easily to her feet. He did not let her go once he had her standing, but bent slightly again and she felt his hands moving over her body. For a fleeting moment she thought that she was being sexually assaulted as his fingers roamed over her, feeling more surprise than alarm. But she quickly recognized the skilled hands of a field medic and helped his check of her, mumbling with deaf imprecision as he hit sore points. A few moments later his hands completed their search and he left her leaning against the ejected seat again and bent to the sand, sweeping away their previous words and replacing them with:

'broke collar
+ 2 ribs
need sling 4 arm'

She nodded when he looked up and pointed to a compartment in the back of the chair above its spent boosters, which was marked with a small, red cross. But he was already there, unclipping the compartment door and extracting the box inside.

Working with impassioned speed, Lord Mantil opened the field med box and extracted what he needed. As he did so he turned his attention to the Major. He couldn't know how much the woman knew about what was happening, but he needed to look inside the man and find what was causing his unconsciousness. Staring with increased intensity, he scanned his limp friend with his powerful eyes. He saw it almost instantaneously, a swelling against the front portal lobe, heavy sub-cranial bruising and a hairline fracture of the parietal.

Mentally he checked his time. A list of tasks appearing and prioritizing in his mind as he assessed how much he could do before the approaching Iranian army were upon them. As he did this he speedily fashioned a sling with the expertise and secured it around Captain Jennifer Falster's shoulder, manhandling her as he worked but carefully avoiding aggravating her wounds. He thought of the Major. Lord Mantil needed to relieve the pressure.

Turning back to the captain, he looked at her a moment and considered his next move. Deciding a course of action, he touched his finger to the sandy floor once more and began to write.

'I now do strange thing
trust me?'

He looked at her imploringly. She nodded. Gently, he reached his hand up to her face and touched her cheek. She instinctively went to flinch but his eyes stayed fixed to hers, and she tried to mirror their steadfastness. His index finger came to rest at the entrance to her ear. Inside the finger, he activated the tendrils that were wired into it to enable him to open locks, or worm their way into any other tight spot the Agent needed to probe.

The tiny fibers snaked out of slits in his armored skin and into the captain's ear canal, sensors at their tips reporting back to Lord Mantil on the rip in the thin tympanic membrane of the woman's eardrum. The cataclysmic drop in air pressure when she and Major Toranssen had ejected from the B-2 had torn through the woman's eardrums. They would heal, to a degree, but for weeks she would hear nothing more than thrumming and mumbled thumps.

He could help the healing along by cauterizing and sealing the wound, but it would still take time for her hearing to mend and adjust, and he needed to speak to her now. The fibrous black wires surveyed her eardrum and the tiny, jointed ossicles behind it that linked it to the cochlea, her brain's microphone. With infinitesimal care, one of the thin wires slipped through the tear in her eardrum and wrapped around one of the tiny ossicles known as the malleus or 'hammer.' In doing so, he literally took hold of the very mechanism of her hearing and, with his finger firmly planted against her ear, he held her head still with his other hand and started to send infinitesimal vibrations through the tiny little joint.

She felt it instantly, like a blind man opening transplanted eyes. With disjointed clarity, the voice of Lord Mantil projected itself directly into her ear without his lips ever moving an inch.

"Captain, please do not be alarmed. I must ask that you trust me when I say that this will all be explained in time."

She stared at him dumbfounded. She tried to nod but his firm grip did not allow her head to move even slightly, so she mouthed her assent. He smiled at her. And while his face begged for her trust, his voice echoed in her head once more.

"We need to move … immediately. We are currently in Iran and helicopters are searching this area. When they find us, troops will no doubt be close behind. While I could easily handle them, I do not want there be anymore killing unless absolutely necessary. Unfortunately, before we can leave I have to operate on the major. He has a cranial hemorrhage that needs to be relieved before it does permanent damage to his brain. I can do the operation now, and I can do it relatively quickly, but in order to do it I am going to have to use some tools that may … alarm you."

She looked at him, her mouth repeating his words: alarm me? He nodded. "Like I said, this will all be explained soon enough. I am going to make a quick repair to your ear. Your hearing should begin to return within the hour. But for now I am going to have to ask you to trust me."

Silence returned as the tendril from his finger released her malleus and then gently cauterized the tear in her ear with a minuscule laser built into one of the tendrils. With her eardrum sealed once more, he gently removed his hand, allowing her to watch the fibers retract into his finger. She looked back at him amazed.

His smile was sympathetic, like he was looking at someone who is about to discover they are the butt of an elaborate but tasteless practical joke, and with one of his many 'talents' stowed, he engaged another. Her disbelief doubled as his left eye twisted, unlocked, and rolled aside to leave a black cavity beneath. Despite having already seen the tendrils in Shahim's hand, this new wonder hit at her on a more primal level, and she recoiled. As she stared at the hole in Shahim's face where his left eye had been, something in her told her that her life as she knew it was over.

Somehow the utter silence from her damaged ears made the few seconds even more surreal, but also, in a way, more digestible; and so she allowed curiosity to take over and leaned back in to look more closely into the black socket that had been revealed behind Shahim's false left eye.

From within, a black lens extruded itself, surrounded by a host of spines and needles. Lord Mantil did his best to make his expression gentle and unthreatening but the sight was, without doubt, the most terrifying thing she had ever seen. And yet she was transfixed. She stared at it. A second more passed.

With an apologetic expression, he turned away from her. He had only a couple of minutes left, at most, before the helicopters came, and so he turned his attention to his other ward, bringing the apparatus that was his Tactical Contact Weapons Complement to bear on the sleeping major.

Gripping the unconscious man's head with both his hands, he focused in on the center of the hemorrhage he had detected inside the man's skull, and set his machinery to work. His scalpel was invisible. A mere flicker of bluish green in the dusty air as it lanced the major's skull. Watching in awe, Captain Jennifer Falster saw the major's hair singe and burn away before she saw the black spot appear on the top of his forehead. A small circle of the skin flayed away along with the thin layer of flesh beneath it and in a moment she was staring at a tiny patch of her colleague's bleached white skull.

The hole that the laser then burrowed in the unconscious major's skull was barely two millimeters across, but as soon as the laser broke through, the sudden release of pressure caused a spurt of blood to squirt from the gap. It sprayed across Shahim's chest and lap, a line of red relieving the oppression of the major's mind.

With the skull penetrated, Lord Mantil lifted his index finger and pressed it to the tiny hole. Once more, the minute fibers wormed out, this time into the major's head, fanning out as soon as they passed through the hole in his skull into the gap between the brain and the cranial bone that cradled it. As they spread out, they found the broken capillaries and veins that were causing the hemorrhage and they began to heat up. The heat from them singed the tiny blood vessels, making them contract and seal and then the wires began to rotate in Major Jack Toranssen's head, cauterizing the other broken blood vessels as they went.

After a moment, he withdrew his finger and focused his left eye once more, sealing and anaesthetizing the small wound even as his hands prepared a bandage from the med kit. Jennifer watched in fascination as the Agent worked, his hands moving with speed and precision, her mind working to keep up with him. In a moment it was over and he turned to her once more, his hand rising to touch her other ear this time. She let him touch her, giving in to the strangeness of it all and his voice sounded in her deaf ears once more.

"It is done. I do not know how long he will sleep, but we must move, and we must move now. Captain, can I ask you to trust me one more time?"

She paused a moment, more surprised that she was even being asked than actually debating her answer. She had just seen a man perform brain surgery with his eyes, and now that man was talking to her with wires in his fingers. What was she going to do? Run away? Ask the Iranians for help? Wait here for a cavalry that she knew would never arrive?

She mouthed yes to him, and followed it with a hesitant shrug, like a child trusting her mother before she pulls off a band-aid.

"Thank you," his voice rang in her ear. He quickly performed the same simple but incredibly precise surgery on her right ear as he had her left, and then he removed his hand from her cheek and stood. She stood as well, a little unsteady, but her strength returning with every minute. He turned and motioned for her to climb on his back. Sparing a thought for how they were going to move the major, she shook her head, mumbling that he should carry the major, she would be fine.

But his face became insistent, the face of a father not wanting a child to argue, not this time. Just do it, his expression said, and she reacted with a trust born of a lack of options. Wrapping her good arm around his neck, she climbed meekly onto his back, wrapping her legs around his waist as she did so. He anticipated her movements and bent to meet her, lifting her easily, and then bending at the knee to scoop up the major. She felt amazement blossom afresh inside her as he stood with ease, bearing their combined weight like they were but rag dolls.

He turned his face to her and he mouthed, 'Hold on' and then he winked, a conspiratorial smile spreading across his face.

And with that, he leaned into the wind and leapt forward, bounding with a single momentous thrust into a headlong sprint, their negligible weight upon him like feathers on an eagle's back as he flew across the plain.

They were fleeing the helicopters. Fleeing the innocent Iranian soldiers he longed not to fight. Heading north, they sprinted toward the large city of Mashhad, kicking up dust in their trail as his herculean legs pistoned under them, propelling them forward.

He did not know how they were going to make it to safety. He would figure that out as they went. He would have to circle the city and try to find a way to the sparsely populated border with Turkmenistan and then across it and on to the American embassy in that nation's capital, Ashgabat. But that was a long way off; first he had to get them away from the closing Iranian troops.

Chapter 2: Floods of Exodus

"Aw, gimme the damn remote, ya silly bitch," said Jason to his wife. She stared at him with indignant fury at the use of the 'b' word and he rolled his eyes, knowing he was about to get the bitch speech again. "Here we go ..."

"*Here we go*?!" she shouted, "I'll give ya somethin' to roll ya fuckin' eyes about, ya jackass. I told you thousand times, I do *not* appreciate bein' called a bitch. Now, if ya don't mind, I am *tryin'* to watch the pastor."

Jason sat sullenly for a while, staring at the screen while a smiling man in an expensive suit fabricated from broken promises explained the vast benefits of his unique ministry to his viewers, "So you see, ma children, only through the voice of God can you be saved from the terrible plague sweeping our great nation. For the sinners have brought this down upon them, and are reaping the rewards of their godless ways."

The pastor went on at some length about how the purchase of his particular version of the bible, with his particular audio CD, would help ensure salvation, hinting at but never actually promising that it would save people from the terror that was indeed sweeping the nation, killing thousands as it went. Jason watched begrudgingly, unaware that the pastor's well-placed words were sinking into his psyche, unaware of how many of them he would be repeating when he had another argument about this at his local watering hole the next day.

It would never occur to him or his wife that the pastor was just trying to profit out of the misery of others by selling more of his trite products. Or that if the man that claimed to be a shepherd believed anything his god had ever said he would be telling his flock that they should be giving their money to the victims of the terrible disaster on the Eastern seaboard, and not to his parasitic ministry.

But this pastor had a new CD out and he needed to move the vast stocks he had paid the printers in China to ship to him. His followers were there to provide him an income, their misguided faith in him and the platitudes he preached leading them to sacrifice their menial disposable income like lambs to his ethical slaughterhouse.

After a while, Jason's wife stood, groaning as she levered her rotund frame out of their plush La-Z-Boy couch, and headed to the trailer's commode, farting as she went. Like a child spotting a forbidden treat, Jason took the opportunity to claim the remote control, and with a satisfied grin he changed the channel to where he knew reruns of *Cops* should be playing. But they weren't. Instead, another special report on the events in southern Georgia was looping here as well and Jason cursed.

"Goddamn it," he said.

A shout came through the thin wall between him and the toilet. "Damn it, Jason, don't take the Lord's fuckin' name in vain," admonished Jason's wife, Theresa. Unfortunately, the strain of her shout forced out a particularly loud and potent fart, and after a moment they both started laughing.

The reporter on the television was showing one of many sites outside Atlanta where tens of thousands of people were being put up in temporary housing set up by the National Guard. They represented only a fraction of the millions who were being displaced by the disaster, but the sight was sobering even for Jason, and his laughter faded as he took it in.

"Damn," he said quietly, as the woman on the TV explained the extent of the evacuation.

"This site, which is one of fifteen outside Atlanta, is estimated to house nearly ten thousand people, a number which has been growing every day in the week since the disaster. As you saw when I spoke with the camp's coordinator, Colonel McAvoy, the biggest problem at this point has been security, keeping the belongings people have insisted on bringing with them safe, even though it is taking away from the space left for other refugees. But this camp is up and running now, and nearly full. And as they complete others like it from Alabama to Pennsylvania, the question has become not where will these people go, but how long they will have to stay here before they can return home?"

The reporter went on with her explanation and Jason sat, enthralled by the sheer scale of the spectacle. Theresa emerged from the toilet, her *Duck Dynasty* sweatpants still down around her ankles, while she pulled up her sweatshirt so she could pull her pants up over her potbelly. But she paused with her hefty midriff and well-worn thong exposed when she noticed her husband's intent expression. He sensed her scrutiny and said in an aside, "This shit is unreal, Terry. They've, like, totally evacuated the entire coast of Georgia and the Carolinas just like they said they would. I mean, this shit is really happening. I can't believe it."

She turned to face the screen, her panties and belly still showing as her limited attention span was absorbed by the images. The view had shifted to a CGI map of the Eastern seaboard of the United States. Overlaying it was a large grey arrow moving north from the coastal border between Georgia and Florida, up the coast all the way to southern Virginia. Its root was the King's Bay Naval Base, where a massive explosion a week beforehand had incinerated two Ohio class nuclear submarines, laying open their radioactive cores and warheads to the North Atlantic trade winds.

In a massive evacuation, the coastal population that lived in the cloud's path had been driven and cajoled out of their homes, assisted by school buses, military trucks, and the conversion of every highway in the area into one-way, six-lane floods of exodus. But many of them had not escaped its effects in time. Many were even now showing varying levels of radiation sickness: hair loss, lethargy, the many symptoms of overexposure to the weapons-grade plutonium dust that was irradiating everything in the cloud's wake.

The scale of the area it now covered combined with the half-life of the material was already diminishing the cloud's effects to some degree as it came to southern Maryland and Delaware, but unseen tumors were already blossoming in thousands of innocent bodies as they sat in traffic or settled into tents, football stadiums, and school gymnasiums, unaware of the embryonic death starting take root inside them.

Theresa eventually finished pulling up her sweatpants and sank slowly into the La-Z-Boy next to Jason, her eyes locked on the screen as the scale of the disaster hit her as well.

"You know, Sara-Beth told me they're setting up one of those refugee camps over at the Sharp's Farm, right here, in Slocomb," she said, an effort to seem open-minded not disguising the air of disgust in her voice. Jason and Theresa lived in a trailer. They had always lived in a trailer. Theresa's sister and two cousins lived in another trailer in the same park. Heading to one of the camps might actually be a move up in the world for some of their neighbors. At least they would have running hot water.

Jason picked up on her tone and reacted, "Terry, these folks have it real shitty. Surely you're not gonna begrudge some of 'em comin' to Slocomb?"

"Yeah, I'll begrudge the fuckers comin'," she replied, turning her head sharply to him, "These snooty fuckers sure-as-shit wouldn't put *us* up if this shit happened in Alabama."

"Hey, these aren't all rich folk, some of 'em are good Christian folk like us." he replied.

"Christian? They're nothin' but a bunch of liberal, pansy-ass, anti-American motherfuckers, and there ain't one single real fuckin' Christian among 'em. I don't care if they all die out there, I don't want them in 'bama, freeloadin' off of us hard-workin' real Americans."

Their argument continued, their raised voices blending with the mixed aroma of Cheetos and methane floating out the window, along with the irony of the fact that neither of these two hard workers had held a steady job in ten years. Outside their trailer, the mix of TV chatter and inane conversation could be heard from a hundred other trailers just like Jason and Theresa's, the clamor settling on the humid night air. But amongst the banal repetitiveness of their surroundings, Jason and Theresa's home was, in fact, quite unique.

For, unknown to them, a dark presence lay in silence underneath it. Amongst the pipes and trash and poorly connected wiring, lay a black figure. Blacker than the shadow that enveloped her. She was perfectly still, perfectly silent. Only the whites of her eyes betrayed any movement at all. She had been present at the explosions in King's Bay. In fact, she had been the cause of the death spreading up the coast. But the massive fireball that had ripped the two subs apart had also flayed off her synthetic skin, leaving her black battle armor exposed beneath.

Agent Lana Wilson lay in the darkness, amongst food wrappers and used tires, with a rage boiling inside her. Her systems were slowly repairing themselves after the massive damage she had suffered, but it would take time. With nothing to do while she recuperated, she had taken to putting her mind in a kind of machine hibernation, relying on a subroutine to monitor her surroundings while she 'slept' away the days.

Each night she awoke, reviewed her status, and briefly reviewed the bits and pieces of information her brain had stored away during the day. The system's status was relatively unchanged. Her weapons were semi-functional again; the laser systems almost fully repaired, while the more delicate sonic punch was only a week away from operational readiness. But those were not the systems that had been most affected. To put it bluntly, she had been stripped bare of every external sensor and apparatus on her body. Everything had been wiped clean down to the black superconducting shielding that lay beneath all the Agents' skins.

She could repair many of those lost senses. But her fake earlobes were gone, along with her hair, leaving her head smooth and featureless. She could rebuild the infinitesimal radar arrays and audio receptors that had been built into her ocular cavities, so she would be able to hear and interact with her surroundings again, but the woven, chameleon skin that had allowed her to blend in with the humans was gone forever. A gash or tear in the skin would have repaired itself with time, but the loss of the entire structure was like the loss of an entire limb, and even her extensive regenerative systems could not rebuild it.

There was a factory, unbeknownst to her, where the human conspiracy that had orchestrated the death of the satellites had built a resonance manipulator, a machine capable of rebuilding even her dermal systems. But she did not even know of its existence, let alone its location, so as far as she was concerned, nothing on Earth could replace the main tool of her disguise. So she had become as black outwardly as the dark purpose that simmered within her. And she would stay that way.

It would limit her movements, hinder her as it forced her into the shadows, but her plans now would have made blending in difficult at best anyway. For her mind was set. She was going to find them, the conspirators, the people that had launched the missiles that had destroyed her precious satellites, the people that had created the antigen that had saved humanity. She was going to find every one of them, starting with Neal Danielson and Madeline Cavanagh, and she was going to kill them all ... slowly.

Chapter 3: Triptych

In a wide room at the center of a large building sheltered within a massive compound, a center of thought was forming. The room was an office, still embryonic in its layout and systems. It was a new office. As new as the newly created governmental position its occupant had been appointed to.

Two large windows, each adjacent, filled its one outside wall. The other walls were blank, bereft of the accumulated pictures and paraphernalia that typically adorned offices this large, the attempts by their occupants to make their workspaces seem like a home or to give them the air of prestige they assume befits their lofty rank. But this office lacked the history it would have needed to form a homely feel and its occupant lacked the arrogance that would have led him to drape icons on his walls to impress his visitors.

But he had an arrogance of sorts. He believed he was one of the main reasons that the single greatest danger in the history of Earth had been discovered in time to do something about it. And he was right. Because of that fact, the man who only two years ago had been a lonely and lowly researcher in a neglected field now found himself the appointed head of an international taskforce with an unprecedented mandate.

For with the help of a diverse team of scientists, air force and naval officers, and three agents with wildly different backgrounds, Dr. Neal Danielson had been tasked with preparing for the arrival of a force more powerful than any imagined in earth's long, bloody history. An Armada that wanted only the eradication of humanity so that it could claim that most precious of commodities in all the galaxy: a life-sustaining planet, irrespective of the life it was already sustaining.

Neal sat at his desk and tried to focus his thoughts. A thousand different aspects of his task whirled about in his head like feathers in a whirlwind, illusive and possessed, but he knew that in order to construct some meaningful seed of a plan he must grasp each and every one of them and focus on it. On its particular implications, on its particular attributes, and how to fit it into the wing that he must form, the wing upon which Earth's defense must fly.

The task of identifying and codifying all of the component parts of the plan they must form was gargantuan in and of itself, but the doctorate student in Neal knew that he must work piece by piece, taking one aspect and building from there. He would never sleep unless he started to think of it all in manageable segments.

So he plucked a thought and centered on it, choosing to start with the subject of his next meeting. He would start with the macro, the leadership; on how he was going to frame the team he was building. Before he could build the larger army, Neal knew he must surround himself with capable and trustworthy lieutenants, starting with those who had shared the first perilous stage of their long journey. Most had already been corralled, but three of them remained unaccounted for: Shahim, Jack, and Martin.

As if summoned by his thoughts of his friends, a knock on the door came and two men walked in, each of them a part of that same auspicious group.

"Gentlemen!" said Neal, rising to greet the men. The first man was Agent John Hunt, any mark of his incarceration now completely banished from his tall, strong frame and boyish face, as he returned Neal's handshake with a smile. Neal turned to the second man with a special affection born of deep mutual respect, a respect that had been hard earned between people from very different backgrounds, and who had made up very different but equally crucial parts of their diverse conspiracy.

Neal allowed a broad grin to spread across his lips as he reached up to finger the new stars adorning the general's lapel, a liberty very few could have taken with the stern-looking air force officer. But the seeming affront was only met with a roll of the deep blue eyes in the rugged man's face as he turned briskly away and went to the conference table that took up one-third of the large office, laying a sheaf of papers and a laptop case on top of it.

"Let's get started, shall we?" said General Barrett Milton. "As you asked, we've been working on refining the teaming structure we're going to need, working on three key branches: Research, Construction, and Execution." The other two men came and joined him around the table as he spoke, remaining standing as they looked at the organization charts Barrett was spreading out. Neal recognized the brisk perfection of John's machine hand in the crisp lines and words on the charts, one of the Agent's many talents.

"Let's start with first: the Research Team will focus on the design and development of the array of tools we will need for the various main milestones for our preparations which we are even now laying out. Eventually they will refocus on the designs of the machinery that will make up our planetary defenses. But we are a ways off from that yet.

"The Construction Team, meanwhile, will focus on the location and allocation of the extensive resources we are going to require, and the construction efforts that will eventually be undertaken, both here on earth and …" he paused as the next words eased themselves from his lips, "… in orbit."

They were all keenly aware that this effort was going to lift humanity on to a new technological plane, the gifts of knowledge that Agent John Hunt was bestowing upon them were the products of many decades of research by his own people, and they would represent an evolutionary leap for us. But every now and then some simple concept brought reality home, and the thought of how much of the coming battle was going to be waged in space was one of those concepts.

"Finally, the Operations Group will be the military branch, that will eventually encompass the various land-based, orbital, and exo-orbital defensive bodies that will be trained to man the defenses the other two teams will be designing and constructing. Now, clearly these three teams are working on very different timelines, and no doubt one or the other will take center stage as the next few years progress, but to some extent we thought we should start considering all their component parts now in order to plan accordingly."

Neal nodded but offered up a point, "What about oversight, management … politicians?"

General Milton winced, then nodded with resignation, "That will, of course, be a massive factor, but we have deliberately not included it in these plans. Not to put too fine a point on it, but that will be a whole beast unto itself, and I strongly believe that we need to manage it completely separately. To allow that to become an integral part of these core teams could undermine our very purpose." Neal nodded again appreciatively and recognized the seed of Barrett's thought here. Barrett went on, confirming Neal's assumption, "We must think of this as a military organization, one without national allegiance, like a much larger and more autonomous version of the United Nations."

He shrugged a little at his own comparison then went on, "That said we certainly don't want to come under the bureaucratic auspices of that group either. In the end, I believe it is essential that we operate as independently as possible, but with the mandate of an international political body. One that must be formed specifically and solely for this purpose."

Neal nodded emphatically now, "My thoughts exactly. And to support this we must try to source the team without regard for national origin, and I don't mean balanced across nations, I mean *without regard for national origin*. From the start we must seek the best people for the job. Only then will we be able to escape the mandating of political appointees into key positions. Appointees with their own agendas."

They all nodded, again they were in agreement. These were vital points and they would need to be immovably firm on them from the very start.

Neal went on, "Of course, it wouldn't hurt our cause if we were to make some deliberate nominations at the beginning that make our team more diverse. To date we do have an unreasonably large number of Americans on the team and that will stick in the craw of many a European state, not to mention the Asian powers we are going to need to bring into this effort."

"I think that, as we already hinted at," said Barrett, "it is clear that our ability to do all this, with both the independence from and the unwavering support of all the major world powers, is going to depend very much on our ability to maintain a buffer between our teams and the politicians, because attempts at oversight are going to be … incessant."

"No doubt." replied Neal, nodding thoughtfully.

"A buffer," went on Barrett, with a wry smile, "that is probably going to rely on the stubbornness and pigheadedness of whatever poor fool ends up running this circus."

Neal looked up at the general, then smiled, chuckling quietly to himself. "Well, then I guess they got the right fool for the job," he replied drily, as his eyes moved back to the organization charts. They all smiled. It was a joke, but it was so very true, and Neal knew he was going to have to dig in hard in the coming months to handle the pressure from above. If he was successful, then such concerns would hopefully not affect Barrett and the others too much, and he was more than a little jealous of them for that. But he would not give anyone else the job in a lifetime. It was too important, and he was going to see it through.

"OK," Neal said, moving on, "Research: I see Madeline in charge, of course, we couldn't hope for a more qualified or experienced person there, but it is the field leads that I am most concerned about."

He indicated the main branches that John had already helped them lay out. In some ways this team would be one of the easiest to bring together, scientists usually lacking some measure of the maniacal national pride of their military counterparts. That, and it would be a foolish scientist that would refuse an offer to work with the kind of fantastically advanced concepts and technologies they were planning on delving into. But many of the skills and categories that John had helped them define were of an ilk not seen by even the most open-minded in Earth's scientific community.

Head of Tension Material Development. Spastic Elevation Mechanics. Pummeled Extrusion Weaving. Direct Spinal Interfaces. Extensible Manifold Lances. Those were the ones that were outside even DARPA's enthusiastic imagination. Then there were some entries they recognized from the team's early forays into Mobiliei science: Resonance Manipulation, Superconductive Shielding, Sonic Field Weaponry, and Subspace Communication. And finally there were those things that humanity's imagination had managed to conjure but not yet realize, things that excited Neal's scientific soul: Fusion Fuel Management, Gravitational Convergence and Dispersal, and Neutronium Lasers.

His mind momentarily narrowed with curiosity and a longing to devote a hundred lives to each and every one of these wonders, and for a moment he mourned the passing of humanity's innocence and the loss of the pride that each of these discoveries would have brought if made on our own. The Edisons and Einsteins of these fields that would never be.

But he allowed himself to wonder for only a moment. For what was any discovery if not the platform on which to explore further? What would the John Harrisons of our future be able to grasp from this newfound plateau of knowledge? Wonder, grief, and hope mingled bitterly in him for a moment, and then he came back to the conversation at hand.

For laying out these ambitious plans for vast teams of hyper-catalyzed thought was going to be the easy part. As Barrett had so eruditely emphasized, getting the world to unite behind them as they moved forward was going to be the hard part. And move forward they must, by any means necessary.

Chapter 4: Estados Unidos del Mundo

"Good evening, ladies and gentlemen. If we may begin." Jim Hacker spoke with practiced authority, and the room responded, quieting in anticipation of his next words. "If everyone could take their seats, I believe we are about to begin." He looked around, a little nervously. The last few days had been hectic, disastrous even.

As the chief of staff for the US president, Jim had seen his world churn in the wake of the attacks on the satellites. After the initial shock of the revelations brought by Neal Danielson and his team, there had come the stunning but victorious attack on the satellites. But their celebrations had been short lived as the first evidence of the threat still among them emerged. The short but vicious firefight between the American Agent Lana Wilson and the team sent to subdue her had triggered a horrific explosion, an explosion that had belched tons of radioactive death into the coastal winds. Jim had barely slept since. Between coordinating relief efforts with the National Guard and FEMA, and helping quell public discord, he had been on overdrive, his acute political instincts flitting him from problem to problem, decision after decision.

It was not the first major disaster he had been party to. Not the first time he had found himself completely consumed for days or even weeks in a spasmic reaction to something that threatened his country, and thus his president, and thus his job. But for the first time he realized that his job, and this radioactive crisis, were overshadowed by something even more crucial, and the fuel that drove him to excel had always been his desire to be at the very epicenter of it all, not handling some subsidiary, if very serious issue.

And so, despite the thousand other draws on his time, and despite the fact that Red Bull and adrenalin had been his sole protection from absolute exhaustion in the last week and a half, Jim Hacker found himself here.

'Here' was a large, oak-paneled conference room in Camp David. In the room were assembled an array of extremely prominent personages from Great Britain, France, Germany, Japan, India, and Brazil. The prime minister of Great Britain was one of only three actual premiers present, the others being the US President and the German chancellor, who had been on a scheduled visit to the United States anyway.

The other nations had sent various senior cabinet members, from the minister of the interior from France, to the senior envoys from Japan, India, and Brazil. Also seated at the main table were the US president and Dr. Neal Danielson. Jim stood behind them, while a wide variety of individuals sat around the outside of the room, somewhat cloaked in shadow. These included the rest of Neal's team: General Milton, John Hunt, Madeline, and Ayala. And, among others, Shinobu Matsuoka of Matsuoka Industries, who had received a special invite from the Japanese envoy at the bequest of the president, and had also been called upon by Madeline and Ayala to attend.

Various other assistants and senior staff members sat in the wings as well, but outside of Neal's team they all shared a common thread: they were all here because of imperative instructions from their country's leaders born of an urgent request from the president himself, and they were all utterly in the dark as to where the meeting was going to take them.

Because of this lack of information, the room silenced with surprising rapidity, and the president took his cue. Nodding to Jim, who assumed a seat around the outside of the room, the president began.

"I must start by thanking you all for coming on such short notice. My staff have made me aware of the pains you have all taken to get here, and I wanted to express my heartfelt thanks for your attendance, especially considering the lack of information provided in advance about the subject of this extraordinary session. I hope what you will see and hear today will give ample support to the urgency with which this session was called, and the secrecy under which it is being held."

He took a breath and looked around the room, engaging each person in turn, making sure that he leveled the playing field amongst the diverse spectrum of representatives that each nation had been willing and/or able to send on such short notice.

"I do not want to delay things any further, but before we get to the meat of the meeting, I wanted to also let you know why this particular group has been formed. In the spirit of complete transparency, I will tell you that not all the nations that were invited to this meeting have accepted. Most notable among those that refused to come without more information were representatives of Russia and the People's Republic of China. I cannot say I am not sad they were unwilling to join us, as they will be an important part of the solution to what you are about hear about. For, along with those two countries, the nations represented here today account for over 75% of the world's economy. And we are going to need to pull together if we are to face what you are about to see. Nothing less than a united front will suffice to deal with what is coming."

He let the words hang a while, the dramatic effect reverberating around the room, and then he allowed his hand to rest lightly on the forearm of the doctor sitting to his right. Without turning to the man, he then said, "With that said, I would like to introduce Dr. Neal Danielson."

The doctor nodded in acknowledgement, then slowly stood up and took a long look around the room. He surveyed each face in turn, assessing how best to begin, which tone to use, what route to take to the bombshell he was about to drop on them.

He spared himself a brief glance at the people he knew had already been informed. Shinobu sitting with a pensive frown behind the Japanese ambassador, the British prime minister who had been told in private by the president in order to help Neal secure the release of John Hunt, and of course his own team, who each had roles in the coming presentation. It was a short list but it was all he needed. He cleared his throat somewhat unnecessarily and began.

- - -

"Even if I agree that this threat is real, what you are telling us would require ... mein Gott ... it would require the mobilization of a planet." the German Chancellor said.

Along with the French minister, she was one of the main skeptics in the room. After an hour of intense presentations by Neal and General Milton, the room had become divided into two camps: those that were vocally resisting the information being presented to them, and those that were sitting in mute shock from it. On the whole, Neal was more worried about the silent ones, because they represented an unknown. He could not refute an argument if a person did not make it, and he did not believe for a moment that the shyer members of the conference lacked their objections. He had a series of trump cards to pull, some subtle, some more obvious, and at last he decided what order he was going to use them in.

"You raise a fine point, Chancellor, if what we say is true then it is going to require an unparalleled mobilization. All the more reason we cannot afford even the slightest shadow of a doubt as to whether what I am saying is indeed true. So why don't we focus on that first. If, after we have finished saying what we have to say, you still harbor doubts as to the scale and validity of the threat, then there will be little point in discussing next steps. That said, I think you will find that find we have some very persuasive evidence to show you."

With that he turned to Madeline and invited her to the table. Her subtle beauty was a waft of fresh air into the conversation, and she smiled as they all sighed inaudibly, relieved at the change of speaker. But her sharp eyes left no doubt as to the intelligence behind them, and she took a deep breath and looked around them each in turn, as if to say: do not think me just a pretty face, my friends.

Her silent point made, she stepped to the table and placed a small case upon it with a black-gloved hand. She looked at the case, almost hesitatingly, and then returned her focus to the room.

"Good evening, everyone. For those of you that do not know me, my name is Dr. Madeline Cavanagh. For the last year I have been working on the cure to the virus Dr. Danielson has already mentioned. I could spend some significant time demonstrating how the cure works to show you just how advanced it is, or I could show the process by which it was manufactured, which I assure you is nothing short of miraculous. But I have decided to show you something else that I have been able to manufacture with the tools and designs given to us by our new allies. Something more ... tangible."

With that, she walked around the table to stand in the middle of the large U, allowing everyone to see her. Then, without hesitation, she began unbuttoning her blouse. The room was stunned a moment, but she turned slowly as she undressed, and underneath the silky material they could see some kind of black undergarment that matched the black gloves she was wearing. At first the room seemed relieved. The meeting had appeared to be taking a strange turn. But then, as the blouse was allowed to drop from her shoulders, they saw that the undergarment was not as it seemed. Almost as one they all leaned forward. They were trying to see a fold, a crease, any kind of texture, a shadow, or reflection. But there was only blackness. Pure, unreflected light, an absorption of all around it.

If the material was capable of revealing something of its shape, it would have been possible to see fine ribs, pistons, and spars running down the arms and spine of the strange suit. These ribs were linked by angular joints at the shoulder, elbow, and down her back that mimicked her own skeletal structure. But such details were hidden in plain sight, as the suit gave no hint of the way it hugged Madeline's taut figure beneath.

The room's fascination with her second skin was such that they barely flinched when she unbuttoned her jeans, showing that the suit enveloped her entire body, the same framing of joints and rods covering her hips, legs and feet as well. With a couple of flicks of her slender legs, she kicked off her shoes and the last of her clothing and stood there, black as blindness, her head and long red hair seemingly disembodied on her inhumanly midnight body.

"What you are looking at, ladies and gentlemen, is a suit made of the same material as the shielding that took our missiles through the satellites' laser defenses. This one is woven rather than plated, giving it a necessary flexibility with only a minor loss of strength. It is light, the entire suit weighs less than twenty pounds. But it gives me more protection than a military issue bomb disposal suit."

She let the statement hang a moment, and then she did what they all feared, and kind of morbidly hoped she would do. She set about proving it.

First she pulled out a lighter. Flicking its flint wheel, she sparked it to life, and brought the small orange flame under her right hand. They waited … waited … waited. Nothing happened. After about a minute of expectant silence, she walked slowly over and stood in front of the British prime minister.

"Prime Minister, if you don't mind, could you verify something for me?" Behind him, two of the important man's staff tensed as if to intervene, but he raised his hand. He was more aware of what was going on than most in the room, and he knew that if he couldn't keep an open mind then he could not expect the rest of them to. He stood, and when Madeline extinguished the lighter he took her proffered hand, straight from over the flame.

"It's cold!" he exclaimed, despite himself, a broad, childlike grin spreading over his face as he shook her black hand. She smiled in return, thanking him with candid gratitude for being a good sport, and then she offered her hand to other members of a now curious group. They reached out one by one and she explained as they did so.

"The material has phenomenal conductive properties, which means it almost instantaneously conducts any energy applied to one part of its mass across its entirety, taking the heat from a cigarette lighter that would have quickly burned my fingers and spreading it out across my entire body. I could not even feel a change in the temperature, any more than the lighter made the room feel warmer as a whole." She looked around, sensing the room's mood before she went to the next level, and then stepped gingerly over to the case once more. From it she extracted a small wooden board about six inches by six inches, with four long nails protruding from it, their sharp points facing outward.

"Heat is one kind of energy. When a bullet hits someone it carries another kind: kinetic. Its momentum is in itself a form of energy, and focused into a point that energy can be devastating. But spread out …" She let the sentence hang as she placed the board on the floor nails up, and without equivocation she stepped firmly onto their sharp points. The room cringed as she placed her entire weight onto her right foot, pressing its sole onto the large spikes.

But nothing happened. She stood there, the suit spreading the pressure out evenly, disseminating the needlepoints of pressure into a flat platform.

"I had wanted to do my final demonstration live, but I was informed in no uncertain terms that it would not be advisable to bring a weapon of any kind into such an auspicious gathering," she smiled broadly, and for the first time that day something akin to a laugh echoed around the room, "but we did manage to capture the most dramatic feature of this armor on video, and I think we would like to share that with you now."

She turned to Neal who nodded and smiled his friendly approval at her eloquent demonstration, and with that an image appeared on the large screen that had been used to show so many powerpoint slides earlier in the meeting. The room was silent as they watched an unknown woman's hands load a small revolver with copper-tipped bullets. Without breaking camera shot, the scene panned out, revealing the woman holding the gun to be Ayala Zubaideh, a fact that was not lost on the French minister sitting quietly in his chair. The sight of her face banished any last thoughts he had of further dissent, though he would not share that with anyone. In her chair back in the shadows, Ayala saw his expression shift and smiled discreetly.

But the rest of the room was unaware of such nuances. They only saw with some trepidation a dark-set, serious-looking woman raise her gun and point it with clear professionalism at the heart of a black-suited figure standing not ten feet from her. They were in some white room, a laboratory perhaps. Shinobu Matsuoka recognized it as his company's lab in the Midwest, but again the point was lost as suddenly the gun flared and Madeline rocked back on her feet as if the floor had shifted under her.

A moment's stunned silence from the people on the screen and the members of the gathered meeting, and then the image of Madeline shrugged and laughed a little, saying, "Is that all you've got?" The other woman on the screen shook her head, also smiling but with eyebrows raised as if to say, 'oh sister, do you really want to go there?'

Shaking her head, Ayala turned to an unseen table, her hands returning with a much larger, longer revolver. The Magnum looked ridiculous in her delicate-seeming hands, but she wielded it with practiced confidence, bracing herself and holding it up with two, outstretched arms.

Madeline looked momentarily trepidatious and then BAM!

The gun was significantly louder than the first, and Madeline was thrown bodily off her feet as Ayala rocked back from the tremendous blast. At first it seemed like the black-suited woman on the screen was crying, and the room momentarily forgot that the woman they were watching was standing, strong as sunshine, in the room with them, and fear for her life filled them.

But the sound soon revealed itself as laughter. The laughter of a child who has been wrestling with her father, the overwhelming strength of the apparent giant combining with a feeling a complete safety to induce a mild hysteria: joy and fear summed. As the suited Madeline on the screen stood, laughing breathlessly, and clearly none the worse for wear, the screen went blank and the room returned its amazed gaze to the woman standing amongst them.

There was a sense of awe and respect, mixed with surprise and some doubts for her sanity, but none doubted the veracity of her demonstration. What they were witnessing was far outside the capabilities of known science, that much was painfully clear. She smiled and then shrugged a little apologetically for her display on the screen, wondering what they would be thinking if they had seen what else the two women had tried.

Before either of them had tried them out themselves they had tested the suits with a few watermelons, then with a crash-test dummy, sensors in it wired to a nearby bank of computers. When that had gone well, they had gone the whole hog.

Both suited, they had spent nearly an hour shooting, stabbing, mauling, clubbing, and all round beating the living crap out of each other. At one point Madeline had walloped Ayala in the stomach with a sledgehammer. Seeing Ayala tumble across the room had sent them both into fits of laughter. They soon realized their 'tests' had descended into something akin to two children checking their bicycle helmets by daring each other to run headfirst into a wall.

The suit was the ultimate toy, making a joke of the most dangerous things on earth. It didn't make you invincible, far from it. In fact, they had both had a strange whole body bruising after their 'experiments', along with a throbbing headache and what might best be termed an unsavory dietary aftermath. But they had survived countless things that would have easily ripped their unprotected bodies apart, and it had been the most fun they'd had in years.

Neal nodded and reassumed control of the room, thanking Madeline for her persuasive demonstration.

"I asked Dr. Cavanagh to speak today for a couple of reasons. Firstly, I wanted you to see something tangible to support what we have been saying, and secondly I wanted that to be something that we have made, something that shows what we can do if we set our minds to the task I am laying out for you today."

He paused, and then with all the gravitas he could muster, "But most of all I wanted you to see something *we* have made before you see something *they* have made."

The room was ripped back from the revelry of Madeline's demonstration by Neal's words. He had expected it. And he had wanted them to have the image of Madeline's seeming invincibility in their heads before they met the last of his team members.

John saw his cue and stood. He did so quietly and calmly, but his movement in the shadow of Neal's last words gave his quiet entrance a truck's worth of weight, and the room's attention shifted completely to him as he walked slowly into its center.

"Ladies and gentlemen. My name is John Hunt. My friend Dr. Danielson has mentioned a source of information, a source of tools and materials such as Dr. Cavanagh's intriguing black suit. He has also spoken of something *they* have made. I am here to tell you that I am the answer to both those riddles. For I am an Agent of the race coming to conquer you."

What noise the room had been making, mostly only the light whisper of their breathing, stopped.

John went on, "I was part of the team sent to subdue you and mute your nuclear response to the coming attack. Not because my people believed you could win, but because they feared that in fighting for your lives you might destroy the very thing they have travelled all these light-years to claim. Your planet."

Some of the room were remembering to breathe, but most stared wide-eyed as he went on, passionate now, "But I tell you that you *can* win. Because we are not united, like my friend Neal is hoping you will be. My people do not all believe in this terrible enterprise. If we have overpopulated our own planet that is no justification for taking yours. And so I was sent by the people I represent to help you. I am not a convert, I am one of the many who believe this cannot be allowed to come to pass, and I have dedicated myself to stopping it.

"But, to demonstrate Neal's point, and to emphasize my own, I should tell you that I am not what I seem. I am but a copy, an esoteric construct overlaid with the characteristics and traits of the real me to allow me to possess this machine body that allows me to walk among you. A body capable of surviving the blistering speed with which I entered your atmosphere nearly two years ago. A body that represents some measure of what you now face."

With that he stopped talking a moment and he bent and placed the thumb and two fingers of his right hand on the floor. He then proceeded to lift himself easily into the air, supporting his entire weight upside-down on the three fingers he had placed on the wooden paneled flooring. He ignored the gaping looks and continued talking, turning himself on his three superhuman fingers to face this way and that in a demonstration of how easy this feat was for him.

"See me. Know that I represent what is coming. I am what they can do." He lowered himself now, supporting himself still on those three fingers, but flattening his body parallel to the floor until he lay flat, raised off the ground only a few inches, in the most impossible yoga position ever imagined. Then, with a flick of his arm, he threw himself up in a smooth arching somersault to land with alarming grace on his two feet once more.

Facing them normally, he now said, "If you think for one moment that this is something that can be ignored, I warn you that you doom everyone you love to certain death by doing so. You must resist. You must devote yourselves to defending this earth. I will help, and there are others who share my beliefs aboard the coming Armada even now, waiting to sabotage some measure of its strength. But do not think we can come close to stopping them alone. We must all stand together."

The room was with him, completely, they were transfixed, and so he said his final piece: "You should know, also, that even as we begin to prepare for the greater fight ahead, we must also address the remnants of the threat that still walks among us. For I did not come alone, and my colleagues are just as capable as I, and harbor nothing but ill-will toward you and your kind."

They all recoiled. John raised his hands placatingly.

"Now, we believe two of my colleagues are already dead. One more has joined me, his will for genocide ebbed from him by his time living amongst you. But four other Agents still hide amongst you. And we must find them. They carry terrible purpose and awesome power, and they must be destroyed if we are to have a chance in our enterprise."

Into the silence, a question came unexpectedly, "Where is this … friend of yours? Your ally." came a meek voice, it was the Japanese ambassador.

John paused, and many noticed Neal and the other members of his team flinch at the mention of the other Agent.

But John did not avoid the thought of his brother-in-arms for long, "A good question." John eventually replied, "He was last seen helping the team that was trying to limit the spread of the virus we discussed earlier. They were shot down over the Middle East, a place we were unable to fully inoculate with our antigen."

John looked at several of the military people in the room, and noted their stoic expressions. Finally he looked at Neal, and found in his intense stare the resolve he sought.

"I am assured we are doing everything we can to find him." he said, and Neal nodded.

Chapter 5: Running Wild

In the late 1950s the first spy satellites were launched by the United States and Russia as they sought to peek over the iron curtain that hung between them. In the days before digital media, several interposed film cameras were used to capture images on film four times the size of our household standard. Used film reels were then ejected from the satellite in large, heat-resistant canisters to fall to back into the atmosphere, and were intercepted in midair by specially designed planes as they parachuted down. Each Corona spy satellite carried two film reels each, totaling more than six miles in length if unspooled.

In a stark demonstration of the evolution of our information age, a single iPod touch available in any of a thousand stores could easily store hundreds of times the information those reels held, and could transmit it wirelessly in less than an hour.

Just as our ability to record and transmit images has evolved exponentially, so has our ability to capture them. So it is an incredibly powerful camera, two hundred miles above the surface of the earth, looking through a four-meter-wide lens of astonishing acuity, that spots the unfolding chase far below.

It is one of many such eyes around the globe, and it reports back its images in near real-time to USSTRATCOM in Offutt, Nebraska. The images contain the answer to a vital question.

"Neal, this is Barrett," came the voice over the phone. It was after 11pm, and as usual, Neal was in his new office.

"Barrett, what's up?" came Neal's distracted reply. He had spent the day after their conference at Camp David in teleconference meetings with a series of world leaders whose envoys had vigorously opined them to become involved personally.

Recognizing Neal's distracted tone, Barrett changed his own in order to bring his friend around, "Neal, I have just gotten off the line with STRATCOM. They've found Shahim."

Neal came to with a start, "Where?"

"He seems to be heading away from the crash sites we found yesterday, and he isn't alone. But he has been pinned down near Mashhad by a platoon of Iranian Commandos. I have requested that they patch through the link to the SecCom in Conference Room 527, can you meet me there?"

"Immediately. What about John and the others?" Neal was already standing and grabbing his laptop.

"John's already there, Madeline's driving in as we speak." said the general.

"Good. I'll be there momentarily."

- - -

Lord Mantil knelt in the center of a shabby, dank room, his senses on high alert, his every system primed and ready. He had made it as far through the desert as he could have hoped before being spotted. In the end, he couldn't have known that a lone pair of army scouts in a jeep had stopped for a rest just beyond a ridge, out of his line of sight, or that one of them had stepped behind a rock to take a pee. Unbeknownst to a heavily burdened Lord Mantil as he sprinted at inhuman speed across the desert, the startled man had watched him from just behind that rock. The lowly infantryman's brain had refused to register what he was seeing at first, squinting ever harder to make out the motorbike that his mind insisted must be there for the apparition to be moving so fast. Despairing at last, the soldier had summoned his colleague with a wild jerk of his hand, and together they had watched the figure head off down the valley before trying in vain to report the full measure of what they had seen to their superiors.

Shahim had heard the helicopters long before he saw them and bolted for cover. Hiding there, he had seen the choppers hove into view and had instantly seen that they were not transports but attack helicopters, and that they were flying in a search pattern, flaring along ridges and valleys this way and that. Their path was too close to his, their timing to coincidental. They were on his trail.

Also unbeknownst to Shahim, Jennifer, and the still unconscious Jack Toranssen, an eagle-eyed satellite above them had also spotted his hair-raising progress across the desert, and its report had gone to a wholly different command team in the US. But they were a long way away, and in no position to offer him any assistance yet anyway.

Navigating more slowly now, moving from cover to cover, Shahim carried his injured cargo ever farther away from the path that they had been taking. Away from the helicopters that were probing the very route of his intended escape. His plethora of sensors also searched; they searched the wavelengths, listening for information about the men that hunted him. The first reports of the ground forces came through not fifteen minutes before he heard their throttled report. Not much more than dune buggies with a machine-gun emplacement behind its driver's seat, the buggies went where even a jeep or Humvee would hesitate. A team of them were spreading out in a grid from the point where the three fugitives had last been spotted. And they were moving fast. He couldn't tell how many there were exactly, or their exact paths, but his every route was now being covered by keen eyes and ears, and his chances of evading them completely were getting slimmer by the moment.

But he was resourceful and quick of mind, and he managed to make it another twenty kilometers before he was spotted again. The radio signal from the buggy was like a flare in his mind. They were zeroing in. All priorities changed. He must find shelter. He must find cover. He must prepare for the battle he could no longer avoid.

The village was little more than a collection of huts, and most of those deserted. The families had headed to the city ahead of the disease that was clearly sweeping amongst them. The first had fallen ill within a day of the virus being dropped, the rest could not know that they were also fatally infected. Maybe in the city they would inadvertently catch the antigen from one of the inoculated. Maybe it would work in time to save them. But probably not. Whether they survived or not, they would never know the source of their death or that their government was hunting one of the sources of their salvation.

Amongst these huts Lord Mantil darted, laying Jack gently down in one and leaving Jennifer to tend to him, and then going in search of anything that might save them. Some kind of transportation. But there was none. The donkeys and camels had been taken to the city, bearing the ill on their forgiving backs. There were no weapons to speak of. He did not want to kill all these people hunting them, but his choices were narrowing. He heard the radio reports, he knew they were closing in. Helicopters and armed dune buggies were converging on him. It was just a matter of time.

"Listen," he said to Jennifer, "I am going to go out and meet them. At the moment they can have no way of knowing how many of us there are. You must stay here, and you must wait. I will try and keep them away from here. I can move faster alone, and I can withstand a fight better without you than I can if I am carrying you. If you are with me I will not be able to protect you from the firepower they are bringing. I cannot know how long it will take me to get back here, and I must leave Major Toranssen in your hands until I return."

He looked down at the sleeping man. His brief surgery had relieved the pressure and stemmed the hemorrhaging, but he was far from well. He would need tending and delicate care until he awoke, which could be in five minutes or five days. Lord Mantil looked back at Captain Jennifer Falster, the woman Jack had kidnapped in order to steal her command, whose copilot had died in the explosion that had also killed Martin Sobleski. He knew how she must feel about what had happened to her since she was rendered unconscious on the bridge of her own command, how angry and confused she must still be.

"Jennifer, I can only imagine how hard this has been for you, and confusing. I wish I had the time to tell you everything you need to know but that is not an option for us now. So I must focus on telling you what you need to know right now." she looked at him with dubious eyes, her fury at what had happened to her and her copilot battling with her incredulity over what she had witnessed the Agent do since his shocking arrival onto the scene.

He saw her doubt and reached out to it, "Jennifer, there is more at stake here than you can know. I am sure you can tell that I am not like you. Well, the truth is you still have no idea just how unlike you I am. But we share a common bond more important than any of our differences, we are part of something greater, something tasked with protecting the innocent from harm. And I can tell you that no one represents that selfless defense of the innocent more than this man."

He reached out and touched the arm of the sleeping Jack Toranssen, and then, to give the moment even greater gravity, he took her hand and rested it on the major's gently heaving chest, "I know it must feel like this man has done you a great wrong, and a part of you must long for revenge. I cannot explain this to you now but you must believe me, on the strength of what you have seen me do to try to save you both, when I say that to let him die here would be the greatest crime imaginable. One day, in a safer place, on a quieter night, I will tell you everything. And you will hear it not only from me, but from the most trusted sources you can imagine, you will get the answers to all your questions. And I promise you that if you let this man die tonight, then when that day comes you will regret it more than you can possibly imagine."

A flash of fear came across her face, only slight, and he assured her, "That is not a threat. I will not judge you for what you do when I am gone from here, I promise you. But I cannot tell you firmly enough that once you know the truth about this man and what you have become embroiled in over the past week, you will judge yourself based on what you do here, tonight. So please, tend to him, just trust me and look after him. All will be explained soon enough, I promise. And if you still want some kind of revenge when you know the truth, I feel certain the major will be the first to offer it to you."

And with that he stood, leaving her hand resting on the unconscious major. He waited a moment while he looked into her eyes. It was a horrible burden to leave a person, the care of someone they despised, a man so recently responsible for the death of her friend. But Shahim had no choice. He had to go into battle and they would not survive what he was about to face if he took them with him.

With nothing more to be said, he resigned himself to the overriding imperatives of their situation and left the small, slovenly hovel he had laid his charges in. It was not the largest house in the camp. In fact, it was the most ignominious, and also one of the farthest from the Iranian's angle of approach. Hopefully it would be the last they would check if they searched the camp. But Shahim was going to set his mind and body to stopping the Iranian forces from ever getting to the small settlement, and they were going to be in for the fight of their lives.

- - -

"There he is again," said John Hunt, full of frustration that he could not get to his colleague to help him. Could not at least tell him what he faced. They needed to work on a subspace tweeter network and soon. This lack of communication was going to be their end. He stared at the big screen impotently and decided to set his mind to something useful. Turning to Madeline, who had also joined them in the conference room, he said, "Madeline, I can't watch this. I cannot just *watch* it. There is so much we should be able to do about this. If we had but one Mobiliei fighter craft I could have been there in less than three hours, and these helicopters and buggies closing in on Shahim would have fallen before me like paper dolls. Shahim would be home before lunchtime."

Madeline looked at him, curiosity and a desire to avert his attention from the frustrating sight on the screen leading her to ask the obvious question: "What kind of craft?"

He smiled, bleakly, but then glanced back at the screen and his face set once more in frustration and mute fury.

Taking her arm and leading her to a laptop, "In my Citadel's language we call them Skalm. They are named for a breed of airborne predator not dissimilar to vampiric bats. They are highly agile and famous hunters, often catching their prey midair and killing it with somewhat brutal efficiency with the four sharp maws that line their underbelly and wings. They have been synonymous with hunting for eons on Mobilius, a source of cautionary tales for our children since time immemorial."

She looked at him somewhat squeamishly at the mental image, and he opened one of the laptops on the desk and pressed his finger against its USB port. The fibers in his hand jutted out into the port and found its metallic contacts, binding to them, and his connection was quick to form. With the equivalent of a mouse and keyboard directly plugged into his brain, he began to manipulate the machine, and images and designs began to flow across its screen. Madeline stared at the images and started asking questions, and in spite of himself Neal stepped over to them and joined the conversation.

Only Barrett remained fixed to the big screen, long practice allowing him to suppress the feelings of impotence that came from watching his subordinates, and often his friends, from well behind the front lines. He also longed to have the power to act that John was discussing with Madeline and Neal, but for now he would leave such hypothesizing to them. He watched. He watched as the black figure on his screen darted out from the huts, tracing a wide curve to flank the coming force. He watched as the hunted turned on his unknowing pursuers, bringing the battle to them and a part of him felt sorry for the troops descending on the small collection of huts. They had no idea what was about to hit them.

- - -

Lord Mantil also felt a measure of sadness and guilt at what he was going to have to do. He knew that he had to choose between the deaths of Jack and Jennifer and the death of these soldiers descending on them. He knew it was not a choice he wanted to make. Neither party truly knew what they were fighting for, neither knew what they faced. Neither knew that they were all, in fact, on the same side of the coming conflict. And so it came down to a simple choice between the hundred or so Iranian soldiers and the two American pilots. Simple mathematics should have led him to kill Jennifer and Jack himself and then leave the remains to the Iranians. Shahim could easily avoid soldiers on his own, especially as they would not come looking for him once they found the two pilots. But such things were never mathematical.

However misguided the Iranian soldiers may be, however justified their actions might be in the face of an illegal incursion by an American B-2 bomber into their airspace, the truth remained that Jack had been shot down solely because he sought to save the very people who now hunted him. And Jennifer was as innocent of the crimes of her captors as she could possibly be. Should she suffer an ignominious death for her unwitting part in the battle that had killed Martin and her copilot?

In the end it came down to one thing. Jack had willingly risked his life to protect others, and had saved hundreds of thousands in the process, maybe more. That alone justified protecting him. That the threat Jack had been fighting against had been brought on the same wing that had delivered Shahim himself to Earth only strengthened the Agent's resolve.

These soldiers had every intention of capturing and then killing the captain and the major. Ignorant as they all were of the greater picture, it was time to choose a side and Lord Mantil had decided. It was time to fight once more.

Lacking the overhead view his cohorts were watching him on, he instead used his hypersensitive hearing like a passive sonar, listening to the hums and thrums of his quarry as they approached with the coming night. As he arced away from the small village, he triangulated the sounds of his prey in his head, picking out buggies and helicopters, and then codifying each one of the copters and cars by the minutest differences in the beat of their engines. Imperceptible irregularities in the walls of their thumping pistons or the explosive firing of their spark plugs leaving an audio fingerprint on each part of the faint cacophony that was starting to fill the night. He found them, he mapped them, and he started to plot their courses. Over time his map resolved; the longer he listened and the wider the range of his run the more clearly he could triangulate their routes. His path altered, his speed changing as he picked out the closest buggy.

A quarter of a mile away, the buggy came on, travelling at twenty miles per hour. Lord Mantil set himself to intercept. Thirty seconds.

The driver focused hard on the terrain in front of him, driving wildly around small rocks, shrubs, and ruts in the grit soil beneath his tires. The dusk was closing in, and the light his powerful headlamps were spreading out in front of him was starting to hold sway over the fading natural light. He switched on the larger bank of spotlights above him and his view brightened further. Behind him the gunner slowly swiveled left and right, the large spotlight mounted beside his machine gun following his sights as he panned the scene scrolling towards them.

Lord Mantil came in from their right, firing his legs in a final burst of speed as he approached; a blur in their vision. He leapt at the last moment just as the gunner spotted him, a shout rising up from his soul as the apparition appeared from the twilight. Lord Mantil landed hard against the steel cage of the buggy, his thundering momentum sending it skidding to the left. He grabbed the gunner by the collar and deftly ripped him from his seat, plucking his sidearm from its holster as he flung him, screaming, from the car.

The driver slammed on the breaks and the Agent used the change in speed as he was flung forward. Grasping the bar above the driver's head, he swung over, bringing his two feet over and around like a swinging axe. But he did not need to kill these men, so he parted his feet at the last moment to fall either side of the stunned driver's shoulders, allowing Shahim to come to rest facing the man, sitting neatly on the buggy's small dashboard. Without hesitation, Lord Mantil neatly stripped the man of his helmet and sidearm and wrenched him bodily from the seat, propelling him out and away from the car as it skidded across the sand. No doubt both men would suffer a couple of broken bones to go with their dazed memories of the lightning-fast attack, but Shahim gave them little thought as he swiveled around and dropped into the driver's still-warm seat, placing the man's helmet and its radio receiver on his own head as he did so.

He was already gunning the throttle and swerving the buggy sharply right before the driver even hit the ground, killing its lights and relying on his acute vision to guide him through the dusk to find the buggy's cohorts.

Wrenching the car around, he used the vehicle in ways it had never been driven before, cutting in a frenzied slice through the paths of other assault buggies in the platoon.

While he had been able to spare the first two, he could not afford such leniency with all of them. There were simply too many. Ripping the machine gun from its mount above his head, he wielded it like a scythe as he crossed each car's path, his speed far outstripping the cautious twenty miles per hour the human drivers were managing in the fading light. He tried to maim rather than kill, but at the speeds he needed to drive at in order to catch them all before they reached the huts, even he could not place all his shots as accurately as he wanted.

One after one the bullets ripped through legs and shoulders as he bisected the paths of the oncoming trucks. The shots carved brutal paths through flesh and bone, and screams filled the helmets of the remaining pilots, drivers, and gunners as dark death swept through their ranks. It did not take long for them to see the pattern of their assailant's movement in the order of the buggies being attacked, and the helicopters shifted their massive firepower to face whatever was tearing them apart in the night.

The light Shahed 285 Iranian Attack Helicopter carried twin autocannons and a barrage of air-to-ground missiles. They were homebred in Iran, and while not a match for their American or European cousins, they still brought vastly more guns to the game than the plethora of buggies whose drivers Lord Mantil was busy maiming or worse.

Shahim sensed the nearest helicopter veering toward him and saw it only a moment before its infrared-enabled pilot saw him too. The pilot shouted to his gunner. The buggy in their sights was going the wrong way and was coming at them from the direction of the death cries rattling their radios.

There was no way they were going to wait for orders on how to handle this apparition, and the gunner went weapons hot. Shahim did not hesitate either, leveling his machine gun and emptying its belt at the coming chopper. The pilot saw the muzzle flash in the distance an instant before the rounds started to impact his armored chopper. The sound was like an angry lead hail pelting the screen in front of him, which started to crack and shatter almost instantly. He instinctively veered hard right and responded in kind, his helmet-targeted front machine gun whirring to life as he squeezed the trigger, glaring furiously at the spot where he had last seen the buggy.

A thousand bullets ripped from the spinning cannon and raced toward Shahim, vastly larger and more deadly than the hail his popgun could return. Shahim's reactions were fast but the fire was wild, and a storm of lead erupted the sand around him as it rained outward from the helicopter. The buggy's sharp turn brought his left side to bear on the metal needles as they blurred the space between him and the damaged chopper, and the line of destruction that the bullets were burning into the ground scythed across the buggy like a chainsaw. The rear left tire shredded a moment before the empty gunner's seat behind spat foam, and the next bullets hit Shahim square. The woven skin on his left shoulder ripped open as a hypersonic bullet bounced off the armor beneath and the next hit him hard in the ribs. Internal alarms sprang to life in his mind as his systems reported damage from the hits.

Deciding with machine rapidity that the buggy was now little more than a hindrance, Shahim propelled himself upward out of the seat, leaving the car to stumble onward into the night.

The copilot in the chopper was hard at work as well, sighting his first missile group on the car, he fired immediately, and two small but deadly heat-seeking missiles rocketed outward toward the small vehicle even as Lord Mantil landed in a roll and began sprinting away from it. Lord Mantil watched the rockets flame from the chopper toward him and then past him into the car. Their brilliant blue flames lighting up the ground and their smoke trails in the flash before they smothered the buggy in bright orange flame. Thud, thud, came the quick impacts and the car was gone, obliterated, not even a hulk.

Even as the missiles' smoke trails wafted in the wind, Lord Mantil was bolting back along their path toward the helicopter, his cold machine body invisible to their infrared sensors and his movements but a blur in the twilight. The two men never knew what hit them, a weight suddenly landed bodily on the front of the helicopter and a moment later a fist came through the window with blinding power. They were both dead before their bodies hit the ground below.

- - -

"Jesus," whispered Barrett at the sight. He couldn't make out exactly what had happened but the results were clear. The image was grey and faded with the passing of the day, but he had seen the inhumanly fast figure from the huts leap onto the unsuspecting buggy, had seen two men fly from it a moment later. Then he had watched as the car tore bloody murder down through the ranks of the coming forces as they approached the huts Barrett knew harbored his friends.

He had then seen the first of the two attack helicopters in the squadron engage the man he knew was Lord Mantil and seen as it destroyed the car that had born Shahim down on his prey. But a moment later the chopper had visibly faltered in the evening air. Then it had become a slaughter. Barrett assumed the original pilots of the chopper were no longer onboard because he had watched as it turned its guns on the rest of the squadron. The next few minutes were ugly, the remainders of the squadron dying quickly as what was clearly now Lord Mantil piloting the chopper wielded the agile machine's guns and missiles like a samurai.

- - -

Shahim watched his radar as the last of the terrified soldiers eventually fled. Shahim let them go, turning the helicopter back toward the huts. He landed in the deserted settlement and barely hesitated. In a matter of moments he had taken his two charges aboard and was on his way, flying hard for the border.

Chapter 6: Ghazzat

A deep heat lay on the city of Gaza. A dry, dusty heat that desiccates the bones and forces you to squint. It had been a long, long time since Saul had been outside his homeland of Israel. Indeed in some ways he still wasn't. But though the Palestinian National Authority was hypothetically part of the nation of Israel, Saul Moskowitz could not have been farther from home.

It was not the first time he had been in Palestinian territory, but the last time he was here it had been under the orders of the feared and respected Israeli intelligence agency, the Mossad. Plus he had been thirty years younger. He had been fitter and at the peak of his trade.

Since then he had gone into a form of retirement. He had reached a point when he had felt his sharpness fading, his skills dulling, and he had been faced with three choices: take a desk job in analysis, stay in the field until the day he finally met his match, or turn his long experience to the aid and guidance of the next generation. He had chosen the third. And so for two decades he had handled a wide variety of agents as they worked their way into the plethora of political and militia bodies that wished Israel harm. Even this job had faded with time, his age leading him to manage fewer and fewer assets in the field. Attrition had slowly whittled down that list, either through retirement or death, typically the latter. Eventually, inevitably, he had been left with none.

Until one had reemerged. The day Ayala had called him he had been stunned, but his long training had kept his voice steady. You can train yourself not to show surprise. To remain placid even during the most shocking of events. It takes a long time, and a lot of practice, but every agent learns quickly that the slightest facial tick or inflection of voice is all a trained spy needs to read you like a book. So you learn to keep a phenomenally tight rein on your reactions if you hope to live very long. So tight, that in the course of normal life you find yourself having to remember how you are supposed to react to important news, consciously triggering smiles and laughter as friends and loved ones share themselves with you, unaware of the calculated method behind your responses.

He had shown no such emotion when Ayala had called. He had greeted her offhandedly, and they had agreed to a meeting, using the long-outdated codes she had used in her time as an active asset. They had met, and they had spoken, and it had taken Saul a few hours to realize that Ayala, his former agent, had just turned the tables, and had activated him, the handler.

He had spent the next few weeks travelling around Israel, contacting agents, speaking with former colleagues, spreading an inoculating contagion that Ayala had given to him to administer. He had been spreading the antigen, and his work had gone a long way toward inoculating the region. But that had been but the first of two tasks given him by Ayala. He had also been given the name of an innocent-seeming junior officer in the Israeli Air Force and been told that she was the single greatest threat to Israel in the nation's short and bloody history.

It had been hard to believe, and Saul had known that he was only being told half the truth, but he had also trusted his old ally enough to believe that the measure she was not giving away would not be something he needed to know in order to survive. Sure enough, she had told him to keep his distance, and he had. She had told him that the woman was not as she seemed and soon enough that had been proven beyond any reasonable doubt. Finally Ayala had warned him that the woman was part of something far larger, something that spanned the globe, and that one day he would know why he had been kept in the dark.

And when the world had gone mad on that strange autumn night, the sky alight with missiles and explosions, stories of deadly dogfights over Afghanistan, and nuclear hell breaking loose in America, Raz Shellet had fled. He had been watching her, as was his mandate, from a distance. He had used his not inconsiderable talents to gain an understanding of her movements without triggering any unwanted alarms, and he had watched, almost expectantly, as she had calmly walked off the base and vanished from her old life.

He had followed her. It had not been easy. He had not been prepared for her flight and had not been carrying any but the most basic amenities, not nearly enough for a prolonged pursuit. Most of all he had been unprepared for where she was going. But he should have known. Israel had allies in most of the civilized nations of the world, and information sharing treaties came as part of those allegiances. If you wanted to hide from Israel's eyes, you needed to do so among her enemies. And there were few places with more enmity toward mother Israel than in the Islamic strongholds of Gaza and the West Bank.

The city of Gaza, the largest of all the Palestinian cities, held more than four hundred thousand souls spread along the coast almost to the border with Israel, only fifty miles south of Tel Aviv. But the trip had taken days, days marked by long nights and hitchhiked rides, at first with dubious and mistrusting Jews and then, as they got closer to the fortified border with the Gaza Strip, the rides had become even less savory.

It had been an exhausted Saul, showing all of his sixty-five years in his gray tufted beard, who had called upon an old colleague in the middle of the night in Gaza. The friend had been startled and afraid but he had granted his colleague shelter and food. Saul knew he had ruined his colleague's cover and probably endangered the man's life, but every part of him had told him that this was more important than that. More dangerous to Israel. More valuable than either his life or that of his associate.

Saul woke from a deep sleep with an aching body. While he showered, his friend made him some coffee in the local tradition, roasting the fat green beans in a pan with some cardamom, then grinding them with a big wooden al-houn. As Saul explained the situation the other agent poured the steaming hot brew … repeatedly. Saul did not wave his fingers over his cup until he had downed his fifth.

He did not shave. He had too many enemies here. Anything he could do to disguise his identity was welcome. With fresh clothes and a gun, he ordered his colleague to leave the city as soon as possible, and then Saul returned to the place he had watched Raz rent a room.

For several hours he veered toward despair that she had moved on, knowing that if she had, he would probably never regain her scent. His relief was palpable when she returned to the lowly guesthouse, a heavy duffle bag of supplies slung over her shoulder. Canisters of food, perhaps, he could not make them out. But seeing that she was settling in for a long stay he settled himself as well, mentally and literally, seeking out and then renting himself a room in the building across the street before sending for help. Help from the only person he was certain he could trust.

- - -

"I'm still getting used to the fact that we can talk on the phone." said Ayala into her cell, catching up with Neal on what she had missed on the satellite images from Iran. It was one of many things she was getting used to. Travelling first class at the US's expense was another, as was sitting in the executive lounge she now found herself in at Heathrow airport. Starting to openly work with senior members of the CIA, MI6, French DGSE, and assorted other agencies across the globe was yet another.

She had been trying furiously to organize some semblance of an intelligence network to track down the remaining four Agents still at large when her old friend Saul had called her. It could only be in reference to one thing. And the location code he had used could only mean that his target had gone in the dragon's den, and he had followed her. She had immediately boarded a flight to Europe and on to Tel Aviv, making arrangements as she went. The Mossad, the CIA, all had assets she could use on the ground. And she intended to use all of them.

She had been in the air when US StratCom had managed to identify and pass back images of Shahim in Iran, and had heard only secondhand the story of his clash with the Iranian Commandoes. As she swelled with pride at this evidence of what her allies John and Shahim could do, she also reminded herself that the tale also foretold the capabilities of her foes. All four of them.

"I know," said Neal in response to her comment about using the phone, "it still seems forbidden. I hadn't even paid my phone bill in three months. Apparently it has affected my credit." He chuckled at the futility of such things, and Ayala smiled. She had tried to impress upon the team the need to be mindful of such things, sudden changes in that kind of behavior being the key signs someone such as herself might look for as they tried to identify a spy or a recently converted asset. But as they had approached zero hour they had all begun to quite simply say fuck it.

Since then, the inclusion of the leviathan political machines that were now joining their cause had put a quick end to such considerations. The identities she had carefully crafted for her team had become moot as they started to enjoy the full support of some of the most powerful governments, armed forces, and intelligence agencies on earth. There were not many doors you could not open with the blessing of the leaders of the US, UK, France, Germany, Japan, India, and Brazil. Unless those doors were in Russia or China, of course.

It was a Mossad liaison that greeted Ayala when she landed in Tel Aviv. It was the first time since she was eighteen that she had flown into the airport under her own identity and it felt deeply unnatural. But she was left little time for reveling in the newness of it as she brusquely refused a meeting at Mossad headquarters in favor of making her way toward the border immediately. Despite the liaison's protestations, her summation of the Israelis' readiness for her arrival was true to her own long experience, and her small team was indeed prepped and ready to move. She had joined them at a warehouse close to the border, two vans at the ready. The men were shoddily dressed, poorly shaven, slovenly and unkempt: clearly professionals, and she did not expect nor ask them to salute as she entered.

"Gentlemen, as you may or may not have been told, your mission today will take you into Gaza. But let me assure that we are not tracking anything so pedestrian as a Hamas cell today." She allowed her offhanded dismissal of their longtime foe to sink in. A foe to whom they had all lost friends and colleagues and dedicated their very lives to battling. Seeing that they were all equal parts offended and piqued by the nature of her opening remark, she built upon it.

"No, by comparison to the quarry we track today, our friends at Hamas are but a nuisance. In fact, what you face today is so exponentially more dangerous that we may even call our friends at Hamas *allies* before this year is out, if we cannot defeat this entity on our own." Again she allowed that bombshell to wash over them, and looked each of them in the eye, matching their rising anger with her own intensity of purpose until they each recognized the seriousness with which she delivered her words.

"Gentlemen, please open your packets." They did so, and photographs of Raz Shellet were clipped at the top of each of the sheaves of papers inside. "Our first and only priority is the *tracking* of this single target. Not interception. The only way I can make it clear enough that interception is not an option, is to tell you that I will happily sacrifice any and all of you to her lethal abilities rather than provoke a full-scale conflict with her.

"I could tell you that I fear the conflict, or that I know we would lose it, no matter how well we all believe we have been trained. But instead I will tell you that the last time a team tried to take down one of this woman's colleagues, it led to the disaster that is even now spreading up the East Coast of the United States." They all looked up at her as one, aghast at her statement. Terrorism was an ever-present threat for everyone who lived in Israel, and a nuclear related attack, though it had never actually happened, was the specter that defined their greatest fear.

"She is a member of a team you have never heard of. Over the next few months and years you may hear more of them, but hopefully not. Hopefully we will defeat them before this all necessarily becomes public. For now our first priority is to find them. To find them and find out what they are planning. Only when we have done that will we have a chance of mitigating the threat they pose.

"So, I repeat to you, gentlemen, we are *not* to engage this woman under *any* circumstances. We are to assume at all times that she is hostile and vigilant. We are also never to use radio communications near her, or any other form of wireless communications, for it is very possible she can hear anything that is said over them. We are to assume positions around her last known location and monitor her behavior. And we are to do so while maintaining maximum cover and distance, we are going to place hard taps on her building's phone lines and transmit the information back to Herzliya for analysis via hard line."

Ayala turned to the liaison and spoke, "You will coordinate with our American and British friends to see that my team is involved in the process."

He nodded, as this was also detailed inside his extraordinary package of orders for this mission. This woman had complete carte blanche. In his fifteen years at the agency, she had been given an unprecedented level of clearance. This had clearly come from the very top, and with enough weight behind it that it had received no resistance on its way down.

She turned back to the team, "Very well, gentlemen, let us begin. I want maps of the neighborhood, electric and sewage lines, known assets and threats in the vicinity, let's go, gentlemen!"

They sprang to life, gathering laptops and locating information points on the fly. They all worked with rapid efficiency, quickly forming into the team they would need to be, skilled, amorphous agents slipping into roles as needed, taking and giving orders, and finding solutions as problems arose. Specialization was a luxury of regular troops. Field agents may or may not have a preferred field, but they were trained to be proficient in all: explosives, marksmanship, hand-to-hand combat, physical and electronic surveillance. They set to their task, and over the next two hours their plan formed.

Within a few hours of landing, Ayala was in the second of two deceptively dilapidated old vans, each carrying half her new team. Each was following a different route. Everyone on the team now had defined roles, along with the various weaponry, bugs, and other equipment they would need. A specialized group was also working with the liaison to ease their vans' passages through the Gaza Strip's strict border security.

Her team members' respective roles were clear and she had every confidence that they would execute against them. What she could not predict was how Raz Shellet would behave. She had not been blowing smoke up the team's proverbial ass when she said that the last time someone tried to take down one of these beasts it had caused the greatest single disaster in history.

For many years Ayala had enjoyed the quiet confidence of someone who is trained to a lethal standard, who can assume she is probably more deadly than any single person she might come up against. It was tempered by a healthy humility, but all of that confidence was banished by the thought of what she faced now. If she went up against this bitch, she knew she would be deader than Davy Crockett, and as she contemplated the recent demise of a squadron of heavily armed Iranian Commandoes, she reached for the black suit that lay in her bag and began to unwrap it.

She had thought of handing them out to the rest of the team, but unfortunately for them the risk of having one of the Agents discover the extent of their new abilities was greater than the risk of these men dying. It was a callous decision on her part, but it was not the first she had made, and it most certainly would not be the last.

Chapter 7: Let's Come Together

Banu sat with a haunted expression on her soft, six-year-old face. It was late and she should be asleep, but she couldn't, not tonight, not with that incessant coughing from her father and two of her brothers. So she had crept out of the small, three-room cabin that she lived in with her father, mother, grandfather, spinster aunt, and three brothers.

Even out here she could still hear the hacking coughs and wheezing snore of her father, but it was dulled and softened by the breathing of the wind in the valley and warm embrace of the sounds of the vivid fauna busying themselves, unseen, in their nocturnal world all around her.

She did not dare wander too far from the cabin. They lived only half a mile from their nearest neighbor, a larger house, with five separate rooms and only seven people living in it. Of course her family was sullenly jealous of them, but that family in turn was equally envious of the battered old Toyota truck that Banu's father owned, a prized possession indeed. Banu had once been friends with the eldest son of the neighboring family, Mabatim, but he was two years older, and was no longer interested in spending time with a 'child'. One of the many tribulations of her young life.

Now, late at night, she wanted to walk away from the cabin. To escape the incessant hacking, to lose herself in the night. But if she was missed inside and she was not near the cabin, the consequences would be extreme indeed. Fearing a beating or worse, she sat, shivering in the night air, trying to shut her ears to the sounds of her family succumbing to the virus she could not know was well on its way to killing them all.

- - -

Miles away, a damaged helicopter flew low and fast over the rugged ridges and valleys. Jennifer and Jack were bitterly cold, a powerful wind blowing over them from the damaged window Lord Mantil had been forced to kick out. But the shuddering breeze had served to awaken Jack at last. He had been disoriented at first, but it had not taken him long to ask after Martin and Jennifer's copilot. As Jennifer told him what had happened, the grief and self-loathing in his eyes had been tangible, and had finally broken Jennifer of her hatred for him.

Huddling against the cold in the gunner's seat of the helicopter, they had talked into each other's ears, she updating him on Lord Mantil's activities, he telling her the full truth behind what she had become unwittingly embroiled in. After what she had seen Lord Mantil accomplish, it had not been difficult to believe what Jack had said, and a bond of sorts had formed between them, breaking through the crustal remnant of mistrust and the pain of recently lost friends.

With fuel running low, Lord Mantil surveyed their progress. They were twenty miles from the border, but reports of fighters being deployed were coming over the radio. Fighters sent to seek the murderer of the squadron whose helicopter he had co-opted. He needed to land and get his charges away from the easily detectable chopper before the planes found them.

- - -

Banu sat in silence. She had never left the valley in her entire life. Its noises and sights were her whole world and she knew them intimately. The sounds of the seasons spoke to her and she could tell the changes in the weather like the rest of her farming family, from the humidity of the air and the thrum of the wind through the trees.

Before she could place a finger on it, something unsettled Banu. More than the ragged coughing, more than the cold wind, something new was in the air. After a moment, a faint swirling noise began to swell out of the night, and the insects and other creatures of the dark seemed to fade to silence in response, as if trying to identify the sound as well.

It was still but a whisper, but it was undeniable, echoing across the blackness like a demon. Banu sat up, straining her ears to identify it, but even as she did so it was becoming more and more pronounced by the moment. It grew and grew until it filled her ears and became a tangible breath on her face, rising to a gale, her ragged sleeping gown whipping this way and that as the shouted voice of hell thundered out of the night at her. The monstrous black shape emerged from the dark sky without lights or warning, descending upon her world like a dragon, and she shook with fear, tears streaming down her face. A sea of soil and grit pelted her and the house behind her and she shielded her face against the storm.

Her father and brothers came rushing from the house even as the whirlwind sank to the ground in front of her, settling on the sandy soil with improbable lightness. From its side, a man sprang nimbly, running up to her family with long strides. They could only stare bewildered at the apparition in front of them as the beast he had been born on whined, its roar slowly diminishing.

As the blades that spun over the beast's head started to slow, the man shouted over the dissipating tornado he had arrived on. He spoke in the lyrical Persian dialect that was their tongue, "I am sorry but I require your truck, give it to me and you will not be harmed, attempt to stop me and I will be forced to kill you. Is that clear?"

Lord Mantil had no time for diplomacy. He needed to move. More than that he recognized the initial signs of the virus in these people, and knew that their lives were essentially already sacrificed to the first of humanity's battles with the Mobiliei. Hoping that the dramatic nature of his arrival amongst these people would overwhelm any desire to resist him, Lord Mantil stood, bold as day, and demanded that they acquiesce.

They shook in front of him, Banu's father trembling with equal parts fear and impotent rage, but he said nothing. After a moment, Lord Mantil nodded with finality and stepped past them to walk toward the truck that sat under a tarpaulin on the other side of the house. He started the old Toyota with ease, his capable fingers caressing the wires of the ordinarily unreliable starter motor in ways the truck's keys had failed to do in years. As Shahim drove the old truck round to the side of the now idling helicopter, a growing anger boiled in Banu.

She could not help it. She was overwhelmed with contempt for her cowardly father. That truck was all that separated them from the nomads and lowly serfs of the plains, and her father had put up no more resistance than if the powerful-looking man had asked for an ear of corn.

Her father glanced at her and caught her look of disdain, seeing her plain-faced disgust at his cowardice. Unwilling and unable to face the man who was stealing their livelihood, he lashed out at her instead, delivering all his rage at his lack of courage into a vicious backhanded blow across his young daughter's face. She staggered back, her vision swimming as her cheek swelled, blood filling her mouth. Her father sensed shock from his sons and turned on them with the threat of the same, but their looks of fear were not for their father as they stared at something behind their enraged patriarch. The man turned to see what they were looking at, but was greeted instead with the cold solidity of Shahim's fist connecting with his jaw. He flew back, unconscious before he hit the ground, and Shahim turned to the stunned girl. She was sitting on the dusty soil, her lip and nose bleeding, trying to compute what was happening.

The Agent stared at her. Though the little girl did not know it yet, her whole family was about to die. There was, unfortunately, very little that Shahim could do about that. Within a week, maybe two, everyone she knew would be dead, and if Shahim left her here she would be dead too.

But worse than that, somehow, she would suffer the fury and rage of her cowardly father in those last few days, adding brutality and cruelty to an already tragic end. Shahim could not help but be overcome by a sudden desire to save this single life, one amongst thousands, a single drop of mercy in a bloody sea of atonement. He looked at her. He could do it. It was not much, but he could save her.

He held out his hand and indicated the truck idling by the helicopter.

She looked at him, then at her father slumped on the floor, then at her brothers staring back at her with shock and admonishment in their eyes. She could have no idea what she was really being offered by the stranger. She only knew that if she stayed here she faced reprisals from both her father and brothers. She could not know that she also faced an unpleasant and ignominious death, but the life she saw laid out in front of her did not seem much better than that at that moment. She looked into the black eyes of the stranger. He was massive, and his face carried a threat of violence.

But as she looked at the black eyes of the man in front of her she also saw sadness, and then something different in his proffered hand: an offer of protection. Unlimited and undying protection. And as she sensed the depth of his commitment, her hand lifted from her side as if on a string. He took it, smiling gently and with fathomless empathy, and then he started to step back toward the truck, pulling her gently along with him. She followed, like a puppy on a loose leash, gently propelled toward a new life, more by the draw of his eyes than the gentle pull of his hand.

When they arrived at the door of the truck, she saw the surprise on the eyes of the man and woman now seated on its bench seat, and for a moment she shrank from their stares. But words exchanged in a language she did not understand quickly changed their mood. She watched the woman's expression as she shot a look of dark anger back at where Banu's unconscious father lay, and then with outstretched arms the strange lady pulled Banu onto her lap.

A moment later they were gone. Leaving Banu's old life behind her. A way of life that would soon be smote by the disease that was even now multiplying in her veins.

One of the many mysteries Banu would struggle to understand in the months to come was the minuscule cell that even then was floating on a whispered comfort from Jennifer's mouth, to be drawn in by Banu's own hesitant breath. It quickly found purchase in Banu's lungs, found its way into her bloodstream and began to multiply. Alone it would not be enough. Not even hundreds of its kind would have been able to stem the tide of viral growth already spreading through her veins.

But supplemented with the tens of thousands of others of its kind that she would inherit from Jack and Jennifer over the next few days, the combined horde would seek out and destroy the alien virus that was dividing busily inside her. In fact, it would seek out a host of foreign bacteria and viruses that infested the blood stream of her slightly malnourished body, and cleanse her of them. It would be the first of many changes she would undergo in the coming months. Changes the most open minded and well educated of children would have trouble grasping. Maybe on some level the parochial nature of her education may save her sanity as her world expanded exponentially before her eyes. Maybe it would even be a blessing, thought Shahim, trying to rationalize what he had just done.

- - -

Lieutenant Malcolm Granger of the British Consulate's military detachment sped along, the alert voice of his colonel back at the embassy compound shouting through a satellite phone at him. Malcolm's two-year stint at the embassy had been sorely disappointing to him at first, because of a lack of any hint of excitement. But that was all behind him now. After reconciling himself to the humdrum nature of the job, Malcolm had actually begun to appreciate the simple beauty of the country he had been sent to.

Turkmenistan may have played a relatively small role on the world stage in recent centuries, but with its borders with Iran, Afghanistan, and Pakistan, among others, it had been witness to some of the most important events in recent history. After a long run as a Soviet state, acting as one of the staging points for the forces that invaded Afghanistan in the first of the terrible wars that would ravage that hitherto peaceful and progressive country, Turkmenistan had made a slow return to its own tolerant roots, raising a generation marked, but not broken, by the scars of its totalitarian past.

Now an ally of the West and a burgeoning democracy, it harbored embassies from most of the major economies of the world at its economic and political heart: Ashgabat. But it was still a relatively poor nation, and the growing power of the Islamic regime ruling its burly Iranian neighbor to the south had forced it to establish strong outposts along that long border.

It was to the one of these many border outposts that Malcolm had been brusquely ordered, there to intercept and aid three American nationals that were apparently approaching the border even as they spoke. At first he had been confused by the request: why send a British soldier to meet American nationals? But his slight but growing grasp of the Turkmen dialect of Russian had not gone unnoticed by his superiors, and apparently it was a rare commodity indeed.

By his side in the embassy car was the Turkmenistan liaison to the British consulate, a man Malcolm had formed a burgeoning friendship with. Ruslan carried with him quickly processed papers for the fugitives, written under order of the Turkmen State Department who, in turn, had been implored by both the US and UK governments to make the three nationals welcome.

They actually had papers for five people, but they had been told that they should expect only three from that list to actually be at the border; which three they did not yet know. What that said of the fate of whichever two had not made it was something Malcolm did not want to ponder too closely.

- - -

The Iranian farmer's old truck rolled up to the border gate, slowing as it approached in order to minimize suspicion. It was a minor factor, though, and unlikely to make this any less of an ordeal. They were two Caucasian adults, an Arabic-looking gentleman, and a young Iranian girl, traveling without just cause or permission. Their chances of getting across without a fight were slim, to say the least.

With that in mind, Shahim scanned the various guards and emplacements, surveying their firepower and angles of fire, formulating a plan. His machine mind calculated options for him, arraying statistics and probabilities of casualties on either side, and he sorted them quietly, refining his choices as the short line of trucks, cars, and carts shuffled slowly forward.

Their turn came.

As the guards approached the truck, Shahim could see the tension on their faces. The plague was spreading fast now, and the first trickle of refugees was starting to flow across the region, through border crossings like this one. But the disease was really still just taking hold, only a few deaths had been reported so far. The spreading coughs and wheezing chest infections only hinting at the scale of the epidemic that was around the corner. Once it came, the borders would start to close, maybe in a week, maybe in a few days, only time would tell.

A thick Northern Persian dialect barked surly words through his window, "Papers, please."

Shahim withdrew a sheave of poorly faked papers that he had drawn from memory, his mind transposing an image from his databanks onto the sheets in minute detail. They were supposed to be letters from the Turkmen ministry, listing four names to match the size of his small party. The text, seals, and verbiage on the sheets were almost perfect, but the paper they were printed on, and their monochromatic tones, fell far short of authenticity. The guard was clearly suspicious, and with good cause. The papers were a sham. A second glance, a third.

Bending, the guard peered into the truck. Shahim had told Banu to pretend to be asleep across Jack and Jennifer's laps. For Jack and Jennifer, Lord Mantil had thoroughly and somewhat brutally rubbed dirt into their white-skinned faces. He had done so with almost bruising force, but the effect had been pronounced: aging them and making them look impoverished, meager even. He had told them under no circumstances to show their teeth, a certain tell of the ardent attentions of American orthodontists.

He had also rubbed soil and even some fecal matter into his own teeth to disguise their uniform whiteness. A thick film of muck inside your mouth was not something he imagined a human would be able to stand for long, and neither would a Mobiliei, for that matter. But Shahim was neither human nor Mobiliei, he was a machine, and he grinned a dirty brown grin at the guard as he spoke in broken Iranian at him, his voice lilted with a feigned hoarseness, his body stooped, a rancid stench wafting from his breath as he calculatedly emanated poverty.

And so, looking into the cabin of the truck, the guard saw three dirty, stinking adults, clearly poor, clearly farmers, and a sleeping child. The driver's filthy teeth and foul breath disgusted the guard. Stinking peasants, he thought with the bitter snobbery of the poor judging the poorer. He surveyed the papers once more, dubiously.

They *looked* right but they *felt* false. The paper was too thin, the ink too light. Something was clearly wrong with them. He knew he should investigate further but the idea of searching these peasants turned his stomach. He glanced at the driver once more. In the end the guard was tasked with stopping money, drugs and wanted criminals from leaving Iran and he had no reason to believe these were any of those. That they had papers that were probably forgeries was Turkmenistan's problem. Let them deal with these scrubs.

Shahim watched the guard from behind deliberately glazed eyes, and read the man. He was not surprised when he was waved through; he had assumed that getting out of Iran would be the easy part. The farmers he had stolen the truck from had no telephone, and it would be a while yet before it was light enough for the grounded helicopter to be easily spotted from the air. Only then would the Iranian forces searching for them know that the fugitives had taken a truck. Only then would the border be notified. The problem now lay not in getting out of Iran, but with the second set of guards ahead. It lay with getting into Turkmenistan.

He edged forward. His systems primed. If it came to it he would gun the car through the gate and then leap out, leaving Jennifer to drive onward while Lord Mantil took care of any pursuers and drew their fire away from the truck and the more vulnerable humans inside. But as they rolled up to the gate, they were greeted not by a Turkmen guard, but by a formal British accent.

- - -

Malcolm struggled to contain his reaction to the overpowering smell of the driver's breath. Could this be right?

"Umm, Lord Mantil?"

It was a strange name, but he had been told to use that name specifically, and to deliver the following message, "I am Lieutenant Malcolm Granger of her Majesty's Ambassadorial Detail, attached to the British embassy. My friend over there, our liaison to the Turkmen government, is expediting your passage into the country. I was told to get your friends to the embassy immediately to await further instructions. A 'Neal Danielson' sends his regards."

Shahim allowed a smile to show on his lips and glanced at the palpably relieved Americans next to him. Jack slumped forward, the tension ebbing from his frame like a burst damn.

"Neal, you fabulous son of a bitch," Jack mumbled into his lap, laughing weakly. Shahim noticed the Englishman's crinkled up nose and remembered his deliberately potent breath. He deliberately minimized the air wafting over his grit-covered teeth, and as the aroma subsided, the officer's politeness became easier, more natural, and the Englishman continued.

"For confirmation I was told to ask you …" he consulted his notes, "what are you the …" the next part was said with clear doubt, Malcolm certain it must have been incorrectly transcribed in some way. But he said it anyway, his orders clear: "what are you the *second … arberator* of?"

His brow crinkled and he looked back at the disheveled man in front of him. As he watched the truck driver's black eyes, the man seemed to straighten, his whole demeanor changing. The lowly peasant he had seen only moments before surged, his back straightening, his expression setting in an iron look, the man behind the machine allowing the full measure of his pride to show in his expression and demeanor. Malcolm watched as Lord Mantil became the warrior before whom thousands had fallen, first to appease his race's greed, and then to appease his own conscience.

"I am the Second Arberator of the *Orbital*, Lieutenant Granger: Lord Mantil of the Mantilatchi." said the man.

Malcolm was transfixed by the powerful stare of the transformed man. The black eyes were piercing. The mention of the strange title seemed to have given a surge of power to the suddenly imperious looking man, and Malcolm managed only a nod at the reply he had been told to expect to the cryptic question.

"Well," Malcolm managed after a moment, "for you I have special instructions, Lord Mantil." he said, and the Agent looked at him curiously, "I am to get you to the airport immediately. You are booked on the first flight out to London. You'll be met there with new papers and then you are to head to Tel Aviv, I believe. There to meet a … John Hunt … who has further instructions for you."

The message told him a great deal. That it came from a British soldier told Lord Mantil that the team was alive and thriving, and spreading out to gather new allies. That it mentioned John Hunt meant his colleague was also alive, and had not fallen prey to the satellites before they were destroyed. Finally that it mentioned Tel Aviv could only mean that they were seeking Raz Shellet.

Shahim proverbially licked his lips. A worthy opponent. And another chance to bring the shame he felt to bear on a just recipient.

Lord Mantil nodded, and Malcolm told them to follow him back to the embassy. He would get them all clean clothes, a shower, and any medical attention they required, then Shahim would leave with Malcolm for the airport per their instructions.

Malcolm did not inquire as to the identity of the mysterious child, nor did the border guards or Turkmen liaison. Many a stranger had been given passage through this border with far less of an invite than the one being extended to these refugees, and no one saw the need to be officious in that invite's application.

Chapter 8: Team Mechanics

"The problem does not lie in the structure, but in the scale." said Birgit, frustrated. Madeline looked at her with anger in her blood. The German scientist had joined Madeline only a day before in what was now Madeline's personal laboratory in North Dakota.

In a surprisingly efficient move, the Japanese and US governments had jointly leased the entire site from Matsuoka Industries for an indefinite period. Neal had let Madeline know the news along with a host of other developments only yesterday, while sitting in his office in DC. The rest of the meeting had focused on the initial members of her new team, and the initial projects she was to focus on.

It had felt strange, taking orders from Neal. But they had not been delivered as a set of orders so much as a list of requests made of an equal, and after discussion he had willingly modified his expectations based on her feedback. Appreciative of the auspicious start to this new phase in their relationship, she had returned to North Dakota just ahead of the first of her new team members, Dr. Birgit Hauptman.

Dr. Hauptman was a surprisingly slovenly dressed woman in her fifties, shedding the stern stereotype of her German heritage along with several office dress codes that Madeline had not been aware she was a stickler for. They had met at the airport in Minnesota, and Birgit had joined Madeline in the back of the government Suburban driven by a member of the security detail now assigned to Madeline. They had talked of their backgrounds, and Birgit had quizzed Madeline on all that had happened over the last two years before her inclusion in the project. Most notably the revelations of John Hunt and the workings of the resonance manipulator.

Then their conversation had shifted to wave dynamics. While a little outside Birgit's field, she had dabbled in them as part of her experiments. Like the many people experimenting in her area of expertise, Birgit had exhausted so many options looking for ever-better methods of containment. For Dr. Hauptman was a nuclear physicist. But she worked well outside the standard electricity generation and weapons antics of modern day nuclear science. She was among the many researchers who were exploring the alchemist's dream of a practical fusion reaction.

Fusion was the controlled driving together of atoms to replicate the hot, potent release of pure atomic power occurring every day in the heart of every functioning star in the universe. Unlike fission, it did not require the use of heavy metals like plutonium and uranium, with all of their associated dangers and costs. Fusion yielded more energy, required no specialized fuels, and left no radioactive by-product.

An ideal to strive for? No doubt. But for fusion to occur, so much heat and pressure was required that the only place it happened naturally was at the core of a star. And so, to date, no one had been able to make a fusion reactor that didn't take more energy to run than it actually created. Birgit did not know it yet, but by the end of this week those inefficient

Tokomak reactors of her career to date would have joined the zeppelin as yet another impractical foible of the past.

Before the two accomplished women could reach that goal, however, they would have to surmount hurdles even John couldn't help them with. For John could tell them how it could work, and his papers were like a treasure map to a wide-eyed, childlike Birgit; he could even give them a precise design that matched the small but potent reactor that burned within each and every Agent that still walked the earth. But they needed to replicate that design on a massive diversity of scales, and for that they needed not only a design but an understanding of how it worked.

With Birgit's already extensive knowledge and expertise, that shouldn't be too much of a problem, but they were playing with fire. Not the fire the first cavemen ignited eons ago, but a flame that could not only burn their curious fingers, but vaporize anyone within a blast radius they had yet to even calculate. They had to step very carefully indeed, as any misstep could cost them their lives.

But patience was an elusive virtue indeed when you had a machine in your laboratory that could almost instantly execute any design you could conceive of. Deus ex machina could easily become diabolus ex machina.

Hours later, in the lab now, their conversation having taken turns and twists neither could have expected, Madeline pressed the look of frustration from her face, her restraint like an iron on the frown that Birgit's obstinacy was wrinkling into her brow.

"I understand that scaling is an issue here, *Dr.* Hauptman, and that is exactly why I think we should start by replicating *exactly* what was given to us and testing how that unit wor …"

Birgit cut Madeline off, "We have discussed this, Madeline, and I fail to see the benefit of building something we already know works." Birgit's German accent somehow made her interruption even more annoying, though Madeline knew how unreasonable that was, and she snapped.

"It is useful *because* we know it works. And because we know it is *safe,*" she shouted suddenly, with undisguised anger. "I for one have no desire to add to the deaths this team has already suffered this week."

Birgit was stunned silent, first by Madeline's tone, Birgit's own ire rising at the other woman's faltering professionalism, and then by the revelation of a loss within the team. She saw the subsurface grief hiding behind Madeline's glazing eyes, and she started to soften.

For her part, Madeline's anger had already extinguished itself in the act of flaring, consuming all her rage like oxygen in a moment and leaving only sadness afterward, an ember smoldering in the dark, empty cavern that she felt herself shivering in.

After more than a week of uncertainty, Madeline had heard third-hand that her friend Martin was dead. The confirmation had eventually come from the British embassy in Ashgabat. Only Jack and one of the co-opted pilots had been among the survivors Shahim had shepherded safely away from the closing jaws of an enraged Iranian army.

Martin's death had revived the feelings of helplessness and impending defeat that had started long ago on a terrible night in India. She would never know exactly how Laurie and James had died. What her lover James had been thinking as the crew of the *King's Transom* had become the first to die at the hands of the Mobiliei. But since then she had been skating on a razor thin sheet of hope as the threat they had gradually uncovered loomed ever darker and colder around them.

While the destruction of the satellites had brought some measure of relief from the ever-present fear, Madeline's own encounter with one of the Agents, Lana Wilson, stood as a stark reminder of what still hunted them even now.

Birgit watched the American silently. She had just met this woman, and though she obliquely understood that Madeline and her colleagues had been through an ordeal, she saw now that she had not truly appreciated the strain it must have put them under.

She also knew she could be abrasive and stubborn, and that she typically came across as somewhat arrogant. She normally did not really care. But maybe she should listen to this woman, if only for the sake of her new colleague's sanity, but also because, for perhaps the first time in years, Birgit might be out of her depth. Standing suddenly, Birgit crossed to one of her bags and started to ruffle through it.

"You are right, of course." she said, rummaging for something. Madeline stared at the German woman's back as she laid her wheel-aboard bag down and unzipped it. Was she being pitied? She did not want pity. Pity was second only to having been given an easy time by some of her older, more lecherous professors on the list of things that really, really pissed Madeline off. She was at the junction between grief and anger when the other woman suddenly stood up, clasping a faded, multicolored jacket.

Birgit turned back to Madeline with a childlike smile on her face. "My lucky lab coat!" she said, as though it was the most important thing in the world. She pulled on the tie-dyed atrocity and smiled. Eccentricity was the luxury of the rich and the successful, and Birgit had been one of the leaders in her field for long enough now that she was usually the most important person in any lab she found herself in. Thus she had long forgotten how completely ridiculous she looked in the old, beaten throwback to her childhood in the seventies.

Without meaning to, Madeline started to laugh, immediately trying to hold it back as the initial chuckles brought a hurt look from Birgit. But attempts at restraining her mirth only exacerbated it. She shook her head. Trying to speak and apologize, but after a moment she recognized in the German woman's surprised look the posturing of someone deliberately making fun of herself, and knew that Birgit was offering an olive branch. Her laughter faded and was replaced by an affectionate smile, and a look of understanding passed between them. It was obvious they were going to rip each other apart in here, but they could at least do so with a mutual respect.

"If you are finished mocking me, shall we get on with some actual work?" said Birgit, indignantly.

"Yes, of course." said Madeline. She turned back to her computer screen and began mapping the design John had given them into the Resonance Manipulator's control parameters. Birgit came over and stood behind her, watching her work with growing fascination. She offered the occasional comment, more often on the design than the way

Madeline was entering it, and soon Madeline began to see how much she could learn from her new colleague. She may be an arrogant, well, you know what, but aren't we all, thought Madeline.

An almost identical, though less censored thought was crossing Birgit's mind as well.

- - -

Hours later they gave up. They had tried to manage it, but had eventually resigned themselves to just letting the grid do it. The long, complex process of initiating the device they had birthed in the golden womb of the resonance manipulator had been fraught with a growing trepidation.

They had known from their schematics that the small machine would yield something disproportionate, and they had planned ahead. Thick cables interwoven with now familiar superconductive fiber worked hard to sap the electricity from the little parcel of pressure and power humming in a corner of the room.

Well, it was not humming, so much as the systems being barraged by it were. They watched the spiking voltages as the machine drove a phenomenal surge into the facility's transformer network. The research campus's grid had been designed to feed the many projects, both large and small, that the electronics giant had conducted over the years. Now it was doing the opposite, driving voltage outward, back into the high-voltage power lines that had once fed it.

Birgit stared in amazement. Decades of research had come to this. A part of her may have been capable of anger. Anger at the wasted years she had spent trying to get to this point, when in the end, one day, *this* day, the answer would be presented to her on a platter. But the simple, artistic beauty of the solution was such perfection to her, a lost piece in a puzzle she had sought to solve for so long, the crucial page in a book that had been full of confusion, suddenly becoming clear as the misplaced paragraphs were revealed. So many questions answered.

Her scientific soul rejoiced at it.

Even as it did so, she also started to look outward from this point. Seeking how to take it forward. In time she would battle nightmarish fears at what Earth's enemies must already have accomplished with this knowledge, she may even have moments of despondency as she contemplated how long ago their enemies had been walking down this road that she was just now starting upon. But the scientist in her would always respond with grim determination to outstrip them even from here, to show them that she had not needed their help to find this start to her new path. She was an excellent and vibrant mind, and she would prove it to them, through victory.

But all that was a long way from now. For now, she simply sat next to her equally mute companion trying to absorb some measure of what they were witnessing.

The state electric board would be seeing something extraordinary as well: their demand would be falling off dramatically. Their dispatching systems were even now struggling to manage the variance, peak generation stations powering down, transformers dumping load as this new, tiny power source flooded the grid with energy.

After half an hour, they eventually turned away from the machine, leaving it to generate, leaving it to add of itself to the world. They had greater miracles to perpetuate. They had just germinated the first shoots of the end of fossil fuel. The small device they had just made with a day's work could generate more power from a pint of water than the building they occupied would use in a century.

Madeline thought of the space-based fighter known as a "Skalm" that John Hunt had shown her in a fit of frustration while watching his friend Shahim fight alone in Iran. The quixotic engines that humanity would need to make that ship possible would need exponentially more power than even their little friend over there could deliver. Add to that the fact that the coming Armada they faced brought with it over a thousand of these Skalms, and the task ahead of them started to seem inconceivable. But seeing this machine and knowing that they had an insider's knowledge of their enemy's capabilities couldn't help but spark some measure of hope.

The two women set to. They needed a plan. Not just to develop individual systems, but to encompass how they are going to be able to escalate their abilities. A plan to help them capitalize on their new source of knowledge. Birgit's and Madeline's imaginations were wide open as their talk turned to how to protect themselves, and the world, from the boundless experiments they knew they must soon undertake.

Talk of containment. Talk of remote, uninhabited locales where potential collateral damage might be limited. Experiments that expanded out past humanity's known boundaries into fantastic new avenues. Madeline and Birgit talked of the only place that they could conceive of where they could truly stretch the legs of the fabulous new creatures they had to breed, and so it was not long before their unleashed imaginations took their sights skyward, into the vacuum.

Chapter 9: Street Fighters

They rode in the car together, itself a strange sensation. John drove. He had downloaded the detailed information coming in about the whereabouts of Ayala and her team, along with the reports on the activities of their target.

The two Agents could share information in ways hard to conceive of. When they were in close proximity, their onboard subspace tweeters were able to communicate directly and instantaneously with each other, tiny hammers in their brains thrumming the fabric of space, sending out minuscule vibrations that instantly reached anywhere in their radius. Their range was linked directly to the power of their internal hammers, and the Agents had a range of almost a mile. Since they had been within range of each other, John had communicated a lengthy and exhaustive account of what had happened in the last weeks directly into Lord Mantil's own memory.

In return, John had felt a surge of information from Lord Mantil. He saw the launch of the missiles in Pakistan, he saw the death of Preeti Parikh, and he felt the speed and devastation of the battle that ended with the searing laser bolt into Jean-Paul Merard's brain. When they were done, Lord Mantil knew all that John knew, and John knew all that Lord Mantil knew. Not in terms of access to files, but in terms of knowledge as accessible and known as the most vivid of memories. The two men were up to date.

Once they were on the same page, Lord Mantil considered the reports of Agent Raz Shellet's movements and, like John had before him, he saw that they were calm and calculated, the actions of an aspiring terrorist. From her pattern of purchases, she was clearly constructing an arsenal, and a considerable one at that. Primitive but brutal bombs appeared to be her staple, but no doubt she was using some of the more exotic materials she was managing to get her hands on to create more complex devices. Lengths of copper wire and amounts of substrate, old computer chips from calculators and defunct PCs, spoke of homemade computing machines that may be used for any number of projects. Detonators perhaps. Monitoring devices. They could not know. But it was clear that she was not being idle. What her intended targets were was pure conjecture, and maybe she was merely preparing herself so that she could respond to what humanity, and its new allies, would do next.

How she had been getting hold of her raw materials had been a mystery at first. But it had not taken long for the experienced if cautious team tracking her to discover her clandestine sources. She was prostituting herself to several local men of varying prominence and power. Each was giving her different parts of the list of ingredients she sought, both in terms of money and access. All seemed ignorant of her destructive intentions. Certainly they were unaware of who her ire was aimed at, for even if they had managed to surmise that she was using them to enable an unparalleled campaign of terrorism, they would naturally have assumed it was against the usurping Israeli state that they all lived in the shadow of.

As they drove the final miles to Ayala's position, John considered a completely unrelated question that had been bothering him. In Mobiliei society it was normal, as it was here, for someone to have a given name and a family or clan name. For Lord Mantil, that family name was one of tremendous age. The name of the heir to the Protectorate of Hamprect, the highest office other than king in his country. But it was not a name. Its owner took it as his name when the title became his, and often the memory of his original name faded with time. His inner circle still knew it, no doubt, but outside of that, such things were taboo, the most vulgar of conceit to even discuss.

But John Hunt and Lord Mantil shared a danger and ideological solidarity that brought them far closer than any inner circle Agent Hunt had ever known, and if Agent Shahim Al Khazar had decided that his Agent's name was tainted by its bloody cause, then John felt a desire to know what name he might call his brother in arms in its place.

Deciding that the subject was too delicate to discuss over their open link, John spoke out loud, "Lord Mantil. May I ask you a question?"

The other Agent turned in surprise, and John felt a system's query ping in his subconscious to check that their link was still active.

"I did not want to use subspace to ask this." John said.

<Go Ahead> came through John's link, and then Lord Mantil smiled. "Go ahead." he said aloud, shaking his head a little.

John paused a moment, deciding whether this was really appropriate, and then went forward. Lord Mantil had proven many things to John over the months since his violent conversion, not least of which was that he was, above all, reasonable.

"I certainly do not want to broach any protocols, or make you feel uncomfortable, Lord Mantil, so please do not feel any pressure to answer this if it makes you feel in the slightest bit uneasy …"

"Quavoce-Annat," said Lord Mantil.

John's eyes left the road for a moment, and he looked confusedly at his sometime friend.

"My name," said Lord Mantil. The phonetic and local spellings appeared via the link in John's mind: kwa- vōs, ən-ət.

"Quavoce-Annat." said John.

"Quavoce. My family calls me Quavoce." and after a pause, Lord Mantil continued, "In truth, I miss hearing it. If it would not make you uncomfortable, I would be honored if you would refer to me by it, when we are not in company."

John restrained a friendly laugh at the noble's polite manner, a laugh that the real him would have found impossible to contain. But the Agents' control over their bodies was absolute, and he remained politely grave as he replied, "I would be honored to, Quavoce, and I would be equally honored if you would call me by my real name."

"A pleasure. Shtat-Palpatam? It is an unusual name," Quavoce went on, calling up the name of the man he had met at the ceremony where their personalities were downloaded.

But John shook his head, smiling.

"No, no, my friend. A traitor to the cause would never have passed the plethora of mental tests and probes that you all underwent in the lengthy approval process the nominees all had to endure. No, I could not have gotten past those exams, my real purpose would have shown up like a beacon. I was implanted at the last minute. When the transfer was being completed, I was one of the men operating the port into the Nomadi nominee's mind, only our link was not as it seemed, and my personality instead of his was implanted, along with a virus that allowed me to fake my way through the final confirmations that followed."

As John Hunt spoke, a thought struck Quavoce. A terrible thought. And as John went to tell Lord Mantil his real name, Lord Mantil spoke and signaled John at the same time, shouting: <stop!>

John fell mute, shocked, and Quavoce went on more calmly, "I had assumed you were Shtat. But this, this changes everything. I must ask you to not to tell me your real name."

John sent a mental query at Quavoce who went on, "John, I do not know where the real you *is* right now, whether it is back on Mobiliei or with the Armada, but the real Lord Quavoce Mantil deshamer Annat rides aboard the fleet that is even now descending upon us, Representative to the Council and the Captain of the Mantilatchi fleet contingent. If they manage to get close enough in the coming war, the AIs aboard his ... or rather *my* capital ship will begin probing the earth for signs of my mind in the hope of reestablishing contact and updating the link between my real mind and the copy that inhabits this body."

John nodded and pinged his understanding but Quavoce went on, "It is strange to imagine, but we must remember that it is only this version of me that has undergone the fundamental change in ideology that has brought us together since we were all downloaded back on Mobilius."

The reality of the divide that Lord Mantil faced hit John for first time. John had known at the time of his transference to this body that he stood firmly against the invasion. When his two minds met again they would be exchanging only memories. But Quavoce would be exchanging two opposing sides of a war, a war that would then rage within himself, and it would be like two enemies uniting in one mind.

Lord Mantil went on, quietly, his machine body expressing freely the reticence he felt, "I now stand on the opposite side of a chasm from the *real* me. We cannot know how the coming war is going to play out. I am sure you have plans, a set of strategies that you know each version of you will try to accomplish, but we both know there is a very real chance we will fail here.

"If we do, then at some time in the not-too-distant future the real me will stand in orbit over this planet and upload the memories that now make me who I am. Maybe they will overpower me, maybe I will come to the same conclusions that this copy of me has. But if I don't, then the less I know about the identities of you and your fellow conspirators the better."

They both contemplated that, and then Quavoce finished, "It would be a cruel fate indeed if your trust in me ended in me being your executioner."

Quiet descended as this enigma hung over them. John had prepared himself for the fact that either this copy of himself or the real him may die in the coming war. He had even known that it may be both, or worse, that this more hardy copy may outlive the real him. But that he may form friendships with his enemy had been beyond him. The real Quavoce Mantil may kill the real him in battle. He and the other members of the resistance may kill Quavoce, they may have already, back aboard the Armada, if the opportunity has presented itself.

After a moment, John nodded and said, "Thank you, Quavoce. You are right, of course. And your desire to protect me, even from yourself, is yet another sign of what an honorable man you truly are. I would like to believe that the real you will come to the same conclusions that this version of you has. But you are right, unfortunately, when you say that we cannot know that for certain. He won't have seen what you have, won't have lived through what you have, and will have had ten more years among our Mobiliei brethren than you and I have."

There was silence for a long time. They were trying to reconcile the concept that at this moment they were both the closest of allies, and the very worst of enemies, sworn to both save each other, and kill each other.

They drove on into the night.

After a long while, John said, "When I was a child my mother called me Batim. It is not my real name, of course, but in many ways it is just as much my name as the one my parents gave me before they actually knew what a troublemaker I was. You could call me that, if you wish."

Quavoce appeared relieved at this gesture of friendship, his infrequent but genuine smile spreading across his face once more. "Batim? The swamp rat?" A chuckle escaped Quavoce's lips, "What a wonderful child you must have been to earn such a name."

John ... Batim, laughed, "One would like to think she was being ironic ..." Quavoce shot a doubting glance at John who smirked in reply, "Yes ... well ... like I said, one would *like* to think that."

They were approaching the center of Gaza City, and John slowed as the muddiness of the evening traffic clogged the roads around them. But they would not drive all the way to their destination anyway.

Abandoning the car that they had been given by a contact in Tel Aviv, they walked the final quarter of a mile in silence. Side by side, they were a walking army. Their legs moving in unison as they passed, unnoticed, through the scarred streets of Gaza at night. John had tainted his skin to give himself a darkness that went some way toward disguising his systemically British look. He could not do much more. They were not designed to be shape shifters, but he used his malleable facial muscles to tighten his jawline, giving it an angularity, and to sharpen his nose a little to give his face something of the strength of the local Arabic complexion.

Their feet moved in unison, not in a march, but in the quiet agreement of two old friends walking in step. Each of those feet that could propel them farther and faster than any of the passing locals could have imagined.

Their hands were tucked into their jacket pockets against the forgiving and imperceptibly cool Mediterranean evening. Hands that could so easily wrench apart any of the fragile bodies of the innocent and ignorant that they encountered in the night.

And as they walked, their eyes stayed always on the path ahead, but they missed nothing. Eyes hiding their most lethal secrets. Eyes that had locked on each other in battle only months beforehand. Eyes that now faced an uncertain future, but did so together, as they went to confront one of the Agents they had betrayed.

They both noted one of Ayala's team in his spot down the road from Raz's building. They would not have seen him there but for the fact that his reports had told them indirectly of his position relative to Raz. He was well hidden and appropriately subtle, they each thought in unison. A fact that had no doubt saved his life. They did not feel the need to point these things out to each other, knowing like identical twins exactly what each could and could not see. They just walked on, another block and then a turn into a faceless, rundown apartment building. They did not glance at the building they knew was Raz's. They would be visiting her soon enough. It would not be a pleasant reunion.

- - -

Across the globe, America was still writhing from the pain of the radioactive wound it had suffered. Twisting and turning in discomfort as it got used to the deep gash that was driving up through eastern Georgia. People moved away in massive waves like concentric circles, either bouncing off or washing into the swelling cities inland from the radioactive coast. Millions were uprooted, and the economy bled in response. The emergency funds of the wealthiest nation on earth pumped through its veins to dull the pain of the unprecedented upheaval.

The monies acted like adrenalin, numbing the nation to the extent of its wound, but its energizing effects would eventually fade, and the reality would come through, surging into focus as the full, stunning aftermath of what had happened sank in. Even a day as tragic as September 11th would be but a headache compared to the long-lasting effects of the invisible radiation poisoning that had bathed so many.

Jason and Theresa Stevens of Slocomb, Alabama, continued to argue over which victim deserved what, and how affected *they* were by the disaster. They bickered, as politically and ethically ignorant of the world around them as they were unaware of the sleeping presence beneath them. It had been a week. As America's wounds still throbbed with bloody newness, Lana's body busily repaired itself. Millions of tiny tendrils and nano machines diagnosed and repaired subsystem upon subsystem in her almost biologically complex body. The fusion reactor at her core pumped energy throughout her systems, reaching more and more components as they came back online.

She would remain as black as midnight for good now, none of her systems could fix that. Outwardly she would be absorbent of all light, a pariah. But as she lay beneath the home of the two imbeciles above her, Lana was coming to appreciate a certain poetic beauty in her new form. She would use it to strike fear into the world. She would become a nightmare, a cautionary tale told to children. And her midnight black silhouette would be the last sight of any who dared to stand with Neal Danielson and his cohorts.

Lana inwardly flinched at a particularly vulgar flatulent burst from the moronic pair above her and thought offhandedly about how she was going to kill them. Responding to her wish with virtual immediacy, her machine subconsciousness began to list out tactical options, arraying a stream of wildly diverse methods of ending the lives of the two people she had been forced to cower under.

She smiled as the list grew, laughing to herself when the artificial intelligence that supported her every whim was forced to begin breaking the list into categories to make it more manageable. She realized she could search the list based on the amount of pain she wanted to inflict, the length of time she wanted the death to take, the amount of scarring and external damage that would be visible afterward. Deliberate disease infection, specific blows that would cause degenerative heart arrhythmia or terminal brain hemorrhages, and onward down the list. The options got ever more vulgar until she reached one that piqued the level of pain and misery she wished to inflict, and combined it with an immediacy and poetic cruelty that somewhat satiated her psychopathic urges.

She thought about, it, and began modeling the ways in which she could use it, analyzing in minute detail every aspect of it as the concept developed like a science in her mind. Yes. This would be her calling card. Using direct manipulation of the spinal cord via electric pulse, she would be able to induce an acute and all-encompassing agony so great it would cause convulsions that would turn her victims inside out.

She smiled inwardly at the vision and saved it, savoring the pleasure of what it was going to feel like. Then, with nothing else to do, she started to think of each of her intended victims as they suffered this death, creating detailed, vivid virtual images of each gruesome end, and drinking them in like a dark, red wine.

Chapter 10: Blowing Minds

Professor Ignacio de Prado walked along a long, ancient corridor in Coimbra University's Faculdade de Ciências e Tecnologia. Yellowed flagstones polished with age met his black, creased shoes, which were softened with seemingly equal age as he scuffed toward the office he had called home for the bulk of his professional career. As he rounded a final corner and started down one side of a cloistered, manicured courtyard, he saw two unfamiliar figures standing outside his office. He was used to many people waiting for him, students of his various classes awaiting him with a pressing question or a spurious excuse, typically the latter. But these two stood with a purpose few students would learn before they were deposited out into the real world, and Ignacio surveyed them with more than his usual cursory glance as he approached.

"Professor Ignacio do Prado, se faz favor?" said the woman in the grey jacket and black skirt. Her white shirt was starchly pressed, as was the one of the man standing next to her. But he wore his with less practice. This was a man not used to wearing a suit.

The professor nodded his slightly chubby, well-worn face at them both with expected hesitance, frowning as he searched for something he recognized in both of them. But he would not find it. This was outside his experience.

In a polite, well-formed Portuguese accent from Lisbon, or maybe Cascais, the woman went on, "My name is Maria Eça, I am with the Ministerio da Defesa Nacional." she handed the professor her card as she went on, "This man is an American who represents an international body that is interested in speaking with you about an important matter. May we have a moment of your time, Professor?"

- - -

"I don't know what it is about, Amadeu," said a frustrated assistant at the door of the university dean's office, "They told me to find you and bring you here, immediately. They did not say why."

Amadeu looked at her skeptically, without any attempt at disguising his fear and concern. There was a long list of reasons he could be being summoned here, ranging from expellable to jailable, and to top it off he was more than a little stoned. He had been smoking alone, in his room, as usual. Fantasizing about a fellow student he had just seen entering the communal showers. That and the woman that had driven the bus on his way to the store last night, and the lady who had bent over in front of him in a hallway two days before, and his high school gym coach. The knock on his door had sent him reeling, only to be followed by the stern voice of the dean's secretary to add to his panic.

He had nagged the woman all the way to the office where he was apparently awaited, but she clearly knew nothing. It was becoming plain that he was going to have to face the music, and then think on his feet about what his tune.

- - -

"I am sorry for this delay, ladies, gentlemen." said the dean once more, his frustration starting show behind his obsequious smile. Maria Eça shook her head once more with a pleasant smile, having already said not to worry countless times. While the man she was with sat mute, unclear what was happening as the people around him communicated in a foreign tongue. But sensing from Maria's lack of translation that the dean was apologizing once more, the man aped Maria's ingratiating nod and the room fell back into awkward silence.

Professor de Prado decided to fill the void with conversation, "Like I said, Senhora, the paper you referred to was not written by me, but by a team of students with my … limited supervision. But the part of the paper that clearly interests you, and our American friend," he nodded a smile at the stiff-looking man who he knew could not understand his lilting, flowing Portuguese, "was written mostly by one particularly bright boy. Only a master's student, and not the best of my students by far." the professor's smile flinched a little as a memory fluttered through him but he went on, "but his ideas about direct spinal interfaces are, indeed, quite striking, if a little far-fetched."

The stiff looking man clearly understood the words 'spinal interfaces' and nodded appreciatively. Maria was beginning to translate the professor's words to him when there was a knock on the door and an apologetic but triumphant assistant poked her head into the room.

"Professore, desculpe. Amadeu Esposinho …" she said almost breathlessly, and at the dean's nod she opened the door fully and herded a nervous-looking boy in his early twenties into the room.

The room rose to greet him and Amadeu looked even more concerned. But he was greeted warmly by the dean, and by a new face, an attractive face belonging to someone called Maria Eça, and he blushed mute as the smart-looking lady extended her hand to him.

"Amadeu, fala-se um pouco Inglese?" she said. The boy stared at her. What the foda was going on, he thought.

"Sim … yes, of course." he replied, and noticed that the stiff-looking man that stood by her side perked up a little.

"Amadeu," the woman went on in English, "I would like to introduce you to General Milton of the United States Air Force."

Amadeu went wide-eyed, and mentally checked and rechecked that he understood her correctly. But suddenly the rugged-looking man was stepping past the woman and extending his hand, his eyes surveying and clearly assessing Amadeu with cold efficiency.

The general's voice was slow, speaking with forethought for the boy's lack of experience with English, and for the shock that he must be under from being summoned here, "Amadeu, please, call me Barrett. I am here because we would like to ask you to help us with something."

Everyone in the room looked surprised, their limited English making them struggle to make sure they had heard correctly. But Amadeu was actually far from a slouch in English, it was the language of the internet, the language of coders, and the internet was his life, even if it played a backseat to the medical studies his father had forced him to pursue.

His reply came out hesitantly, "My help? Can I ask with what?" He had visions of some college think tank. Maybe it could be interesting, but typically they were sad attempts by blowhards to get extracurricular credit. He was profoundly unprepared for the general's next statement.

"Well, Amadeu, I won't beat around the bush here. We are forming a team. A team that is planning to build the direct spinal interface that you recently wrote about so astutely, and finish it within the year…" the boy stared at Barrett with undisguised astonishment and not a little glee, "…any chance that might interest you?"

- - -

As General Milton bounced around Europe and Asia on a prolonged recruitment tour, Madeline was in the middle of a lengthy meeting with several members of NASA's Institute for Advanced Concepts, in an office on the campus of Berkley.

There were numerous fields that the cutting edge agency was working in that were of interest to Madeline and her colleagues, but one in particular was the focus of today's conversation. After years of conceptualizing and scientific dreaming about one of the most fantastic and yet feasible hopes of the twenty-first century, this team had labored through many a mocking remark and disparaging magazine article. But Madeline had in her toolbox of fabulous machines the key to unlocking the bonds that, until now, had kept this particular dream earthbound.

In a conversation that became ever more heated and impassioned, the horizon was beginning to come into focus for these brilliant thinkers. A horizon that had on it a structure so large and so magnificent as to defy imagination. Thousands of miles long, reaching from the earth's surface out past the ranges of geosynchronous orbit to an anchor in space, the tether they were envisioning would link humanity to the stars.

No more rockets and boosters, no more heavy-lifting ourselves into space piece by piece. Instead, a smooth ride up a tether of carbon nanotubing extending into the blackness, a trillion tiny fibers interwoven into a band of material so enduring it could support thousands of tons with its unimaginable tensile strength.

It had been first conceived by Arthur C. Clarke in the 1970s and refined by countless scientists since. Humanity had even managed to invent the first carbon nanotubes. But they had yet to develop the technology to anything close to the levels they would need. Now, on the table in front of them, were the equations and methods necessary to close that gap. And there was a sample of this magical material. The perfect carbon nanotube, the bootstrap by which humanity would truly lift itself into space at last.

- - -

She sat, shivering in the middle seat. It was too wide for her. A small window to their side showed the ground twenty feet below, but she dared not look. The plane was larger than any building she had ever seen in her life, and when it had moved it had been like the earth shifting. No amount of explanation and comforting could reconcile six-year-old Banu to the concept of this building being able to fly. Having seen planes flying far overhead and hearing her brothers explain them to her, she had thought she might be able to accept this.

Maybe if her savior had been here with her she might have felt safe; the man who she had learned was named Quavoce Mantil. But he had vanished with the same mystery as he had arrived, taking his strange name and bottomless eyes with him. After a long and tender good-bye, he had promised that he would see her again soon, that for now she should go with the other two strangers that had been with him that night, and they would make sure she was safe until he came back from whatever mission had taken him away from her.

But the two Americans did not speak a word of her language. Not even the translator they had hired was able to grasp in full the local dialect she had spoken all her life. Quavoce had been able to speak with the gravel of a local. He could speak to anyone, she had discovered, no matter what language they spoke.

So Banu Ahmedisavi, or Banu Mantil, as she had already started to call herself, found herself sitting between a strange man that knew enough of her tongue to emphasize just how lonely she was, and the female friend of Quavoce, Jennifer, who spoke none at all.

The rumbling began. She screamed weakly as the ground surged forward and her chair drove into her back. The translator tried to comfort her, speaking in quiet tones and reaching out to her, but she recoiled from him and clung to Jennifer instead.

The strong military woman wrapped her arms around the child and pulled her close, unbuckling her belt so she could envelop the little girl. Banu sobbed quietly into her chest. The translator tried to speak again, but Jennifer shook her head ever so subtly and the man fell silent.

Jennifer squeezed Banu tight and began to hum a lullaby into the poor girl's ear, soothing the terror of a little girl from a small farm in the hinterlands of Iran, as she felt the deafening might of the immense Rolls-Royce engines powering the massive plane into the sky.

Chapter 11: Two on One

Back in Gaza, the bulk of Ayala's team gathered for the first time since their first meeting with her back in Tel Aviv. They had spent nearly a week watching the mysterious woman Raz Shellet, and had seen a disturbing amount of activity in that time.

After a while, the woman had stopped collecting materials and started spending more time in her rented apartment. Then, yesterday, she had taken the first of several large boxes with her and set off out of the city. Long after she had left the box buried in a field near a local military base, still under the distant eye of one of the well-hidden Mossad team members, John had gone to the sight and scanned the buried box. He had come back to the team and told them they had to move. She was planting massive explosive devices at key locations, probably as stockpiles, and they probably did not have much more time until whatever she was planning began in earnest.

By that night Raz had already planted five more of the boxes. And so, leaving one lookout in place at a key vantage point, the team gathered in a small rented room nearby. After a brief introduction, Ayala handed the process over to John Hunt, who stood and looked at the men gathered in front of him.

"Gentlemen. As you may have guessed, the time has come to engage our target. I say engage rather than take down because I am afraid taking her down will not be a simple task. For, as you have no doubt also guessed, Raz Shellet is no ordinary terrorist. Raz Shellet represents an evolutionary step in capability from anything you have ever witnessed. She is faster, stronger, and more deadly than all of you combined."

They started at this, not least of which because they were far from harmless tikes, and the implication that anyone at all was better than the lot of them was a touch hard to swallow. But John was not about to spend time debating the point with them. He needed them to believe it, not academically, but in reality.

"Allow me to demonstrate. Stand up," he said with authority, and the men rose to the challenge, literally. John turned to Lord Mantil … Quavoce, and smiled, "Quavoce, my friend, would you mind hitting me with that chair?"

The room was curious, if also more than a little skeptical about where this was going. Quavoce looked at John with an expression that asked if this was really necessary. John nodded and turned to face the group.

Seeing the looks on the team's faces, Quavoce saw that it was, indeed, quite necessary. Once he agreed, Quavoce moved with such force and speed that the room involuntarily stepped back. In a blur, the machine man darted forward, grabbed the legs of one of the small, folding metal chairs in the room, and whipped it around. Just missing the men watching, he spun, accelerating the metal frame around at a speed his mind told him was in excess of a hundred miles per hour by the time it hit John's stomach. John did not flinch, he merely took one step back to brace his body against the blow … and WHACK.

John skidded back a foot or so and then regained his composure. Quavoce's hands still held the aluminum legs of the chair but he soon realized that was now moot. The chair was wrapped around John's torso like a cummerbund. Lord Mantil released his grip and John smiled at the group as he bent the groaning metal from around his middle. They stared at him as he plied it from his body and then, holding the warped frame in one hand, John pulled up his shirt and showed them his unblemished stomach.

"Now, gentlemen," John said, dropping the metal to the floor and stepping toward them, "you are trained professionals so I won't beat around the bush. My friend and I represent what you face tonight." He stepped closer to one of them and the man assumed a defensive stance without thinking.

"You cannot beat us, you cannot kill us," John said calmly, and then his hand whipped out and gripped the first man's wrist. The trained Mossad agent instinctively fought his grasp. John continued talking, "If you try …" the man twisted and brought his elbow up into John's face but John's hand was there in an instant, "… then she will …" holding the breathless Mossad agent by his wrist and elbow John now twisted him, careful not to hurt any more than his pride, "… without doubt …" two of his colleagues stepped forward to help their friend. The first came in low, a sweeping leg to unbalance John, the second came around the other side and sent a series of well-placed kicks and punches to try and force John to release his friend. "… kill every last one of you."

As the final two words of John's sentence came out, he thrust the initial man forward. In the same flash, his right foot lashed backward and upward, catching the sweeping leg of the second man as it went, kicking it up and away and sending him with it. The third man's fist came in low and fast, straight for John's face. Bending away from this blow with ease, John's hands whipped out in unison, the first grasped the wrist of the man grazing past his head, the second shot downward to grab his ankle.

They had no idea what happened next, but before the rest of the group could gather themselves to come against John as well, the two men were tossed lightly into the four other men, sending them all sprawling.

"Enough!" shouted Ayala, but John silenced her.

"No!" John said with venom, "Not enough! I won't go into battle tonight unless these men understand what they're up against!"

He came to stand over them and looked at them one by one. He saw fear in some, anger in the others, and confusion in them all, "I am sorry to have done that to you, gentlemen, but I am afraid I had to make my point beyond any doubt."

They stared at him and he went on, "Like me and my friend here, our target tonight is bulletproof, knife proof, fireproof, and radiation proof. She can blind you at a hundred paces, and fold you in half like a rag doll with one look from her left eye. I know this without any shadow of a doubt because I can do all those things too. So here's the deal. You leave the fighting to *me and my friend*. Not because you are cowards, or because you don't know your job, but because you *do* know your job, and you know when to fight and when to run."

Ayala stepped up to John and rested her hand on his shoulder, and John saw the instinctive fear for her life in the men in front of him, even the willingness to continue fighting in order to protect her. These were good men, brave men, but that was all the more reason not to sacrifice them needlessly to the coming battle.

Ayala spoke to her men now, "I would tell you not to be afraid of John here, but that would be very bad advice indeed. He has sacrificed more than you can know to come here and fight for us, and I have absolutely no doubt that he will sacrifice you too if need be. As will I, for that matter. I can only ask that you not force him to make that decision tonight. Now, if you are all absolutely clear on your place in this operation, we will begin the briefing. Though you cannot join in the actual fight with these two men, you *do* have an important role to fill. If you will take your seats again, we can begin."

She stepped over to the warped remnants of the chair on the floor and pointed to it. With a wry smile, she turned to the British Agent, "John, you can sit here."

- - -

Spread out in a wide star from a given point in the center of Gaza City, seven marksmen lay. They lay on their backs, listening to the receivers in their ears, their long, black rifles resting on their chests as they rested in a semi-sleep, allowing their minds to relax without allowing them to completely slip away. The hours ticked by. At the center of this star two other men lay on two rooftops, facing each other, a wide main street between them.

They all waited.

The street was all but deserted. A man was pushing a cart along, laden with various car parts and other dross, while a keen street vendor, arriving early, was beginning to set up his stall. Between the two waiting men were four empty lanes, two in each direction, pockmarked with the occasional scar of the many conflicts the city had suffered.

At twelve minutes past three in the morning, Raz Shellet appeared from her building's front door. She was carrying a large duffel bag not dissimilar to the ones she had carried out of her building at regular intervals for the last day. It was the second time she had left her building since the team had set up their positions. Unlike the previous time, she turned left instead of right.

They waited.

- - -

Raz felt something was wrong as she left her building. The people of this town were evolutionarily wired to be sensitive to war, they had seen far too much of it in their lifetimes, and she could tell the town was waiting for something, bracing itself. She could feel it. Shutters were closed. Less people were on the streets. People had seen things and they were preparing for something.

It could be nothing, it could be an attack by one of the many groups that had terrorized these people over the years, from the Israeli forces that claimed to be only enforcing the peace to the many insurgent groups that claimed to be defending their rights even as they fundamentally abused them. Maybe they sensed some small part of the battle she was, herself, bringing to this town. Perhaps they sensed that in two days she planned to set off an unprecedented series of explosions across the city. Explosions designed to look like mortar raids. To look like slaughter. To look like genocide. Explosions designed to destabilize this region and plunge it into war.

Her hair hung loosely over her left eye. Like it always did now. She did not really fear these people, whatever attack was coming on them she would welcome it as another step in the direction she wanted to take the world, into a war that would distract it from the real threat that was coming. But even though these men, women, and children held no threat for her, there was something out there that did. For she, like her colleagues, knew that at least one of their fellow Agents had betrayed them. So, unlike Jean-Paul Merard and Preeti Parikh before her, Raz Shellet had pre-computed defense tactics for a fight with another Agent. These were lined up at all times, ready to autoactivate should the need arise.

As she walked down the street, Raz Shellet instinctively scanned every person she saw and every doorway she approached for signs of a waiting Agent, waiting for the traitor to come. And unlike Jean-Paul or Preeti Parikh, Raz's drooping hair covered her left eye, and hid a fully deployed weapons array, standing at the ready.

- - -

John and Quavoce could not use the subspace link between them for fear it would alert Raz to their presence. For even though they could scramble the signal between them in order to hide their meaning, the very use of the medium in an otherwise subspace-mute world would set off alarms in Raz's mind.

So they looked at each other across the road, just out of sight of the street below. The seven Mossad agents had been alerted by a single pip on their radios from the lone spotter covering the door when Raz had emerged, and another when she had turned toward them. The seven heavily trained men checked their rifles. They were not to fire more than once from one location. Shoot once then move … quickly. Once the fight had started they were allowed to use the radio, but they should assume that anything they said over it could be heard by their target. They had noted that neither of the two superhuman-seeming men had asked for actual receivers, but they had said they would also be able to hear whatever was said over the channel.

Two of the Mossad men prayed. One more pulled out a small photo of his young son and kissed it gently, then replaced it in his jacket. Underneath their clothes they all now wore black body suits that Ayala had given them. They had all pulled the black hoods up over their heads like balaclavas when they had gotten into position. And they all sensed that no matter how much the Agents had tried to warn them, they were about to see something bordering on insanity.

Another pip came and in their various positions they all sprang to a waiting crouch, still just out of sight in their various hiding spots. The one spotter who was in plain sight watched Raz as she came down the street, his finger poised as he sent pips to his colleagues. First as she left her building. Next as she turned their way. Then as she crossed the first street. Now, as she approached the corner they had agreed upon, he got ready to count down till she was in the kill zone.

pip … pip … pip … pip …

Pip. They all leapt to their knees and seven long-range rifles were leveled at the same moment, seeking their target, four sighting her right away as they had clear lines from their spots. The others were arranged along her potential escape routes and they waited. As they all span, John and Lord Mantil were already airborne, launching themselves off their rooftop purchases above their prey.

Raz heard the pips and instinctively began scanning the area with her various arrays. Suddenly she sensed movement above her, and down each street, in uncanny unison with the telltale pips on the radio, and she flipped her head upward just as she was hit with the first blast from John's sonic punch. The power snapped her head back but her array was already deployed and she fired instantaneously in return. But her shot went wide as John's first blast hit her.

Her onboard systems raced as her odds were recalculated. Two assailants. Two Agents. She bent as Quavoce hit her as well, and sensed their lasers already hitting her, and then she suddenly hurled the big bag in her hand into the air between her falling assailants. They saw it coming up and turned their fire on it instead. But it was not naturally combustible and its detonator was hidden deep within. As it came level with them, they both turned their heads away from the blast they knew was coming.

She detonated the bag with her mind, even as four supersonic bullets raced at her through the night. Two missed because of her lightning-fast maneuvering in the second since the fight had begun, but the other two hit her from both sides at once in the instant before the bag exploded.

A ball of flame erupted in the center of the junction. John and Quavoce hung in midair on either side of it and it blasted them outward into the walls of the buildings they had been hiding on a moment before. Raz felt the bullets hit her and instantly computed their sources. She did not wait to see the traitor Agents hit the wall. She was running from her assailants, the fireball she had set off still expanding above her head.

She sighted the window her systems said had been the source of one of the shots ahead of her, and bathed it in laser heat as she started to run. The man inside had listened to the warnings. He was already turning to leave. But the explosion had made him hesitate. If his back had been turned, the beam would have been absorbed by the black suit he had been given. But it hit him square in his exposed face and his skin erupted in flame, his eyes instantly and permanently ruined.

The beam lasted less than half a second. Raz had to get out of there, and her feet weren't moving fast enough. The explosion would not stop John and Shahim for long. So she brought her feet together and bent into a crouch, and then thrusted her legs with all her might, catapulting herself into the air as the man she had just fired upon fell to the floor in his scorched hiding place, clutching his ruined face and screaming.

One of the remaining six agents watched her leap and swore, "Kusemek, what in the name of God almighty was that?"

Without hesitation, a reply came over the radio, "That was your target, where did she go?"

The Mossad agent was stunned. He had been the one spotting for the team and his mike was still open. He recognized the voice of one of the strange men whom he had just seen blown to smithereens. Instinctively, he replied, "She jumped, west-south-west. About four blocks. Holy shit. Yes, four damn blocks, maybe more, toward the harbor."

Suddenly he saw one, then another figure catapult out of the fireball into the air in the same direction as their target.

As the two Agents soared away into the night, the spotter looked at the four buildings that marked the wrecked junction's corners. They were demolished, obliterated, the only thing coming out of them alive had already jumped away into the night. Their five hundred sleeping occupants would make up the first victims of a bloody morning.

Raz heard the brief conversation over the radio and knew they were coming after her. She could not rely on jumping again, they would see her in the air. Landing with a thud that cracked the concrete pavement, she rolled and set off at a sprint north, up through the city.

Thud, thud. A block apart, John and Quavoce landed in quick succession, communicating with each other now through a scrambled subspace connection.

John at Quavoce: 'i see her landing point.'

Quavoce at John: 'confirmed. i have visual, a quarter mile ahead.'

He was already sprinting after her, and John was soon coming up a parallel street. Quavoce beamed his sight of their quarry directly into John's head, and John judged the distance and leapt into the air four blocks forward to land on a rooftop just ahead of Raz. But his rolling impact was heavy on the old building's weak roof, and Raz heard the crumbling concrete under his skidding feet and reacted.

Suddenly she broke hard right, away from him. Quavoce saw John's view as well as his own, saw that he was already propelling himself from roof to roof in her pursuit and so swerved right as well, trying to keep Raz penned between them.

The race went on through the streets, stunned pedestrians and car drivers frightened by the explosion across town ducking out of the way of the inhumanly fast Agents. Soon they would be out of the city, thought John with relief, not wanting to fight Raz in the densely populated streets. He deliberately did not try to overtake her, precisely so she would leave the tight confines of the sleeping city. A new line flickered on his tactical screen as he landed on another building. The next building was one Raz had visited earlier that day.

His machine mind calculated the risk a moment too late. He had just launched himself onto the roof of the building when it seemed to tremble. A fireball emerged from within, engulfing the building as it expanded outward, sucking plaster and furniture into its gaping maw along with its two hundred fifty inhabitants. John saw himself falling into the flame and knew there was nothing he could do about it. This was not going to be pretty.

Quavoce witnessed his friend's plummet into the fireball as if he was experiencing it himself, and his mind started a new computation. Raz knew she was still being followed. She had just run John into a trap, and no doubt she would try the same thing with Quavoce. She would try to lead him into another explosion. He called up the sights of her day's visits and anticipated her course. The nearest was half a mile ahead. Bracing his legs, he set his trajectory and leapt.

Raz ran on, knowing that she had just consumed one of her pursuers. He would, no doubt, survive it, but even he couldn't leap out of a disintegrating building with ease. She assumed her other pursuer was still on her tail. She did not turn. She stayed en route. She slowed a little to make sure he was keeping up. She knew he was running parallel to her but no doubt he would try to converge now that his cohort was detained. He needed a fix on her. She ran on toward her next site. This would be just as fun, she told herself.

The full weight of a sonic punch hit her in the head from above, and what was left of her clothing flamed orange red as she was bathed in laser. She spun on her attacker but he had timed it to perfection. As her head turned to him, his fist crashed into it with all his weight, driving her neck-first into the street's rough tarmac. Her feet came bursting up to meet him, flinging him from her as her battered head flexed with the tremendous blow. His fist had cracked a little on her skull, but multiple systems were down on her side. Her right eye was not working and her positioning systems were malfunctioning. Her world seemed to warp as her machine mind tried to get a handle on it all, but her left eye was still undamaged and she unleashed it, firing wildly.

Lasers and sonic blasts ripped up the building facades around them as she tumbled along the street, curtains flaming to life in windows even as wide patches of wall shook under the blows. Quavoce tried to right himself and turn back to face Raz as he slid along the street behind her, and his feet and hands began to grip the concrete as he started to drive himself forward into her once more. She met him full on and they came together like a thunderclap. Lasers burning into each other and sonic punches pounding their frames as they clung to each other, not willing to let the other fall away again as they pounded their rage into their nemeses. The two goliaths flung from one side of the street to another, pounding into walls as the terrible power of their fight propelled them about. A truck parked ahead of them crumpled and exploded as they crashed into its cab, a dodged fist from Quavoce crushing the engine block and igniting the remnant fuel within.

The fight was destroying them both, and Quavoce was perfectly happy with that. His rage at another slew of needless deaths that night driving him to ruin. He coldheartedly selected the most brutal tactical options one after the other regardless of the cost. She must die.

But Raz was, if she was realistic, happy with that as well. This machine version of her had no more need to live than Quavoce did, and she knew that while there were only two of the traitors, there were four of her true brethren left. One-for-one attrition would favor her side very well indeed.

A signal penetrated Quavoce's bloody rage. A simple request and with it he simply released his hold on Raz. She flew away from him with the force of a blow she had just landed on his torso. As she spun through the air, she considered her sudden release. Maybe she had damaged him irrevocably, hit some vital system.

She did not pause to consider this too long but began to twist in the air so that when she landed she could propel herself back at her foe. But as she span, a powerful fist connected with the back of her neck and she felt herself propelled to the ground with phenomenal force. As she tried to turn on her new attacker, she was greeted by a boot crashing into her head with the force of a jackhammer. Her already damaged cranial shielding buckled further from the blow as her head was ground into the street, the black asphalt cracking under the pressure.

She felt her wrists being gripped from behind by two hands. Strong hands. Hands unfettered by the pounding of fists into machine bodies. And these fresh, undamaged hands wrenched her arms behind her, while a well-placed boot in the small of her back gave her second attacker an unbreakable purchase. As her arms were pulled behind her, she felt her shoulders cracking. The closing vice behind her snapping her arms as immense power was applied on the fulcrum boot in her back. She knew it was John. It could only be John. He had managed to free himself from the inferno trap she had sprung on him and now he was trying to snap her in half.

She writhed under the pressure, but his grip was too sure, and her body already too damaged from the fight with Lord Mantil. She tried to turn her head to the traitor she knew was John Hunt, fresh from the fiery trap she had set for him, but two new hands suddenly grasped her turning head while John's continued their bone snapping pressure.

She felt the twist as a blanking of systems. Her tactical options flashed off as her brain went to some auxiliary power. Her mind cut off from its main power source as her head was brutally ripped from her body. Her weapons devoid of real power, her body gone, she looked her killers in the eye as, eviscerated, Quavoce held her head up to his furious stare.

John at Quavoce: 'Can she still send the kill command?'

Said John, as Quavoce began to sear out her brain with his laser. She could not actually hear John, but the thought had already occurred to her. As Quavoce's laser dug into her, routing her out, she summoned up her final reserves of power and in a last act of spite, expended her life sending out a signal across the city.

Thirty different boxes and bags of skillfully crafted explosives placed around the city clicked in response, and the town shook with a violent deathblow: thousands of Gaza City's residents consumed in fire in a final flare of genocidal malice.

Chapter 12: Real Estate

On the other side of the planet, still unaware of the events unfolding in Palestine, a far more peaceful, but no less important, meeting was occurring.

They had settled on the Oval Office for the location, because of its unquestionable cache. The president sat at his chair behind his famous desk and awaited their guest. The president had asked his chief of staff to go and greet the foreign head of state visiting him, but had noted, as he had many times recently, that Jim Hacker deferred to the ever more strident Neal Danielson before agreeing to be involved. The president knew that he should be angry at his chief of staff for plainly courting the other man's approval, but like so many before him, the president saw only the seemingly harmless scientist, and not the capable mind beneath.

Jim Hacker saw something else, he saw Neal for the acutely sharp man he was. Jim was not alone in this, devoted as the rest of Neal's team was from their long time as an underground operation, but Jim was among the growing cadre of extremely capable allies that was starting to look to Neal for leadership every day.

For his part, Neal sat, relaxed, to one side. His part in this meeting would be limited. He was there to make sure his team got what he needed, he was not here to get involved in negotiations. That he would leave to Jim Hacker, the president, the secretary of state, and the British Foreign Secretary, who was also present to give his country's blessing and support to the negotiation.

They were meeting a man who had something they needed, a particular spot of land.

As you span the globe there are various nations, territories, and protectorates that fall directly on the equator. The line sweeps through the nations of Ecuador, Columbia, and Brazil in South America, swamped by the oppressive heat of the Amazon River along the way. It touches a small island off the coast of Cameroon, and then drives east through the ironically named Democratic Republic of Congo, to Uganda and Kenya, before passing into the Indian Ocean. It slips between two tiny atolls of the Maldives archipelago, then heads to Indonesia, the nation most touched by this forty-thousand-kilometer circumference of the globe. Sumatra, Borneo, and a host of smaller islands are then skipped over before the long journey across the Pacific to the Galapagos, and so back to the appropriately named Ecuador once more.

As Madeline's already large Research Team started to bring to fruition a concept that had fueled the visions of space's most ambitious dreamers for decades, a plan was forming to actually build an elevator to space. But there were only a few places this tenuous but spectacular structure could be rooted. The elevator would rely on Earth's own centrifugal momentum to hold its massive length stretched taut, and so it must be tethered to somewhere on Earth's portly waistline. It must be anchored in one of those nations, protectorates, territories, or atolls that fall on that line.

So many considerations factored into the choice that Neal, Barrett, and Jim Hacker had spent days arguing over it. Calling upon a throng of political experts from the CIA and NSA, they had plumbed through the options.

It was clear that the place would need to be incredibly well guarded. A carbon strip into space provided a phenomenally tempting target for every terrorist, insurgent, freedom fighter, and other assorted nut job that claimed some random cause as justification for enforced societal atrophy. This meant an island would be best, which catapulted the Galapagos to the top of the list. But taking over one of the most famous and well-protected nature reserves in the world and building the huge port, airport, military structures, and plethora of ancillary buildings that would be necessary would be far from ideal.

There were several islands at the mouth of the Amazon that fell along the line, but this was one of the most inhospitable places on earth, and none were far enough from the mainland to provide much protection anyway. Indonesia had a host of islands that would fit the bill, but they were all densely populated and tightly squeezed. And the population in question was not famed for hospitality to foreigners, the pirate raids in this region falling second only to the famous pirate alley off the coast of Somalia.

So that left one small, rocky island, little more than a vacation resort, off the coast of the African island nation of Sao Tome e Principe.

And that brought them to this man:

"Good Afternoon, Mr. President," said the president of the United States, and the comment was quickly translated into the native Portuguese of their guest's home.

The man being escorted into the auspicious office had a solid look of calm on his face, glued there by a strong paste of confusion and concern at the sudden overtures his office had received to visit the US. Though he was in theory the head of sovereign nation, the president of Sao Tome e Principe held sway over the second smallest nation in Africa, with only the tiny and dispersed nation of the Seychelles having a smaller population.

Not that the people of Fradique de Menezes' country were not proud, and prosperous even. But with a smaller population than the Upper West Side of Manhattan, one could see why the president did not often consider himself a member of the world's political elite.

Formalities were exchanged, introductions were made, pleasantries bandied. As the toothy smiles faded, Jim Hacker took his cue and, through a translator, began to delicately guide the meeting down its winding path. He did not immediately start with financial statements or overtures of support for the various aspects of Menezes's burgeoning economy, but they got there relatively quickly. As the conversation veered down this avenue, it soon became clear to all that this was not simply an opening of relations between these wildly different nations.

The Sao Tome premier started to suspect something of the true nature of the meeting when the secretary of state stepped in and reiterated a point about a 'mutually beneficial relationship;' but still he did not really understand the full scale of the discussion until they started to talk about what they could 'offer.'

When numbers in excess of his nation's GDP started being discussed, his mind began to swim, searching for some source or reason in the sudden outpouring of generosity. Words like 'cooperative facilities' and 'base of operations' were being used, and he sensed that here lay the true price for the help being offered. But mentions of a national highway and an international port and allusions to new schools and a modernized telephone network were so far beyond the normal talk of subsidies and loosely termed loans that he was caught up in the heady promise of it all.

After a while, though, he held up his hands and stopped the conversation. The men stopped talking, and waited with polite smiles, these men with untold power and influence waiting on his opinion with bated breath.

In his native Portuguese, Fradique asked the first completely direct and honest question of the day, "Gentlemen, Mr. President, your talk is enticing indeed, but I cannot help the feeling that maybe we are skirting the real conversation here. I think, perhaps, that you do not talk of *exactly* what you desire from us. May I ask, please, that someone clearly describes what, precisely, you would like in return for all this very generous support?"

The room was silent a moment, and then the British Foreign Secretary thought of a parallel that could help their cause. Sitting forward, he took the lead. With a nod and a hesitant look from his American colleagues, he said, "Mr. President, how much do you know of the history of the island of Hong Kong?"

The man's blank look at the translation which he then received prompted the British man to continue, "Years ago, the Chinese and British came to an agreement. The British wanted a port in the Far East, and the Chinese wanted a way of opening up relations with the West without giving up too much of their sovereignty.

"So Great Britain 'leased' an unused patch of land on the coast near a deserted island, from which to maintain their growing and prosperous relationship with the nation of China. A relationship that thrives even to this day, to the great advantage of both parties. Even after the lease ended, China continued to benefit from the massive investment the British empire had made in the tiny plot of land.

"So," the British minister adjusted himself so he could look directly into the eyes of the foreign premier, then went on, "what we would like to explore is the possibility of an arrangement not nearly as widespread, but just as profitable to Sao Tome e Principe as that relationship. We want the rights to develop a small, almost uninhabited island off your coast, and a small portion of the nearby mainland, into a small but modern commercial port that will employ many members of the nearby community and bring significant and ongoing income to your nation. The port would be divided into two sections, one for commercial use by the influx of companies that will come with the surge of investment, and another for military use to supply the small island with what it needs to function."

The president of Sao Tome sat back and crossed his fingers. Once upon a time there had been frequent talks with many European, American, and even Russian envoys about establishing military bases on Sao Tome island or its less inhabited sister island Principe. But adverse political pressure had always stifled the plans, and in the end most countries had always been more interested in stopping others from establishing a base than actually building one themselves.

But since the end of the cold war interest had flagged, and with it economic support, and even at its height nothing of this scale had ever been proposed. The president considered his options. His time in office had been filled with propaganda and demagoguery, just like his predecessors'. There was rarely anything a person could do in four years that would appreciably improve the lives of his constituents, at least not in comparison with the preposterous campaign claims they were all forced to make. But this. This was different. This was very appreciable indeed, and it would no doubt be very beneficial for his constituents, if it was done correctly. But he kept his face placid, trying to maintain his bargaining position. He would try to take these wealthy Westerners for all he could get.

Jim, Neal, and the various powerful politicians in the room watched the other man think. They all looked pensive and humble, but every one of them saw the moment they had him. He started to tell them his conditions, and how he would not compromise the needs of his people. But the very fact that numbers were starting to be discussed told them it was no longer a question of if, but how much.

On the small island in question there was actually only a lone resort, until recently owned by the only residents of Ilhéu das Rolas. A resort that, coincidentally, had just been purchased by a CIA cover company operating out of Nigeria. And so a slice of the compensation they were discussing would end up coming back to them anyway, after President Menezes and his cronies had taken their share, of course.

And so it went. The United States and Great Britain entered negotiations proper for the first operational site of an equatorial space elevator and the massive infrastructure that would be needed to support it.

Chapter 13: Calling Card

It would take another two days for all of her systems to come to full power, but Lana decided it was time. She had reached a point where she was capable of beginning her new mission. As dusk fell on Slocomb, Alabama, Lana Wilson counted the minutes, then the seconds, until the moonless night would be dark enough.

Theresa and Jason Stevens sat, as always, in their trailer, eating a noxious combination of Doritos and Ramen noodles, served with Bud Light. They did not notice the light slowly fading outside. They were transfixed by the TV where *Desperate Housewives of New York* was playing. The stations no longer reported every day on the tented communities of people waiting to return to their irradiated hometowns, or the devastating effect it was having on the economy. Apparently people were bored with the topic and wanted something more entertaining, so the stations had started running shows once more, and filling the news with stories that were more heartwarming, despite the seriousness of the eco-political shockwaves washing outward from the once affluent East Coast.

Oblivious, night fell on the community of aluminium and plywood trailers that dotted the park where the Stevenses lived, as inevitable as the rising danger in its wake from under their home. As the darkness set in, Lana stretched her arms for the first time in three weeks. Levering herself up on her elbows and heels, she crab walked sideways to a point next to where two breeze blocks formed the steps to the door of the Stevens' cabin. Scanning the area, she checked the heat signatures of the neighboring domiciles, plotting the whereabouts of the various characters she had come to know and loathe over the past few weeks. Sliding out from under the trailer, the lithe shadow that was her skinned black presence stood and flexed, checking her systems one by one.

She smiled. She was ready.

The knock was so light. So innocent. Jason shouted a question at their visitor but no reply came. Just another quiet knock.

"Jesus fucking christ, who is it?" he shouted again.

Again, silence.

He levered himself out of the couch and cursed as Theresa looked on curiously, "Better be fuckin' important!" Jason threatened.

It was, in many ways, the most important knock of his life, for it was the knock of death's own hand. Theresa watched from the couch as the door opened toward her, unable to see outside. Jason paused and stared out, uncharacteristically silent. He seemed confused by what he saw. A black silhouette rose through the opening and Jason seemed transfixed as it reached up to his neck. A flick from one pitch-black finger to his throat sent Jason stumbling back, clasping his neck and rasping for breath.

His silence, at first due to shock, was enforced now by a neatly ruptured voice box. Neither he nor his wife could know what a precise and calculated death monger had just dealt the tiny blow. Theresa stared up at the black, smooth female figure that was stepping into their home and closing the door, baffled and mute, like her husband.

- - -

The next hour was an ever-increasing swarm of terror for the poor couple.

After throwing the muted Jason on the couch by his wife, still clutching at his throat, Lana had turned on Theresa. The woman had risen, ill-placed bravado fueling her rage as she faced the black apparition invading their home, but as harsh words formed in her throat, they were suddenly stifled by a black hand striking out to grip her by the neck.

Theresa's eyes widened as she felt herself pinned inside the black graphite grip. Jason muted, Theresa leashed, they both stared at the nightmare that had come to them as it spoke at last, a sultry woman's voice emerging from her black lips, "Ahh, peace and quiet. At last you two are silent. You have no idea how long I have endured your inane bickering."

The woman stared at them a moment longer, seeming to savor the peace and quiet, and then went on, "Tonight, my friends. Oh tonight you will sing a different tune, one for my benefit alone. Tonight you will sing a tune I will conduct, using you like the dull instruments you truly are."

She smiled viciously. Then, as she placed one of her feet firmly onto Jason's torso, pinning him to the couch, she stared into Theresa's terrified eyes. Theresa stared back at the woman gripping her by the neck and tried in vain to release herself from her clasp. Then she felt something strange on the back of her neck. It was like the woman's black fingers were probing the back of her spine. Then there was a sensation like a hundred tiny needles in the back of her head, like ants were in her skull.

Lana felt the probes snake out of her fingers and penetrate the woman's skin, reveling in the pathetic human's struggle. She felt as the fibers worked their way into the gelatinous tissue between the links in the woman's spinal cord, seeking the soft core within. She could feel the signals flowing inside the all-important cord of nerve fibers inside, she could feel the ebb and flow of Theresa's fear as the woman amplified her futile attempts to release herself. And as the fibers pushed deeper, the pulses became louder and clearer, refining into audible signals until her fibers finally broke through to the hot cable within.

Jason stared up at his struggling wife and wrenched at the leg pinning him. He tried to scream but the noise wouldn't come. Only a hoarse whisper and searing agony as the air ripped over his fractured vocal cords. He paused as the black figure spoke.

"OK," Lana said, "we have connection. Now, let's see how this works, shall we?"

With that, Theresa's entire body spasmed, tensing as a whole. Jason watched as his wife bucked back and forth. He stared in fear and disbelief. What the hell was the woman doing to her?

Lana looked at the sweat dripping down Theresa's face. Fear and pain poured from her eyes as a thick flow of tears, spilling from them like the spittle coagulating at the sides of her gasping, mute mouth.

"OK, that was a bit amateurish. Sorry about that!" said Lana with a chuckle, an incongruously pleasant smile on her lips. "Let's try that again, shall we?"

Based on the woman's thrashing response to the first assault, Lana's systems had compiled a map of her victim's central nervous system. Using that map, Lana selected a limb. Theresa's left arm tensed suddenly, unnaturally rigid, neither flexing or extending, but tensing inhumanly as each muscle group fought each other with antagonistic intensity.

"Good, that's a bit less … hectic, isn't it?" Lana beamed as a hoarse scream rattled from the poor woman's throat. "But those aren't called antagonistic muscles for nothing, now are they?" and with that Lana cut the signal to Theresa's biceps, but kept the triceps flexed to capacity. Now Theresa tensed for a whole new reason, as the muscles in her arm tried to bend it backward, wrenching at the elbow with unnatural imbalance. Theresa grasped at her rigid left arm with her right, trying to stop the growing tide of agony, and the tears flowed even more liberally as the muscle started to tear. But muscle is surprisingly tough stuff, and suddenly she felt a new level of pain, an electric shock of grinding, splintering torture as her humerus bone started to bend under the strain.

"Not going to give, is it?" said Lana eventually, and with psychopathic glee Lana changed the signal ripping Theresa's arm apart, from constant to pulsing. On the third wrenching tug, the bone in her upper arm parted and Jason recoiled in new horror as his wife's left arm suddenly snapped just above the elbow, shattered bone slicing out through the skin like some alien animal trying to escape.

"One bone down …" said Lana, laughing as Theresa wept and gargled with unparalleled suffering, wetting and soiling herself as she convulsed. Lana smiled a disturbingly beatific smile, and then went on, "… two hundred and five to go."

- - -

An hour later, Lana was leaving the now still trailer, and appropriating Jason's old Dodge Ram for the long drive to Florida. Her two disproportionately unfortunate former hosts lay on the floor of their home, shattered and broken. The police and coroner would struggle for days to discover what had caused the gut wrenching disfiguration that had left them so contorted. But it would not be until the senior government officials sent to investigate Lana's next crime heard of the Stevens' unfortunate ends that a link would be made, and some answer be given for the terrible way Theresa and Jason had died.

The authorities were left in no doubt as to the profound evil that had emerged that night, but no one would have guessed that this marked but the beginning of an epic rampage.

- - -

In the end Lana had gotten bored long before she had broken their bodies completely, but not before inducing unbearable pain, fractured pelvises and shattered collar bones. The two had hung limp when she had decided to end it. Unable to move, but also unable to slip into the unconsciousness their minds sought because of the link she had to their spines.

When she had finally decided to end it, Lana had sent a signal that lit their every nerve ablaze and laughed as their muscles twitched, broken limbs contracting inhumanly, like poorly strung marionettes twisting and flopping on the stage. The spasms in their intercostal muscles and diaphragm finally tensed inward, crushing their lungs, driving their last breath out through clenched jaws and tear streaked cheeks as their alveoli collapsed and surged up their bronchi, filling their mouths with blood.

Lana had dropped their wrecked bodies with undisguised loathing and turned to leave, her fury satiated for now, but keen to start the real killing. These two had been but test subjects, poor rats in her maze. Though she had a little bit of murder in her for every human, her real wrath was focused elsewhere in the chaos that America was becoming.

She commandeered Jason's truck and drove out of the trailer park at last. She did not know exactly where the true targets of her expansive rage were just yet, but she would find them soon enough.

Her first lead was an easy one: it was the only place she had ever seen one of them in person.

She drove through the night, arriving at Madeline's mother's retirement community just after one o'clock in the morning. The place was already quiet, but Lana waited until the last of the building's countless TVs and radios had gone quiet before entering through a side entrance. A security camera blithely recorded her unobtrusive ingress, but she tripped no alarms. Nor did she awake any of the building's slumbering guards with her quiet departure an hour later.

In the morning, the small community awoke unaware that anything was wrong. It would be one of the resident nurses, checking in after Madeline's mother missed breakfast, that would discover the horror.

Part 2

Chapter 14: Catalogue

Ayala arrived at her regular meeting with Madeline with her usual sense of trepidation. She had nothing new to report and she was frustrated. Over the last two months she had built up an unprecedented intelligence network in the search for Lana. With full access to the US/UK program called Echelon, her team had set the ears and eyes of the massive processing power it encompassed to scour massive swathes of the world's phone calls and e-mail traffic for any mention of a black-suited figure, or any other description that might fit the woman who had begun terrorizing them. But after the FBI and local police had pursued a thousand hoaxes, false alarms, and even some near misses, they were still no closer to catching the Agent known as Lana Wilson.

As she had too many times before, Ayala had come to update Madeline on the situation. Though the updates had become more and more self-defeating, she had continued to answer her friend's requests for information without complaint, knowing it was the least she could do in the face of her continued failure to find her quarry.

Usually their meetings were by teleconference, what with the wildly different locations Ayala's work now took her to. But because of this day's particularly important event, this meeting was going to be face-to-face, Madeline having a key role in the auspicious launch about to happen, and Ayala's specialized team being in charge of security. Still well in advance of the countdown, the two women met in a private conference room at Cape Canaveral.

The meeting did not go well.

"What the hell does she have to do, Ayala?" screamed Madeline. "Come up and punch you in the fucking face?"

Ayala did not reply in kind, but in a calm voice reiterated her point, "We have been working around the clock to catch her, Madeline. I know that is no comfort to you, but it is all we can do. She is very clever and extremely resourceful."

"She is utterly fucking skinned! How difficult can it be to find a hairless, earless, pitch-black robot? For Christ's fucking sake, Ayala, how many of our family and friends does she have to kill before we stop her?"

Ayala started to reply, again in her calm, conciliatory tone, but before she could, Madeline let a throaty scream of frustration escape her lips, her face turning red as she slammed her balled fists on the table. Ayala fell silent, standing across the table from her tormented friend and waiting. Waiting to see if there was something else she could say.

Knowing that she truly was doing everything she could to find their stalker, Ayala stood her ground and waited for her friend's tumultuous rage to subside.

Madeline let her head fall into her hands and the tears started to come again. Months before, they had tried to keep the pictures of her mother's corpse from her, but Madeline was almost as resourceful and well connected as Ayala. Thoughts of what she had seen still haunted Madeline more often than she cared to admit. Madeline raised her head again, opening her bloodshot eyes wide. Whenever she closed them the sight of her mother's naked, brutalized body came back to her, and so she kept her eyes transfixed on the far wall and gathered herself.

Ayala watched her, drawing from a profoundly deep well of patience for her friend's grief. What had happened to Madeline's mother had been a terrifying return of the enemy they knew as Lana Wilson. After the initial shock, they had responded by gathering all of the team's close relatives together, secreting them in one of the nuclear fallout bunkers that lay hidden in the Colorado mountains to protect them from further attacks. Their plan had been simple: even Lana was not strong enough to break into those deep, atomic-bomb proof bunkers, and if she tried to attack them, the team assigned to guard them would seal the doors and wait for John and Quavoce to come to their aid.

But Lana had not been so blunt or predictable. She had spread her net wider, and first Neal's aunt's entire family, and then two of Madeline's college-age cousins had been found. All had suffered the same horrifying fate that had become Lana's trademark, and it had become ever harder to keep the whole string of deaths secret. Moving as if at random, Lana would strike and then vanish. Each time she struck, a massive team would descend on the area in an attempt to flush her out. Three times one of the many FBI teams searching for her had found her, at least that was what Ayala and her advisors assumed had happened. No one from the ill-fated teams had survived the encounters to report on what had actually transpired.

As Lana's net widened, so did the group of people sequestered, and a race had formed between Lana's appetite for cold-blooded murder and the FBI's ability to gather every cousin, best friend, ex-boyfriend, college mentor, or other randomly associated character from Neal or Madeline's past. Intermingled amongst the killings, Lana then started more wholesale attacks. Neal's hometown high school was first to go. Lana left nothing but a burning hulk to mark the graves of the children who had been unable to escape the inferno. Then the Marine Research Institute, where Neal had first met Madeline and the doomed James Hawkson, had been spectacularly demolished. Since then the Array Neal had worked at had been shut down, and Madeline's high school had been temporarily closed due to 'fire hazards.'

Lana had turned Neal and Madeline into pariahs. Anything they had ever touched in their lives was being systematically turned to dust. Any relationships that predated the madness that had been the last two years had been utterly violated. But in the end Madeline had suffered the greatest loss, and the first, with the gruesome murder of her mother, and she was still the most devastated.

Madeline stared at the wall through eyes strained by the weight of her grief, and anger tempered her breathing. Ayala had given up trying to console her with hugs or kind words, at Madeline's strong request. She had had enough of that. Madeline needed action. She needed Ayala to find the bitch, and then she needed John and Quavoce to kill her, and in the meantime Madeline needed to throw herself into her work.

Madeline sensed that Ayala was about to speak and held up her hand. Her own voice came out shakily at first, but became stronger as she spoke, "Don't, Ayala, I know there is nothing more you can do. And I know that you don't begrudge me my tantrums, which I am grateful for. That's why I let it rip on you rather than on my team." She looked at Ayala and managed an askew smile, which was answered by a simple nod.

"How long do we have till takeoff?" said Ayala, taking Madeline's cue.

"Two hours. But there's really nothing more for my team to do. It's in the hands of NASA and the ESA now."

Ayala nodded, "Shall we head down to mission control, or do you need a minute?"

Madeline shook her head firmly and stood, her chair grinding on the concrete floor as her legs pushed it back.

- - -

Two hours later, Madeline stood amongst a seemingly chaotic throng of people, some standing and some sitting at terminals. Voices rang out with updates and confirmations, checklists ticking down through the exhaustive process of the last of five launches from this site in only a few weeks.

Technicians typed furiously on keyboards as swathes of information slid across screens in the final, frenetic buildup to takeoff. The massive volume of information passed out of mission control, through a thick vein of optic cables surging under a concrete plain for over a quarter of a mile, to the tall scaffolding that supported the vehicle they were prepping. The cables then joined a maze of wires, hoses, and pipes that converged on the base of the launch pad like roots, carrying their wares to every one of the thousand systems they fed. From fuel stirrers to ignition control, from bridge retraction motors to the still hardwired telemetry that linked them to the astronauts on board.

07:34:44 PM ... Countdown begins (T minus 9 minutes)
The frantic activity of a thousand technicians stops for a moment's peace as the countdown begins, an enforced time of careful review and consideration.

07:36:14 PM ... Access arm retracts
The crew aboard the Orion Multi-Purpose Crew Vehicle, nervous despite their countless hours of training, busy themselves throughout the retraction of their access bridge, symbolic of their cutting off from the ground below.

07:38:44 PM ... Launch window open; hydraulic power system (APU) start

Stepping into their window of opportunity, the sense of urgency builds. The reality of the launch becomes tangible. Nerves tingle as possibility turns into imminent reality.

07:38:49 PM … LO2 replenish terminates
Fuel loaded, systems ready. Cool liquid oxygen propellant stirs in the rockets' vast tanks, waiting to expend itself in flaming glory as the rocket surges into space.

07:39:44 PM … Purge sequence four hydraulic test, IMUs to inertial
Systems begin to reconfigure themselves for the coming press of acceleration, and the ensuing escape from gravity. Years of perfection hone their delicate structures to the brief but glorious task only moments away.

07:40:14 PM … Main engine steering test
Nozzles designed to focus the stupendous energy of launch flex and turn under the watchful eyes of expendable cameras, which are soon to be consumed in the fury.

07:40:49 PM … LO2 tank pressurization
07:41:09 PM … Fuel cells to internal reactants
07:41:44 PM … Crew close visors
07:41:47 PM … LH2 tank pressurization

07:43:13 PM … Orion's own GPCs takes control of countdown.
Mission Control gives up control of the launch to those that will live or die by it.

07:43:37 PM … Main engine start (T minus 6.6 seconds)

5, 4, 3, 2, 1 …

07:43:44 PM … CBC ignition

go

Years of experience don't even slightly blunt the feeling of being driven back into their harnesses as the rocket powers upward. No amount of appreciation for the vast forces at work can possibly temper the sheer, childlike joy that comes from being catapulted by humanity's greatest achievement into the greater void.

With nothing left to do but watch, the four men and women grin broadly. Leaving common sense behind, they reconcile themselves to the spectacularly dangerous career they have dedicated themselves to by smiling and thinking:

if you have to go, you might as well go big …

- - -

Below them, the earth shakes with the thunderous roar of fifty-seven million horsepower as seven massive boosters send four tiny astronauts surging into space. The Delta IV Heavy was already one of the most powerful rockets in the world. When they attached four extra CBC boosters to it, they made it the biggest, most powerful machine ever made.

The big rockets' cones vibrate with insane abandon as they fight to tame the mayhem exploding out of them. At six thousand degrees, the fiery plume from the combustion of their liquid hydrogen fuel is hot enough to boil iron. The engine burns its liquid fuels so quickly it could drain a swimming pool in twenty seconds.

After only eight minutes of this mad burn, the rocket has reached seventeen thousand miles per hour and is already passing Low-Earth Orbit, two hundred miles above Earth's surface.

But this rocket's mission will take it much farther. For they are going far outside their ordinary orbit, and they are not alone. Like their sister ships that are already in space, Cable Lift Vehicle-19 (CLV-19) carries an unusual cargo. For along with the small module carrying the four astronauts is a massive length of nanotube cable wound into twenty spools. It is the nineteenth section of a greater whole to be hefted into space over the past month by US Delta IV Super-Heavies and modified European Ariane-5 MEs. But this is only the second one that has been manned, and it will hopefully be the last.

Sixteen hours into the mission, the commander acquires their destination visually, a lonely white dot floating in a strange-looking cloud of grey dots. Like an explosion of grey that has been paused, the first of the CLV manned Orion modules sits among the loosely tethered batch of more than seven hundred tons of cable, like a shepherd keeping eye over a grazing flock of grey sheep.

As CLV-19 approaches her rendezvous, she is now only a fraction of her launch weight, her First Stage Rocket along with its six CBC boosters have long since been jettisoned. Left behind as empty husks, mere memories of their former glory, after they wantonly expended the hundreds of tons of fuel that had made up 90 percent of their mass at launch.

CLV-19 is now left, a long, thick cylinder, and after the might of its exit from Earth's embrace, it takes only small attitude thrusters on her sides spraying gas to maneuver her, to roll her over, spinning her gently and silently. For her pilot and commander looking out of her cockpit, the glittering white globe of Earth seems to rotate around the module, the clouds swirling on its panoramic surface adding to the eerily beautiful effect. Her other two crew members are prepping for egress as the module closes in, attitude thrusters in her nose slowing her as she slides closer to her sister.

In the final meters, the pilot has a disconcerting view of the other module's large final stage booster, cold now, and silent in the vacuum. Along her near side, the commander and pilot see two white-clad figures tethered to four powerful-looking clamps. They are matched by the two other members of their own crew now outside in the vacuum.

Various thrusters tweak the module's speed and position in tiny increments as she slides quietly by, their jets silent in the vacuum of space, no air to transmit their sound to the few ears that could hear. Barely three meters apart in all the vastness of space, the two members of each crew tethered to the side of the modules wave to each other with big white gloved hands as they slide slowly past, two of them actually reaching out for a once-in-a-lifetime high five.

Radio chatter bounces between the modules as the pilots and crew coordinate the final crucial seconds of the coupling. Unlike the other US and European rockets that had brought the other loads of nanotube cabling into space, these two modules are going to link together. As four massive clamps are bolted shut by the crew, the huge modules ease to a virtual halt relative to each other, moving millimeters at a time in the final moments. Finally the clamps seal, one by one, resounding, metallic clanks transmitting through both hulls. The two modules are now one, and the process of attaching a portal between their modified cabins begins.

"Mission Control, this is CLV-1, clamp seal confirmed."

"Mission Control, this is CLV-19, clamp seal confirmed."

"CLV-1 and CLV-19, Mission Control, clamp seal confirmed. CLV-1, what is your status on system linkage?"

"Mission Control, CLV-1, crew reports primary socket seal, and control board linkage is confirmed on my board."

"Confirmed, Mission Control, this is CLV-19, showing linkage complete here as well, initiating systems tests. Estimate portal seal in five minutes."

"CLVs 1 and 19, this is Mission Control, as of this moment, your combined designation is officially changed to Terminus One. Congratulations Terminus One. Commander Cashman, you have the com."

"Thank you and confirmed, Mission Control, this is Commander Cashman of Terminus One. Beginning Systems Integration Test now."

As the two modules complete the process of fusing themselves into one cohesive whole, the crews return to their now connected command modules to prepare for the next stage. The connection process has been relatively quick, but still exhausting, and they are sweaty from the thick spacesuits they have been working in. The irony of overheating in the cold vacuum of space passes without comment, and seeing that they have time, Commander Cashman sends the members of his crew that had gone extravehicular to clean up and get some food.

With controls synced and switched to one board, the remaining crew meets to discuss the next stage. The commander of the now defunct CLV-19 assumes his role as second in command of the newly designated Terminus One and they go over their plans one last time. If all goes well, neither of the modules now forming Terminus One will ever return to Earth. In fact, if all goes to plan, their crews will be the first people ever to ride a train there.

Chapter 15: SpacePort One

The HMS *Dauntless* followed her patrol vector with typical precision. Though it was never mentioned, her crew was still ashamed by the way their former Lieutenant John Hunt had fooled them. In the captain's chair on the bridge, Lieutenant Commander Joe Waters sat in for Captain Bhade, who was at a meeting of senior officers.

"Jesus, she's big," said Tac Officer Thomas McDonald at the comms desk. He was surveying the various ships and submarines tied into the tactical radar network that made up the Joint Task Force. The USS *Ronald Reagan* formed the core of the taskforce's defense network, and it was anchored only a quarter of a mile offshore. It represented the largest runway within over two hundred miles. The international airport on the island of Sao Tome was in the far north of the island, and until they had their shore-based facilities completed, the *Ronald Reagan* was serving as both the new base's airport and strategic headquarters.

Aboard her, Captain Bhade looked around the low-slung briefing room. It was as crowded as it could be, not a seat was empty, and the senior captain stood amongst the more junior of the officers gathered in the room. Filling the room were a host of senior captains and admirals, colonels and generals from around the world gathered to discuss the defense net being set up around the previously backwater southern tip of Sao Tome island.

Pinned to the wall at the front of the room was a map of the island showing the small country's infrastructure. As the captain of the most advanced anti-aircraft battery in the taskforce, Captain Bhade had been put in charge of coordinating the fleet's air traffic control network. His ship's vastly capable tracking systems forming the hub of a network of radar systems spreading out like overlapping petals. At the front of the room, a man that introduced himself as General Milton was briefing the senior team on the next stages of the project.

"I know that you must all have been wondering what military priority would warrant the force size that has been assigned to this location, and I am happy to tell you that today I have received approval to release that information to this group," said General Milton to the room, his powerful voice filling the space. "But before I get to that, I wanted to take this opportunity when we are all in one place to introduce the various team leads on the ground here, and have them talk through their plans. Then I will walk the group through the final plan for the base once all our work is complete.

"First of all, I would like to introduce Admiral Terence Cochrane of the Royal Navy, who is in charge of our sea-based defensive network here at Rolas Base."

A slight-looking gentleman stood, familiar to most of the officers in the room as one of the most senior admirals in the British Royal Navy. The very fact that Admiral Cochrane was involved in the project was comment enough on its importance, even if one didn't factor in the scale of the naval taskforce assigned to the project.

But despite his slight-seeming frame, Admiral Cochrane was a famously sharp mind, known throughout the international military community as a stalwart of the Falklands war, and thus one of the very few naval officers in the world with actual naval ship-to-ship combat experience. Standing, the man stepped behind a podium and spoke into the microphone, his voice not used to barking across a room. But its tenor lacked nothing of the force of the general's for all of its subtlety and seeming finesse.

"Gentlemen, ladies, fellow officers, let me start by saying that it is an honor to see such an unprecedented collection of international allies working together toward one concerted goal. Let me assure you that once you all understand the nature of our mission here you will appreciate, as I do, the extreme importance of our role in putting in place an impenetrable defense network around this location." He allowed a mischievous smile to spread across his face and went on, "I am sure all of you want to get to that point in our discussion as soon as possible, but when General Milton and the rest of the command team discussed this briefing, we decided that once we have shared that information, the last thing you will want to do is discuss patrol matrixes or construction plans.

"With that in mind, let us focus on the different aspects of our taskforce here first, and then we will get to the big event. So please bear with me as I run through the core aspects of our naval operations here." Though cordial, his carefully enunciated English accent managed to demand their attention, and few were in doubt as to how little tolerance he would have for anyone who didn't give him their undivided attention. "As most of you know, our naval operations here are split into three divisions. Firstly our Surface operations are under the command of Vice Admiral Alicia Burns of the United States Navy, based here on the *Ronald Reagan*.

"Vice Admiral Burns commands the USS *Reagan*, along with two Ticonderoga-Class cruisers, the USS *Port Royal* and the USS *Lake Erie*, providing large gun and missile fire support, these ships will coordinate the base's defense around the east and west coast patrol fields."

A projector overlaid two circles onto the map of Sao Tome on the wall, showing how the two powerful cruisers were stationed on either side of the island, providing overlapping fire support that covered the entire island and extended several miles out to sea in either direction. Highlighted on the map was the island of Rolas, a quarter of a mile off of the uninhabited southern coast of the main island of Sao Tome. Also marked was the semi-dirt road down along the east coast of the island from the only large city on the island, the capital in the far north. The road ended at the tiny fishing village of Porto Alegrè, overlooking a large bay, which was to become the hub of operations once base construction was complete.

"The cruisers and the *Reagan* are supported by a joint force of several ships, including one Japanese destroyer, the JMDF *Chokai*, two French stealth frigates, the *Surcouf* and the *Courbet*; and the British destroyer, the HMS *Dauntless*.

"Our subsurface operations are being run through Admiral Takano aboard the JMDF *Chokai*. The admiral commands a powerful taskforce of submarines consisting of three Oyashi-Class multi-role submarines and two Asashio-Class attack submarines. Together with our surface ships and the air fleet based off of the *Reagan*, this force constitutes a naval defensive position unparalleled since World War Two, and from a sheer firepower perspective not surpassed in history."

The admiral let that point sit out there a moment with not a small amount of pride, then continued with the introduction of the captain of the *Dauntless*. "Directing our air traffic defensive matrix is Captain Bhade on board the HMS *Dauntless*, using the first ever multinational coordinated radar array. The network connects the radar systems of every ship in the taskforce to create a panoramic, auto-validating picture of any movement in a two-hundred-fifty-mile radius, with fixed-weapon response capability out to ninety miles, and airborne response out to two hundred miles on permanent rotating patrol."

The map continued to update as the admiral spoke, showing the various force deployments around the island as the taskforce spread out to clamp down all movement in and out of the sensitive space they needed to protect. The admiral continued with a detailed explanation of the priorities and movement criteria agreed to with the government of Sao Tome. The system was now tracking any and all movement off the coast of the island, separating it into two groups: intra-island traffic, such as fishing boats, and inter-island traffic, such as cargo ships and commercial air traffic into the civilian airport at the far north of the island. Wrapping up his briefing, the admiral thanked the group and handed back to General Milton.

"Thank you, Admiral. We can take questions now or later, what would you prefer, Admiral?" The admiral shrugged and Barrett looked around the room to see if there were any pressing thoughts. Seeing none, he moved on, "Well, if no one has any immediate questions on the naval force deployments, we will press on. If you do have any questions at any point, you can find the Allied Chain of Command in your briefing documents, please feel free to escalate any questions up through your commanding officer."

The general looked down and consulted his notes before continuing. "Now I would like to introduce General Braldinho of the Brazilian Army who has been coordinating the construction of our land-based perimeter defenses."

A stolid-looking man with graying temples and sparkling eyes stood, stepped over to the podium, and said in hesitant English, "You must to forgive me, my fellow officers, but English is not so good as my fellow admirales e generales. I have asked to one of my younger and better-looking subordinates for conduct today briefing." A muted laugh fluttered through the room at the self-deprecating joke.

At a wave from General Braldinho another man stood, a man the general introduced as Major Garrincha. Only a handful of those present knew this was a pseudonym, the second one that the man in question had adopted in as many years. Under his first disguise, the man had struck fear across the Middle East before leading one of the most terrible guerilla attacks in modern history. Sharply dressed in a well-cut uniform, his hair cut short against his head, his chin closely shaven for the first time since his arrival on earth, the man Barrett had only recently come to know as Lord Mantil spoke out with a smooth, crisp, pleasantly lilted accent to the gathered officers.

"Obrigado, meo Generale. My fellow officers, I wanted to lay out the three stages of our land-based defensive construction, the first of which is nearly complete, and the second of which is underway as we speak."

At a nod from the faux-major, a new projection came over the map on the wall, showing the single road connecting the only town on the south of the island with the more heavily populated northern side.

"Our first job, and one which has proven surprisingly problem free, was to relocate the two hundred inhabitants of the small villages of Puerto Alegrè and Monte Mario, as well as the employees of the small resort that was located on the island of Rolas, to another location designated by our hosts, the government of Sao Tome e Principe." Quavoce used a laser pointer to highlight the two towns in question as he spoke.

"With that completed, we began the job of isolating the island, Ilhéu de Rolas, from the civilian population, for a radius of ten miles from the island proper." A circle appeared on the map showing a ten-mile radius around the small island off the southern coast of Principe. "To do this we had to clear a path across the island to provide a clear defensive barrier. The path is a minimum of four hundred feet wide and has been dynamited, burn-cleared, and then bulldozed. We have constructed two parallel, twenty-five-foot, razor wire fences to stop any 'accidental' ingress across the border.

"To stop any *deliberate* ingress, in the no-man's land between the fences we have placed a series of movement sensors, seismic monitors, and active radar arrays linked to a series of German MLG-27 automated cannons, spaced at two-hundred-foot intervals along the land-border's length, and set to automatically take out anything moving in or above the perimeter with their 1,700-round-per-minute fire of depleted uranium, 27mm rounds."

Several of the officers in the room inadvertently whistled at the statement. While the size of the naval presence had already proven the severe approach the taskforce was taking to defending the site, the use of automated cannons to defend a land-based perimeter was both unprecedented and unflinchingly brutal.

The cannons were completely without mercy, and the amassed group knew that they would shred anyone unfortunate to wander into the area into mincemeat in less than a second. But Quavoce and Barrett knew that the step was absolutely necessary, because though they were saddened by what would happen if some local foolishly tried to cross the perimeter, they also knew that if Lana or one of the other two surviving Agents tried to get close enough to the Rolas Island to launch a handheld surface-to-surface missile, they had to be stopped at all costs. Those missiles had a range of up to seven miles. Any longer-range munition fired over the perimeter would meet the same end as anyone trying to carry a handheld missile launcher into range. Anything and everything that crossed the fire lane that the Brazilians and Germans had constructed would be pummeled into oblivion. It was a necessary evil.

Already the system was proving reassuringly, if brutally, effective on any birds and animals small enough to get through the razor wire, the patch of land between the fences becoming a grisly graveyard for their torn carcasses. The system was capable of tracking and killing up to forty separate targets at any point along the fence. In time, the local animals would learn to avoid the area; until then their deaths would be mourned, but not avoided.

"As you all know, a strict no-fly zone is in place over the perimeter, and our Japanese colleagues are maintaining a rotating submarine presence at the shore-points at either end, where the land perimeter joins the wider water perimeter, providing constant coverage of the coastal portions with their more than effective subsurface capability.

"There is only one access point through the perimeter, on the west coast, at which we have set up a two-stage, 'airlock' autocannon system that can be deactivated in steps to allow ground access without losing perimeter integrity at any point. Air support from a rotating Tiger Attack Helicopter Squadron also provided by our German colleagues will enforce the no-fly zone, with longer-range support provided by the F-35Ns aboard the *Reagan*."

With the ground defenses covered, the proxy Brazilian Major Garrincha moved his briefing on to the second stage of construction that was occurring on Rolas Island itself. They had started by extending the small pier on the island to allow midsized ships to dock and unload building materials to supply the rest of their building work. The small hotel had been converted and massively expanded into accommodations for the Brazilian construction workers who were employed on the central project of the island, where a massive concrete platform was being constructed.

Nearly half a mile on each side, the foundation of the platform had already smothered half the island. They were building the anchor for the greatest structure ever conceived by man, and as the designs slowly unfolded in front of the room, the group's curiosity steadily grew until eventually Major Garrincha finished his part of the brief and took a seat, giving the floor back to General Milton.

"And now we come to the part of the agenda that I imagine most of you have been waiting for: the reason why we have gone to such extreme measures to secure this area against any and all possible attack or infiltration. Gentlemen, I am proud to announce to you that you are part of one of the most ambitious and significant projects in human history. For there is a reason why we have chosen this particular island. Its location puts it on a phenomenally short list of candidates for what we are trying to accomplish. For the massive platform my colleague Major Garrincha has described will be the anchor for a nanotube cable over fifty-*thousand* miles long.

"A cable that will be attached to counterweight that will hold it out perpendicular to the earth's equator. A cable that will extend directly into space, and form the very first elevator out of Earth's atmosphere."

- - -

Two hours later, the meeting of the senior officers of the Rolas Defense Task Force finally broke up. The meeting had become an engaging question-and-answer session after the general's explanation of the purpose of the new international base. The general and Lord Mantil left together, a helicopter taking them both to their accommodations on Rolas Island as they talked more about the meeting.

"I think that went well, Lord Mantil." The general was still getting used to the Agent's real name, but as his respect for his alien ally continued to march steadily upward, so too did his desire to show that respect in no uncertain terms.

"Indeed, General Milton," said Quavoce, "they seemed surprisingly receptive to our plans once they had gotten over the initial shock. I think once we start to initiate the connection procedures, it will start to feel more real to them."

"For me too, Lord Mantil," said Barrett with a smile. "I have to admit I am still having trouble dealing with the concept. I suppose you must have these on your home world, but it is still difficult to envision this, even having seen the plans." He shook his head and then leaned in close to the Mobiliei, "Have you ever ridden up one of them?"

Quavoce allowed a pleasant smile to spread across his lips and said, "Of course, General." He paused, then went on with as little condescension as possible, "There are literally thousands of these elevators spanning the equator of our world. Most spaceports have several strands running up from the same location. Some of the larger ones have a hundred or more, with staging posts along the way to allow egress at different orbital levels and direct links to orbital hubs and space stations.

"A lot of our intercontinental travel is now via elevator, with glide planes using them to climb out of the atmosphere then be released at the appropriate level to then glide down through the atmosphere to their destinations, like your space shuttles do." Quavoce went on in a reassuring voice, "Elevator travel is as commonplace as airplane travel is to you, as safe and as a part of life as trains or cargo ships. As a child, my school even went on field trips into space … several times."

Though Quavoce's face stayed pleasant, Barrett had a sense that behind that mask, the Agent was remembering something, straying back to a time before he had set himself against his country and his race. The general was right, but Quavoce set the thought aside and returned to the present, looking into Barrett's eyes. "General, once this is complete, a whole new era will begin for your race. This step will open up space like the invention of the compass unleashed our respective ancestors upon each of our world's oceans. I only wish you were discovering it with the innocence and simple curiosity we did, instead of in response to the threat of annihilation."

Barrett could feel the shame emanating from the humanoid sitting next to him on the helicopter, and he felt the need to say something, but what, he had no idea. They sat in silence for a minute, each man unsure of how to get past this point, until the general found a change of topic to bridge the void, "I understand from Major Toranssen that you rescued a refugee when escaping Iran. How is she doing?"

While Captain Falster had eventually returned to America to work on another project, she had first dropped Banu off at Rolas to reunite with Quavoce. It had been a surprisingly heartfelt reunion given the brief time they had had together, but Banu held Quavoce up as a savior, a guardian, and felt the weight of the unspoken promise he had made to protect her as her only solid foundation in her fast changing universe. This was compounded by the fact that he remained the only person she knew that could speak with her in the local dialect of her home, a home that no longer existed.

Quavoce looked up at Barrett, "Young Banu is as well as can be expected. She had not yet learned to read, though she is trying hard to catch up now, and it will be a while before she is comfortable with any language other than her native dialect. But she is a quick learner, a function of her young age. Hopefully soon I will no longer be her only real access to the outside world."

Inwardly he sighed, but he did not let the emotion show. "I have tried to explain some measure of what is happening to her, but I fear she still does not really understand. She still talks of home and I fear it will be a long time before she truly grasps the extent of the devastation in that region." Barrett nodded, thinking of the plague that still ravished the rural parts of the Middle East, as well as a swathe of Southern America and sub-Saharan Africa, and many backwater locales in Cambodia, Laos, Vietnam, northern India, and Nepal. In total it had claimed nearly two million lives across the planet, a figure that would have been far greater had Martin and Jack not been so successful blocking it in the most unprotected regions. But it had still wiped out whole communities where isolation or political strife had not allowed the inoculation developed by Madeline Cavanagh and Ayala Zubaideh to spread.

The northern Iranian region where Banu had spent every day of her eleven-year life had been one of those communities that had gone unnoticed by the antigen. Everyone Banu had ever met before the night Quavoce took her away was now dead. A thousand ghost towns haunting the countryside of stricken nations in the aftermath of the satellite's final solution. The plague had sparked a string of political posturing across the region that was only redoubled by Russia's implacable anger over the launch of HATV missiles from Pakistan. Arguments still raged about what reparations must be made, as America and Europe tried desperately to calm the enraged parties on both sides. Tanks still amassed along Russia's borders with its former allies of Kurdistan and Uzbekistan, as Russia threatened to roll through them en route to Islamabad.

On the other side of the region, the devastation of Gaza City had sent the Muslim world into a frenzy and fueled claims of genocide by the Israelis. While few truly believed the Jews were responsible for the plague that had taken its strangely dispersed toll around the globe, there were those for whom anti-Semitic demagoguery was the only fuel in their political engines, and their rhetoric was rampant.

The general and Lord Mantil went silent as the helicopter approached Rolas Island. The first signs of the bridge that would eventually join the island to the mainland were already evident as construction proceeded apace. Crews continued their work into the night, cycling out as long shifts came to a close, fresh men and women replacing them.

General Barrett looked out over the work as the helicopter came into land. They were rushing, he knew that, but they could only keep their intentions secret for so long. Ayala's new friends at the CIA and MI6 had told her that rumors were already spreading about the sudden arrival of forces in Sao Tome. While a wide variety of speculations were apparently floating around, Barrett was sure that once any of the three remaining Agents heard about the work they were doing they would link it with the island's particular location along the equator and figure out what they were up to. After that, it was only a matter of time before one or all of them came knocking, and they had to be ready when they did. As ready as they could be.

Key senior officers on the station already knew the full nature of the threat they faced, including Admirals Cochrane, Burns, and Takano, and Captain Bhade of the *Dauntless*, of course. Once they publically announced the base's purpose, Barrett would also brief the permanent detachment that they were training to man the defenses. They all knew there was going to come a time when it would no longer be possible to hide the base's purpose. When the incomprehensibly long cable began to literally lower from the heavens to the ingenious catchment mechanism they were building, the secret would be out. It was simply not possible to hide a fifty-thousand-mile-long elevator into space.

- - -

They had kept the resort's pool as a retreat for the senior officers stationed on the island, most of whom had been billeted in the old hotel complex, often two to a room. There had been some talk amongst the other officers about the young girl that had accompanied the Major Garrincha to the base, families having not yet been permitted on base for the other officers. But the others soon noticed that the major enjoyed the special attention of all of the company's most senior staff, and talk died down accordingly.

The resort encircled the kidney-shaped pool, its light blue ripples bracketed on all sides by the buildings that had once been the home of sauntering tourists. But now the pool seemed at odds with the busy purpose of the tourists' usurpers, and was a lonely area of calm amongst an ever-growing sea of prefabricated buildings, fast-poured roads, and the behemoth platform that was to be the keystone to Earth's bridge to the stars.

Back at the old resort, Banu stood by the window of the strange place that had become her home, staring down at the small pool's crystal blue waters. Growing up, even the water she drank had been less clear than the shimmering blues and turquoises of that strange pond. It was one of a thousand wonders she was still trying to come to terms with. But today, like most days, she merely sat and wondered at it all, avoiding the questions that swam just out of focus in the back of her mind.

She heard the strange electronic lock click, and the clunk as the door to their room opened, but she did not turn. She knew Quavoce's sound and his smell and she did not need to confirm it was him. Instead she stayed there, contemplating the man who had shattered her world, and wondered for the hundredth time whether he had saved her or damned her. Feeling her fears climb in her throat again, she turned to him suddenly, needing to see his eyes, needing to see the boundless assurance and confidence that they offered.

He was just standing there, behind her, watching her with his seemingly limitless patience. She greeted him in English.

"Hello, Quavoce. Welcome home."

His smile was broad and from the heart and she returned it, turning somewhat sheepish under his gaze. He looked at the little girl and felt for her as a father would, ever hopeful, but unsure of what the future would hold. In his heart he feared that because of her tragic circumstances this progeny may be forever on the eve of going out into the world, a chick that may never be able to fly. He stifled a shudder at the thought.

He still did not know exactly why he had saved her, but the thought of leaving her there, as yet another life lost to expedience, had simply been too much for him. Smiling still, he turned now to the small kitchenette and took in the simple but hearty meal she had prepared for him. It was beyond him to tell her that he did not need such things, and somehow this food, prepared for him by this young girl, did give him a sustenance of sorts.

Reverting to her native tongue, she invited him to sit at the table, and began to serve him, agreeing to join him with the same reluctance she always had. Only newlyweds ate together in her culture, and even then only if for some reason they were not sharing their house with one or other of their families.

In larger groups, women did not eat with the men. And as she sat with him, she felt again how alien it all was. But the sense of the affection this man clearly had for her was palpable. She had never seen such a thing, not from her father, or even her mother, not to this depth, and despite that, it felt as natural to her as breathing. And so, as the man she knew as Quavoce ate the meal she had prepared, and urged her into a conversation in her fledgling English, she looked at him and felt the stirrings of something she instinctively knew was her first brush with love.

Chapter 16: Escalation

Ayala's understanding of Middle Eastern politics made her a logical choice for the conversation she was heading to as she walked down the famous corridor.

But her background also made her shun the spotlight of such an auspicious setting, and she had to forcibly resist the urge to lie about her name as she passed through countless security checkpoints. Over the last few months she had developed a network she could only have dreamt of in her days as an active agent of the Mossad. Though her efforts had failed to pin down the atrocity that was Lana Wilson, Ayala's obvious talents in intelligence gathering had not gone unnoticed by the powers that be.

By her side was her former handler turned assistant Saul Moskowitz, more at home in the corridors of power than she, perhaps, but also far from comfortable as they passed yet another burly looking Secret Service agent. With officious precision, this one raised his wrist to his mouth and reported their approach as the others had, but did not stop them. They were, after all, expected. Yet another thing that Ayala never liked to be.

"Mr. President, Ms. Zubaideh and Mr. Moskowitz," said the president's secretary as they were ushered into the room. Neal nodded to them from where he was seated on one of the two couches in the room, with Jim Hacker standing behind him like the shadow he had become. Sitting next to Neal was Peter Cusick, the director of the CIA, and a man Ayala had come to know well in the last few weeks. The president leaned against his desk, facing the entire assembled group.

"Thank you for coming," said the president, sensing that his guests did not particularly enjoy being called to the White House.

"Of course, Mr. President. An honor as always," said Ayala with consummate diplomacy, and the president waved them to a seat. They sat facing Neal, and could see an apology of sorts on his face.

"OK then," said the president, "I asked you to come by because you may be one of the few people that both fully appreciates the scale of our 'mission' and also has an appreciation of this new crisis."

Ayala quirked an eyebrow at him with a genuine surprise she would normally have hidden, and in the pause that followed, Neal spoke up.

"Normally this would be a subject for the joint chiefs, but before the president goes in front of them he wanted to get our opinion. Actually, he wanted to get my opinion, but I told him that you were far more qualified to speak on this than I am." Again the apologetic expression flashed onto his face, though without contrition, only sympathy, and he carried on, "The stalemate in Pakistan has been broken."

Ayala felt Saul tense at his side, aware that she had done the same thing. Ever since the conflagration that had killed the four satellites, Russia had been, quite reasonably, screaming bloody murder over the launch of missiles into their airspace by Pakistan. Frantic attempts by the UN, US, UK, EU, and every other union we could wrangle had stayed their hand for a while, but apparently not for good.

"As we already knew, the government of Tajikistan had allowed some Russian troop movements in the Badom-Dara region across from Northern Pakistan. Well, at twenty-three hundred hours eastern standard time, four Russian tank divisions crossed the thin swathe of Afghani territory that separates them from Pakistan and began rolling south toward Chitral and the main roadway to Islamabad. Satellite imagery confirms that Pakistani troops moved to intercept them, and we can also confirm that three Russian armored paratroop divisions began to deploy via Russian heavy-lift just north of Islamabad. Those are the deployments we know about. We also have unsubstantiated reports of landing craft along the coast and cruise missile launches from Russian submarines, as well as other disturbing events.

"At this point we have to assume that a full-scale invasion of Pakistan is underway, though we can have no way of knowing just how far they have gotten, or how far they intend to go."

Ayala was stunned. The last time Russian troops had been in the region they had forcibly occupied Afghanistan for more than twenty years. How could they not have seen this coming? These kinds of decisions took months, years. How had the buildup to a decision to actually invade escaped their channels?

Peter Cusick offered up a comment, "As far as we can tell they have already secured the airport and major communications hubs around the capital, and at key points along the border. As of half an hour ago, no official information has been coming in or out of the country. That said, informal reports are still flowing, and all indications point to the beginnings of a significant occupation force."

"Mr. President?" interjected Ayala. "I have been focused on other things, I admit, but I have been meeting weekly with the heads of more than ten of the world's most capable intelligence agencies, including Mr. Cusick here. I simply cannot believe that this could have passed unnoticed. How could this happen? How could we not have known?"

"Actually, I had invited you here precisely because I was hoping you could help shed some light on that," said the president with evident candor.

The director of the CIA went on, "We had reports of their troop buildup, of course, as you know. And even knew of their contingency plans for invasion. But every source we had in the Kremlin, and since the fall of the Iron Curtain we have a fairly significant number, told us that invasion was not being seriously considered. Posturing. That is what *all* of our sources said. Posturing. And this was confirmed at the highest possible levels in back channel conversations between our state departments."

The room was silent for a moment until a new voice interjected meekly, "May I ask something?" said Saul Moskowitz, in his heavy Israeli accent.

He took the room's silence as consent, and went on, "What have our assets in Moscow been saying *since* the attack?"

Peter shook his head, "We have not had time to contact them via the usual paths since the attack. We should know more from them soon." He appeared comfortable with the statement, but both Ayala and Saul saw the twitch as he said 'soon.' He was not comfortable with the silence and they knew it. Come to think of it, neither was Saul.

The old Jew spoke again with deference, "Umm, surely the news has spread in Moscow far faster than it has here. Shouldn't we have heard something from them by now? Shouldn't at least some of them have initiated contact?"

It was what he would have done. Unless he perceived he was in danger. Or he was already dead.

The president looked at the director, who sighed and ground his jaw a bit, staring intensely at a point on the floor as he considered his response.

"Under ordinary circumstances I would say yes, but this is so unprecedented that I have to believe that our sources are as surprised as we are." But he did not seem convinced, and neither was anyone else.

Ayala looked at Saul, then at Neal, and then spoke, "I think we should consider another factor in our calculations here. I am not sure how it plays into this, but this is, as you say, Peter, unprecedented, and I can't help but draw a parallel."

The room waited and she went on, "Not that any of us could easily forget it, but there are still three Agents out there. One of whom was last seen vanishing into the Siberian mountains. In view of the unexpected nature of this move, I don't think we should discount the possibility that Mr. Kovalenko is somehow involved."

Their conversation was interrupted by a knock on the door. The president's secretary poked her head in, "I'm sorry to disturb you, Mr. President, but the secretary of state is on line two and requests to speak with you urgently."

She was well aware of the seriousness of the meeting the president was in, but equally aware of how to prioritize his calls. Appreciating the urgency with which the secretary must have pressed to force the interruption, the president nodded and stepped to his desk.

"If you'll excuse me a moment." It was not a request they could deny, and they went to stand but he waved them back into their seats as he picked up the phone on his desk.

They all pretended not to listen, except Neal, who openly stared at the president as he frowned into the phone, nodding and grunting his understanding occasionally.

"I think you should get over here as soon as you can, Judy. And please have your staff prepare a brief on this immediately. I'll need you to give an update in the SitRoom ASAP."

He bid her farewell and hung up.

"Well, it appears that our contacts have been even more remiss than we thought, gentlemen," said the president with evident concern, his eyes glazed as he tried to bring new information into focus. Ayala did not comment on the mild slight at having been referred to as one of the 'gentlemen' by the clearly disconcerted president as he continued, "We have received a formal dispatch from the president of Russia saying that in response to 'hostile attacks' on the sovereign republic of Russia, they have taken 'defensive measures' against their attackers."

He delivered the final blow with greater intensity, "The message came from the office of President *Svidrigaïlov*." The room reacted to the name, just as the president had when he had heard it. Svidrigaïlov was one of the few remaining true hard-liners in the Russian leadership, but he had been perceived as marginalized and virtually bankrupt of real power in the Kremlin.

Apparently they had been wrong about more than just the Russian's intentions in Pakistan. If this message was correct, and Svidrigaïlov had somehow grabbed power, then they were not only facing the collapse of the Pakistani government, but an inestimably greater threat. If this message was correct, then in one ill-fated evening a fifth of the world's nuclear weapons had just fallen into the hands of a red-blooded, hard-line communist to rival Kryuchkov and Yanayev.

- - -

Emilia drove just within city speed limits in order to avoid arousing suspicion. Something was very wrong, and she had get away from Borodino immediately. It had started with a muted call from an old colleague. No words, just a silent line and three distinct taps from the other end. It was a standard signal, and it meant only one thing: get out, and get out now. Without hesitation she had switched off her cell phone and removed the battery, hidden them both behind some books in the library, and exited by a side door.

Stepping away from the old stone building, she had walked down a side street, not even trusting her own car as she headed for the trolley stop nearby. She had hesitated then. Wondering if she was being paranoid. It was all or nothing in these types of situations. You either went completely off the grid and bolted, potentially blowing any cover you had managed to build, or you stayed put. With all the tension of the last few weeks, was it possible she had just been rattled by the strange call?

Outside the library, with the day's grey light darkening to twilight, she had thought about abandoning her fears altogether and stepping back inside. But the sudden sight of four black Zil sedans approaching the library from different directions had banished her doubts.

After stepping into a nearby store to let the Zils pass by, she had headed for the trolley stop once more. The trolley had taken her away from the scene, she had not even looked where it was going, and after ten minutes of rumbling through the suburbs of Moscow, she had gotten off. Finding an appropriately inconspicuous and dilapidated Lada amongst the sea of old Russian cars that covered the city, she had broken its meager security and headed off into Moscow, seeking a way into the British embassy, and an escape from whoever was pursuing her.

- - -

The British embassy in Moscow sits in the middle of the Moskva River, on an island known as the Balchug, formed by one of the many canals that parallel the main river along its winding path. There are countless bridges going to and from the long island from either side, but its north shore faces onto the Kremlin itself, and Emilia had no intention of veering near there. So it was dark by the time her circuitous route took her to a spot south of the river.

Leaving the car in a side street, she began to weave her way toward the embassy, alert for anyone watching as she went. She knew that if they were looking for her, they would probably post some kind of lookout near the embassy. It would be their job to stop her from getting to the gates. If she got inside she was, by all intents and purposes, as safe as if she was back home in Yorkshire, or such was the theory.

Coming up from the south, she strolled over one of the smaller, less used bridges, and began her long walk east along the island to the embassy. She could sense tension in the air and knew that something was wrong. People were nervous, no one was making eye contact.

She saw the flashing blue and red lights reflected in office building windows before she saw the cars themselves. At first her heart began to race with fear at the sight of the flashing lights. And then it sank when she saw where they were coming from. Parked in a dense circle near the entrance to the British embassy was a gaggle of police cars and bicycles. A van was unloading more officers. Amongst them she could see some men in suits arguing loudly. It was against countless international treaties to block the entrance to an embassy, but as she looked on surreptitiously, she saw these policemen were not guarding the entrance but surrounding a body.

The words started to filter through. The suited men were from the British consulate. The person lying in a congealing pool of their own blood had been shot. From the enraged voices of the embassy personnel, it was clear that whoever it was had been trying to reach the embassy's gates. A feeling of peering over a great precipice came over Emilia, and she suppressed a sense of nausea. This could not be a coincidence. Something terrible was afoot, and she needed to disappear.

Turning to walk away, she tried to think of options. An exit strategy. Her Russian was excellent, naturally, so maybe she should try to flee to one of the countless satellite towns and cities around Moscow. Mozhaysk, where she had been living up until two hours ago, was out of the question, but there were more than ten million people living in and around the Russian capital, and surely she could lose herself amongst them. Walking north so as not to retrace her steps, Emilia came upon the banks of the Moskva.

A momentary glance across the river to the Kremlin revealed tanks and troop carriers in Red Square, and the pieces started to come together. It was clear that this was much larger than her. Red Army in the city, foreign operatives being rounded up, maybe even killed, if that had indeed been one of her colleagues leaking life into the cement in front of the embassy. These things could only mean a coup.

She set aside thoughts of who might have attempted such a thing, focusing instead on how she might avoid joining her colleagues in the grave, or worse, in the dark basements of Lubyanka.

She did not sense the eyes looking down on her from a high rooftop behind her, nor did she see the figure leap silently from that lofty height to the smaller block to her right. A minute later some part of her mind registered a dull thud around the corner ahead of her, and her eyes flashed in that direction. Her pace remaining steady even as adrenalin pumped into her veins.

As she rounded the corner, she saw a lone man walking toward her. Behind him she could see a set of concentric cracks in the pavement circling from what looked a very shallow crater. The man was looking at her as they approached each other. She resisted the urge to run. That would be futile. If she did, he would only alert his colleagues who were no doubt nearby, and they would seal the bridges. If she ran she was as good as dead. Slipping her left hand into her pocket she grasped her keys in her fist. The loose chain that bound them allowed her to arrange the three keys so they were pointing out from the gaps between the fingers of her bunched fist, turning her hand into a makeshift maul.

As they came abreast of each other, he stepped into her path and she slipped her hand from her pocket, her training kicking in. Without hesitation, she thrust her hand in an upward curl to connect with the soft tissue of his throat, hoping the keys would make it a short fight. Her eyes were locked on his, looking for the telltale signs of his repost, but she saw only blackness as he walked calmly into her blow. Sensing the coming impact, she pushed upward from her waist, hoping to drive her fist home, but instead felt her hand impact solidity. The man did not flinch. Her hand drove into his chin and she felt the keys twist in her fingers as they met the immovability of his synthetic skin. Instead of driving her metal keys into his throat, she felt as they stopped dead and her fist's momentum drove the metal back down into her palm.

A moment later she was kneeling on the floor, clutching her left wrist as she stared at the impossible pain of the keys driven backward into her flesh. Blood spilled out from where the three shards of bronze had cut deep gashes back along the inside of her hand and stuck out of her palm, as burning agony screamed up her arm. She was dizzy with the pain, as though hot, noxious fumes of hurt were coming off of her wound to cloud her vision.

She did not see the fist coming down on the back of her neck, nor did she have time to sense the rush of air before it crashed down upon her. Her head snapped downward, snapping the life from her body as it did so, and she slumped to the ground. Without opening his lips, the strange man used a handheld radio to tell FSB personnel nearby that another of the foreign agents had been spotted. He gave them the location of Emilia's body and, after flexing his powerful legs, catapulted himself up onto the tower block's roof once more, and from there back out into the Moscow night.

It had been a long day, and it would probably be a long night. After he had helped decapitate the elected Russian government, he had spent the evening covertly coordinating the FSB's movements. The FSB operatives, many of whom still remembered when they were known as the KGB, had been sent on a string of missions to track down 'dissenters' and 'terrorists,' guided by an unseen voice to the bulk of the West's agents in the city. They had all but finished cutting out the Alliance's eyes and ears in Russia. Now it was just a case of tracking down the few who, like Emilia, had escaped the net thrown out by the FSB forces loyal to Svidrigaïlov.

With an ally like Mikhail in their midst, it would not be a fair fight. Tonight would be a manhunt, pockmarked with quick slaughters across the city's dark streets.

Chapter 17: Fine Tuning

The gentle notes of a grand piano swam in the air of the laboratory. It was long before dawn, and Birgit reveled in the serenity of having the huge space to herself. Behind her was the original resonance manipulator, long since superseded by its ever more powerful successors, but still useful for the smaller experiments the teams were working on.

Birgit's head swayed gently back and forth ever so slightly with the pianissimo tap of the music, as an unknown virtuoso in a long-forgotten studio slid seamlessly through Beethoven's twelfth piano sonata. The lonesome notes echoed through the darkened laboratory as Birgit worked, sometimes solemn, sometimes forte, but always pensive, focusing Birgit's thoughts as she, in turn, tapped away on one of the powerful PCs that dotted the room. The only light in the vaulting space was the desk lamp illuminating Birgit's dashing fingers, the big overhead fluorescent bulbs dimmed for the night.

Every now and then she would break from her annotations to grasp a plastic stylus and brush deftly across the pad to her right, spinning and delving into complex diagrams in front of her as she worked on her latest schematic.

Over the two months since her recruitment, she had become an artist. No longer slaving over theoretical sciences, no more straining within the suffocating confines of penny-pinching university budgets. Freed from the limitations of humanity's embryonic mechanical expertise, she had taken the resonance manipulator and surged outward to the very bounds of her imagination.

She had long ago left behind even the most ambitious dreams of her forbears. The facility she now worked in, buried deep in the secret stone fortress that had become her home, was powered by a reactor the size of a football. It took in air and a tiny amount of distilled water, parsing them for the ingredients it needed, and exhausting only helium and an isotopic charge similar to that of an air ionizer. That and more power than a conventional coal power plant consuming more than five hundred tons of coal per day.

Unlike its coal equivalent, though, it was not particularly flexible, and once initiated, it could only vary its yield 15% through the recycling of fuel into an energy-loosing fission reaction and the dripping of power into some tritium breeding in its tiny core.

So its prodigious output needed to be used, and used it was. In another part of the facility, three huge domes rose out of the concrete floor of a vast cavern. Representing the single largest investment of the operation to date, matching even the phenomenal investment in Sao Tome, the three domes were the top halves of three golden resonance manipulators, each thirty feet across, each capable of taking several tons of raw materials and twisting them into anything up to the size of a Mack Truck in only a few hours.

Their capacity was incredible, limited only by the need to pull raw materials to the site. In a rolling line they had two of the domes working at any given moment, while the other one was open, either to be loaded with raw materials for the next cycle or having the results of their efforts lifted by gantry cranes out onto the rolling stock that ran alongside the domes.

For their first month of operation, they had focused on producing the vast cables of carbon nanotubing for shipment to Florida. Now they were making the components of the complex system that would help guide that cable to its anchorage in Sao Tome, and the elevators that would clamp to that great cable. Next they would begin on the components for the massive facility they had planned in space, components that would append to the two conjoined shuttles that now made up Terminus One, and the fledgling space station they were going to build along the elevator's path in Low-Earth Orbit, creating Earth's first true space station.

But all those operations were the realm of General Milton and his team, and were but the echoes of the work of Birgit and the various other teams of the Research Group. While the three gold domes digested and formed the ingredients of the Research Group's many creations, Birgit sat at the other end of their work, the cutting edge of the effort's arrowhead, as she conceived the machines and weapons that humanity would send out against the coming Armada.

And now, in the early hours of the morning, as the majority of the minds that made up the Research Group slept, Birgit worked away, enjoying the abandon of playing her music in the huge laboratory, filling its void with the muses that fed her vivid imagination.

But she was not the only scientist awake at this lonely hour. Down the hall, a curious Amadeu Esposinho slaved away in the smaller laboratory that had become his team's home, or the Lair, as his two English colleagues liked to call it. They were both brilliant computer scientists from Oxford, products of one of the greatest universities on earth, and highly intelligent even by its standards. But they were socially awkward at best, and he was frustrated with their inability to accept the fact that the fundamental roadblocks that they were encountering were not due to inadequacies on the side of the programming, but inadequacies on the part of their subjects.

Of all the complex Mobiliei technologies the Research Group had been tasked with, emulating the neural interface was by far the hardest. For the majority of the tasks they faced, from the spiderweb strong nanotubing that made the space elevator possible, to the fusion reactors that now powered their many ambitious experiments, the group had been able to take the designs supplied by John Hunt and Quavoce Mantil and simply extrapolate them to their own need.

But the technology their alien counterparts had developed to *interface* with their machines was based on a wholly different physiology and psychology than humanity's. And with the expansion of war into space came an equally great expansion in the speed and lethality of the machines that waged that war. At the quickness these machines needed to work, no hand-eye interface could possibly keep up with events, let alone control them.

So the young Amadeu, pulled from his seemingly hypothetical musings in Coimbra University in Portugal, faced what was possibly the hardest task of all of the teams that made up Madeline's Research Group. He had to tap into the very wellspring of human thought, and bridge the gap between mind and machine. Amadeu was working on linking the brain directly to the tools it was going to need to control, exchanging arms and legs for flight and throttle control, eyes for visual sensors and radar arrays, ears for gravitic wave sensors and mass accelerometers.

There had been discussion at first of not even attempting to perfect the link, of focusing instead on building the kind of Artificial Intelligence that could operate independent of the limitations of biologic communication. But Amadeu and his team had received word from whatever source of information was mysteriously driving all their research that this was akin to saying you would try to avoid debates on issues by instead having a bunch of children and teaching them over the course of a lifetime, to think exactly the same way you did.

For the programming of artificial intelligences was as complex as the lengthy programming our own intellects required through the years of childhood and adolescence. Then they were told that while it could be condensed to something far faster than the decades we took to reach intellectual maturity, such acceleration also depended on the kind of cerebral links that Amadeu was struggling with, and thus they were back to square one.

Once they had exhausted such shortcuts, Amadeu had redoubled his efforts into making the technology of the spinal interface work with the unique biology of the human mind.

He worked with every hour he had. Alone, now, he enjoyed his solitude, allowing himself an occasional whistle, a frequent grunt, and many a soliloquy to the air about whatever challenge he was considering at that point.

"Cale a boca!" he shouted suddenly at his screen, telling it to shut up, to stop telling him it couldn't be done.

He whistled as another model begun, then waited, waited, his eyes hopeful, his hands wringing, his lips contorted as he waited, waited, waited …

"No! No se fala!" A small stream of obscenities escaped his lips as the model finished inconclusively. His words at first out loud, and then vanishing into a whisper as if they were walking out of the room in disgust.

Despite his frustration, working at night was so much better than during the day. For in the day he felt just the same frustration, only he had to keep it bottled up inside him. Plus he felt a freedom once the computer whizzes left the room. A freedom to explore avenues of inquiry that they tended to mock.

He might not have solved any of the plethora of problems they still faced, but he felt like he was closer. Like when he worked on one of his pet puzzles, crosswords, or brain teasers, he felt like he was in that moment before the solution dawned on him, when he could see the holes in the walls before him, the path through the maze, when the world seemed to flatten into a perceivable map, readable, understandable, and decipherable. It was resolving, he could feel it.

He suddenly realized, as he often did, that his back was a ball of tension. Stretching, groaning, he pushed his hands out and up, pulling at his knotted muscles like separating dough.

Finding himself at a momentary impasse, his mind wandered, and, as his world expanded from the screen in front of him, he heard the music for the first time. It was beautiful. Familiar but foreign, a taste he remembered, but from where he could not recall.

He decided to investigate its source. Stepping into the rock corridor that joined his lab with the larger Fusion Team's laboratory, and the even larger Subspace Mechanics Team's space, he traced the source of the gentle music to a dimly lit doorway and gently pushed it open. Entering the bedrock chamber that held the font, it suddenly resolved itself into something magnificent. Amadeu felt as it touched him deep inside.

His eyes came to rest on the single woman working in the room, the head of both the Fusion and Subspace Teams, and perhaps one of the most brilliant women he had ever had the privilege to meet. Stepping quietly into the room, he stood watching her. While her eyes seemed transfixed by her computer screen, her hands danced on the keyboard, and waved the stylus on the computer-aided design board with an artist's flare. But though she was clearly utterly absorbed by her work, he could see the way the music was reaching into her in the way her head bobbed almost imperceptibly to the music.

A crescendo in the piece passed, and her whole body seemed to reverberate with the emotion from the music. But her fingers never missed a beat in their own sonata as her eyes remained on the screen, feeding her brain the information it sought as her hands fed her responses back to the machine.

"Did you ever play the piano as a child?" he asked, suddenly.

She leapt out of her chair, a scream bursting out of her as she sent her chair sprawling backward, its little wheels trying to stay under it like tiny legs scrambling for balance. He took two steps backward as well, as stunned by her response as she had been by his sudden statement.

"Oh. Oh, Dr. Hauptman, I am *so* sorry," he said, mortified, his accent strong. "I was ... I was down the hall. Oh no, I am so very sorry for ..."

Birgit held up her hand, silencing him, and took several deep breaths, trying to tame her racing pulse. It was like being awoken from a sleepwalk, and she struggled to orient herself. But the music still played, and after a few moments she was able to reconcile the intruder at her door with the mild-mannered boy that worked down the hall from her. She had met him once, maybe twice, but only in passing after one of the lunchtime talks they had started giving to increase inter-team information sharing and camaraderie. He looked distraught, and clearly panicked, and she realized he was about as little of a threat to her as he no doubt had been to the girls at his high school and university.

"Relax, relax," she said taking a breath. "You just startled me, that's all."

"I know. I'm so sorry, please, oh my ... I ..."

He stammered onwards, and she smiled, "It's Amadeu, isn't it?"

"Si ... yes."

She waited, but he was at a loss, so she prompted him with a pleasant but expectant expression, her eyes saying 'go on'.

"Yes," he said, "like I said, I was just working down the hall and ... well ... I heard the music, and I recognized it. Well, I didn't really recognize it, but I remembered it from years ago and ..." He realized he was babbling, and that it was only made worse by his broken

English. But looking through the haze of his embarrassment, he saw that she was smiling conciliatorily, and he went silent and meek. It was a maternal smile, a supportive smile, and it set him at ease.

"Beethoven," she said.

He looked puzzled a moment, then smiled back, the music breaking through to him once more as the level of adrenalin dropped from in front of his eyes, and his sense of his surroundings returned.

"It's wonderful," he said.

A moment of silence passed as they both listened to the thrum of unknown fingers on ebony and ivory keys. After a long but pleasant lull in the conversation, Birgit felt the tug of an unanswered question.

"I am Birgit Hauptman, by the way. And you are the Portuguese wünderkind that has been working on the 'spinal tap,' is that right?" She smiled at her little joke, and he was about respond when she then said, "I'm sorry, what did you say when you came in?"

He stumbled at this, his mind rewinding back through the last minute to find the thread of thought that had led him to blurt his question at the poor woman. It took a moment, but when he found it, his young olive features illuminated with the memory.

"Err, yes, Dr. Hauptman, err, I asked only, well, if you had ever learned the piano as a child," he said, feeling the inanity of the question as he said it, out of context as it was.

She looked at him quizzically, curious as to the root of it, but then shrugged and said, "No, I never had lessons on the piano." Then a simple blush escaped her, "But I've played the French horn pretty much every day for at least forty years."

A shared smile spread across their faces as they both allowed the image of her with the burlesque brass instrument to come to mind. But in a moment, she saw his candid amusement turn to curiosity, and a hesitant request form just behind his lips.

Curious, she prompted him, "Tell me, Amadeu, were you simply curious about my musical training because you wanted to see if I was qualified to listen to Beethoven, or did your question have import to something else?"

The question bridged the gap between Amadeu's stammering voice and his insightful mind, and the original flow of his thoughts came through like a surge of confidence. "Actually, Dr. Hauptman, I think it may be more relevant to my work than you can imagine. You see, my team and I have been wrestling with a problem for weeks now, months, really, as we try to tap into the mess of wiring that is the human brain. And I think you may have just given me a clue to deciphering it."

- - -

The sound of the French horn was a strange addition to the typical whir of the air recycling plant and countless computers of the laboratory space. John Hunt had picked up on it as soon as he passed through the pressure sealed doors that guarded the Research Group's multifaceted space.

John had been working with the teams over the last couple of months as they developed their own version of the scientific knowledge he had managed to bring with him. He would download patches of information to teams and give guidance on application and dangers through discussions with the team leads.

Only a handful of the leads knew of John's real identity, and along with Neal and Madeline they decided on the ebb and flow from the massive reservoir of information John had at his disposal. They needed to balance the desire to move forwards speedily with the need to not overwhelm the teams too early with the sheer scale of the task at hand. Everyone had, of course, been given an overview of the enemy they faced, and the Armada's approach that dictated their timeline. But to scare them with the depth of the Mobiliei's true technological advantage risked paralyzing them with the size of the mountain they had to climb.

But a phone call this morning from one of the Research Group's younger members had intrigued him. Amadeu was among the more engaging and creative scientists in the group, due in no small part to the fact that the scientific establishment and the rigmarole of growing up in it had had less time to beat his creativity into submission. But then one of the other truly enigmatic geniuses he had encountered in the team was Birgit Hauptman, thirty years Amadeu's senior and the preeminent leader in her field, so it was more than just his age that made him interesting. The fact that Amadeu had mentioned Birgit during his brief call had only fueled John's curiosity more.

As he approached the Spinal Interface Team's lab, the sound of the double horn became ever clearer, and his acute hearing told him it was not a recording he was hearing, but someone playing live. The music stopped abruptly when he knocked on the door, and a moment later he stepped into the room to find Amadeu and his two English colleagues standing around a bemused-looking Birgit Hauptman.

The esteemed scientist was sitting amongst a sea of wires and monitoring equipment that looked like a Dr. Frankenstein experiment gone right. Pads were stuck to her temples and wired under her salt and pepper shoulder-length hair to monitor her brain activity. Amadeu rose with evident excitement as John stepped into the room, and the Agent found himself sharing a quizzical glance with Birgit as the boy ran over to greet him.

"Come in, Mr. Hunt. Come in." John noted that the other two computer whizzes were silent as Amadeu ushered John round to where the results of his experiments were scrolling across his computer screen.

"As you know, Mr. Hunt, the way our brain is designed is fundamentally at odds with the neurology of the Mobiliei. This is natural, of course, as we evolved in completely different ways," Amadeu said, skipping any formalities in his excitement, and getting straight down to business. But he was unlikely to outstrip John's capacity to process new information, so John let the young scientist run.

"Well," continued Amadeu, "one of the biggest differences that makes the human mind so very different is the separation of function into two distinct lobes: the right and the left. The left lobe, as you are no doubt aware, is responsible for language and mathematics, all things logical and rational. The right side is more esoteric: spatial dynamics, facial recognition, what we like to call intuition."

He paused to see if John was keeping up, and got a nod as a sign he should proceed. A glance at Birgit told John that the woman was as keen for John to hear Amadeu's point as the boy clearly was, and seeing that Amadeu had impressed the German doctor was high praise indeed.

The boy went on, "So, as you know, the linking software that we have been working on has managed to tap that logical side of the brain with ease. Our test subjects have been able to communicate simple commands to our machines. But we have been unable to establish a link with the right side of the brain, where intuition and spatial dynamics is processed. The link allows basic systems operation, but if our pilots and tactical officers are to have a chance in combat, we will need a real-time link to the more intuitive and creative side of the brain, without having to process things through the corpus callosum."

Amadeu referred to the thick cable of neurons that linked the two sides of the brain: two hundred fifty million wires parsing information between our logical and creative minds.

"Well," said Amadeu now, his eyes becoming even more intent as a broad smile spread across his face, "after an enlightening conversation with Dr. Hauptman this morning, it occurred to me that the problem we were facing was that we were relying on language as the method by which we got information out of the brain. But we know from years of working with epilepsy sufferers and stroke victims that language is the sole domain of the left side of the brain." He smiled broadly. "For the right side of the brain to be heard clearly, we were going to need something more … inspiring."

Amadeu nodded emphatically to Dr. Hauptman, who could not help but laugh at his untethered enthusiasm. Shaking her head slightly, and causing the twenty or so wires springing from it to sway a little, she shrugged and brought the tip of her big, brass horn to her lips, an instrument born out of a childhood whim of a much younger Birgit, and now spurring something wholly unexpected in a strange young Portuguese boy's imagination.

Her first few notes were a little skewed, her dry lips not forming the close bond they needed with the mouth of the instrument.

"Sorry," she said, licking them quickly. Her next note was clear and true, her left hand tracing tiny patterns on the brass levers at the center of the instrument's twirl of brass, and sending her notes swimming up and down the scale as she tripped through a basic piece. As she played, Amadeu pointed to the screen and John watched as the notes flared in the left side of her brain.

"Faster, Birgit, have fun with it," said Amadeu, and John and the other two computer programmers' eyebrows rose in surprise at the familiarity. But Birgit didn't flinch. Straying from the simple piece she had started out with, she broke into something more elastic, moving from classical into jazz, and starting to improvise, her stream breaking into lyrical twists and turns.

The screen danced with the signals flowing from her mind, the left side vibrant as usual, but now supported and outshone by the right side as it flowed at a speed and coordination that the left side could not match. The left side just spent too much time processing its signals into interpretable language that could be shared, but the right side glided down valleys of thought and surged up intuitive avenues that the left side simply couldn't follow.

John sat down by the computer and surreptitiously pressed his finger to the computer's USB port under the desk, connecting himself to the machine and allowing the signal to flow into him. Powerful and pure. There was a crispness and speed that matched or even exceeded even the best of the neural links back on Mobilius, while the previous links Amadeu had worked on had been a sad approximation of the taps his generation had grown up with back home.

Certainly it would mean learning to communicate with the machine the same way that you learned to play an instrument, but maybe they could find a way around that with time. Either way, Amadeu had found the Rosetta stone. He had found a way to tap into the human mind's creative well, and it was going to make an astronomical difference in the efficiency of the link. The splitting of the human mind down the middle was one of those foibles of evolution that had no practical application, but because it had no downsides great enough to have prompted natural selection to weed it out, it had remained.

But the Mobiliei had no such division, their brains' many lobes were each globularly attached and acted as one, each module of the mind had evolved with a distinct purpose, and it served that purpose, be it motion, language, mathematics, lyricism, or short-and long-term memory. But the grouping in the human mind was what led to humanity's strange separation of intuitiveness and logic. Up to now it had been a hindrance, but now they might have found a way to turn that to their advantage.

The discussion moved to next steps. To methods of interpreting this powerful signal and turning it to their ends. To ways of 'learning' to adapt both the mind and the machine to best take advantage of this potent discovery.

Amadeu was as quick as ever, and Birgit and John enjoyed working with him. His colleagues were clearly disgruntled at being subjugated, but the auspicious reputations of both Dr. Hauptman and Mr. Hunt kept them focused on the task at hand, and over the next hour the diverse team explored a set of methods that may take them to the next level.

Eventually Birgit and John left the young programmers to their devices. The two of them had a multitude of other less exciting, but no less important topics to discuss. But as they walked off down the corridor, Amadeu came running after them.

"Do you have time for one more question, Mr. Hunt?" Amadeu asked, and John nodded, Birgit smiling and excusing herself to return to her own laboratory at last.

"How can I help you, Amadeu?" asked John.

"Actually, I just wanted to confirm a theory I have," said Amadeu with a penetrating stare.

They waited a moment while Amadeu scrutinized the man he knew as John Hunt, and then the young Portuguese neurologist suddenly said, with quiet curiosity, "Are you one of them?"

At Amadeu's junior level, he had not been made privy to John's true identity. They did not need everyone knowing that an alien assassin was wondering in their midst, no matter how benign his intentions.

John looked at him, curious as to how to respond.

Amadeu did so for him, "Over the last hour, I referred to the alien ... I mean Mobiliei technology, as *yours* twice, Mr. Hunt, and I noticed that neither you nor Dr. Hauptman corrected me."

John smiled. The boy was smart, but surely that was a tenuous starting point from which to leap to the conclusion that Amadeu had come to. But that was the whole point, wasn't it. That single piece of the puzzle was just the boy's logical brain confirming something that his extraordinarily capable intuitive brain had surmised from a thousand seemingly innocent hints and clues. Intuition. It was what separated humans from Mobiliei. It was why humans seemed so obsessed with seeming irrelevancies. It was why they took so much more pleasure from art and literature and music than his own culture did.

Of course, it was also why they were so obsessed with superstition, their pervasive organized religions being the greatest incarnation of that particular foible. But as ignorance diminished, so would the sway of such beliefs, as it had in his own culture.

But that did not address how John should handle the boy's question.

He stared at the boy, and Amadeu's expectant expression seemed to deflate as he started to worry about what his mouth had spurted without his mind's approval. Sensing the boy's apprehension, John smiled.

"Amadeu, I think you had better come with me," said John, starting toward Birgit's lab. It was still early and, unlike Amadeu's rudely awoken cohorts, the rest of Birgit's team had yet to arrive.

"Birgit?" said John as he walked into her space. "It appears we have a new recruit to our inner circle, as it were. Young Amadeu has had a busy morning, and it appears he has figured out something else from our already productive conversation."

Birgit looked passed John to the student standing in her doorway and was reminded of his frail frame standing in just that spot only a few hours beforehand. She frowned at him a little, and then waved him in, asking him to close the door behind him. And, in a hidden and highly secret man-made cave, a long forgotten military facility from the Second World War, deep under the Yatsugatake Mountains of Japan, a German scientist and an alien agent told a young, Portuguese neurolinguist into their circle.

Chapter 18: City Counciling

On a dark night in the small city of Johnstown, a group gathered in anger. Shouts ran rampant through city hall as the mayor tried to wrestle words with the crowd. But they would not be calmed. Federal, state, and even local taxes were going up again, and they weren't going to stand for it.

"Mayor Karmen, this is too much, surely you can see that?" said a woman's voice from the crowd.

On some level, Paul Karmen recognized the woman's voice, but he was too harried to place it. They were angry, and it seemed like he did not have a friend amongst them. These were his people, heck, many of them were related to him. But this was out of control.

"Now, of course I see that this is a lot to ask. The last few months have been tough on us all, and I know it seems like the world's going to hell in a handbasket, but people, I don't know what you want me to do about it. There's wars going on, and we have a responsibility as Americans to do our part."

The room did not like that, but the voices quelled to a dull rumble until another familiar voice spoke up. This one Paul did recognize, and Al Schneyer raised his powerful voice as he spoke. The man was in his fifties, the veteran of many a town hall meeting, his large frame delivering an appropriately powerful opinion that always seemed to be at odds with Paul's, but which was always couched in the nicest of terms. Al was a farmer turned businessman, who had seen a great deal of expansion over the last ten years as he had turned his family farm into a corn-growing concern. But as the Schneyers had enveloped their neighbors' farmland, they had also taken on airs. Tonight Schneyer wore his somewhat trademark suit that was a little small for him, but apparently expensive, and he was clearly freshly shaven, one of the few there who was, including the mayor.

"Now, now, folks, the mayor's right. We're Americans and we have a duty to pay our fair share," said Al in a deep bass.

And here we go, thought Paul, "Of course we should support our troops during a war, and where the government is involved in supporting the folks in Palestine and finding these damn terrorists that've been tearing up things back home, we have a duty to back them up." The room nodded and commented their assent to this, but he wasn't done. Oh crap, thought Paul. "Of course, if they were actually out looking for these damn terrorists that'd be another story. But have they found them? No, they haven't. Three months of attacks and murders—sickening murders, devil's work—and not one culprit caught, not one arrest in all this time."

The room rallied behind him. Paul went to speak, but as he opened his mouth, Al boomed out again, smiting Paul's response before it had started, "And what about that war spending? Where are our dollars going? To the Middle East, to help the folks dyin' a thousand deaths from the plague ripping apart those poor countries? No, their goin' to shit is where they're goin'!"

The room broke into angry talk at this last point, and Paul called out for order. "Please, ladies and gentlemen. Please." But his voice was lost in the confused shouts and rants filling the room. His eyes met Al's, who looked back at him with the immovability of the self-righteous, and Paul wanted to punch him right in his smug little face. Lowering his head awhile, Paul wondered why he had taken this job at all.

"Everyone, please!" shouted Paul in a rare moment of exasperation, his outburst knocking the wind out of the room. "No one is more frustrated than I by the horrific attacks across our country." Paul felt the pang of his own loss in the last few months, and his voice wavered a moment.

The room was momentarily silent. "I just fail to see what all this shouting is going to do about it. We sent a letter to Congressman Hartley, we know other towns, cities, and concerned citizens have done it too. God knows we already didn't vote for the man sitting in the Oval Office, and I'm pretty sure none of us will next time either." A murmur broke through at that comment, and Paul worried he was going down the wrong track. Finishing with marked conviction, he said, "But while he's in office, he is still our president, and what he says goes … that's it, folks. We can send another letter to Congress, but bar that, this town isn't about to start acting like a bunch of liberal whiners."

The room fell silent again, and it seemed for a moment that Paul had assuaged further dissent. He dared not look at Al Schneyer. He didn't want to encourage him further. But he heard the man clear his throat, saw with the corner of his eye that the burly man was glancing around for support, and Paul's shoulders sagged.

But as Al went to speak further, to hit home his point about refusing to pay this last property tax increase as so many had proposed earlier that day, the room started to twitch. A part of their brains was telling them something was wrong. A smell. Smoke.

They saw the smoke before they saw the flames. The vents in the ceiling started belching it even as the first licks of orange started to appear outside the windows of the big hall. A single shout catalyzed the room's impending panic, and the mob reacted. Moving as a mass to the double doors at the back of the room, they already felt the heat starting to emanate from the walls. But something was blocking the main doors. They rattled and banged on them, anger and fear rising in intensity, but the doors would not budge. Turning at first in drabs, and then as a whole, the mob started to move to the smaller side exit at the front of the hall, to the left of the now-deserted dais.

Having come down from the stage, the mayor was one of the first to get to the other exit. It too, seemed to be blocked, but it could be opened enough to allow one person at a time to break free. Stepping to one side, Paul tried to urge the women out first, herding people and trying to stop the mad crush to the door. It was hard. People at the back were desperately pushing forward, and the volume of shouting and screaming was drowning all reasonable calls for calm.

The shouting was cut through by the crack of a gun. Then another. Crack, Crack. Through the windows they could see that the flames were not as bad on this side of the building as the other. But they could also see the first of the people that were running free of the fire.

Crack, another fell, her head blown open as she sprinted from the burning building. She joined the several bodies that had already fallen. But the people close to the door could not see through the window to what was happening to their friends and loved ones outside, and they kept pouring out through it.

Crack, crack, crack. They fell with brutal efficiency, one after another. No one was getting more than a few meters from the door. As the group near the window started to back away in horror, the pressure at the front relieved until a woman trying to escape had barely gotten a step before she saw the bodies in front of her. She stepped back instinctively toward the doorway and as the shot hit her, she was blown back into the man behind her, her blood splashing over him as he caught her and stumbled back into the hall.

The sight sent the remaining thirty people in the hall into a mad frenzy. Paul stared in horror at the man clutching the woman … her face gone … her head punctured and run through. Another man made a mad dash for the door and Paul reached out for him but he was too late. The shooter allowed the man to get a few steps then dropped the sprinting man as he leaped over another body. Spinning him in midair as his head was stopped dead by the bullet. The man fell like a rag doll to the paving stones outside the hall and lay there limp, unmoving.

Paul stared at the man's body from the doorway in astonishment. Behind him the room had gone mad. People were shattering windows on the far side of the hall, but the fire was fully fledged there, clearly deliberately set to herd people out onto the killing field that was this lone exit. The broken windows only let the flames leap inward, and Paul felt the heat behind him increase.

Suddenly a chair came flying through the window to Paul's right, soaring through the air in a cloud of shattered glass to land on the pavement amongst the bodies. A man followed behind it and the crack of the gun came clear again. Paul saw the muzzle flash down the street. Staring at it, a part of him said run. But where to? The rest of the people in the hall began to climb out the shattered window, driven to primal insanity by the flames on the other side of the building. Paul watched as the muzzle flashed once, twice, crack, crack, dropping them as they climbed out, a gruesome pile of bodies draped over the window's sill and over each other. As he stared at the flashes in the darkness, Paul saw its source start to move. Slowly. Deliberately, it started to come closer.

Inexorably the flashes stepped toward the hall, their vicious crack sounding amongst the din of the fire and screams. Regular. The thump of a heartbeat that was silencing the hearts and shouts of the crazed people climbing out of the only window not ablaze. And as it approached, Paul saw a figure resolve behind the flash. Black as the darkness it was stepping out of. Blacker even than the night sky above them.

Without thought, Paul stepped forward, out of the doorway, peering into the night to see what thing could be doing this. What shadow was wielding that gun. But as he stepped forward, none of the shots were for him. They flew past him into the last of the terrified people weeping as they tried to clamber over their dead husbands and wives.

As he stepped slowly from the building, Paul saw the black figure step into the dim light of a streetlamp. Her lithe figure walked with grace, an assault rifle braced at her shoulder, firing with calm ease. With a start, Paul realized that the figure was not even looking at the building as she slayed the last of the town's people.

She was staring at him. He froze in the focus of her black stare, suddenly aware that he was shaking. She lowered her rifle at last. No more screams came from the hall. Only the sound of the fire devouring it. Without warning, his fear boiled up in him, and suddenly he was running, sprinting away from her. He didn't see where he was going, his legs grabbed at the asphalt with abandon as he felt the full weight of his impending death clawing at him for the first time. The fist that suddenly grabbed his calf was like iron. Cold and hard, it clamped on to him and stopped him dead, his leg dislocating as he was hauled bodily backward and up, his face barely missing the tarmac was wrenched upside down.

He cried in pain as his weight swung from his dislocated leg. It took him a moment to realize he was upside down. Hanging from his ankle. He drew his attention from the pain in his hip, like drawing iron from a magnet, and focused his eyes. He saw her feet first. Planted firmly in front of his face as she stood holding him by his ankle like nothing more than a sack of potatoes. He felt her stoop, and with her free hand, grab him by the neck. She pulled his face to hers and held him there, grasped by one bruised ankle and his neck. He felt like a doll. Like paper in her hands. He realized that his hundred-eighty-pound frame was nothing to her, that he was but a joke, and he saw mockery in her black eyes.

When she eventually spoke, it was with incongruous gentility, her soft, almost sultry voice at horrific odds with the way she had handily slaughtered half the town. "Paul Karmen. Hello. My name is Princess Lamati. I want you to remember my name. It is very important that you remember it, and tell it to the people who are going to come and 'rescue' you. I am Princess Lamati of the Hamprect Empire, and I am here to eradicate you. *All* of you. But that can wait. First I have a message for an old friend of yours. In fact, I believe you somehow managed to get her to go to the prom with you, a long, long time ago."

Paul tried to comprehend her words, to wrap his head around them, and found himself morbidly curious as to where this was going. A whimper escaped his lips, an echo of the question that her statement begged for. But he could manage no more than that through his shock.

She went on, "When she comes to see you, when Madeline Cavanagh comes to visit her old boyfriend in the hospital, tell her that she can end all of this, end all the slaughter and pain, by simply stepping out into the night. Tell her that all the people who have died at my hands have suffered because of her. Tell her I won't stop. I'll never stop. Tell her that by staying in hiding like a coward she has only caused more death. I will find her eventually. And when I do, all this extra suffering will have been in vain. A sad prelude to the one thing that could have stopped it all: her death. I tell you this now, because in a moment you may black out, and I want you to remember my little message.

"Do you understand me, Paul?"

He managed a nod through the grip around his neck, and Lana smiled, "Good."

Through his discomfort, a new feeling came like an unexpected whisper in a darkened room. A tiny tingling in the back of his neck where Lana's fingers touched his spine. An itch in his very bones. He tried to writhe against it, but she held him firm, and his struggles washed pointlessly against the wall of her strength. Suddenly he felt the itch break through to his soul … and then fire. Fire in every bone, in every inch of his skin, in his mouth and ears and eyes, in his bowels, and under his nails. Fire like a thousand red hot needles coursing voltage into his veins. He screamed in his brain, the final image he would remember that night seared into his mind, along with her words.

"Tell her I won't stop. I'll never stop."

His mind tried to close itself off. He prayed for death.

- - -

As the phalanx of helicopters came in over the treetops, Ayala went through her preparation ritual. Her team was split into two groups, each with three leads, each lead with two men running with him. The groups were travelling in heavily laden Black Hawk gunships, with high-caliber machine gunners mounted on either side for suppression support.

Leading the two burly choppers were two latest generation Apache attack helicopters mounting a range of armory designed to blanket areas with hailstorms of lead in an instant. Their front cannons, like the side machine guns on the Black Hawks, carried depleted uranium shells designed to explode on impact. As much to mark their target as to try and kill it. The pilots were wired into a real-time network designed by Amadeu and his team. Soon enough they may be the first to start using the new spinal interfaces they were now so close to perfecting, but for now they sufficed with having shared views of the entire squadron mapped to a small square in their peripheral, feeding info to their left eyes, and notably thus the intuitive right side of their brain.

The team came in low, their movements coordinated by an AWACS radar plane circling above them, its potent sensors scouring the ground for information, and updating the team's net. The whole was passed over a degrading code encrypted network designed by John Hunt himself. Even if Lana could hear their signals she would not be able to interpret them.

Sitting in the copilot's seat of the left Black Hawk, Ayala saw the town first as a map on her visor, then as a black smoke stack rooted in orange. They broke the tree line and spread out wide, covering ground fast. The Hawks touched separately on opposite sides of the town, depositing the three-man teams and then immediately lifting to give air cover.

The teams were clad in the second generation of conductive armor. Ribbed with bionic assistance, their every move was exaggerated by machine muscles. Sprinting away, they scattered through the town. One team leapt in smooth bounds across the rooftops, laying down fields of fire to cover their colleagues. The suits made them nigh on invincible against ordinary troops, but they were still no match for the pure machine that they hunted, so they stayed tight. Flanking each other in carefully coordinated maneuvers as they swept the town. Infrared sensors mounted on all their slender but almost indestructible helmets sought anomalies. They sought patches of conductive material. They sought the blackness that covered their quarry like it covered them.

They hunted the shadow of Lana Wilson. In three minutes they were done. Perimeters were set and the greater team was already arriving. The meat wagons began rolling in. The team kept in constant contact with feedback loops to their comms that actively monitored the status of each team member. Even if they never called for help, Ayala would know instantly if any of them were in trouble.

But it was quiet, as it always was.

Jumping the twenty feet or so from her seat in one of the circling choppers, she landed and jogged lightly over to one of her team leads as they coordinated the last of their sweep with the ground forces now surging into the shattered town. They were finding children huddling in houses, teenage babysitters fearfully staring at the husk of the town hall. The place they had last seen their parents.

"Status, Ben?" she spoke in Hebrew. Each of her six team leads were the survivors of the operation in Gaza City three months beforehand. They were on an extremely short list of people who had encountered one of the Agents, seen what they could do, and lived to tell the tale. Combine this with the fact that they had each grown up in various units of Israel's special forces, and you had the beginnings of the hunting party that was tasked with killing the almighty bitch they knew as Lana Wilson.

"Teams count fifty-seven dead. One wounded, looks like he was broken like the others, but he's still alive."

She looked at him quizzically. 'Broken' was the only term they had found for the way Lana mangled her prey. But they had never survived before. "Wounded … but still *alive?*"

He nodded, already starting to move in that direction, and they set off at a run.

Three men kneeled, guns out, surrounding a body not far from the main square. A fourth knelt by the man, tending to his wounds with a field medical kit. Ayala followed Ben to them, using the bionic muscles that lined her own suit to keep up with the team lead.

The nearest of the body's three guards moved smoothly aside to allow them to pass, maintaining his field of fire, and then stepped around them to reclose the circle, returning smoothly to a one-knee position.

Ayala looked down at the man on the floor. His arms and legs were warped and broken, just like the rest. But his face was relatively intact. Not swollen like the rest, the eyes still in their sockets, the tongue not forced out under the jaw.

"Is this our target?" she asked Ben.

"Hard to say at this time, ma'am," said Ben, keeping his eyes outward to guard his CO, "but he fits the description, and he is the only one we have found tonight who has been manipulated. The others were all shot or burned to death."

This was a new tactic. She was sending a message. "Maybe she wanted us to find him. Or maybe we disturbed her." But she shook her head at that. "No, then she would have just ended him when she heard us coming. She meant to leave him alive. She doesn't make mistakes. If he has survived this, then it's because she wanted him to."

Ben turned and looked at Ayala and she met his stare, seeing that he agreed in the way his eyes asked what the next steps were based on such a conclusion.

"OK, whatever happens, I don't want Madeline to know about this. She is on edge enough as it is. This was a gas explosion. All dead. Which means we need to get this one out of here and to a secure location, immediately."

Ben nodded, and she went on, "Get a med team in here, get him stabilized, and then get him evac'd to the fortress." He nodded again and she turned to look once more at the unconscious man on the ground. He was quiet now, but his face showed the strain of the torture he had been subjected to.

But it was not this new turn that bothered her. They had been coming for this man. Before they had even known about the attack, they had dispatched a team to take this man to safety, him being one of the last people left that had known Madeline and Neal as a child and was not either locked away in their bunker in Colorado or already dead.

But Paul had changed his name after getting on the wrong side of some dubious money lending types in his native Florida. Apparently he had managed to shake his past and convince another group people of his spurious good intentions. Until now he had even gone undiscovered by both Lana Wilson and the team that was trying to save him from her. But they had caught a break only two hours beforehand, a random friend that had met Paul at his grandmother's funeral only two years ago remembering the last name that Paul now used.

"I just can't believe that we were this close," Ayala said to Ben as they walked away. "The fire is still fresh, our friend's wounds are still open." They had placed roadblocks for miles around, but they knew that such things would not stop Lana. Not unless they had tanks, and maybe not even then.

He nodded, saying, "We nearly had her. But we are getting closer. Next time we will make contact."

He was half-happy at the thought. He very much wanted a piece of the woman he had tracked all across America, but knew that it may actually be her that got a piece of him when it came down to it. With the battleskins, they were as close to superhuman as any man had ever been, but that may not count for much if they ever came into contact with their quarry.

Ben had asked Ayala several times whether the same technology that made the suits possible would allow them to replicate the Agents' machine bodies and indeed there was talk of such things. For Ben was not alone in dreaming of a platoon of Johns and Quavoces to enable them to truly take the fight to Lana and her two friends still hiding somewhere in Eurasia.

But such things would be impossible until they had the spinal interface finished, and even then it would not be as simple as that. Agent John Hunt had managed to smuggle a veritable treasure trove of schematics, scientific data, and other information to help humanity take the technological leap it would need to make if it was to have a chance of defending itself against the coming Armada, but it was not limitless, and its focus had not been on ground forces. The Agents' machine bodies would be possible to recreate eventually, but the more esoteric parts would need to be reverse engineered, and that would not happen anytime soon.

Of course, talk of fighting the Agents was all moot if they could not find them, and therein lay the issue.

"But that's just it, Ben, we didn't get close, we just happened on the same target at the same time. We were lucky, that's all. Not lucky enough to catch her, but it wasn't skill that got us here."

Ben was not used to seeing frustration cloud the face of the woman that led their team. Drive, yes. Unrelenting pursuit of the woman that was ruining Neal and Madeline's lives, without doubt. But never frustration. She was too good at what she did, and that required a mastery of any emotions that might cloud your thought. But now she was clearly bothered by something.

She grasped his black shoulder and stared into his eyes. As he had gotten used to, it felt not like a firm grasp on his shoulder but a gentle pull on his whole body, his suit transmitting the pressure evenly over its entirety. But he allowed it to stop him and turned to her. Her eyes were intense. Anger? No. What was that emotion flaming in her pupils?

"Paul Karmen has eluded us for three months," she said. "What are the chances that we would both find him, via different paths, on the same night?"

"Slim to none ..." he replied. "Unless we found him by the *same* path."

"Which means that either Paul's old friend decided to tell Lana what he told us, even though he only remembered it after we already had him in custody ... or ..."

He waited for her to finish but then came to the same conclusion as her by himself. "Or she got it from us."

They looked at each other. They couldn't be certain, but they had to assume she had hacked into their network somehow. While their field equipment was infallibly encrypted, it was impossible to secure every piece of data in a search effort as widespread as theirs. That hadn't stopped them from trying, and their operation was phenomenally secure. But not secure enough, apparently.

"We need John or Quavoce, and we need them now," said Ayala, quietly. "We have a leak in our security, and we need to find it."

Ben nodded, "Until then, I'll have all teams go systems silent, even back at base camps. We can unplug everything until the leak is patched." They had set up bases in Washington, DC and Salt Lake City. From one or the other they could be anywhere in the country in less than two hours on the jets they had permanently fueled and waiting. Ayala ran the primary team in DC, the Northeast being the center of most of the attacks, while a secondary team operated out of Utah.

But Ayala was shaking her head, "No, Ben, don't shut things down. If she has found a way to listen in on us, then shutting down our systems will just alert her to the fact that we know about it." She took in a deep breath and then resigned herself to her next comment, "Let's face it, Ben, we're never going to find her like this. She is too quick and too good at staying underground. I mean, maybe we'll get lucky, but it's unlikely. But if we know where she is getting her information from ..."

Her eyes narrowed and he nodded. They may be able to set a trap. Of course, they still had no evidence they could actually kill Lana even if they got hold of her. They may just be grasping the lion's tail. But at least if they had some notion of where she might be, they might be able to get both John and Quavoce away from their duties protecting the spaceport and Research Group's laboratory and onto their side of the fight.

"I'll contact John and ask him when he might be able to conduct a communications sweep," said Ayala. "Until then, this conversation stays between us. Is that clear, Ben?" The agent nodded his assent and they returned their attention to the mutilated man on the ground behind them. Ayala only hoped she had made the right choice. If Lana had hacked their systems, then she may also know who the members of her teams were and where they were located. That made them all targets as well. Hopefully she wouldn't come after them, but Ayala had to assume that it was a possibility. She knew Ben understood this too. He was cold to such things, but others on the team had families, wives at home, friends … vulnerabilities.

- - -

Despite their ardent search in the smoldering wreckage of the town, Lana is, in fact, only half a mile away, sitting in a tree, covered from head to toe in mud and dead leaves, hiding her energy-absorbent skin from the helicopters and planes circling above.

She listens to their chatter, frustrated at the encryption hiding their voices from her. More because she longs to hear their anger and fear than any need she has to hear what they are saying. No doubt they are trying to figure out how she got to Paul first. No doubt they will try to find some bug or other method by which she might have hacked their systems, but they won't find what they seek. It is far simpler than that. She found one of them instead. Mr. Moskowitz had proven most cooperative. Not through her usual coercion; she needed him alive if he was to remain useful to her. No, she had simply found his home and placed in its basement the black bag that had once been her lifeline. It didn't bother with hacking his systems, they were too well encrypted for her to break them without setting off the alarms the traitor John had no doubt helped build into them.

But if she couldn't hack into their systems, she could listen to and watch Saul as he did. For two days now Saul had carried with him a tiny robotic spider lurking in his clothes. Sliding out of sight on nimble legs, it listened diligently to his every move. It never transmitted until he had gotten home in the evening. It remained passive and invisible all day as he went about his business. So it never set off the plethora of sensors and proverbial trip wires that now surrounded the White House and a growing number of technologically secure facilities across the world.

She had hoped to get a bead on where Neal and Madeline were hiding, and maybe she still would. But for now she had gotten only the gift of listening in on a scrambled phone call to Saul in the middle of the night, saying that they had found another of Madeline's old friends. Saul had left for the Pentagon immediately to help coordinate operations.

Lana, meanwhile, had set off herself. From that day's hiding place in a sewer under a town near Pittsburgh, she had converged on Paul's small town ahead of the crew coming to take him into protective custody.

Now she watched. Looking at the team working to secure the area. She saw how they moved and knew that they had the beginnings of the encounter suits that her race had once called battleskins, before the advent of machine avatars like the one she now inhabited. She studied the weapons and sensors on the helicopters scouring the area and knew that they had armed them with bullets that would sting her thick skin. Burn her fibrous armor. Weapons that could, if fired with enough accuracy and persistence, actually kill her.

She raged at the rare feeling of vulnerability. She couldn't help but bring up visions of the fight in King's Bay. The thousand bullets tearing into her. Her synthetic humanoid outer skin that had allowed her to walk amongst her prey flaying off her. The long weeks waiting while her systems recovered.

As she pondered that fateful day, her machine mind continued to monitor the activity over in the devastated town. Sifting radio signals, tracking the Apaches and Black Hawks overhead, watching the black-suited personnel moving over and around the buildings. Through the noise, her mind notified her of something interesting. Over the networks a story was emerging. Not about the town, the airwaves were notably silent about that still. A press conference was being held in Washington. It was being mirrored by conferences in the UK, France, Germany, Japan, India and Brazil. It was discussing a new space project.

Lana switched her attention to the reports, monitoring each of them in real-time. Images flashed on various channels, all clearly from the same source. Stock footage, no doubt. They started with an amateurish-looking photo taken from a telescope at a university in Cameroon. It showed a line dropping from the sky, seemingly from nowhere.

Lana did not need to see more to understand its implications, but her mind continued to track the story as she thought about what she was seeing. She knew immediately what that line was. She had seen ones like it a thousand times.

She had first travelled on a space elevator when she was five. She had never seen a cable being strung before, as on Mobilius they just passed new ones up existing cables once they had the main hubs in place. But she had seen old footage of the first tethers being lowered to Mobilius. They were moving faster than she had expected. Even with massive unrest across the planet, they had managed to get this far in only three months since the fall of the satellites.

She pondered the implications and began to build a system request for her machine mind to start modeling how quickly they would be able to start construction of significant space-based manufacturing facilities.

As she did so, her mind continued to monitor the various reports. It watched as the president wrapped up his speech and then handed over to one Admiral Hamilton to field questions. She smiled. Her old friend Admiral Hamilton. He was on her list too, along with his son. But they were way down the pecking order.

Her real attention was elsewhere as her subroutines continued to monitor the feed. It watched as the president thanked the assembled members of the press and then stepped out of a side door. Then it saw something.

Suddenly her view changed.

She had programmed the system rule long ago. As a subroutine of her mind, the rule searched for any sign of her targets and was to notify her instantaneously if it located any such sign. The alarm sounded in her head, clearing her field of vision and instantly updating her on the tiny piece of information that had catalyzed it. As the side door had opened for the president, it had caught sight of half a face. It was nothing more than a profile of a nose and the front of one man's cheek. But it was enough. The door closed behind the president and the view was lost.

But it was all her mind had needed. In the White House, waiting for the president to leave the press conference, supposedly out of sight, was Neal Danielson.

Sitting up, Lana did something all her systems told her was unnecessarily risky. She started to move. Not too quickly, but any movement at all might give away her position to the helicopters circling above. She needed to get out of the valley, over the ridge, so she could start to make her way to DC.

She sensed one of the Apache's coming close and leapt lithely out of sight.

Inside the chopper, the systems sighted the movement momentarily as she leapt and the pilot saw a blip. They instantly went weapons hot, calling out to the rest of the team that they might have seen something.

They had trained hard for this. They knew that Lana might be able to bring down one of the deadly attack copters, having seen the images of Quavoce co-opting one in midair in Iran. To that end, they had installed kill switches into the weapons controls in case of attack. But this was no attack. After a minute of silence following the blip, they came down from high alert and decided they must have been mistaken.

But they still circled the spot where it had happened with backup from their sister ship. Lana moved more carefully now. Picking her moments with precision, she moved from shadow to shadow as the choppers banked in low and tight overhead, picking exact moments when she was obscured by the dense foliage of the canopy until she was out of their area of focus.

With no more movement the blip was eventually dismissed and twenty minutes later the Black Hawks had picked up Ayala, Ben and rest of the ground team. They would leave the final clean up to the local and state forces that had arrived to take over the scene. In company with the two Apaches, the group headed back to their base in Reston, Virginia, just outside DC.

On the ground a black figure moved through the muggy evening air amongst thick undergrowth along the bank of a river. It was one o'clock in the morning and she was forty-five miles from the White House, so she headed toward a nearby highway. She would leap aboard a passing truck headed into the big city and hitch a ride.

Until now, she had given the entire DC area a wide berth because of the heavy military presence throughout the city. But now she had a reason to risk it. With all its layers of protection, and with Ayala and her team nearby, she would have precious few minutes to find her quarry once she attacked the White House. Even if she moved quickly, she knew she would no doubt need to fight her way out afterward.

At least she knew what was going to be coming in after her, she thought, and her mind started calculating how to handle the potent force she had watched scouring the countryside for her, sorting through weaknesses, formulating combat tactics.

Chapter 19: Chopper

Viewed from ten miles away, it looked like an error in the world. A scratch on the sky like a paper cut, ending in the slightest of dots. It looked like the sky was about open up, revealing blackness behind the façade of blue and white. Hanging down from thousands of miles above, the cable dangled at a slight angle, the prevalent winds over a thousand miles of atmosphere pushing at it gently, although from a distance it seemed still, the forces spread over such distances as to become epic in nature.

As the three Royal Navy Chinook helicopters approached it, they kept in a strict formation. They had been specially configured for a unique task. Two pilots flew each, and they had heavy fuel tanks taking up their extensive cargo space. Tight band communications linked them together, patched through the HMS *Dauntless* below as it tracked the cable's every movement. But the most notable modification was strung between them. Hanging on steel cables linking the front two heavy-lift choppers was a huge C clamp, facing forward like an open claw. Attached to the back of the clamp, the third chopper acted as an anchor, and, if something were to go wrong with either of its cohorts, they could detach from the team, and the third chopper could bank left or right to take its place as appropriate.

The helicopter team's job was simple: latch on to the slowly swaying cable and help guide it down to the concrete and steel platform that now dominated the small island of Rolas, south of Sao Tome.

As the three big choppers came within a mile of the cable, it began to resolve, and the six pilots started to see how it gently moved in the jet stream. But as they got even closer, they saw that the gentle movements were on a massive scale, and they also began to make out the ball that hung at the end of this incredibly long chain.

The ball was trying to control the chain's slow, ponderous movements as it lolled through ten-mile-wide swings, at first with bursts from its thrusters, always driving down, pulling the cable taut as it was slowly unreeled by the station above. It had been a constant balance, matching forces that had grown and grown over the weeks it had taken to get to this point. Changes in pressure at either end took days to reverberate along the cable's length. So they were always calculating, predicting, a team of scientists and engineers focused solely on modeling and remodeling the cable's behavior as it was lowered to earth.

Now the ball's thrusters were all but silent, its job now more as counterweight, relying on its own weight to hem the great line as the final miles of its massive journey were closed as it approached home.

The helicopter pilots had practiced for weeks to lock in their maneuvers to the pendulous swing of the cable, they watched and they spoke in a constant flow of chatter, a language formed just for this moment, but rooted in the precise, high-speed chatter of aircraft carrier controllers, guiding their charges down to a moving runway.

As the tripod of helicopters swooped closer, they matched the lazy rhythm of the black line with a skill that bordered on art form. The clamp slung between them in its steel web, seeking its target. The cable towered above them, making them ever tinier by comparison. In the final moments, the rotors seemed to chug ever slower, the cable loomed ever larger, only a meter across, but reaching farther than they could imagine, up to the stars above.

Finally, the moment came. Eyes were focused, breaths were held, and, at the last moment, the ball at the end of the chain came to life again, as planned. It gave one more breath of fire, as if in protest at the cable's capture. But in fact it was calling for its leash, a bark of acquiescence, to shake any final tremors from the line above, where the collar was being clipped.

They were in perfect sync, and the two lead helicopters slid either side of cable as it moved slowly from left to right. They felt the tremor as it glanced off one of the steel cables a meter shy of the clamp, and all three pilots watched with bated breath as the resultant wave went reverberating up the cable into the sky.

The carbon nanotubing that made up the nearly indestructible cable was extremely light, especially considering its incredible strength. But tens of thousands of miles of it still amounted to a spectacular weight, and an even more spectacular momentum. As the cable slid into the clamp, sensors closed it neatly and they had it.

Or rather, it had them.

The first tug was like a truck starting to roll down a hill, so slow it almost seemed gentle, but completely unstoppable. The left Chinook strained as it was drawn to the right, its partner veering wildly away from the cable tugging toward its rotors. As they had practiced, the rear chopper slid to the left and joined the tug, the two heavy-lifting helicopters exerting their full might to slowly tame the snaking beast between them. Over fifty thousand pounds of thrust clawed at the air, rotors screaming to halt the cable's untenable sway.

From below, the HMS *Dauntless* tracked the operation, and watched as the cable began to bow gently. It would take many hours for the wave to reach the two shuttles anchoring its end. But in order to compensate, they were already applying a gentle thrust outward, tensioning the cable as it twisted to this new pressure. By the time the wave of energy from the tackle below reached the twelve men and women on Terminus, it would feel like a moment's gravity as their ship quietly moved with the energy, and they would laugh as they momentarily 'stood' on walls and bulkheads, the illusion of gravity alien to them now.

With deliberate and powerful movements, and the help of the cable's counterweight pulling at its length below, the three helicopters slowly wrestled the cable into submission, dampening fifty thousand miles of momentum.

Now began the long process of bringing the leashed cable to the waiting bars and piles of its Earth-based terminus.

- - -

Neal continued his lengthy explanation of what was happening on the big screen in front of them. His audience was small but auspicious: the president, Jim Hacker, and the CIA chief,

Peter Cusick. The screen showed an image from the deck of the *Dauntless* as it tracked the three brave Chinooks, and the vast cable that dwarfed them.

"Now, I cannot stress enough how impressive that work is, Mr. President," said Neal as he nodded his appreciation for the job the six pilots were doing. "Believe me when I tell you that the task those men are doing is both extremely difficult and extremely dangerous. If they stray into that cable it will mean a very unpleasant end for them, and possibly for the whole enterprise. They could, in theory, become ensnared. It is unlikely, but not impossible, and the sudden additional weight on the line without prior adjustment by Captain Cashman on Terminus could hypothetically bring the entire cable down."

The room looked concerned at the apparent flimsiness of the whole plan, and Neal held up his hands placatingly, "Now, that is just a worst case scenario, and once the cable is anchored, Terminus can apply what we are calling contingency pressure, making the entire cable weight negative, essentially pulling constantly at the anchors we are going to attach.

"For now, the captain of the *Dauntless* is also under orders to intervene if the worst happens. With force if necessary, to protect the cable should anything go wrong. But I digress, and the hardest part is already behind us, anyway. Initial contact was always going to be the point of greatest disparity, and they have handled it with aplomb. From here on it should be plain sailing."

They seemed somewhat mollified by his qualification, but still uneasy with the whole operation. Peter Cusick seemed particularly uncomfortable, and Neal suspected this was at least somewhat due to an ignorance about the science behind it. He was about to embark on an explanation of how an elevator to space made of carbon nanotubing had been an idea under active development by NASA for years, long before the Mobiliei's arrival, when an alarm caught his ear.

Around the perimeter of the White House were a host of motion sensors and cameras. Outside these was a permanent cordon of police, while inside them was the first line of the Secret Service patrols. Lana had leapfrogged all of them.

- - -

Pulling to a halt in a stolen car, Lana parked illegally on the far side of Lafayette Park. She catapulted from the car at a sprint before it had even fully come to rest, her powerful legs accelerating hard across a small park, directly toward Pennsylvania Avenue. Barring the surprised shout of a policeman at the sight of her black silhouette powering down on him, the only announcement of her arrival was a small alarm set off by a motion sensor as she hurled herself into the air over the avenue and went soaring out over the White House lawn.

Two Secret Service men tried to track her black figure against the night sky as they shouted into their microphones, "Perimeter breach, north quadrant. Suspect fits description of Lana Wils ..."

Their voices were cut off as they ran headlong into her weapons systems aiming down from where she was sailing through the night sky, a laser opening them up and spraying them across the pristine lawn as they ran to intercept her. As her long leap started to angle downward, she focused on four other Secret Service men arrayed in front of the house. They, in turn were bringing their Glocks up to bear on her.

She started to work her way through them, still in midair, taking the first down by lazing his face with fire, and then the second. She was about forty feet from hitting the destination of her massive arching jump, a window into one of the many halls of the White House, when she felt the return, two shells impacting heavily into her. It was a stark reminder of her last encounter with US special forces as two of the snipers arrayed around the roof of the White House brought their weapons to bear. The rounds were hot and fast and they visibly halted her progress.

Lana changed her target priorities, even as the two Secret Servicemen on the ground started to fire as well. She ignored them now, and their small arms fire, and instead sought out each sniper emplacement and assaulted it, sacrificing her momentum further as she unleashed her sonic weaponry as well.

Her flight seemed to falter in mid air as more rounds hit her and suddenly she was hitting the ground, desecrating the serenity of the famous lawn as she wantonly dug into it, propelling herself forward more like a panther than a human. More guards were already converging. More guns were coming to bear. This was a fiercely well-guarded place and she could not take them all.

But she did not plan to. She planned to get inside. To take the fight into the corridors and offices. She planned to do her killing up close, where the advantage swung wildly in her direction. And so she drove herself bodily into the remaining two guards directly in front of her.

As more and more rounds now pounded into her torso from above and from either side the bullets threw her off track. As she collided with the last guard in front of her, her black body was thrown to one side, and into the pillar to the left of the window she had planned to leap through, cracking the plaster.

But still she did not relent. She used the poor guard's snapping body as a lever and wrenched him around to give her a final blast of forward momentum. Hurling herself into and through the window at last she snatched a chunk of the shattering glass in mid-air, and without even looking in the last guard's direction she hurled the shard at the man. The two-pound splinter of tempered glass was travelling at thirty miles an hour when it caved his face in, throwing him backward and sending his instantly limp body reeling across the cloistered balcony to join his colleagues.

- - -

In another part of the building, Neal's briefing went silent in the wake of the distant alarm. Within seconds of the perimeter breach, Secret Service men were crashing through the doors to the briefing room and dragging the president to his feet. They had heard the stifled warning from the first men to fall and knew it was Lana.

Assuming she had at last come for the president himself, they responded to the training Ayala had given them. Under their trademark suits they all wore black of a different kind, battleskin. Like that which Ayala's team wore, it protected their bodies, and they now pulled black hoods out from under their collars, sealing them around their faces to extend the protection further. As they hustled the president out, they formed a phalanx around him.

A moment later, Neal, Jim, and Peter Cusick were left alone. Neal stared after them as Peter turned to him, "Guess we're on our own."

They shared a bewildered look in the wake of the shouts of the president's guards as they coordinated his evacuation.

Peter's face turned grave, "I'd suggest sticking with them, but honestly I think that you would only …"

Peter left the point unfinished, and Neal nodded. While the Secret Service agents secreted the president away to safety, Neal could only make things worse by joining them. The CIA chief had long since expressed his concern with Neal hiding away at the president's location. He knew that Neal needed to stay connected with the commander in chief, but he also knew that the maniac known as Lana Wilson was not after the government, not yet. She was after Neal and Madeline, and as long as Neal was there he only increased the risk of an attack just like this one. But Peter also knew that if Lana ever satiated her desire to kill Neal, then it wouldn't be long before she turned her focus to the president anyway.

And deep down, Peter also knew that at this point Neal was as important as most world leaders, even this one, and it was this thought that led him to now wave to the far door, opposite the one the president's men had just used, and urge Neal toward it.

Following his meaning, Neal followed Peter, and Jim Hacker was not far behind. Sounds of fighting could be heard in the building. A loud burst of gunshot would suddenly shout out across the night, only to be silenced a moment later. Running now, Neal and Jim followed Peter down a deserted corridor.

After a couple of turns, Peter flagged the other two to a halt. He tried a door handle, cursed quietly, and then stepped back. The blow his foot delivered to the door just left of its handle carried all the weight of his field training as a junior operative more than three decades before. Still, the heavy door took two hard kicks to rip the lock through the framing, the loud cracks tearing at Jim's and Neal's cool as they glanced warily this way and that.

Pushing through the crippled bolt, Peter led them through the now open door into one of the building's hundred offices. It was very late, and even the dedicated White House staff had mostly retired for the night. But a secretary whimpered as the three men burst in.

"Georgina," said Peter in a quiet voice, "come with us." She hesitated, "Now, Georgina! I don't have time to talk about it." Sobered by his harsh words, she climbed to her feet and followed them all into one of the inner offices branching off this one. Slamming the door shut behind them, Peter pulled a slew of jackets from the hooks on the inside of the door to reveal a thick steel shank. The shank turned as he grabbed it, clicking into two unobtrusive-looking notches either side of the door with resounding thuds, sealing it shut.

"Welcome to my office, gentlemen. A room that doubles as one of the White House's safe rooms," said Peter to Jim's surprised look.

But Neal was shaking his head, "I'm afraid that won't stop her," Neal said. ·But Peter knew this. He had attended the same briefings Ayala had given the Secret Service. The door and frame were lined with the same reinforced steel that gave the shank its strength, but Peter was already jumping behind the desk, and busily retrieving some potent firepower from the coded lockbox that was its bottom drawer. If they were going to go down, they would go down fighting, thought Peter. And hopefully the highly trained agents helping the president escape would be able to keep the bitch busy till the cavalry got here.

His thoughts of the president and his guards fleeing away through the building's halls were crystallized when a prolonged firefight started ringing out in some other part of the West Wing. They had to assume she had found them.

- - -

She came at them like a lightning bolt. Five men fell in the first swathe of her sonic punch. But they were only downed, not out, their suits having absorbed the power of the blow before it could crush any bones. They responded fast. Part of the throng pushed the president onward at a run, and the bulk turned to face her, ten well-aimed Glocks meeting her headlong attack with twenty bullets a second.

The hail slowed her, but did not stop her. They were harder to kill, these ones. They wore the superconductive armor John had given humanity, and it made them infinitely tougher. But inside their protective shells, they were still soft, like candy, thought Lana. She just needed to crack the coating to get to the sweetness beneath. So she leapt into their bullets, shielding the weapons system protruding from her eye from the flying lead until she was at point-blank range. As she barreled into their wall, she began firing at each face in turn. Felling them as she pounded through their formation. She registered damage from the hundred or so bullets that had hit her, but nothing major was affected. These were just handguns. She had faced a squad of assault rifles, machine guns, and sniper rifles, and she had survived, albeit barely. By comparison to that, these were mere gnats.

As she bloodied the hallway with the ten brave men, she heard the faint whir of approaching copters and recognized them instantly. She could hear their telltale signatures and knew it was the same team of gunships that she had left not long ago. They had come with disturbing alacrity, and she grimly set to finishing off the ten men in her way so she could get on with the job at hand. She assumed Neal would be with the president and his men, so as she broke the last of the guards blocking her path, she set off at speed after the rest of the group.

As she rounded the corner, she encountered better-armed resistance. Blocking the way was a six-man team, armed with close-quarters assault rifles of the kind used by SWAT teams. Completing their armor were black helmets of the same material as their battleskin. They laid down a fire with fabulous accuracy, and she felt the hot sting of incendiary rounds exploding against her. In a confined space, firing these would normally be suicidal, but protected by the suits they were able to employ this far more destructive ammunition. Her machine mind whined at the searing magnesium eating at her armor. In a flash she dropped, twisted, and leapt back the way she had come.

A second later, the six men were ready as she came swinging around the corner again. They laid fire across her once more, but as their target slumped to the ground they realized it was not her at all. They quickly stopped firing at the dead body of one of their compatriots. Then another came, then a third. They were wasting fire on each, not daring to confirm that it was Lana before beginning to shoot.

The next body came around with more speed, and as they pounded it with the last of their magazines' bullets, she followed it around, brandishing the fifth limp soul in front of her like a shield and driving forward. The last of their ammunition petered out, and with no hope of reloading in time, so went their hope of surviving. She set about the six men with efficient brutality.

- - -

Crouching behind the desk with Jim and Peter, Neal could also hear the choppers coming and hoped it was Ayala. He knew they had gone out on a mission that night to try to track down another errant friend from Madeline's past, but they should be back in DC by now, he thought.

They were, and they had been barely out of their battleskins when the call had come in. They had resealed their armor while they flew out over the city once more, priority clearance granted as Air Traffic Control cleared the skies. Landing in front of and behind the auspicious house, they spread out. Ayala joined them, heading into the fray as well to help save the president and the friend she knew was also in there. Reports were coming in from the surviving Secret Service detail that they were holed in the heavily guarded SitRoom, under the West Wing. The teams converged on the firefight.

- - -

The sound of the bionic teams pounding through the House was very different from the sound of the Secret Service detail, and Lana knew instantly that she was about to face her first real challenge since King's Bay. But she wasn't going to run yet. She could tell she was close. She could tell there was not much fight left in the agents protecting the building. Surging onward, she found the last line of defense around the president as he cowered in the SitRoom and drove herself into the pack of guards, her weaponry exploding on them like a grenade.

- - -

The shouts and screams of the guards coming through the comms ended after ten long, gruesome seconds, and the band went quiet. Ayala knew she must assume Lana now had the president. Her teams continued to close in, until a new voice over the Secret Service radio band halted them.

"Good evening, ladies and gentlemen. It's been a long night, hasn't it? I am speaking to you, Ayala, I know you must be here by now."

They all paused, and Ayala went to reply, but Lana went on, "What with the bonfire in West Virginia and now this fun little hunting party here, you have been quite the busy girl, haven't you!" Her voice was sultry. Her accent so American, so normal, so human. But her next words silenced any doubts as to her purpose, "Now here is the situation. I have your president. I want Neal Danielson. I know he's here somewhere. A simple exchange. What do you say?"

So Neal was still alive. That was something. Ayala opened her link before anyone else could, speaking with an equally incongruous pleasantness, "Ah, yes, Lana. A great offer, indeed. We hand you yet another victim so you can torture and kill him, in return for a promise of mercy from a brutal and cold-blooded mass murderer. You know that isn't how this is going to work, Lana."

Ben turned to her as she said it, his face saying: surely we have to negotiate for the president's release? But they all knew from hard experience that there was no reasoning with this woman. When you are dealing with a self-confessed genocidal maniac, all the standard negotiating tactics are simply moot.

Lana had committed too many atrocities. She knew that she was speaking with a team whose sole purpose was to hunt her and kill her. And Lana knew that there was nothing she could offer them that would deter them from that goal. Just as Ayala knew that to discuss terms with Lana would be like negotiating with Hitler to exchange half the world's innocents for the other half; an exercise in futility that could only lead to more bloodshed. If Lana had the president then the man was dead. It was as simple as that.

Opening a closed channel to her teams, Ayala spoke crisply and firmly, "All teams move in on her position. I want her penned. If you see her and she has the president, you are to hold fire unless she attacks. But if she does attack, then you are to open fire. I repeat, if attacked you are to return fire, whether she has the president or not. We cannot let her use him as a shield. If we can stall her we may be able get into a position that allows a firing solution without going through the president, but we can only do that if we are willing to fight her despite her hostage." She doubted it could be done without hurting the President, knew it really, but to leave no avenue in her orders that ended with the president surviving would have been both callous and difficult to defend later.

- - -

But even as Ayala gave her orders events were accelerating ahead of her. Lana knew that her situation could only get worse as time went by, so she had decided to act even as she spoke over the radio. She did not carry the president ahead of her, that seemed pointless in the face of Ayala's defiance, and she had other plans for him. As she came on one of the teams penning her in, she threw the president's unconscious body up and over the three-man team and then came at them, running straight into their blistering fire as they tried to compute the suddenness of her onslaught.

The fight was short but potent. These men had trained specifically to the goal of taking her down, and their shots came hard and fast in the seconds before she closed the gap. The hot rounds drove her back and she was forced to use all of her limbs to dig into carpet, wall, and ceiling to propel herself through the wall of fire. But her powerful limbs were relentless, and though the three men emptied ninety magnesium-hot rounds into her, denting and ripping at her armor, she was eventually on them.

They used every ounce of their strength to fight her, but their bionically enhanced muscles were no match for the pure machine power of the hellcat in their midst. The strength of their fight only escalated her brutality, and inside their battleskins they were slowly battered to death. The first blacked out from the rending force of being slammed into the floor with all Lana's massive might. Though his armor absorbed the bulk of the energy and dissipated it across his body, the momentum of his brain inside his skull crushed it against the inside of his cranium, and he went limp. And through attrition of snapped legs, shattered hands and crushed vertebrae, the other two were soon quiet, alive on some level, perhaps, but not for long.

Though she longed to properly finish them off, Lana could hear the pounding of more power-assisted feet as their colleagues converged on her, and she fled. She could not face many more of them. She had surprised these three and still they had exacted a steep toll on her systems. The next time it might be six or nine, each with another sea of white-hot metal to tear at her armor, each with a fresh, angry, bionic soldier willing to throw his life at the task of ending hers.

She knew she needed to escape this madness. And so she left these soldiers writhing on the floor and ran, scooping up the limp president as she went and sprinting out onto the White House lawn.

She wasn't sure if the man was still alive, he had definitely suffered in the taking, and she knew that shrapnel from her altercation with Ayala's commandoes had hit him at least twice, but she didn't care. They had denied her the true prize she sought, and she was going to make them pay for it. As she stepped into the night, Lana gripped the president by the calves and started to swing him around herself like a discus, spinning him once, twice, three times, building up a tremendous speed, and then flinging the man's body with all her might, out over the Mall, watching for just a moment to see if her aim was true.

Seeing that it was, she went running after one of the Apaches circling the House. Mimicking Quavoce's maneuver in Iran she leapt up onto it as it turned on her. A moment too late the pilot sighted his cannon on her, but it could not angle upward fast enough to meet her as she connected with the side of the chopper and both pilots knew they were all but dead.

They managed to kill the weapons systems before they were thrown from their mount, and a hail of bullets hit the helicopter's armored sides as it banked away. The other gunship fled in pursuit, but Lana's machine reflexes were simply better than the pilot pursuing her, and she soon pulled away, ducking and diving between the city's low-slung office buildings.

She knew that she could not fly in these skies for long. Sure enough, within moments of her shaking the pursuing Apache, three F-18 hornets just scrambled from nearby Langley Air Force Base came in hard and fast, acquiring the rogue as it flew west out of the city. They did not wait for further confirmation. They had all the clearance they needed. For the first time in US history the US Air Force fired in aggression over the nation's capital.

But by the time three hypersonic missiles blanketed space around the chopper, enveloping it in volcanic fire, its cockpit was empty. In the moments between the second Apache losing sight of her and the jet fighters coming in on her tail, Lana had switched to autopilot and leapt into the Potomac River as it rushed by beneath her.

Her systems damaged again, her real target still alive, she swam away in shame and fury.

Chapter 20: Lockdown

Quavoce stood on a lower tier of the fortress that Rolas Island had become. He looked north over the channel that separated the island from the mainland, visible some quarter of a mile away.

The massive platform was a quarter of a mile along each side, and its bulk utterly dominated the small island. It towered up some two hundred feet from the rocky shore, its steep walls touching the water at several points. Some part of Quavoce was sad at the obscuring of the equatorial paradise, but necessity must sometimes mandate callousness, as it had so many other times since he had landed on Earth.

The SpacePort was built like a fortress of old, surrounded on all sides by fortifications and weaponry. The building itself was a steep, blunted pyramid made of two vast blocks. The lower block, accounting for more than half of the base's volume, was solid, a massive, heavy mass of concrete and crushed stone held together by a lattice of steel girders, reinforced with fibers of carbon nanotubing. The whole was woven into the bedrock of the island through deep piles that gripped the earth. On top of this stupendous foundation, the SpacePort proper rose. Slightly smaller across than the solid base, the building that housed the machinery of the SpacePort was without window. Built into the twenty-foot-thick walls were a series of guard posts and maintenance ports that were accessed by a network of tunnels that ran through the wall, but only opened onto the central space at four broad gateways, each sealable behind a series of thick blast doors. The central space itself was an open plan, allowing the movement of the huge cable riders on to and off the main dock.

In the center of the cavern's roof, a wide square was laid open to the sky. Guarded by the interlaced fire of twenty autocannons mounted on the building's roof that left the nearby sky clear of anything larger than a mosquito, this wide skylight was where the space elevator came to ground. Coming down from the Terminus station in geosynchronous orbit thousands of miles above, through the square hole in the ceiling, to the central quad of the SpacePort.

Finishing a quick tour of the armament on the lower tier of the SpacePort, Quavoce came to one of the four gatehouses and started heading through its extensive security procedures. Five minutes later, he was walking down one of the 'avenues' that led to the central square. The area was a hive of activity. Once the skilled three-helicopter team had brought the cable's end to ground, they had been working round the clock.

They were getting ready to attach the first rider, itself another wonder coming out of the Research Group. Powered by another of Birgit Hauptman's fusion reactors, it would drive upward along the tether using a long string of thick rubber tires clamping the cable from either side. This first pod would carry the end of the next tether, pulling the second cable up to allow two-way traffic to pass into and out of the SpacePort.

Birgit had travelled with the elevator machinery from the Research Team's base, along with Amadeu and several other members of the pod's design team.

"Major Garrincha," said Dr. Hauptman in greeting as Quavoce walked up to the table where she was working. She was looking intently at the machine and Quavoce was happy to see it was working diligently away under her gaze. A strap around her neck secured a primitive prototype of an interface to her spine. It was not intrusive, relying only on information it could glean through her skin. As such, it could not send information back to the brain, only take instruction from it. But Amadeu had done well, and it was surprisingly efficient at acting out her whims on the computer in front of her.

The text on the screen momentarily stopped scrolling, pausing after a 'reflexive command' was registered from her mind. A clever device, Quavoce thought. He had been able to get hold of some of Amadeu's papers and schematics via his colleague John Hunt. John himself remained with the rest of the Research Group, but they updated each other on progress remotely, John stressing that Amadeu's team was ever closer to fully codifying the essential spinal interface lexicon.

They had also discussed the stunning attack in Washington two days beforehand. Neal had considered fleeing the country, coming to join the efforts at SpacePort One or heading to join the Research Group. Both were well outside the United States, and both were protected by either John Hunt or Quavoce Mantil. But as riots began to spring up all over the United States, the situation was turning critical there and he needed to stay with the vice president and try to stem calls for the return of US components of the forces currently deployed around Sao Tome and the nearly operational SpacePort.

"How are you, Dr. Hauptman?" said Quavoce as she disconnected her interface. He used her native German, lilting his voice to the softer accent of her hometown of Munich. "Everything seems to be proceeding according to plan?"

She nodded, standing. "Indeed, Major, I am happy to say things seem to be going very smoothly here. Though I worry about some of my American colleagues," she replied, also in German. John had told Quavoce that Birgit knew about he and Quavoce's real identities, as did the young Amadeu. Knowing this, Quavoce had decided to talk with both of them in their native languages, ignoring their unease at how easily he slipped between them.

Quavoce did not ignore the woman's comment, but limited his acknowledgement to a nod. There was enough tension in the group already, and it was best to focus on the task at hand. So he talked instead of the planned attachment of the rider, and the final preparations for the second cable's long ascent.

But while they chatted, Quavoce did study the American members of their team. Though this was an international enterprise, there were numerous US scientists and military folks involved across the gambit of their efforts.

It was clear that no one could be unaffected by the tragedy in Washington. The authorities had shut down the area around the White House and the Washington Memorial since the terrible attack. But even late at night, when Lana had perpetrated her treason, there had been hundreds of people on the Mall, and photos of the horrific way the president had died had circulated the planet on youtube, facebook and a million forwarded e-mails and text messages.

There was no real way to identify what had been left of the man. He had been thrown, bodily, over a quarter of a mile. Though he had apparently been unconscious when he was sling-shotted into the night sky, his death had not actually come until his body, travelling at over forty miles per hour, impacted the Washington Monument itself. A bloody, red flower of gore marked the spot he had hit the hard stone, underlined by a long red stain running down the white marble obelisk to the ground where his shattered body had finally come to rest.

Riots raged around the country. People were demanding to know what could possibly have happened. The government was still denying all details of the event, including that the remains at the base of the monument were even human, let alone the pulped body of the president himself. But trying to deny that the president was indeed dead would have been next to impossible.

With all the uproar around the country, a president who was absent in office would have been even worse than a dead one. So the vice president had come forward and, in a closed statement that did not allow questions, he had told the world that the president of the United States had been assassinated, and that he, Frank Denchey, was assuming the office of president for the remainder of the term.

The gravity of the announcement had sparked a storm of conjecture. Media speculation was running ever further into paranoia. It was ironic for those working in Sao Tome, and the Research Group's underground vaults, that some of the more outlandish pundits were now positing that this was all linked to some alien conspiracy. If there was room for laughter amidst the turmoil, Neal and his colleagues might have found this amusing.

But no one was laughing.

And so Neal had to stay in the US, for now. He was trying desperately to stop the vice president from recalling all of the US personnel from abroad, most notably pulling the battle group from around Sao Tome. Ayala was trying to rebuild the Secret Service to a new, hardened standard to protect the vice president and Neal from further attacks.

- - -

Neal stalked out of his office in a wing of the White House with fury boiling in his veins. Ayala had called him to yet another meeting with the acting president, this time due to an argument over uniforms.

Neal stomped down the hallway, powering through the sounds of workmen, drills, and hammers without thought. Forty-eight hours after the attack, the House and its grounds were now surrounded by a full battle group; Armored Personnel Carriers, anti-aircraft cannons, and a new breed of Secret Service agent being brought rapidly up to speed. The city was locked down for a mile in every direction, with nothing getting in or out without passing through the full array of firepower the combined might of the US Army and Air Force could lay down.

Inside this cordon, the gloves had been well and truly taken off. Ayala had been tasked with standing up a full-time security team, fully equipped with the latest armament coming off the Research Group's lines. With the requirement that at least one team be permanently suited up at any time on the White House grounds, Ben Miller and the other team leads in Ayala's crack squad took the time to drill over a hundred new recruits on their revolutionary equipment. The recruits had been pulled mostly from the Navy Seals and the British SAS, allowing for commonality of language, with some candidates coming from the French

Foreign Legion and the brutally effective German shock troops known as the Kommando Spezialkräfte.

The troops had been leant to Ayala's command in part because of the critical need to protect a fellow world leader in the face of such unprecedented assault, and in part because of the equally unprecedented opportunity to gain access and training on the new weaponry coming out of the Research Group.

Neal arrived at the West Wing and was faced with two men completely clad in black, their guns leveled at him. But they had been forewarned of his arrival by another team, in another part of the building, and they waved him passed.

"Mr. President," said Neal as he entered the Oval Office. The president sat at his desk, Jim Hacker behind him, clearly cementing his relationship with the new leader. Chuck Crawley sat on one couch facing Ayala. Until two nights ago, Chuck had been a team lead on an advance team preparing Camp David for a visit from the now dead president. Now he was the most senior member of the Secret Service still alive, and therefore its proxy leader.

"Neal," said Frank Denchey, somewhat surprised to see the advisor again so soon.

Ayala interposed, obviously frustrated, "I asked Neal to come and join us, Mr. President, as he is so close to this crisis."

"Yes, well, maybe I should have the advisory group here as well, Ms. Sue-bye-duh." He brutalized her name for the third time that day, and Neal saw shivers of anger run down her arms to her fingertips, as she harnessed it and steadied the ingratiating smile on her face.

Neal held out his hands palms up and smiled, "Mr. President, before we go widening the group that knows about our dilemma ever further, I think maybe we should try to resolve whatever question is at hand amongst ourselves.

"Whatever it is that Ms. *Zubaideh* [he emphasized the correct pronunciation, and noted the slightest hint of a wry smile on Ayala's face] is doing, or wants to do, that does not meet with your approval, I can tell you most adamantly that Ayala does not offer opinions in areas that she is not qualified to speak on, and that her definition of 'qualified' is very, very high indeed."

Ayala did not react to the compliment, but stayed neutral, allowing Neal to try to take control of the situation. The president responded, "Yes, well, I am sure that you are right about Ms. Zubayderr's qualifications," he mumbled his closer but still unpleasant rendition of her name this time, clearly aware, at last, of his misstep. But it did not deter him from his point, "But on this topic I am afraid I just do not agree that she *is* qualified."

Neal cocked his head in candid curiosity, ignoring Ayala's barely contained sigh and the president went on, "You see, I am just not comfortable with the number of new members in the team she is training up. More to the point I am not comfortable with the number of them that are not Americans. Overlooking for the moment that the majority of the team leads are Israelis, as she is herself, more than half of the new recruits are from Europe."

Neal drew a deep breath as the source of Ayala's frustration became clear. "So you are uncomfortable with the number of people in your personal guard that come from the ranks of our allies?" As he clarified the point, Neal glanced at Mr. Crawley to see where he stood.

Chuck Crawley was a new factor in this. At this point, Jim Hacker was a known quantity, and Neal felt confident that he could rely on the ex-president's chief of staff to at least remain neutral, and not argue against Neal. That meant that Mr. Crawley was probably adding to the issue. No doubt trying to gain a handle on his new responsibilities, and seeing Ayala and her 'new recruits' as some kind of competition for the role of Secret Service chief.

The president shrugged at Neal's paraphrasing, "Not uncomfortable, per se. God knows I am grateful for the offer of help from our British, French, and German allies in our time of crisis. And the speed with which they responded is a real demonstration of how close our countries have become in these difficult times."

The president seemed set to go on, but Neal stopped him. There were not many people who could interrupt a president. Even one that was new to the position was very aware of the precedent his opinion took in any room, especially an oval one. But as aware as Frank Denchey was of his new position's authority, he was not fool enough to have missed the growing influence and power of the seemingly diminutive Neal Danielson, in this country and many others.

"Mr. President," said Neal with a look of candor and directness that put the room slightly on edge, "we are all part of the inner circle here, trust me. There is no need to expound upon the virtue which our allies showed by coming to our aid. They did so because America's troubles are Europe's troubles, and vice versa. They also did so because in Ayala's pursuit of the Agent Lana Wilson she has been given access to weaponry that they can only dream of, and this is an opportunity to access that technology."

The president sat there, feeling a little schooled. He looked from Neal's calm but firm expression to the Secret Service man on the sofa, and then his eyes flashed briefly to Ayala before returning to Neal. She had seemed somewhat controllable. But it was clear in Neal's tone that he was no one's to command.

But Neal went on, "But you should know that the reason they responded so quickly was because I called the prime minister, French president, and German chancellor personally, and asked them to. I also called Madeline, the head of my Research Group, and told her to expedite production of the next generation of battleskin in our production facilities, and get them to us."

The president felt the emphasis of Neal's words, as Neal had hoped he would. This was bigger than him. That was what was being rather unsubtly pointed out. Neal was trying to convey that he had plans and priorities that superseded the president's wishes, and Frank's intuition tried to tell him that he should probably not attempt to steam roll the erstwhile White House advisor.

But the new president's ego also told him that he had stumbled into his dream just as the office was being emasculated. Like winning the lottery on the day of the collapse of the currency, he had inherited a moot throne, and something more primal than his intuition rose up in him. Ambition wrestled with instinct, and he felt an ugly emotion wire its way into his being.

Neal watched as the man digested what had been said, but the initial acquiescence that Neal had enjoyed in earlier meetings with the man seemed to be eroding. With a sense of the inevitable, Neal saw the president's next comment brewing in the man's throat, and braced himself.

"That is all very good, Mr. Danielson, and rather familiar. I heard the same from Ayala before you came, so maybe we should move past the showboating, and onto the meat of the issue." Neal stiffened at the president's tone, and noticed Jim Hacker was looking intently at him.

The president continued in a deliberately regal tone, and Neal allowed his expression to slip into a patrician's patient smile. "Let's remember that we are discussing *my* protective detail here, shall we? And that we are doing it in *my* office." The display was rather nauseating for all present, especially given the way by which Mr. Denchey had come by said office. But Neal's expression remained patient and open.

"Of course, Mr. President," Neal said with layered deference, "and as such your wishes are, in the end, paramount." Neal thought also of Jim Hacker, though he avoided his eyes. He knew his next statement would probably place the chief of staff's loyalty firmly with the new president, and he was fine with that. If the wormy little bureaucrat was so easily swayed by petty national politics, then Mr. Denchey was welcome to him.

"If it is your wish to see the group be more unilateral, then we should move immediately to implement that directive." The president and Mr. Hacker seemed somewhat surprised by the change of tone, the first pleased, the second pensive. "May I suggest that Ayala work with Mr. Crawley on bringing the remainder of his men and women up to speed, and equipping them with the latest tools to ensure your safety. Mr. Hacker, meanwhile, can use his considerable organizational skills to help rebuild the infrastructure and staff of the White House with appropriately American personnel, including aiding Mr. Crawley in the difficult task of replenishing his tragically diminished ranks."

The president seemed very pleased with Neal's proposal, and Ayala would have been angry at the way Neal had backpedalled away from the issue at hand, but she was too taken aback by the way her old friend was reacting to this seemingly pointless argument.

She watched as Neal bent to the will of the new president, a man who had clearly just been promoted past his level of competence, and she tried to reason why Neal was giving in. As she watched, he continued his platitudes. They discussed how to structure the new team they needed to build, Jim and the slightly dazed Chuck Crawley offering up points. All the while Neal seemed deferent. OK, here we go, Ayala thought as Neal threw in a little defiance as he stressed a point. But he had conceded so much that the president and his men all met him on that one, ever the humble victors.

She almost smiled at the show, and then had to withhold a frown as she puzzled at his motives. Because there was something else in his demeanor. Something under the subservience. Something in the way he backed away from the essential point of the discussion: ensuring the president's safety.

Because that wasn't the essential point anymore.

It was almost like resignation she saw in him. Almost like he had given something up. But Neal never, ever gave up on a fight that he believed in. It was this same stubbornness that had kept him in the scientific minors for the first thirty years of his life, and it was the trait that had driven him to the spearhead of the effort to save humanity in the last two.

Ayala watched. Every now and then she agreed to something and took a note. Focus on training up Mr. Crawley's team. Select members of a new team that had come from US forces, divert the rest to building up her strike force for hunting Lana, switching out her US team members to Chuck's detail in return.

This would help avoid international strain. There was no need to snub the loaned forces from our allies, suggested Neal, conciliatorily. They would be trained as part of Ayala's force and put to good use.

Of course, of course, agreed all. No need to cause offence.

- - -

Ayala was quiet as she and Neal walked back to his office. They followed the corridors in silence. They passed one of the scars of the attack; freshly plastered bullet wounds in a wall near to the cracked sidings and stained carpet where some of Lana's many victims had fallen. Getting to Neal's office, he switched on a stereo, turned up the volume, and stepped up to Ayala, taking her by the shoulder and bringing his mouth to her ear.

She did not step away. She knew what he was doing. His hand over his mouth, his whisper was quiet but clear.

"What did you think of our little conversation back there?"

She cupped her own hand over her mouth and his ear, and replied, "Honestly, I was more than a little disappointed at how easily you acquiesced to his requests. He was being a schmuck, and if you had let me get a word in, I would have told you that it was really just that bewildered fool Crawley who wanted to establish some control over my team. Denchey was just along for the ride."

She was not harsh in her tone, just honest, and she felt Neal's smile against her cheek as he replied, "Ayala, that was all just a byline. I meant the president. Did you see him? He was posturing. He was trying to establish that he is in control."

"So? Of course he was. He just took on one of the biggest jobs in the world. One we all know he was hoping to take at the next election anyway. He wants to put his stamp on things, that's all. In the end, you could have gotten him to see reason, you know you could. Jim would have backed you. Well . . . he would have until you bent over and took it from the president."

"I wouldn't worry about Jim," whispered Neal. "He was a fair-weather friend. We're better off without him. But the real issue was the way Denchey flared when I tried to tell him that this was part of the greater issue at hand." Neal felt Ayala's head move ever so slightly, her attention focused by his comment. So this was the thing she had seen in Neal. This was the change she had sensed.

He went on, "I spent the last two days briefing him on the single biggest event in human history. I told him that we are engaged in the preparations for the fight for our lives. I told him that we are at the beginning of an effort to construct an intra-stellar navy hundreds of ships strong, anyone of which could outgun an aircraft carrier."

As he whispered to her, she saw it too.

He finished his point as she nodded gently, "America has just lost one president; they can't afford to lose another. The economy is in freefall, the people are almost in open revolt. Given that, a president who, in the face of a war larger than anything any of us has ever known is more worried about his political career than listening to the people he knows full well have more information than him … such a man is worse than useless to us."

He pulled back and looked into her eyes, only inches from her face.

"Ayala, it's time to end this chapter in our work. I need you to arrange for my transport from DC to Sao Tome within the week. We have to assume Lana may be watching us, so I'll need an escort from your team, and I should probably get one of those battleskin suits as well, just in case."

She nodded her understanding, and Neal went on, "You mentioned to me that your team-lead Miller may have a way to entrap Lana. Get on it. Pick a representative to handle the transition to Crawley and then set it up. Once you have everything ready, call in John and Quavoce and proceed. Sao Tome is a veritable fortress now, and our Research Group is holed away enough to fend off any trouble while you bring an end to that almighty bitch. Once that is done, I need you out of the US."

She looked at him. He was saying they were going to leave their single biggest ally to its own devices. The resignation she had seen in him had been his decision that he could no longer rely on America as his primary advocate. She looked at him, and realized the astonishing callousness it took to give up on a nation of over three hundred million people. But as she stared at him, a series of images came to mind: of the riots across the Midwest, of refugee camps, of empty, irradiated Eastern seaboard cities, of a closed stock exchange, and suspended trading in the face of a market in freefall.

She thought of these things, and she thought about Neal's decision, and she knew he was right. It was time to leave.

- - -

In another part of the building, Jim Hacker sat and wrestled with his thoughts. He had seen the resignation in Neal's eyes as well. He had seen it and it had saddened him. Not because it was unjust, but because, deep down, he could not disagree with it.

But he knew full well how badly the US still needed the support of Neal and his team. He thought of how the US needed access to the ever-greater technological leaps coming out of the Research Group's laboratories. How they would need them to fight the coming Armada, of course, but also to win the fight for control of his own country.

If it could be won.

Jim Hacker cursed his role in it all, cursed the way his dedication to had been repaid with this unholy mess. He looked for a way to continue to contribute. He looked for a way to help. Jim Hacker despaired at the future of his country, and the future of the world.

Chapter 21: Sierra Mike Whiskey Eleven

The Black Hawk came in to the helipad on the White House lawn on schedule, as it always did. When the chopper was still twenty feet from the ground, the twelve-person unit aboard it started leaping from its open doors. The black figures landed at speed and sprinted away on bionically assisted legs to replace one of the two units currently onsite at the White House. As they took up their positions, the units they were replacing took off at a run and boarded the helicopter. The whole operation took less than thirty seconds, and the big helicopter barely touched the ground. As the departing team leapt aboard, its engines were already throttling up to take it skyward once more.

Among the departing unit, Lieutenant Hektor Gruler took his place crouching amongst his teammates. Though at least four units were on permanent rotation now, and had been for a week, this was Hektor's last time switching out. It had become clear after an initial push that all the actual White House guards would be sourced from American forces, and Hektor, who had been volunteered by the Deutsche Kommando Spezialkräfte, had joined his French, British, and Israeli counterparts in a series of wholly different exercises.

Then eleven of them had been tapped by the taskforce commander, Ben Miller, and been called to attend a briefing in the early hours of the morning. In the quiet of the predawn, they had been driven to the White House, and then they had broken into threes and quietly rotated out one of the units on guard there. For four hours they had sat in for the other team for the rest of their watch, as per their orders, and then they had boarded the helicopter in the morning just as a team would when going off watch.

They flew low and fast. Every flight path in and out of the White House was now randomly selected from a range of options, never offering a predictable target. But this one was unique in and of itself. About half a mile from the White House, it banked hard left and flew south. A mile later it was landing at the deserted Reagan Airport, closed to civilian traffic since the attack that had claimed the president's life.

Hektor hesitated. Their orders had only included getting onto the helicopter, and they had assumed they would then be returned to the base. He had assumed that they were switching out the other unit so it could perform some other, more important task. It had seemed futile, but then so had calling in some of the very best soldiers from around the world, and then having them play second fiddle to the very people they were there to support.

It was all adding up to a very frustrating deployment for Hektor, despite the opportunity to wear the new power-assisted suits the Americans had access to. He had been one of the top hand-to-hand fighters in his unit back in Koln, and the misleadingly diminutive bulldog had become known by his unit as hektik for his slightly insane fighting style. He had hoped for active deployment, maybe in the Middle East, maybe in Eastern Europe. He had hoped for combat.

But Hektor was not the only one confused by what was happening, or by their landing spot. The pilot had only received his new destination in midair.

With a start, something in Hektor clicked, and he realized that there were too many people on the helicopter. There had been eleven of the black-clad soldiers at the briefing that morning … now there were twelve. He instinctively braced himself, sensing something was very wrong with what was happening.

"Unit Sierra Mike Whiskey, on me," came across their comm links, and without further warning, one of the twelve black-clad men leapt from the chopper and started out across the short distance to a sleek black jet waiting a hundred feet away. Hektor watched him run, and saw that he was a little unsure of his footing. He was not used to the extra power the battleskin gave you. He had not practiced day-in day-out with the thrust and landing of a powered footfall. It did not take a genius to figure out that this was the unannounced addition to their ranks.

The rest of the team stepped from the helicopter warily, covering the ground in sweeps as they approached the plane's hatchway. It lowered as they stepped closer, and a man in US Air Force uniform stepped out. The mysterious twelfth man stepped up to the bottom of the ladder and exchanged a few words with the man. Clearly getting the information he needed, he stepped lightly up the ladder and then turned to the team.

His voice came across the radio once more, "Gentlemen, if you will join me aboard, we will get going," and with that the man disappeared into the plane's cabin.

For want of something else to do, they began filing onto the plane, covering each other's rear as a matter of course, and only lowering and flicking the safety of their stocky custom assault rifles once they were aboard. The Black Hawk was already airborne behind them banking away. The pilot's confusion at what had just happened probably never to be sated, but soon to be lost among the sea of other strange goings-on around the capital.

Inside the cabin, the mysterious twelfth man removed his helmet and looked around his eleven cohorts as they lined the stark, black ribbed interior of the plane's long, thin fuselage.

"Gentlemen, if you will safety and stow your weapons, and make yourselves comfortable, we will be taking off shortly." The man smiled with obvious pleasure at their confusion, but did not elaborate further.

There were no seats in the plane. It was a purely utilitarian interior. But with their suits, they did not need such comforts. Using the limited but adequate space available, they each either sat or lay out, leaning against the walls or each other, happy in far less commodious conditions than this from their years of hard training and less-than-glamorous deployments.

Glancing out the windows, Hektor watched as they approached the runway. We have an escort, he thought, as he saw the two F-22 jets waiting on either side of the broad jetway for their strange black jet to join them. So, whoever this man is, he warrants an air force escort, as well as eleven of the most highly trained and best equipped men in the world.

One had to be a little impressed.

The black jet pulled level with the F-22s, and with that, the two powerful jet fighters gunned their engines and surged forward, taking off in smooth unison less than eight seconds later. It was common for an escort to be airborne before its ward. In fact, they usually met in the air.

But this jet's pilot was not going to wait for the F-22s to bank around and come back for him. He was not so meek. No sooner were the fighters off the ground than their own pilot engaged their jet's mighty engines. The force with which the plane powered forward was phenomenal.

"What the f ..." came over their radios before whoever had said it caught themselves.

They accelerated after the other fighters at astonishing speed, the men aboard sliding backward into each other as they scrambled to get a hold. Powerful black fingers and feet grasped at the ribs that ran along the inside of the plane, and soon they were pulling themselves into a semblance of order, but the pressure remained colossal, and they felt the plane lift into the air only seconds after it had gunned whatever demonic engines must be powering it.

In the cockpit, the pilot, one Major Jack Toranssen, laughed in spite of himself at the show of outrageous power from his new toy. It was the fifth time he had flown the plane, the first three being her maiden flights from the Research Group's test facility; the fourth being the long haul to DC the previous night. By his side, Captain Jennifer Falster grinned broadly as well, sharing his joy at the power that the fusion thrusters Birgit Hauptman had designed gave them.

The F-22s had been surprised by the order to come to heading instead of looping back for the other plane. After all, they were here to escort this passenger jet, albeit an unusually sleek-looking one, so surely they should wait for it. So they throttled back on their engines once airborne, and waited politely for their ward to catch up.

"Escort Squadron, this is Sierra Mike Whiskey One," said Jack, over the radio, "bring your course to 95 degrees, and climb to cruising altitude of 35,000 feet at 900 knots."

"Sierra Mike Whiskey One, this is Escort Squadron, course 95 degrees, altitude 35,000 feet confirmed. Coming to new course now. We have you on our tail. Please confirm airspeed." The two pilots shook off the strange request. Nine hundred knots was supersonic. It was within their planes' abilities, but well outside their effective cruise speed.

Jack glanced at Jennifer as they came up on the two jets. The F-22s were flying about three hundred feet apart, per standard escort formation. They were climbing fast, already past 15,000 feet, and thrusting upward into the thinning air. But they were holding at 550 knots. The black jet slid between them, its jets hugging the rear part of its fuselage. If the pilots had been able to see the plane before taking off, their professional eyes might have seen that the jets were thinner than normal. If they had been able to see their air intakes up close, they would have seen no rotor, only ducts allowing air backward over a smooth, black cone.

As the jet drew level with them, they both glanced at it, and saw the strange-looking engines along its rear. The black cylinders mounted on its side were trailing two luminescent blue flames out of each black pod. Jack opened the comm again, some of his mirth coming through the line as he reiterated his orders, "Escort Squadron, this is Sierra Mike Whiskey One. Let me reiterate that airspeed, gentlemen. That's nine ... hundred ... knots."

And with that, Jack throttled up the two fusion jets powering the missile he called a plane, and the engines amped up their heat output, firing the air to cosmic temperatures. It was like he had opened up portals into the heart of a star, and the two thin blue flames flared sun-bright as the black jet rocketed forward. Stunned, the two fighter pilots gunned their engines and went off in pursuit, watching as the black wings on the animal in front of them slid gently inward, warping smoothly, as they formed into tight fins against the side of the plane's fuselage.

Smoother, faster, the jet powered upward and eastward, the three planes announcing their departure from Virginia with a thunderous crack as they broached the sound barrier.

Back in the black jet's sparse cabin, a grinning Neal Danielson spoke to his daunted colleagues at last.

"I am sorry to have sprung this on you, my friends. But we have some time before we reach our destination, and I promise you I will answer any and all questions I can. For now, I would like to start by telling you that you have been handpicked. You represent the most effective of our new shock troops, and therefore I have selfishly requested that you form the basis of a new team at our main location. I am Dr. Neal Danielson, the head of this taskforce, a taskforce which you are all going to become very familiar with over the next few months. For now, though, know that we are heading to Sao Tome, to the famous SpacePort One you have no doubt heard so much about."

There were some stirs among the men at this news.

Neal went on, "Your personal effects are being gathered and will be sent on separately, and those of you that have families back in DC will be given the opportunity to bring them to Rolas Base once initial operations are set up and the base is secured."

As he filled them in on their new assignment, including details of the training they were going to receive at the hands of Quavoce Mantil once onsite, the F-22s banked away from them, their job complete, their flight path already extending out over the Atlantic.

As their slower escorts left them, the black jet began to climb once more, up, into the stratosphere. They all felt it, and Neal explained, "Gentlemen, as you can no doubt tell we are climbing once more. The plane you are flying on is the first of its kind, but it will not be the last. It is called a StratoJet, and, like the suits you are wearing, it is a little special. We are currently climbing up out of the lower atmosphere, to a cruising altitude of 85,000 feet."

A few helmets were coming off now, revealing surprised looks on the faces of the commandoes crammed into the tight cabin. Hektor was removing his, getting comfortable for the long flight to Africa.

"We are also still accelerating, though not as dramatically as when we took off." Neal said with a smile he simply could not get under control.

"It is six thousand miles to our destination, my friends. A flight that would take a normal passenger jet twelve hours. Concorde could have done it in five …" they waited for the punch line and Neal paused a second to relish it.

Finally he said, with undisguised glee, "We will be there in two. Welcome to the StratoJet, my friends."

- - -

Cutting a swathe through the jungle on the southern peninsula of Sao Tome, the long, broad airstrip ran almost from one side of the island to the other. Though the strip was actually north of the perimeter fence that isolated the southern tip of the island, landings were still strictly controlled. Jack knew he could have easily outrun the Typhoons that came to meet him, but he stayed within the stringent parameters laid out for him and landed at a leisurely 120 knots, his StratoJet's wings now spread wide once more, after the stratospheric Mach 4 flight they had enjoyed.

Quavoce and General Milton greeted them at the landing strip. After saying hello to Neal, and exchanging a heartfelt reunion with Jack and Jennifer, Quavoce turned to the eleven black suits behind them. While the general guided the other three to a jeep, Quavoce walked along the line of men and greeted each of them by name.

On the plane ride down there, Neal had told them that they would be falling under the supervision of a Brazilian major by the name of Garrincha when they arrived at their destination, and that they should prepare for a very rigorous regimen indeed.

Quavoce did indeed have a strict training program planned for them. Though the battleskins vastly magnified their wearers' strength, in the end they were only an extension of the wearer's own skill, and Quavoce intended to expand that skill significantly.

Hektor did not realize it, but everything he had learned about hand-to-hand combat was about to be turned on its head. With Amadeu's help, Quavoce was going to wire these men into their suits and expand their understanding of what their bodies were capable of. Without further ceremony, he ushered them aboard a truck and took them to their barracks.

Ahead of them, Neal, Jack, Barrett, and Jennifer were approaching the first gate on their way into the compound. In the front seats, the general explained to his longtime prodigy Major Toranssen the details of the security procedures they had put in place.

In the backseats, Neal turned to Jennifer, "We haven't really spent much time together, Captain Falster."

The statement seemed open-ended, but Neal left it there.

Jennifer filled in for him, "No, sir. Your colleagues Major Toranssen and Ms. Cavanagh have kept me very busy over the last few months."

He felt like she had been about to say the word 'since,' and he knew what she would have been referring to. Since she had been kidnapped. Since her partner had been killed in the dogfight that had also claimed Neal's friend Martin. Since she had come within a hair's breadth of an ignominious end in a dungeon in Iran. Did she know that Neal had been the one who had come up with the plan for that mission? Did she know he had ordered it?

"Indeed," said Neal. "I understand from Madeline that you have been having quite the time test piloting the new toys coming off their line," said Neal with a fatherly smile. But his smile became more like a laugh when she beamed at him, a hint of embarrassment following her initial flow of happiness at the thought.

She was about to elaborate on the spectacular experiences she had had over the last two months, but something about the man sitting next to her made her stop. Any doubts about the importance of the mission that had claimed her partner Captain Kellar's life had long since been dissuaded. But Jack had described this Neal Danielson as the mastermind behind the ever-larger conspiracy, and as she looked at him she realized that she was looking at the man that had caused all this to happen. It was ... unsettling.

As these thoughts worked through her, she found that she had lost the amusing anecdote that had been waiting to come from her original train of thought, and was forced to merely smile and nod a little, turning to look out the window as they slowed for the next security gate.

They sat in silence, both pretending to listen to the more technical conversation happening in the front of the car.

Eventually, Neal attempted to break the tension, "So did the major let you fly the StratoJet, or did he hog the controls the whole way?"

She chuckled, "No, he lets the rest of us play every now and then."

"Good, good," said Neal. "Have you seen the schematics for the Skalms? I hear they are something to behold."

Jennifer brightened at this, "I have, they've even begun testing the wing designs. The entire Skalm is too large to produce in the existing resonance chambers, so we'll have to wait till they complete the next generation chambers, but even the wings are a thing to see."

"I thought they were all wing?" said Neal, wishing he'd had time to study the forms more closely. He had an image in his mind of a giant X made by two crossed delta wings.

"No, well, yes, I suppose they're actually four wings, rotated around a central drive core, but I am told the whole has to be made as one, as the structural pressures would be too much for any after-chamber join to withstand."

Jesus, thought Neal.

"I know," went on Jennifer, seeing the look of surprise on Neal's face, "given the strength of the materials being used, makes you wonder what the Skalms will be capable of doing."

Neal nodded appreciatively.

It did beggar belief that the capabilities of the new ships would even test materials capable of withstanding tens of thousands of miles of weight, like the cable they could see slicing upward from Rolas Island a few miles away.

But Neal would have to wait a while longer until he had such weaponry as the Skalms at his disposal. Wait until his first massive, apartment block sized Resonance Dome was finished.

"Three months," Neal said offhandedly, thinking of his schedule, and the inexorable slowness at which they were being forced to proceed by politics, the persistent ineptitude of their spinal interfaces, their projects' massive hunger for resources, and the continuing unrest in Russia, the Middle East, and now the US.

Jennifer's smile faded a little as the conversation puttered to a halt once more.

Neal sensed her reticence, and with it, some of the awkwardness of a moment ago, and Neal was brought back to the present as the thought of how he had sent her to die whispered in his ear again. He stepped on another surge of remorse for having put this woman in danger. No, Neal, even if she had died on that mission, it would have been worth it.

As Jennifer went quiet and looked out the window, he staunched a new desire to reprimand her for, even inadvertently, making him feel guilty for his choices. He looked at her and felt a surge of anger, followed by a wave of regret, followed by a sense of confusion. He knew he had been right to order the mission, and he knew he would do it again. He knew he would actually have to, and on a far larger scale, when the real fighting began.

He wanted to say something more, but decided against it. He wallowed in the anticipation of regret.

Jennifer sensed the turmoil of the man sitting next to her, and studied him. As he turned back to her, they smiled at each other, almost bashfully, and in that moment he suddenly became aware of a certain grace in the way her clearly feminine figure suggested a strength and athleticism beneath her androgynous uniform. He balked at the thought. Stopping it almost before it had started, pushing images of her body to the back of his mind, and focusing instead on the anger he had felt a moment ago.

With determination, he parceled away any carnal thoughts of her, and focused on some meaningless small talk to fill the time until they reached the bridge to the island fortress if Ilhéu de Rolas.

But over the twenty years since Jennifer had stumbled through puberty, she had learned to spot how a man looked at her when he was picturing her naked, like all women learned to, eventually. Surprisingly she felt a rush of pleasure at his eyes' momentary straying to her breasts and neck. It was not so much objectifying as flattering, at least for the brief moment the look lasted.

She saw him muster his emotions, and then stifled a smile at his sudden adjunct to small talk. She was not immune to the fact that this was one of most influential figures behind all the revolutionary things happening in the world today. As she looked at him, she found herself seeing the brilliance in his eyes, the weight of the power on his shoulders, and being drawn to it.

Chapter 22: Dangerous Liaisons

Amadeu had worked on the spike for weeks. Using the small resonance manipulator they had brought to SpacePort One for various teams' usage, he had crafted the device based on a modification of the original Mobiliei design. It was a shiny silver spike about two inches long that was no more than a centimeter across at its base. The small underside of the device was the size of a penny, and was almost gelatinous; a dome of semi-transparent spongy material that covered a pattern of golden streaks and copper dots on the small base of the spike.

The device itself was almost an exact copy of the original Mobiliei spinal interface it was based on. Its function and technical specifications were identical, but due to biological diversity on a galactic scale, its application and operation were utterly different. The fundamentally different way Mobiliei and human brains worked had formed a vast chasm that had forced Amadeu to reinvent the basis of mind-machine interface from the ground up.

Sure, they'd had the basic theoretical foundation. And they had been given the technology they would need, but it was like being given a car built for a species that has hands for feet and feet for hands, not even mentioning where they kept their eyes and ears. The system's capabilities were all in place, but no human could use them without completely redesigning the interface.

Progress had been slow at first, and then had taken on a new and promising path when Amadeu had discovered that there was a language that could reach the significantly more capable right side of the human brain. From that day onward, he had completely reprogrammed the way his machines built their bonds with the minds they were plugged into.

He had started with 'dumb' interfaces that merely listened to the signals coming through the spine without actually puncturing the cord itself. With his learning programs becoming ever more effective at interpreting the mind's operation, he had then begun experimenting with his monkey subjects, and begun to physically tap their beings to link them to the machine.

But though this had proven successful, it was all, in the end, academic until they tried it on an animal that could understand what was happening to them and react accordingly. With disturbing candor, Madeline had offered to find a human candidate for trials, flatly refusing his offer of testing the process on himself on the basis that he was too valuable to the team.

He had fought this, at first on purely ethical grounds. But she had eventually convinced him to work with one of her 'volunteers;' a brave green beret from the ranks of Ayala's shock troops who had been briefed on the risks of the procedure. But not long into the tests, Amadeu had realized that his objections were not only ethical, they were practical. In the final days before he and Birgit left for Sao Tome, they had stumbled through a series of unimpressive tests with the brave volunteer. The implant had been successful, the connection clear and true, but there was something missing.

The experiments with the monkeys had been academic not only because of the differences between the ways our minds worked, but also because the monkeys couldn't appreciate the scale of what was happening to them, and in the end neither could this volunteer. Amadeu did not need just any human subject, he needed someone that grasped the full depth of what was happening. It was like a caveman being given a bicycle. Even if he had some idea, some concept of how it is supposed to work, he would still never have seen it done, and would have no one to show him. How many times would this person graze his knees and wrists, crash into trees, and generally risk life and limb before he either gave up or killed himself trying to master the relatively simple but fundamentally counterintuitive process of riding a bike?

And yet, once upon a time, there was indeed a very first person to actually ride a bike, Amadeu told himself, as he sat alone in his laboratory. There was a person who first conquered the initial instability, and formed that bond between bike and rider, who built the muscle memory that turned the seeming impossibility that we all remember from our first days without stabilizers, into the smooth ride we all come to know and love after time.

That man was able to do this not because someone told him what needed to be done, but because he was the one who had conceived of and built that bicycle, and he understood, fundamentally, the logic behind what he was trying to accomplish. He was able to work through his initial shakiness because of his belief in what *could* be done, and how it should, in theory, work.

That was the theory, anyway, thought Amadeu, his heart starting to race. It would do him no good to push another test pilot down a hill on this bicycle of his.

He needed to ride it himself.

He knew that.

Deep down, he was sure of it.

But despite that certainty, he shuddered at the thought of what he was about to do, even more than a young MacMillan must have felt in 1830 when he first rode forth on his strange-looking wheeled device. For Amadeu had watched the way the silver spike wormed its way into the spines of his simian, and then human test subjects, and it made him shiver.

Steadying himself, he wrote a brief note highlighting what he planned to do, and what should be done by anyone discovering him, should he be … unresponsive. He carefully pinned the note to his shirt with a safety pin and then picked up the spike once more.

It was cool to the touch. He dipped the silver device in a whitish liquid preparation Madeline had helped him make. Since the global uptake of the antigen Madeline had created to protect us from biological attack, Amadeu was, like virtually every other member of the human race, effectively immune to any infectious disease that might lurk on the spike's surface.

But this spike was going to snake its way into his very fiber, into his spinal cord. So he dipped it into this white soup that contained a vastly amped up version of the cellular construct that had multiplied across the planet. It was wired specifically to the job of bolstering the consistency and efficacy of the recipient's spinal fluid and its delicate contents. He dipped the spike finger-deep into the solution and removed it, grasping it again by the other end and dipping it again to make sure the solution reached every part of it. He felt a slight tingle on his fingertips where the liquid touched them, as an army of nano-warriors scoured his skin of pollutants.

The spike was designed to remain in him once it was in place. The gelport on its tip would protect the interface while not in use and deter unwanted signals and contact with the complex connective systems it covered. Amadeu stared at it. Assuming this went well, this spike was about to become part of him.

He smiled at it. It was pretty cool-looking, after all, though only the doughy gelport would be visible to anyone else. Soon, he hoped, everyone on his team would have these little gelports on the back of their necks. Then the soldiers being trained by Quavoce. Then ... everyone. This little spike was going to change everything.

Starting with him. Picking up the optic cable that would connect the spike to the computer, he brought the connection up to the gelport of the spike. The plug on the end of the white cable also had a gelatinous penny at its tip, identical to the one on the spike's base, and as Amadeu brought them together, the two seemed to morph out toward each other. Sensing each other's presence, they ballooned ever so slightly, and as Neal allowed them to touch, they melded, connecting the spike to the cable through a thousand molecular highways. The software Amadeu had designed sensed the spike's purpose, and offered him up the option of initiating the interface device to prepare for insertion.

Amadeu selected OK, and the computer began preparing the spike for insertion. A beep from the PC indicated it was about to test the spike. Neal held it up in the air by its base, and waited.

The spike shimmered slightly in the luminescent light, and then, from along its length, a single fiber unpeeled itself. It was micro-thin, and it seemed to fall away from the spike's point like a blade of grass slowly wilting. As it bent away, it then began undulating, waving and twisting as the machine tested its malleability. It was followed quickly by two more hair-thin spines, each beginning to twist and turn like Medusa's reptilian hair, and slowly the spike revealed itself not as a metallic whole, but a thousand tendrils that each twisted and turned independently.

After a few seconds of this testing of probes' flexibility, the hairs began to merge back together again. They followed a precise choreography, leaving no space between them as they slid into each other once more. It was like a building's destruction seen in reverse. The thousand constituent fibers that had made up the spike sliding back into place, to return the whole to a single gleaming point once more.

<Test Complete> said his computer.

Amadeu nodded. It was time. He only had one more thing to do before he took the leap. With his free hand, he pressed the speaker button on his desk phone and called Birgit in her quarters in another part of the complex. Her voice came out of the speaker.

"Hello?"

"Birgit, this is Amadeu. I am sorry to call you so early, but I need you to come to my office as soon as you have a chance."

There was a pause while Birgit no doubt gathered her senses. It was five o'clock in the morning and she was exhausted. They were launching the first climber that morning. Her part in the effort was really over. Tests were complete, and they had run it up as far as twenty thousand feet yesterday without a glitch. The designs were good. The construction was good. The system was not new, it was only new to them, and they had every reason to believe it would work as planned. A luxury which Amadeu did not enjoy in his efforts.

But she wanted to be there in the morning when it departed for real, and she didn't know why Amadeu was waking her at this ungodly hour.

"Is everything all right, Amadeu?" she asked, a hint of anger in her voice.

"Yes, everything is fine, but I need you here as soon as you can make it. I'll explain when you get here."

She did not like being ordered around, least of all by a young boy, albeit it a somewhat loveable one, and she snapped back, "Amadeu, what is this about?"

"I can't tell you, but I need you here, please come. There has been a … breakthrough in my research." It wasn't really a lie. By the time she got here, there would have been. Either for better or worse. He knew she would not let him do this if she was here, but he needed someone here once it was done, in case something went wrong. Maybe even someone to bring him out of it if he passed out, as the first test subject had, though without any long-term aftereffects.

She persisted with her questions and he became impatient, "Listen, please, Birgit, listen. I rarely ask for favors, and when I do I don't do so lightly. I am not asking you to come here for some frivolous chat. I *need* you here. All will become clear when you get here, I promise. It is important. I wouldn't bother you if it wasn't. But I can't tell you anymore over the phone so … just come, will you?"

She was more than a little perturbed by his tone, but on some level she got it. Goodness knows she had made several calls just like this herself in her long career. Sometimes you just needed someone to get something done, not bother you with questions that you didn't have time to answer. "I'll be there in five minutes." she said flatly and she hung up, leaving him to whatever had so possessed him to call her and demand her attendance.

She pulled on some shorts over the underwear she had been sleeping in, clipped on a bra, and threw on a T-shirt. In truth, she was more curious than annoyed, such was the boy's infectious enthusiasm. And so, a moment later, she was walking briskly from her quarters toward the small block of offices where they had been given some rooms to continue their work onsite.

Back in the lab, Amadeu took a breath. The spike was live as he held it up to the back of his neck. This was not really something you should do yourself, but the machine would not allow him to miss the mark. At the meeting point of the line of his shoulders, he felt with his left hand for the bumps of his spine, and with his right hand he guided the point of the spike to the line between them.

The fibers at the end of the spike became mobile as they approached his neck. They could sense the pulse of his heart, the firing of his nerves, all the electrical signals that darted about his body, and at the center of that symphony, they could see the hot core of his spine, and they hungered for it. Amadeu's spine was a superhighway pumping a billion signals back and forth from every corner of his body, and the top of his spine thrummed like a biological IT network, feeding the HQ of his brain with information from every part of the organization it ruled, and delivering the HQ's orders to every element of the whole, both subconsciously and consciously.

Amadeu felt a tingle as it touched his skin. The fibers at the tip of the spike found each nerve at the point of insertion, and dulled them each individually. Like a secret invasion force quietly silencing guards, it pacified Amadeu's defenses, and started to open a small aperture with minute delicacy. Parting the epidermis whilst hardly tearing a single cell of its delicate structure, the multitude of hair-thin fibers of the spike negotiated their way past capillaries and veins, moving them aside without spilling their precious contents. As the gap in Amadeu's skin was opened, the tendrils drove ever deeper, the first already starting to flow passed the thin layer of muscle to the boney discs of his upper spine.

In many ways they were doing what the fatter, blunter fibers in Lana's hand had to her many victims before driving their body to mutation, but this was infinitely subtler. The spike probed Amadeu's delicate nerve endings with needlepoint accuracy, as opposed to the chainsaw brutality Lana had brought to bear on those unfortunate enough to cross her path.

The spike continued its way inside, drawing power through the link coming from the computer. Once it was fully inserted, with only the gel-like connective surface showing, it would form a smooth bond with the skin it had displaced and it would draw what little power it would need from the spine itself. It would only ever respond to a port like itself, and even then only at the direct bequest of its owner, Amadeu.

But now it was just getting its purchase, getting ready to open up a line into Amadeu's mind. Slowly but surely the fibers snaked into his spine, so slowly, so softly, they snaked up to the blue pulsing neurons and merged with them.

Amadeu felt the base of the spike draw level with his skin, and he knew this meant that the full two inches of the spike had now wormed themselves into him. He fought a surge of instinctive repulsion at the thought. He suppressed a feeling of violation and reasoned with his desire to rip out the spike which he had just allowed to invade him.

And then, as he wrestled with this emotion, something happened. A request.

<Open connection?>

It was not on the screen. It was in Amadeu's mind. Not heard, not in his middle ear. No, it was … written across his memory. He remembered it happening, no, he was remembering it happening as it did. Real-time memory, that was the only way to describe it. But it didn't describe it. Amadeu saw that now. When they had experimented before, it had taken the soldier fifteen minutes just to understand he was being asked a question, ten more to understand that question, and an hour to answer that question in a way that the computer could accept.

Amadeu settled his thoughts. He contemplated everything he knew about how his mind worked, and how the software was designed to speak to it. He braced himself for what was to come, and as he did so he envisioned the metallic spike in his neck not as a physical entity, but as a portal, a mouth to speak with, eyes to see with. A new sense. He took a deep breath, closed his eyes, and focused. It took him a few moments to find his tongue in this new language, but soon he isolated that part of his mind where the question had been sent to and, in a way only he truly understood, and with that part of him only he truly knew the computer was listening to, Amadeu replied.

Amadeu: 'open connection.'

- - -

Lana moved her fingers as part of a full systems check. The smaller two fingers of her left hand were still not responding properly. As the fist went to clench, they instead bent backward and out in a horrible mockery of the human hand they were supposed to replicate. She looked at them, and queried her machine mind as to how long it would take to repair them. They were cracked at the skeletal level, as bad as the damages she had incurred in King's Bay, if less widespread, and the machine estimated eleven days without further movement of those joints.

She cursed and noted the date, setting a limit on further action till they were locked back into place. She rose tentatively from her hiding position, shaking off the mud and debris she had used to hide from scans from above, and scanned her position. She started with passive scans, in case a team was nearby, and then went to active sensors.

Comfortable that she was alone, she stood and began to make her way across the late evening toward a nearby town. After a little over a mile, she came to a telephone pole. She tested its sturdiness before applying her weight, and then shimmied up the pole. At the top, she clapped onto the wire with her good hand and used the forefinger of her other hand to link with the wire.

Connection was quick and smooth, her internal systems less affected by the battle than her external ones were. It had already been a week since the fight, and still she was far from whole again. But she would get there soon enough, she calmed herself by saying. She scrolled through various cable channels. News programs flashed across her mind.

Riots in New York, protests in San Francisco. Two militia groups in Grand Rapids, Michigan, had sent mailed declarations of independence to their governor, and several police officers had been killed in the ensuing standoffs. The New York Stock Exchange had reopened briefly to allow a balancing of annual budgets but closed again after strictly limited trading. The new president had fixed prices to stop hyperinflation, and the National Guard were doing spot checks on supermarkets and guarding deliveries of basic groceries.

She smiled vaguely at this news. A pleasant by-product of her efforts, but not what she needed now. Tapping into the phone system, she hacked a local substation and made a fake call to a number in Vermont. The call was rerouted automatically to a number in Reston, Virginia. A voice answered. It greeted the caller and a mild-mannered conversation ensued between a mother and her daughter away at college. But this was not a real conversation, and the mother and daughter did not exist. Hidden within the unobtrusive static that quietly popped and crackled on the line was a second signal. The mother was Lana, the daughter was her bug loitering in Saul Moskowitz's house. The download of information was long and slow, the method horribly limited, but soon Lana was trolling through the details of Saul's past few days at work and at home.

Her machine mind was sorting and arranging the data into neat little packets, cross-referencing subjects and names, categorizing and analyzing the information as quickly as it could come through the slow link. It was well ahead of the flow when the name came through, and recognition was instantaneous.

Neal. The file opened without prompt, such was the level of priority set by Lana on any information pertaining to his whereabouts. The recorded conversation was spotty. It was between Saul and someone on his office phone. The machine tracking Saul was under strict instructions to remain passive when inside Ayala's team's headquarters. The place was rigged with the most persnickety of detection devices, and any unknown signal would set off alarms that would have them soon closing the tap on her little font of information.

But though one-sided, the conversation was nonetheless informative. They were moving Neal, that much was clear, Saul was to arrange transport for Neal's affects to a location in Colorado. Neal would travel separately under close guard. Saul was to arrange things for four days from now. Neal would be moved before then.

She analyzed the information as the last of the updates streamed into her system. Details of the way Saul was going to ship Neal's effects. Details of the timing and hints at the destination, but no more on the arrangements for Neal himself. The upload complete, the mother and her daughter said their good-byes and the conversation ended, Lana dropping to the soil next to the pole's base.

She considered the timing. He would be moved within the next four days. She would never have as good a chance at him as when he was in transit, but getting close to enough to follow him would be difficult, and she had no intention of going anywhere near the White House again, not since Ayala's teams had been so reinforced. That said, she could follow the package Saul was preparing straight to its destination. She knew when and how it was going to be shipped. She knew its rough destination. It would take her right to her target.

Four days. She glanced at her two broken fingers. Seizing them with her good hand, she deployed her weapons array and fired at the already damaged armor at their base. Bending back with all her force, they slowly started to snap, the material around their base giving under the force.

Once the armor around them started to give, they came away smoothly, her black skin finally tearing as she ripped her dead fingers from her body. She only had four days. She had no time for the vestigial little fingers to heal and no need for them anyway. She initiated the process of sealing the stubs left by her blunt surgery and set off to get in position. She needed to carefully maneuver herself into a strategic spot to intercept the delivery Saul was arranging. As she jogged away, she tossed the two fingers to the ground without qualm.

- - -

Amadeu wandered out of his office. He felt slightly discombobulated. He looked left and right, but his vision of the corridor was blurry, like a fog was blocking his view. No, not a fog, more like a wall of cloud. He pushed at the cloudwall and it was cold, like ice crystals touching the tips of his fingers. He thought of the heat of his body, and he pushed through the crystals, feeling them melt against him. Seeing the way they melted away at his touch, he swished his arms through the cloud, wafting it outward and clearing the hallway.

His vision open, he looked up and down the corridor again. No one was there. He felt like he should be expecting someone. Like a visitor should be arriving any moment. He moved on, hoping to meet them. He came to the building's entrance. A guard sat there. Amadeu said good morning, but the guard did not acknowledge him. Outside the building, he looked left and right again. Again there seemed to be a fog, but as he thought of his internal warmth and shook his head, the fog lifted, more easily this time, and he panned around. He saw the entrance to the covered bridge ahead of him. The bridge led away from the mainland peninsula he and his colleagues worked on, to the fortress island. To the SpacePort. He thought of the SpacePort and decided to go there.

He was at the SpacePort. The wall was thick here, not crystals but a sheer block of ice that chilled him when he touched it. It did not give. He worried that he was going blind, but when he thought of it, he knew that his eyes were not the problem. He did not know why, but he knew it was true. He stepped around the edges of the ice wall, and looked for a gap in its cold edifice. He stepped back and he was a thousand feet away, surveying the fortress as a whole. He skated around it, parts of it hidden from him, parts of it covered by a loose fog, parts open. He saw an entrance and stepped into an open door, finding himself in the air-conditioning ducts of the building. He jumped from one fan to the other, aware of his position but blind to his surroundings. He could feel temperature and humidity, he could feel the air as it passed through the system, but he could not see it.

At last his eyes opened. No, only one eye, and he could not move it, but he could see the inside of the great chamber at the heart of the fortress. He could see the Climber, the powerful machine designed to climb the tether, carrying cargo into space. He tried to go to the machine. He tried to study its design, to view it with the critical eye of someone who had participated in its design, but again the fog came, solidifying to ice at key points as he tried to focus on the machine.

Frustrated, he looked for that part he knew best: the machine that controlled it, the simple, non-invasive interface that he had designed for the pilots and engineers to master the complex and powerful machine. Finding it, he saw it was clear, a hint of fog vanishing as his hot eyes focused on it, and suddenly he was in the machine. He looked out, and he felt the bounds of the machine as if it was his own skin.

The climber was essentially a fat cylinder, forty feet high, twenty feet across, with smooth walls. At its top, it began to taper, thinning to ten feet across. A series of flaps arranging like a flower were able to close and form a point around the cable, smoothing the aerodynamics of the craft as it drove up the tether that it was built to ride. On one side, a series of flaps running from the top of the craft to the bottom were open, allowing the climber to be slid around the base of the tether, accepting it into the craft. As the machine enveloped the tether, the flaps closed.

Inside the car, two long lines of big, thick rubber tires lay open like a mouth turned on its side, its rubber teeth ready to clamp down on the tether as it slid into place between them. In total, eighteen tires, nine on each side, ran from the top to the bottom of the cylinder's inside. When the cylinder was in place around the bottom of the tether, then the wheels came together, gripping the nanotube with their malleable but ardent teeth, and the climber was ready. The rest of the engine car's space was taken up by the drives that powered the big wheels, all linked to the main fusion generator, a second backup waiting to take the load, if, for some reason, the first failed.

Amadeu saw the technicians working through the battery of final tests. He felt the pop, tickle, and surge of systems flexing in final preparation. And, seemingly in seconds, the machine was counting down, the gantries were pulling back, and the heavy cylinder began rising up the cable, lifting off the two great trolleys that had slid it into place.

He felt a tug. Like gravity was trying to stop the machine from rising. But not gravity. He could feel that the machine was working perfectly. No, the tug was not on the machine that he was rising with, it was on him.

There was language.

Suddenly words came and he looked at them, seeing their strange shapes and knowing that they held meaning. Knowing even that he knew what that meaning was. He looked at them, and then he felt a part of himself talking to him. No, not a *part* of himself, *he* was asking himself a question, *he* was trying to tell himself what the letters meant.

<Are you OK?>

Yes.

He looked at himself. He nodded to the version of himself that spoke this language, and then he saw that other part of himself talking to someone else.

"Yes," it told them. He wanted to see who *he* was talking to, and instantly he was sitting in his office again. Birgit was in front of him. She looked unhappy. His head swam as his world refocused, and he reclaimed his own senses, a spring of bile begging to rise at the sudden shift in perspective.

"What did you do?" Birgit said to him, angry and concerned all at once.

"I … errr …" a laugh escaped his lips as realization came, "I was talking to the machine."

He was stunned. She thought she understood; he had connected with the machine, he had conversed with it. But she didn't understand, and as she fussed over him, he gripped her shoulders and she stopped, looking into his eyes, stunned, perhaps a little afraid.

"I did it, Birgit. Not just connection, I was *in* the machine. I was over in the fortress, I was in the climber as they prepped it. I was in it as it lifted off. I was in the corridor cameras, the front door security system. The air conditioners." He laughed again as she started to grasp what he was saying, seeing past his mania to the simple joy that was fueling it.

"Birgit," he said, at last, "I looked out from the camera on some technician's laptop as it faced the climber and then at will I leapt into it through the network, finding those systems I had designed and … the fog … the walls … I'll never call them *fire*walls again …" he laughed again, "… *Ice*walls, the walls fell as my mind worked into those systems I had access to, either because they were not well protected or because I had worked on them and knew the passwords."

His intuitive mind had interpreted the system security as haze, some of which he could pass through, some more impenetrable. Simple systems had opened to his highly computer literate mind with ease, more secure ones had been more difficult, but the fog had been clearest on those systems he had designed himself. As the artistic side of his brain had encountered visual blocks, his logical left-brain had been hacking as only it knew how, talking with those systems it knew best and clearing the way.

He had been one with the machine. At the end, Birgit had been speaking with his logical left-brain, and he had been forced to use it to understand and reply to her. That was a little disturbing. Without that conversation, he wouldn't have even known he was under; heck, he hadn't even truly realized he wasn't in his body, not truly. His right brain just made the leap. He needed an anchor, clearly. He would have to work on that.

And as he thought this thought, the computer to his side flickered to life, and code started flashing across the screen. He looked at it and Birgit followed his stare.

"What is it doing?" she asked, her voice tinged with concern as she fretted over the link.

Amadeu was confused at first, then he realized, "Not 'it.' *Me*," he said, "I am studying the program, my right brain is working *with* my left brain to interpret the code driving the interface, and telling it what it needs. It needs my left brain to translate for it, I can feel them talking." He laughed again, amazed at the sensation, the code slowing as his attention veered toward the conversation he was having with Birgit.

Usually the left-brain is the core of what we feel we *are*. He could see it much more clearly now. When people refer to their conscious and subconscious minds, they really mean their left and right brains. The vast majority of people have trouble listening to their intuitive right brains, women are inherently better at it than men, thus women's intuition.

Occasionally some people think more with their right brains than with their left. They are often our greatest artists. They are also often considered insane. But the biggest difference is with age. We forget how to listen to our right brains with time. We imprison them with logic and prejudice until our greatest source of creativity and brilliance is locked behind a wall of assumption and primitive common sense, and then it is heard only as an echo.

He paused, gathering his thoughts, literally.

"Not *it*," he said once more, quietly, "me ..." and he focused on the screen, taking notice of what his subconscious was doing. The scrolling text slowed perceptibly once more as his mind was forced to wait for him to consciously decide what to do next, but still the screen flashed faster than Birgit could comprehend.

"Stop, Amadeu. *Stop* this," said Birgit, dazed. "We need to make sure you are coping with this. That your mind can handle everything that is happening."

"My vitals are fine," Amadeu said, his heart rate appearing on the screen the next moment. A diagnosis program they had used on the volunteer soldier sprang to life as if by magic, and began analyzing the host of biometric information available through the link. Still the window with the code flashed in the background, Amadeu not even looking at it now, as he flicked between screens on the medical program to show Birgit his vitals were steady. His brain function was unusually high, and patterned unusually concentrically across lobes, but it was not alarming by any measure.

But Amadeu saw genuine fear in Birgit's face, and genuine concern for his safety. Realizing he was making his colleague and friend uncomfortable, Amadeu stopped himself deliberately. The screen went blank. As a demonstration of his continued volition, he initiated an end to the link, and reached around behind his neck to catch the cable as it parted from the gel socket that was now a flat grey feature of the back of his neck.

It felt strange to end it. He resisted the urge to cliché and did not compare it to a lost limb or a diminished sense, but he could not deny the profound sense of loss that severing the connection brought. Maybe it was worse the first time, he thought, when the sensation was still fresh and exciting and new. But then maybe it only got worse with time. He had been jacked in for less than fifteen minutes. What would it be like after an hour, or a day? He would have to think about that. They would have to be careful.

At the sight of the cable in his hand, Birgit sighed, her relief palpable. He felt a little pleasure at how much she had worried about him, and she saw it in his eyes, frowning back at him to bring him down to earth before he became too smug.

"That was a *stupid* thing to do." she said, plainly.

"It was the *only* thing to do, Birgit." he replied.

His clear voice, devoid of any hint of remorse, met her stern reprimand as she faced the immutable righteousness of his success. Suddenly she felt like a bureaucrat. After all those arguments with Madeline, telling the younger woman to stop playing it safe, here she was playing that part she always loathed in others.

She stepped away, sinking into a seat across the room, somewhat grumpily. "Yes, well, you can't argue with results, I suppose. But in the end all you've proven is that *you* can do it. In the end, we are no closer to understanding how to get a soldier or pilot to do it, and that is our real goal."

He shook his head, "On the contrary, Birgit. I didn't know what I was asking our 'volunteers' to do until I did it myself. I had no idea how to direct them and they had no idea how to interpret what they were seeing." He shrugged, the simplicity of their previous mistakes seeming so obvious now.

"But now that one of us has learned how to ride this wonderful machine, maybe it will be easier to teach someone else." Amadeu smiled as the possibilities opened up in front of him. "Maybe I can even ride along with them to show them how."

It was a valid point, and Birgit fought an urge to be his first pupil, if only because she had been reprimanding him only moments before. It was an urge she would not end up fighting for very long.

But they both knew the second, even more important truth. They had been forced to wait until this critical step was complete before they initiated one of their most ambitious and most important projects yet. For hidden in the DNA of every human, and layered with the countless interactions and learning experiences of childhood and adolescence, was the key to developing the quantum complexity of sentience. That thing that could not be programmed, that thing that could not be built. Freed by his new ability to commune with the machine, Amadeu had gained the ability to be the first to share his sentience with that machine, in its entirety.

With Birgit's help, Amadeu was going to add his self to another whole, to clone his brain, not to make a copy, but to make something new.

They already had the substrate ready, the processing void they intended to seed with this new mind. That night, after Amadeu had convinced the nominally reluctant Birgit to try the link as well, and after they had both gotten a full soporific-induced eight-hour's sleep, they would begin the process of giving birth to humanity's first artificial mind.

Chapter 23: Triptych

The leadership team took its seats around the table and began to settle. Most of them knew each other by now, and at the very least they all knew each other's names and reputations. At one end sat Neal, scanning his notes on each of the agenda points they had laid out.

To Neal's left sat General Milton. To his right sat Admiral Cochrane of the British Navy. Birgit had a spot between Major Toranssen and Amadeu; Captain Falster sat next to General Braldinho, the man in charge of the Brazilian forces still working on finishing the base's defenses and the construction of the large port they were building on the mainland. Various other senior members of the taskforce surrounding SpacePort One filled the other seats. The stony-faced Quavoce, aka Major Garrincha, stood at Neal's shoulder.

"Ladies and gentlemen, if we can get started?" said Neal, noting how quickly the officers came to attention. It was a pleasing sensation.

"Now, we have a lot to cover today, so I won't waste time on formalities. Before we get into the various project updates, I wanted to talk about one topic in particular, one that impacts us both as taskforce members and citizens of the various allied nations that make up this extraordinary team."

The room was curious both professionally and personally and there was little noise as Neal went on, "I want to talk about a part of the team that has not yet had as prominent a role as the Research and Construction groups we are about to hear updates from.

"I am talking, of course, about the Operations Group. When General Milton and I first started to think about how to organize our efforts, this group was originally envisioned as the team that would eventually be taking all the important work the Research and Construction Groups were going to do and, using it, form the fighting force that would accomplish the goal that we have set ourselves."

Neal was aware that he was not actually saying what they all knew that goal was. People rarely did. At some point they would have to be more forthright about what they were all working toward. But though everyone in the room was well aware of the threat they were facing, most still refrained from talking about the coming conflict openly unless they had to, if only out of respect for their sanity.

"Because of the longer-range nature of the Operations Group's mandate, not much time has been spent yet on that aspect of the taskforce, but part of what I want to discuss here today is the increasingly vital role that this group has.

"Originally I had not planned to fill the role of the head of the Operations Group for some time yet. But in conversations with my advisors, it has become clear that I have already started acting as that lead and it seems wise that I remain in that role for the time being. While this group's mandate is more esoteric at this stage, two key areas of focus have already begun to emerge. I will start first with the work of Major Jack Toranssen and Captain Jennifer Falster."

Jack stayed focused on his hands. He had known Neal intended to talk about what Jack and Jennifer had been working on with Madeline and John, among others, and like a good officer he did not react to the mention of his name.

For some reason she could not put a finger on, though, Jennifer felt the blood rise to her cheeks when Neal said her name and she fought it down with verve. She had been the subject, attendee, and presenter at a thousand such senior briefings, so why this one would be any different was beyond her. Stifling her reaction, she focused on Neal's words as he went on.

"As you know, we have been both privileged and extremely lucky to have the invaluable input and assistance of John Hunt throughout these initial stages of our work. As the members of this closed committee also know, the man known as Major Garrincha behind me is also an extraordinary ally in the work we have set ourselves to and we remain utterly in their debt for all they have already done for us.

"In addition to their many duties as advisors and aids to the Research and Construction Groups, they have also begun prepping Officers Toranssen and Falster on some of the strategic aspects of the coming fight.

"For now, officers Toranssen and Falster have started using that information to start documenting the force's organizational parameters. In time the major will start enlisting each of you as appropriate to help draft force estimates and dispositions for each branch of the fleet. I am pleased to announce, though, that in their efforts, the major and the captain have already recommended a very apropos acronym for the new allied military force: Terrestrial Allied Space Command. I think you will all agree it is very appropriate to the TASC at hand."

A polite laugh rippled throughout the room and Jack and Jennifer smiled and nodded.

But Neal was building up to a much graver point and as the chatter petered out, he began again, his tone more strident this time, "But, my friends, I mentioned two streams of work that the Operations Group has already begun working on, and the second is, I am afraid, much more pressing.

"Most of you have not met Ayala Zubaideh." Neal did not look at Barrett as he mentioned her name. They had been separated by the exigencies of their work for months now and though he knew neither questioned the need for their relationship's long hiatus, he also knew that neither was immune to its emotional effects. Trusting the general's emotional fortitude, Neal went on, "Until a few months ago, mentioning her real name under any circumstances would have been more than my life was worth. But Ayala's role has changed significantly since we destroyed the Mobiliei satellites, and she has been very busy in that time.

"In recent months, Ayala has come out of the shadows and, with the help of Dr. Cavanagh and others, has started building up a team of the most lethal shock troops the Earth has ever known. Utilizing the very latest armor and weaponry coming out of our laboratories, Ayala has trained an ever-growing team of specialists culled from the most elite fighting forces in the world. She has done this so that we can try to hunt the greatest threat our enterprise currently faces.

"A week ago they came face-to-face with one of those threats for the first time in the terrible battle that consumed the presidency of the United States and sent the United States into an uproar. But though I know it will be hard for any of my fellow Americans to believe, the outcome of that confrontation was not ... *entirely* a failure." He raised his hands palms out as if to say, I know, I know, and went on, "For though it was a tragic day for America and the world as a whole, the president was not actually Lana Wilson's target.

"I am sad to say that *I* was, and I am somewhat ashamed to say that, in the end, it appears she killed the president out of frustration at not being able to get to me."

The room listened in silence. Some glancing furtively at the American members of their contingent but most were glued to Neal as he went on, "That meant that, although it was at a terrible price to pay, ladies and gentlemen, Lana was stopped from achieving one of her goals for the first time and was forced back into hiding once more.

"I can tell you that we are putting in place a plan to bring her back out into the open. And I can tell you that if that plan succeeds, and we believe it will, then we will be in position to engage her soon ... and with a very real chance of victory."

He sat back for a moment, his opening points made, and let the weight of that last statement sink in for the many present who had been touched by Lana's insatiable lust for vengeance. Halfway down the table, Admiral Hamilton stared straight forward as if facing a firing squad, his face a mask as he forced down his emotions at the mention of her name.

But Neal was not quite done. "Ayala, are you still on the line?" said Neal to the air, and a voice suddenly resolved itself from the speakers lining the large table they were sat around.

"Yes Neal, I'm here."

Speaking via a secure line being patched from her team's headquarters in DC, Ayala's commanding voice focused the room's attention once more. Without prompting, she took the lead as their attention turned to the errant Russian and Chinese Mobiliei Agents.

"Ladies and gentlemen, Neal asked me to speak today about the renewed Iron Curtain, or the Steel Curtain as some in my team have come to call it in more recent months. As some of you know, my friends and I were aware of all the Agents' identities well before the Mobiliei satellites were destroyed, but we could not move against them for fear of provoking the viral attack before our antigen was dispersed.

"While we were hampered by our need to coordinate our affairs, we did take steps to keep track of them, and I initiated protocols to notify the countries concerned of the traitors in their midst. This was done well in advance, or, in the case of countries where we could not rely on their discretion, as the attacks began.

"Our efforts paid off in Israel where we were able to catch the Agent relatively quickly. Our successful if bloody action there brought about the end of Raz Shellet before she could do even greater damage. There is also reason to believe that our efforts to track the French Agent contributed to our ability to neutralize him immediately after the satellites were destroyed."

As Ayala spoke the room became tense, and everyone knew why. For his part, Admiral Hamilton continued to look stoically forward, as if at attention, as if at court-martial. He feared she was about to talk about his attempt to capture Lana Wilson. An attempt that had caused more widespread devastation and destruction than he could have possibly imagined.

But to his surprise she did not. The gathered military minds could all surmise on their own that Ayala had no doubt put in place some form of plan to apprehend or at least track the US Agent. Plans which, in this case, had been blown wide open by the admiral's premature attempt to have Lana brought into custody.

But this was not the time to revisit the ramifications of the admiral's order. In fact, Ayala's goal today was quite the opposite. Today they wanted to encourage that kind of intervention, not dissuade it.

So Ayala moved past discussion of the situation in the US to the admiral's surprise and relief and instead said, "In Russia and China, my efforts focused simply on warning them of the Agents' identity and malevolent intent, as our ability to intervene and support them was so much more limited than in Europe or the US. All we could realistically have hoped to accomplish was to displace the Agents from their positions of influence until we could negotiate broader access for our people.

"And we thought we had managed to displace them … until a few weeks ago …" said Ayala with emphasis.

"My friends, as you all know, our nations' efforts to encourage China and Russia to come to the negotiating table to date have been unsuccessful. But I think it is time you knew just how severely they have failed."

The room was curious and furtive glances were shared as Ayala's voice continued to flow from the speakers, like children looking at each other at the back of the classroom, out of sight.

"In order to understand the seriousness of the situation, it is time you knew that in the last two months, we have not had one single, formal interaction with a senior official of either Russia or China."

The room was stunned. Everyone knew that relations were strained. Strained by the war in Pakistan. Strained by the viral outbreaks across Africa, the Middle East, and Indonesia. And strained by the economic malaise caused by the ongoing unrest which was affecting everyone. For months the entire world had been on tenterhooks; you would have had to be living under a very big rock indeed to have missed that. But while all had assumed relations with Beijing and Moscow had cooled, for them to have stopped all together was unprecedented.

"I know this must come as a shock to all of you, as I know that our governments have worked to keep the extent of the issue quiet, if only to protect what trade remains with the two nations. Usually management of those trade channels alone would have forced the two governments to at least open a diplomatic back channel, and at some points we have seen hints of that from China, but nothing has ever come of them. Clearly there is something else at work here.

"The last report we had of both Agents said they had vanished from their stations without a trace. In the aftermath of the fall of the satellites, our political contacts confirmed that both governments and all their respective intelligence agencies were aware of the traitors' identities and were actively blocking their access to any military or governmental agencies.

"They were not told where the Agents were from, for that we asked that they send representation to our initial meetings with each of your heads of state. But we were in the process of trying to pass on potential methods of detection they could use to guard key institutions when the process broke down.

"At first talks softened to a murmur, but our spies all confirmed unofficially that each Agent was, indeed, on every official and unofficial blacklist in both countries. So it was unclear how they were influencing both governments to refuse our political forays."

"And then it got worse ... much, much worse."

She did not hold back. She told of the systematic eradication of spy networks in both countries, and of the Stalin-esque clampdown on communications in Pakistan after it was occupied. She painted a picture of a world divided in two in a such a profound way as had not been seen since the Cold War.

After she had done, Neal stepped in, speaking now to a hushed room, and said, "Thank you, Ayala.

"My friends, forgive the dramatics, but we tell you this for a reason. We tell you this because this current state of affairs cannot be allowed to continue. While I know all our respective governments have been using every conventional method at their disposal to reopen diplomatic ties with Russia and China, I am afraid those conventional methods are not working, not nearly quickly enough anyway.

"Ayala's work to track Mikhail Kovalenko and Pei Leong-Lam *must* be allowed to continue. For though they have been less violent in their efforts to stymie our work than Agent Wilson has, they have been no less effective, as evidenced by the ongoing absence of any Russian or Chinese financial or political support for our vital work, support we will most certainly need once construction begins at full scale.

"I know each of our nation's State Departments and Intelligence Agencies have been working to gain a diplomatic and intelligence foothold once more, but I wanted today to formally ask each of you to join me in reaching out to your respective governments to see that no effort is spared in breeching the veil that has fallen over those two countries."

His tone became stern, "I cannot stress enough how important it is that we gain access to them once more so that Ayala and her team can do their jobs."

He looked at them all again, holding their gaze one at a time to emphasize his point.

Then he took a breath, "OK, it is not pretty, but it was time that you all knew the full extent of this crisis. Goodness knows I need your attention to be focused on the work here at Rolas, but I am afraid I need your help with this as well. This impasse *cannot* be allowed to continue. We must push forward, my friends. And that will take the various nations you all represent getting a handle on the situation in Northern Asia and reopening active dialogue with the Russians and Chinese."

There were emphatic nods and stern looks around the table. These were very senior men and women each with a voice in the highest halls in their respective nations. Neal might have wanted to keep them focused on protecting Rolas Base, but at this point the most credible threat to the base's security was from Russia or China and that threat was only going to get worse with time unless Ayala was allowed access to hunt it down.

He did not know what else to do. He simply did not understand why the UN, NATO, and the EU had all failed to get a grasp on the situation and he was running out of patience with the entire process.

"OK," he said, allowing the tension to ebb from his shoulders with a long breath, "with that said, let's get on with the rest of our agenda. General, I believe you are first up. If you would give us an update?"

Neal glanced to his right and General Milton nodded, fully aware of the importance of what Neal had just said. He only hoped that someone here might be able to bring pressure where he and Neal had failed.

But enough of politics, thought Barrett, setting his mind to the task at hand. And so Barrett began his lengthy briefing, deferring to General Braldinho and others as necessary.

The meeting ran on for several hours. They discussed their many projects, involving Birgit and Amadeu as needed without posturing or territorialism. Barrett was proud of how the gathered group of thinkers and leaders were forming into a team, as was Neal. It was just as they had strived for, and it may give them a glimmer of hope.

But they notably avoided discussing one topic any further: the political climate. The point had been made. The message heard. They would do what they could. Neal only hoped it would make a difference.

Chapter 24: Vendetta

Lana reveled in the rioters' fury. The police and National Guard were mobilized in most of the major metropolises of the country, most notably in New York, Chicago, LA, and DC, where protests had turned violent. Many less politically motivated participants had started taking the opportunity to engage in some old-fashioned capitalism, looting the contents from any home or store they could violate.

But this unrest was spreading, onto streets, into homes, into suburbs, and the overflow of angst and fury was spilling into the markets and drowning them. With even Park Avenue's residents affected, a wholly different resistance movement had been mobilized, with the wealthy and formerly wealthy starting to vocally support a forceful crackdown on the protests.

But that was not all Lana had to smile about, for amidst the violence and political rhetoric, Lana's tap into Saul Moskowitz's life had suddenly struck gold, proving more profitable than she had dared hope, and now she faced the very real possibility of bringing one of her intended targets to his knees.

Upon reflection, the attack on the White House had been ill conceived, she knew that. But she had nearly succeeded in spite of her overzealousness. If only she had spent longer assessing her target, or pursued some of the other movement she had tracked in the building, rather than focusing solely on the president's party. But she could not have known that Neal would not stick with the president, and any additional time spent in the capital surveying the area would have brought with it ever-greater risk of discovery.

No, she had seen an opportunity, and she had taken it. And despite her failure to achieve her target, she had still survived the encounter and managed to strike at the very heart of the nation she had been sent to emasculate. She was not sure which of her fellow Agents were still alive, or what they were doing if they were, but surely they weren't proving as successful as she was. Certainly there had been no news from Europe or Asia to indicate anything as spectacular as her reign of terror in the United States, except maybe that gruesome night in Gaza City several months ago.

In fact, Lana thought, there were many powerful nations still relatively untouched by the efforts of Lana and her cohorts. The most notable example of this was the wealthy countries of Western Europe, which, aside from the economic backlash from the various military and societal tremors resonating around the earth, had escaped the current crises relatively unscathed. As she contemplated this, Lana felt a deep-seated desire to redress that imbalance. Maybe once she had dispensed with Neal, and hopefully Madeline (if she could find her), she would head to Europe.

She sat in a new Ford sedan, moving slowly in the evening rush-hour traffic. Her face was heavily painted with makeup, and covered by a baseball cap and sunglasses. Thick black hair hung down about her neck. Not a wig. Real hair. The hair belonged to a Maribel

Braggs of Ashburn, Virginia, as did the clothes Lana was wearing and the car she was driving.

As Lana had stalked the small towns west of DC, she had come across Maribel's home, and the annoying poodle she lived with. She had entered Maribel's home and quickly dealt with the yapping pup, then she had studied Maribel's possessions and surmised that the woman was both single and quite devoid of plans for that weekend. It was a perfect combination for Lana's needs, and a very unfortunate one for Maribel's.

She had watched Maribel come home and heard her call out for 'poochie!' as she closed her front door behind her. But Maribel's little mutt had been quiet. Confused, Maribel had turned around, looking for her pet, and come face-to-face with Lana's night-black visage. She had died quietly and quickly, Lana having temporarily lost her appetite for torturing innocents in the face of the greater target that was almost within her grasp.

Instead she had neatly scalped Maribel's head, dressed herself in Maribel's clothes, and applied liberal amounts of Maribel's makeup to her face. She had then stuffed the overweight Maribel into a corner in the basement, along with her dog's body, and exited the house without an afterthought.

While Washington Reagan Airport was shut to all civilian traffic, Dulles had remained open, and was struggling to move the large volume of travelers coming to and from the political hub of the still mighty United States. As Ayala's administrative lead, Saul Moskowitz had originally planned to have Neal's effects sent to his location on a military transport out of Reagan, but Ayala had said no. She had stressed that there was too great a chance that Lana would be able to track the small volume of traffic coming in and out of that airport, and that he should use a civilian transport out of Dulles.

Saul had argued the point at some length, but Ayala had been adamant, and Lana had been glad she had. The forces in and around downtown DC were now at a level that made even Lana pause for thought. Her attack on the White House had hastened events in America, and Ayala's forces had responded in kind. To venture into that hornet's nest again would be suicide, Lana knew that.

That said, the security around Dulles airport was hardly to be sniffed at, Lana thought. Checkpoints were randomly searching cars approaching the airport, while cordons and motion sensors had been set up in the woods that bordered the runways. Lana had felt their probing sensors as she had stalked the woods the night before, looking for a way to get onto the runways, but she had not dared venture too close to the sensors, as she knew that would bring down the full might of Ayala's forces.

But with the closing of Reagan, over sixty thousand cars were now coming and going from Dulles each day and searching them all would have been impossible. Cameras had been mounted at several points above the highways feeding the airport, scanning the faces of drivers and passengers, but their recognition software was primitive, and Lana could disguise herself well enough to fool these machines even if her hair and makeup would not stand up to close inspection.

If she was pulled over by one of the random roadblocks, it would probably not go well, and she would have to fight her way out of it, but they were not manned full-time with Ayala's shock troops, who were focused on guarding the city proper, and she was reasonably sure she could escape before the shock troops arrived, if it came to that.

But she passed the last checkpoint without incident, and drove onward into the airport's warren of parking lots and access ramps to the day parking lot aside the terminal. She took a parking space on the rooftop where few cars were parked, and climbed out, studying the cameras covering the lot as she did so.

Her mind began to analyze the way the cameras crossed each other. Her view of the world started to change as she overlaid the angles of the various cameras and a path began to emerge, a series of islands on the parking lot's top level not covered by the camera network.

Lana then looked over to the roof of the main terminal building, and slowly her machine mind began to plot a similar map of where the airport's guards there could and could not see.

Without rush, she calmly walked to the far side of the lot, stopping in a hole in the patchwork of camera views that covered the rest of the roof. Here she was hidden from the eyes roaming the lot. Deftly she removed her clothing, and used it to wipe the makeup from her pitch-black face. Looking back across the lot toward her car, and the terminal beyond, she could see her path planned out before her. Her mind was ready with the exact speed she would have to run, and the power and trajectory of her coming leap. Checking the skies, she watched the planes, and waited for the moment when the rush of a landing 747 would confuse the motion sensors they had nearer the terminal, then she ignited her run up.

Several floors below, taxies were pulling to and from the curb in the gap between the parking lot and the terminal. They swarmed around each other, jockeying for curbside position so they could unload their cargo of husbands and wives, lonely businessmen, harried parents, and confused children. From the amateurs with their vast bag of clothes that would never be worn, to the diligent packer with their matching luggage, so shiny and new, and so soon to be eyed by distant thieves.

The madding crowd busied past each other, watched closely by airport police. Couples talked silently about the stringent security, about whether it was even safe to travel in these strange times, about the riots wracking their country. Cameras scrutinized faces and license plates. Men and women twitched at the banging of car doors, and vigilant eyes sought out the unusual, looked for threats, sought signs of anything unusual.

But amid the noise and haste, no eyes or cameras were pointed skyward, and no one saw the naked, black figure silently soaring across the black sky above them. Her long, impossibly graceful leap took her from one patch of camera blindness on the parking lot's roof to another on the terminal's, landing with a skid and a tight roll.

The route here was more convoluted. A darting run here, a well-placed jump there, but soon Lana's black eyes were peering out over the edge of the terminal's far roof, north, to the heavily guarded cargo sheds, where the absence of hordes of civilian traffic had made that approach impossible. She looked and she saw the plane she sought, her acute eyesight picking out the marking on its side and comparing it against the schedule Saul's team had set up and the cargo company manifests she had hacked.

She saw her target and she studied it. She had fifteen minutes till it was scheduled for takeoff. She had deliberately waited till just before the flight, so that she wouldn't leave too much time for her clothing and car to be discovered in the lot behind her. By the time they investigated that, she should be airborne, hitching a ride with Neal's effects, so she could track them back to their owner.

The airport was backed up, and the plane was a few minutes late taxiing to the runway. When it eventually started moving, she saw it leave the cargo terminal and backed up, preparing her machine legs for the next step. She had carefully programmed her body with the coming leap. Because, with the speed and distance she had to go, there would be no time for even her inordinately fast mind to intervene.

Her path was set. The moment came. Without requesting confirmation, her body surged forward, landing with two feet on the edge of the roof. Her legs bent as far as they would go, and then catapulted her skyward with all their might, out over the waiting passenger planes, over the unsuspecting travelers, pilots, and crews busying themselves with preflight rituals.

Her target turned on to the bottom of the runway as it was supposed to and Lana could see its two pilots as they conversed with air traffic control. They did not see her black body against the night sky as she flew, landing just under their starboard wing, using its bulk and the roar of the engines to hide the resounding crack of her landing. The jet was cleared for takeoff, and even now was revving its engines.

Once again her mind was programmed not to wait for her. Her legs wrenched at the tarmac, driving out her momentum in a screeching, ripping skid as she skidded up to the wheels.

Without pause, she was grasping at the plane's undercarriage as it started to accelerate. She caught it in a flash, barely a blur on the runway as she darted under and up to the landing gear. She could not afford to hesitate even slightly. If she was seen here by the pilot of one of the planes approaching the runway or one of the ground crews that busied this way and that, she would be in for a fight.

But it was all over in a flash, a momentary black blur against an already dark night. Her skin was a void that defied sight on the clearest of sunny days, at night she was but a shadow as she flashed through the dark sky, a sky where motion sensors were made pointless by the muddled haste and jet wash of the countless planes plying the runway.

In a moment, she was worming her way up into the plane's fuselage through the landing gear doors, even as the jet started to gather speed.

By the time the plane was airborne, she was nestled amongst the crates in its hold, listening carefully for any signs that her boarding had been witnessed. But the plane did not slow its steep climb, nor did it bank to land again after some warning from the ground. Cautiously confident that she had managed to avoid detection, she sat back and allowed her body to assess the stresses and strains she had just put on it while the plane banked lazily onto its course.

But it was not alone. Far, far above the flight paths of the approaching and departing cargo and passenger planes, two black StratoJets also banked and turned, swooping in from where they had been circling in wait. As the cargo plane took off, they gently dropped into position far behind the bulky jet. Lana had managed to avoid the cameras and guards at the airport because, as usual, they had underestimated her speed, and because they had underestimated her ability to be subtle, when she needed to be. But she had underestimated her enemies too. She had assumed only human guards were watching the airport, and that her true adversaries were far away, guarding more important objectives.

John and Quavoce did not know exactly how Lana had managed to hack Ayala's network security without detection, but their supposition that she had done so had been confirmed when they had seen their old colleague leap aboard the cargo plane far below. They had wanted to fight her right there, but it was too dense a kill zone, there were simply too many ways for a savage killer like Lana to hurt innocent people in such a populated area, and too many ways she might escape as well.

No. They had let her board the plane, and let it take off.

It was a flight that was going to take Lana exactly where they wanted her, so they could face her on their terms.

- - -

Several hours into the flight, Lana was relatively sure that they were over the Midwest. Her internal compass told her what direction they had been flying in, and she could estimate their airspeed by the pitch of the engines' whine coming in through the plane's hull. The cockpit was cut off from the cargo hold by a thick steel door. She had crept close to it to listen to the pilot's conversation after takeoff, but had not loitered. She had nothing to fear from the man and woman if they discovered her, of course, but she knew that if she was to be successful, the crew had to be alive and well when the plane got to wherever it was going.

Hanging back in the plane, she had scanned the packages aboard until she found what she had supposed was Neal's belongings. She had not cracked them open, instead she had inserted one of the last of her tiny bugs in between the cardboard flaps, and watched through its eyes as it slid inside. After using the bug to check the contents, and confirming that she had the right package, she had ordered the little device to slip itself inside one of the many books inside and go silent. She would notify it later, if she needed it to confirm the package's location after it left the plane.

After that, she had been faced with no choice but to wait. So she had sat and waited for the landing cycle, patient and silent in the hold of the lumbering freighter.

Sure enough, as they were somewhere out over the Rockies, she felt the plane starting to descend. After a while her barometric sensors told her they were at about eighteen thousand feet when she suddenly felt a clunk and a thud resounding through the plane's fuselage, almost like the landing gear was being deployed. The plane started to vibrate with a powerful turbulence, but something was amiss. Something was clearly interrupting the airflow over the plane's slick lines, but her senses told her it was not the landing gear. The vibration was imbalanced: it was only coming from one side of the plane, and it was coming from its front.

There was only one logical conclusion: one of the plane's hatches had been blown open. She bolted forward, stopping only to listen for a millisecond at the steel dividing door. No sound except the roar of wind. If there had been an accident then there would have been shouts, assuming both pilots had not been sucked out of whatever opening had interrupted the plane's smooth lines. No noise meant no pilots. No pilots meant no reason not to explore further.

The steel door between the cargo hold and the crew compartment smashed open like cardboard as her foot came through it, and Lana was greeted by a blast of air, and an empty cockpit. Gripping the walls against the hurricane coming through the blown-out hatchway to her left, she climbed to the gaping opening and angled her head out into the thundering blast of night air.

Her mind raced to take in what she saw as she scanned the scene. Below and behind the plane were two dark green parachutes, dropping back fast as the plane surged onward on autopilot, but as her eyes turned toward the rear of the plane her acute pupils found the unmistakable blue flares of a flock of streaking rockets powering towards her.

Without thought, she instantly went to leap clear, throwing herself with all her might out of the open door, but no amount of strength could get her away from the sheer power of the coming explosion. The missiles detonated in quick succession, birthing a rioting cloud of thunder and fire around the plane. They engulfed the big jet in a chorus of demonic flame, combining their fury into one terrible ball of orange-white heat. As the explosion found the plane's jet fuel it gained new strength, and powered outward, sending fire and debris into Lana's falling body like a thousand streaking, flaming meteors.

Her machine mind screamed at her, alarmed at the pounding forces ripping at it. Disaster wrought on her systems as they were alternately fried and beaten, shutting down one by one. A moment later she was tumbling through the sky, the remains of her tactical systems trying to grasp the world flying by her.

Then she saw the black jets. She saw them by their blue engine trails as they swooped in on her.

She sensed the bullets an instant before they rammed into her, thousands of hypersonic shells battering her limbs to pieces as first one then another jet sliced at her. They made several passes as she fell, swooping and darting around her falling body like eagles picking at their prey. But as she neared the ground they stopped their attack and brought their own wild plummet to a halt. Rotating their fusion drives and angling them downward, they ignited the smaller thruster in their planes' noses and brought the fantastic new StratoJets under control.

But Lana had no such ability to halt her fall, and as they reared up, she continued to rocket down toward the earth, one of her legs blown clean off, her right shoulder exploded and flapping free.

Her body slammed into the rock of the blunt hills a hundred miles southeast of Denver like a hammer, and all at once a thousand of her systems went quiet. She lay there, still and broken, in the shallow crater her impact had etched in the stone.

Her remaining systems tried to grapple some semblance of control from her ruined hulk. One eye registered one of the black jets descending like a vengeful angel next to her, she felt the other landing behind her, and then there were two sets of feet crunching through the night to her side.

"Princess Lamati." came John Hunt's voice out of the descending silence.

A pause, and then, in a tone that matched the contained fury of her own seething rage, he went on, "As you lie here, shattered and broken at last, I am only sad that it took so long for us to finally bring an end to the cancer that is your existence." She could hear the first hints of victory in his voice, the building satisfaction combating the frustration of months of failure.

He switched to the native tongue of her homeland, and using the tone reserved for speaking with a servant or vagrant, he went on, "In the end you did not put up much of a fight, but then you were only ever effective against the innocent and the weak. Like a common animal, you only ever picked fights with those who could not defend themselves."

Lana screamed inside her skull, a broken moan escaping her limp mouth while impotent rage roiled inside her, but he did not stop. "How easy it was to kill you once we could actually get you face-to-face, so to speak. I only wish we had brought an audience along to watch you die. But after the cowardly way you lashed out at your attackers in King's Bay, we were forced to insist that we face you alone."

He laughed coldly as he watched Lana's body twitch, impulses flexing her broken limbs, a deeply ironic mimicry of the spasmic torture she had inflicted on so many of her victims.

"Well," said Quavoce now, as she convulsed on the ground, "we are almost alone. One person insisted on being here, even if it meant risking her life, and in the end we could not deny her this moment." His voice returned to English and became a shout, clearly aimed back over his shoulder, at his plane still whirring with contained power not far away, "You can join us now, if you please. She is no longer a threat."

Lana raged at the limits of her failed, impotent body and Quavoce returned to her own tongue, now using the patronizing tone reserved for children or pets, "In the end, we could probably have just sent Ayala's shock troops to kill you, such was the depth of your final failure.

"But we couldn't risk you getting away, oh no, you have caused far too much damage. So we both came. And I must say that we are both extremely happy we did." The two men exchanged a relished smile then stared back down at her, registering her struggling systems, registering the final glimpse of fight in her one functioning eye.

They watched as she tried to aim her laser at them, but her crippled systems could not control the beam. It was weak and wide and they both laughed.

"There's still some fight in this tagnol, yet." said John, comparing her to a carrion-eating, feral pest from back home on Mobiliei; a mangy hyena at best.

Another pathetic, stifled scream came back at them in reply, and Quavoce bent down, saying in English once more, "Princess Lamati, I am here to tell you that you represent everything that is wrong with Mobiliei. And we are going to see to it that you and your murderous, bastard allies do not win the coming war, not without a hell of a fight, at least. Because this place is not yours to own. It already has a civilization, and we are here to help them beat you."

"On that subject," said John, smiling, "do you like our jets? Recognize their design at all? Three months, Lana, the humans have had only three months and they've already mastered fusion drives, stratospheric flight, and superconductive plating. They have eight more years until the rest of your fleet arrives."

Quavoce stood again and added, "And when it does, trust me when I tell you that the real Princess Lamati will be the first to die. But we are getting ahead of ourselves, we have someone that wants to say good-bye before you die. We just need to disarm you first."

And with that they both glared down on her and she felt the combined fire of their weaponry burning into her left eye, turning the remains of her weapons systems to liquid inside her eye socket. She tried to writhe away, then felt their hands as they bent and pinned her down. She felt the strength of their healthy, fully functional machine bodies and she longed for that strength once more.

Then she heard the third set of footsteps approaching. They paused a short distance away, and then stepped closer.

"Is that it?" Lana heard a woman say, her voice lathered with disgust and repulsion.

Lana felt as the human's breath came close, kneeling beside her and leaning in.

After a long silence, she heard the woman's voice as a husky whisper, close, so close, "Can you hear me, Lana? Can you hear me inside that thick skull of yours? I'm still here. Alive and well. All your efforts, all that death and torture for nothing. Neal and I are still thriving, all the more motivated by the sickening, psychopathic bullshit we have had to endure from you." Lana heard the woman's voice break as emotion overtook her, "But my mother isn't, is she, you fucking bitch?" Spittle flew from Madeline's mouth as she spat her fury at Lana's shattered shell.

Madeline breathed deep, John and Quavoce watching her with infinite patience as she let her anger wash over her. After a few moments, Madeline's eyes focused again, grief fueling her rage to a bubbling simmer behind her eyes, a focused, hot wrath in her pupils as she stared at the source of so much sadness.

"We're still here, Lana, or *Princess* Lamati as I hear you are called." Madeline laughed derisively into Lana's prone face. Though it was blind and mute against the barrage of hate facing it, she saw the twitches and spasms of Lana's frustrated fury. She saw them and knew Lana could hear her and the knowledge filled her like a warm medicine.

But nothing compared to the feeling of justice Madeline felt as she hefted the drill she had brought with her. It held a bit made especially for this occasion. A drill bit Madeline would keep in a box on her desk for the rest of the war, as a symbol of their fight, of their victories, and of their losses. Forged of diamonds set into a carbon nanotube bit, it was the hardest substance on earth, harder even than the armored skin of the Agents, and with monstrous satisfaction, Madeline pressed it into Lana's eye.

"Ready, Lana?" said Madeline in a mockingly sweet voice, "I am going to kill you now. Me. Madeline Cavanagh. I am going to drill your fucking brains out. Are you ready for that?

"I hope not.

"I hope you know the depth of your failure.

"I hope that you know that you have achieved none of your goals by coming here.

"I hope you know that everything you have done has only fueled our determination to beat you, and driven good people like John Hunt and Quavoce Mantil to our side.

"They stand with us because of people like you.

"Do you see it now? Do you, Lana? We will survive … not in *spite* of you … but *because* of you."

And with that she leaned into the drill, leaned in with all her weight, and squeezed the thick, plastic trigger. The drill whirred to life, a rending whine in the night, echoed by a warped scream from Lana's lips, and a mountainous shriek of frustration inside her mind. Lana tried to writhe, to escape the drill's incessant surge as it cut through the back of her eye socket and began to encroach on her mind.

But she was pinned down by relentless strength.

Lana Wilson was broken.

Lana Wilson was beaten.

And, as the bit turned her brains to twisted debris, at last, Lana Wilson was dead.

Part 3

Chapter 25: 1979 va

Cold. Black. Limitless vacuum.

Above: a dark void riddled with a billion sparks, white flares too tiny and bright to bring into focus, too distant to perceive.

Below: a seemingly vast orb, bright blue-white, green, swirling vortices, weather, life. Impossibly beautiful, driving awestruck wonder into the most cynical of minds.

The Earth.

Vast, all encompassing. Yet minuscule. Only a spec in our own solar system, completely invisible beyond. Its very fragility and scarcity making it the most prized and valuable entity imaginable. Its stable sun; its temperate, breathable air; its vivacious life; all making it the most precious of oases in the vast, black desert of space.

But what a dichotomy of resource. For while the Earth is, in and of itself, the most precious of jewels, its inhabitants spend lifetimes fighting to claim metals and precious stones that are abundant everywhere else in the solar system and beyond. For the sun's countless other astral satellites are riddled with the noble elements, exotic gasses and the very minerals and crystals that countless men have died to extract from our little orb.

It is another irony, of course, that the same warm embrace holding Earth's inhabitants safely on its surface makes bringing Earth's limited resources out into the vacuum astonishingly difficult.

And so, the solution is obvious. In order to build anything substantial in space, you need raw materials. If you do not want the vast cost and effort of taking them from Earth's surface, you are left with the Moon and the host of asteroids that have what are referred to as 'near-Earth' orbits, circling the sun at the same safe distance that we do.

For even with the completion of SpacePort One, Terminus One, and the tenuous tether that links them, movement of materials on the scale humanity needs in order to build a full-scale battle fleet remains prohibitive.

The four tethers that had finally been connected between Terminus and SpacePort One were now moving people and equipment into orbit at a rate of two hundred tons per month, fifty times the hauling capacity of the defunct Space Shuttle program. And at a thousandth of the cost. They were the bootstraps.

But if we could mine even a single asteroid the size of a football stadium, we would be harnessing a mass of more than two million tons. Moving such an asteroid into orbit would bring more raw materials into play than ten SpacePorts could in a hundred and forty years.

And the average asteroid is made up of massive amounts of frozen oxygen and hydrogen, huge amounts of iron, silicon, and carbon. Not to mention a host of precious metals such as platinum and gold, in quantities the largest Earthbound mine could only dream of.

And so, once the SpacePort was completed, and Terminus One was in permanent, attached orbit, the ever-growing number of scientists involved in Neal's various programs had devoted their collective genius to the possibility of harvesting one or more of the host of asteroids in near-Earth orbit. There had been dissenters in the debate, members of the team who decried the idea as too far-fetched and risky. But in the end, the astrophysicist in Neal had argued them down, and the decision had become not whether to go after an asteroid, but which one.

So the Hubble telescope and its various cousins around the globe had been tasked with studying the band of orbit that might yield a suitable target. Madeline, in her wisdom, had long since tasked a team with proposing a series of vehicles that could go after the meteor they would eventually choose, vehicles whose capabilities now defined the size and distance parameters of the search.

There were many candidates, the band of space in question is proverbially littered with them, but one in particular stood out, a recently captured comet, leashed by the sun's gravitational well to become Asteroid 1979 va.

It was vast, it was close, and it was getting closer, because in nine months, Asteroid 1979 va would reach its aphelion, and come within four million miles of Earth, but a hop and a skip in intra-stellar terms. At only ten times the distance between the Earth and the Moon, this was an opportunity that could not lightly be missed.

Plans were made, the resonance manipulators in Japan were put to work once more, and a crew was sought.

- - -

It had been two months since the final demise of Lana Wilson, and in that time a ship had grown in space. In geosynchronous orbit, the two Orion crew modules that had made up the core of Terminus One had grown into a massive hub at the end of the space elevator.

Attached to them by a series of cables and a flexible corridor barely a meter across was the first spaceship of a new age, the first to be constructed totally in space. It was the first machine that was designed never to touch down on Earth's surface. And the first designed to use the esoteric device that had allowed the Mobiliei to exceed the seemingly unbreakable speed of light. Translated from the Mobiliei language that spawned it, the device was the Accelosphere, the ship was called, simply, New Moon One.

Still thousands of miles below this new ship, a Climber rode one of the tethers up from Rolas Base. It carried materials, fuels, and the final component of the new craft.

Amongst its crew was one of the pivotal minds of Neal's blossoming team, on her way to oversee the final stages of the construction of her brainchild. The cabin was menial, consisting of only the basic amenities needed for the elevator's operators to live on the two-week-long ride up the tether to the Terminus.

They were in the process of building a larger passenger compartment that could be fitted to the Climbers for transporting greater numbers of people, but for now, the focus had been on moving materials for their all-important first project. This was her first ride on the vehicle. She did not mind the inconvenience.

A couple of weeks after completing the elevator's first operational climb, they had sent a fully constructed crew module into space for attachment to the growing Terminus station, and fifteen engineers and astronauts had gone with it. It had then been followed by various pieces of the ship they were constructing and the equipment needed to form those pieces into a cohesive whole.

Finally the true meat of the craft had been hauled up in eight long missions, the eight vast engines that would propel the ship around the sun to catch up with its quarry. Eventually these engines would be detached from each other and arranged around the surface of the asteroid to manhandle it into Earth orbit.

But now the final component of the ship approached, the massive subspace wormhole generator that would form a great sphere around the ship when it was at its most vulnerable, snapping it out of normal space and allowing it to drive forward at phenomenal speed, using first the Earth's and then the sun's primal grips to slingshot the ship after its intended target. Birgit was travelling with this final component: the Accelosphere Generator.

It was incredibly complex, not a design so much as an abstract of science, a convergence of physics, chaos, and imagination that required an artist's mind to bring into the universe. And its construction was only possible because of the breakthroughs already accomplished. It was a compound achievement, another peak along our mountainous journey, a foothill around the base of the Everest we were forcing ourselves to run up, exhausted, excited, exalted.

Because this was a device too complex to have been held in John and Quavoce's memory banks. They had only been able to share the hypothetical possibility, the theoretical madness of it, along with the all important promise that if all went well, if we could find our way through the labyrinthine intricacy of it all, that *it could be done.*

She had succeeded, but only on the back of two other miracles, both born of young Amadeu's brilliance. The first had been the ever more advanced spinal interface. It had been the only way to conceive of and document the micro and macro complexity of the device. And then there had been the still adolescent but nonetheless shockingly capable Artificial Mind that she and Amadeu had seeded from that link, incubated in the substrate, and born into the ether.

She spoke with the AM even now, on the morning of day three of her two-week journey. She would be cut off eventually by the distance, but for now she had access via a small interface module on her neck, which connected via the Climber's own subspace tweeter to the network of subspace communications they continued to build up on and off world.

As though she was in the lab with the young Mind, she communed with it.

Minnie: <good morning, dr. birgit.>

Birgit: 'good morning, minnie.' replied Birgit, via the strange internal voice that she had learned to use.

It was only a part of the way you spoke to the young Mind, as it was capable of communicating directly with both the left and right side of your brain, and, if allowed, it did so at will, often simultaneously.

Minnie: <not far now, your location displacement is going well. soon you will be outside my communications range.>

Birgit's senses swam with a visual sense of her travels so far, a line up and out of the atmosphere, the horizon a flat line of white resolving itself to a curve, and now morphing, so slowly, into a sphere. Minnie was 'talking' with her via images and conceptualized distances as it conveyed its sense of Birgit's physical movement. Minnie had never been out of range with either Amadeu or Birgit since her birth, such was the joy of the subspace tweeter. She did not yet understand the concept.

Birgit: 'yes, minnie, my body and my mind are moving to a new location, in order to support the installation.'

Location, body, movement. Minnie still struggled with the concept that she was not an embodied form like the intelligences that had formed her. She understood it theoretically, as she understood vast swathes of conventional physics, and was even coming to grips with its cousins quantum mechanics and chaos theory. But she was an idiot-savant, or maybe it was just that she was the first of her kind here on Earth. She still struggled with understanding the strange limitations having an embodied form put on her 'Parents,' just as she struggled with how their minds were both impossibly beautiful and complex and yet simultaneously limited in such incongruous ways.

Minnie: <dr. birgit desires proximity, in order to view the fruition of your work, as not all humanity can achieve what birgit can. ?¿>

Minnie was still refining he use of questions, statements, and rhetoric, and she often changed the nature of her statements after the fact.

Birgit: 'i have a desire to see it come to fruition, yes. that is an emotion. and/or I see the benefit of proximity in my ability to connect via this same pure link with the work there, when they need me.'

The combined word 'and/or' appeared like a concept, not a word, one of many eccentricities of mind-language they were still discovering. As Birgit thought ever-so-briefly about that, she felt her right and left brain begin to veer down different conversational avenues, the concept of language being as alien to her intuitive self as an umbrella to a fish.

Minnie: <your proximity is both a desire and a perceived benefit. you are unique, even though you are one of billions.>

Birgit: 'yes, minnie. sometimes we rationalize desires or emotions, and sometimes we develop emotions that support our preferred rational … ' Birgit readied herself to continue their ongoing conversation about the nuances of human decision making, an ongoing debate for both of Minnie's parents, but she could feel her right brain was also engaged with Minnie on another level.

For Minnie was simultaneously communing with Birgit about the Accelosphere's installation, only with Birgit's right brain. Minnie very much enjoyed communing with Birgit's subconscious. That part of Birgit's mind was the closest Minnie had been able to come to understanding the concept of beauty.

Birgit felt it as a disconcerting sense of wonder that she knew meant she was discussing/exchanging concepts with Minnie about a subject near and dear to her heart, but which exceeded the bounds of her left brain's capacity to translate into language. The thought attempted to reunify her mind, and suddenly she was seeing some measure of what her other self was 'saying' to Minnie.

She was envisioning the method of the Accelosphere in image and concept. How the sphere would move the ship into what was fancifully known as hyperspace, where the Einsteinian laws that bound matter were muted, and the leash that held us all under the bounds of relativity was finally breakable.

It was a fascinating area to Birgit, as it would be to anyone brilliant enough to fully grasp it in the coming years, and she had spent night after night communing with Minnie, along with Madeline, Neal, and twenty or so of her more capable and open-minded colleagues, dismantling and reconstructing the theory. For Birgit it had been pure, scientific joy. Trying to understand the variants and apply that theoretical understanding to the very real subspace actuator they had to build.

As she thought of this today on the Climber, her and Minnie's right-brain conversation veered back to the test versions they had built on Earth. Models that, when activated, had vanished just as John and Quavoce had said they would, dropping through floors to reappear a moment later and be caught by waiting canopies below. Eventually a brave astronaut had replaced a disillusioned monkey in the units, and their tests had been complete. The astronaut had spoken of perfect blackness inside the sphere. Of being weightless in relation to his surroundings, even as the orb's mass as a whole was still drawn downward by the earth's gravity.

And so Captain Samuel Harkness of the Royal Air Force had become the first human to move out of what we perceived as normal space, to enter an area that existed only in a fifth and sixth dimension. With all her storied scientific knowledge, Birgit still found it difficult to truly grasp the implications of this.

She and Minnie grappled with mental images, like the diving of a submarine to move underneath the waves, still there, but not visible, but that did not cover anything like the full extent of how this new dimension functioned in relation to ours. Minnie, born as she was from the combined knowledge of Amadeu and Birgit, and lacking the physiological flaws that inadvertently lead to imagination and creativity, was no more capable than Birgit of explaining it fully, though the two of them could come closer than most.

As they communed in the harmonious quasi-language that was the right-brain's codex, Birgit felt the queasy sense of splitting again as Minnie 'spoke' to her left brain once more.

Minnie: <¿maybe I should create an avatar, to allow me to move physically?>

Minnie could feel Birgit's uneasiness at the sudden shift, and computed that she had probably caused it.

Minnie: <i am sorry, dr. birgit.>

Minnie did not mean it.

Birgit: 'no, no, minnie, it is ok. i did say you could do it.'

Nearly everyone else that had 'spoken' with Minnie had quickly demanded she not communicate with both sides of their brain about different things, not only because it was very disconcerting, but also because it implied a level of lack of control over their own thoughts that was profoundly disturbing.

Amadeu got a perverse pleasure out of it, but then he was a very strange young man. For Birgit's part, she allowed it more out of a sense of responsibility for the young mind she and Amadeu had formed. Like a parent allowing a child to ask those uncomfortable questions, or going away for the weekend even though you knew the kids might have a party and wreck the place. You did it because it had been your decision to create this person, not theirs, and you had a responsibility to help them become an independent entity, an adult, no matter how uncomfortable it might sometimes be for you.

In the end, Birgit supposed, she did it out of love.

Which was, of course, another irrational concept Minnie would never truly grasp, and maybe she was the better for it.

Minnie: <you do not want me to understand love?>

And there was that disconcerting feeling again.

Birgit: 'no, minnie, like any parent, i really don't want you to have to go through that, no.'

Birgit laughed, both inside and out, and knew that even though Minnie was still learning, the growing brilliance that was her 'daughter' did get her sense of humor, indeed Minnie shared it, in as much as she had a sense of humor at all. Minnie knew pleasure as a sense of accomplishment, humor as a play on the juxtaposition of reality and perception, and Minnie was capable of 'feeling' it, in her way. Birgit sensed Minnie's reciprocal smile as a warmth in her mind, and their shared amusement was amplified.

- - -

Four hours later, still engaged in conceptual discussions about hyperspace and physical manifestation, Minnie pointed out their location to Birgit.

Minnie: <you are approaching range.>

Their shared experience suddenly leapt outward and downward, and Birgit could see the Climber from the ground, a rising speck moving upward, a smooth bump on the cable, like a meal moving through a preposterously long snake's belly.

As she snapped out of their ongoing game of visualizing dimensional relativity, Birgit was at first queasy and then, just as suddenly, awe-struck by the beauty of *this*, of humanity's new reality.

She realized with a jolt how blasé she had become about the marvelous world they were stepping into. While their motivation may be raw survival, that did not change the fact that Birgit was riding a fusion-powered train into space, carrying with her a machine for generating a gap in reality.

Minnie: <it is impressive.>

Thought Minnie to Birgit, as they studied the view.

Birgit: 'yes, it is. we have achieved a great deal, in a very short time.'

Minnie's sight merged the image from a telescope on the ground with the view coming from Terminus itself, and her own copies of the blueprints of the space station, and the ship that was forming next to it.

The combined conceptualization appeared to Birgit, but it was too much. This moment called for simplicity. Without fear of hurting the young Mind's feelings, Birgit forced the compound image away, returning to the singular view from the ground.

Birgit: 'minnie, every now and then, it can be beneficial to look at it from one perspective at a time.'

Minnie: <¿why?>

Birgit: 'because perspective can be important. understanding becomes more complete when you view things from different angles, not all at the same time, but individually.'

Minnie: <like the perspective of a single human. ¿?>

Birgit: 'exactly. try to *see* this … *just* this.'

Their view focused. As the Climber drew itself up the cable, the full size of the journey became real to Birgit, and, on some level, to Minnie as well. They had all seen images from the ground, telescopes watching the lowering of the cable. And in the distance, as if dangling above the abyss, the construction of the ever-evolving Terminus and the mighty New Moon One.

The station, whose sapling had been the merged hulks of the two Orion modules, had grown to include various living and mechanical modules that sprang from the main mass; rotating wheels set at strange angles to the original hub to provide working and living space for the growing community, each spinning independently to add some modicum of gravity.

Birgit: '¿you see how the station begins to dwarf the original modules? and now, from this perspective, you see how the ship that is forming next to the station dwarfs it all?'

They had built it farther out along the tether that linked them to Earth, using its growing weight as a counterbalance to allow larger loads to be carried by the Climbers ferrying to and from the surface.

Minnie: <the ship is taking shape, i see the beginning of the final design, i see it as it is now, the foundation of its potential. i see it as it is and as it will be ... *if* it will be. plans are not certain. they grow more so as completion nears. ¿this is the perspective of time?>

Birgit felt a wave of pride.

Birgit: 'yes, minnie.'

Two months into their preparations, the ship had indeed truly started to take shape, and its potential was already clear.

Birgit: 'and now i see it for its uniqueness. it is not like any ship we have dared to attempt before. it is an amalgamation of sheer power. ¿what is this the perspective of?'

Minnie: <context¿!?>

Birgit did not reply. She knew Minnie could feel her approval, and she felt Minnie's response. The image of the ship became loaded with new meaning now, as Minnie followed Birgit's line of thought. Each of its eight massive engine shells now gleamed with the vast fusion power that would be their final roles, not as certainty, but as potential. She felt that power, set within the shielded reservoirs of frozen oxygen, nitrogen, and hydrogen that would be their fuel sources, and it was seen as new, as if for the first time.

Now Minnie went further. Focusing on one engine, she understood it within the context of its purpose. The shell outlined the massive cigar shape each engine would form, over three hundred feet long and nearly sixty feet wide at their waists, pointed at one end, and open at the other, and black as night along its entirety. The eight engines were arranged in a circle, each of their smooth, deadly looking bodies pointing toward the sky like a vast Stonehenge.

But they were also each independent and detachable, existing as separate entities linked by a network of nanotube spars to a central, tubular nexus, itself as long and as wide as each of the engines that surrounded it. This tube was currently empty. The back half, level with the exhaust nozzles of the eight black engines around it, would contain the living quarters of the ship's crew. The middle of the central cylinder would eventually house the Accelosphere Generator that would envelope the entire ship in its protective shield.

And eventually the whole was to be capped by a complex array of sensors and the powerful laser armament that would take out any particles the ship would no doubt encounter when maneuvering alongside and tethering to the asteroid.

The Earth was already travelling at over sixty-seven thousand miles per hour on its annual journey around the sun, but the ship needed to complete that journey in less than half that time. Some of that saving would come from cutting the corner on its journey around the sun, but the ship would still reach speeds measured in hundreds of thousands of miles per hour. If all went well, it would catch the asteroid in just over three months from departure, giving it five more months to decelerate the massive rock into Earth's orbit.

All this raced through Birgit's mind for the thousandth time as the Climber approached the range of the Earthbound subspace tweeters through which their connection was possible.

Minnie: <you are here/there.>

Birgit: 'i am here, *you* are *there.*'

Minnie: <this is not like other good-byes. you go, not to sleep, but away. i am not happy at this. it is not pleasant.>

Birgit was touched, and found herself more affected by the coming departure than she had thought she would be.

Birgit: 'yes, but it is not permanent. loss is not pleasant but we have a saying: absence makes the heart grow fonder. the heart in this case ...'

Minnie: <it is metaphorical, yes. you are saying i will enjoy communing with you more when you return. i think this is true. but not enough to offset this displeasure. from my perspective, your leaving is not beneficial.>

Birgit: 'you do not know it, but you are actually quite funny, minnie, and very sweet. all the more so because it is unintentional.'

Minnie: <i intended the juxtaposition.>

Birgit: 'yes, minnie. i know you did.'

Minnie: <goodbye, birgit.>

Birgit: 'goodbye, minnie.'

The emotion she felt from Birgit was powerful in the moments before disconnection. It would be the subject of much conjecture by Minnie over the coming weeks. It was alien to her, but it was also somehow analogous to a sense she had when she contemplated Birgit. Like all children, she was learning that which her parents knew she must, but feared nonetheless.

Chapter 26: Standard Procedure

Thousands of miles below them, and far, far away to the northwest, deep in the forgotten heart of Asia, Lieutenant Malcolm Granger sat back, his feet parked on the desk in front of him, while he flicked through a copy of a cheap but still disconcertingly appealing adult magazine that a friend had sent him from England.

Life on the diplomatic compound in Ashgabat had returned to its usual ambulatory pace after he had been dispatched to help a mysterious group of Americans across the border into Turkmenistan months ago. He had smuggled the strange group into the British embassy, and kept them there for a few days. But then they had departed, taking the discombobulated young girl they'd had in tow away with them, and so life had returned to normal. The whole episode proving to be but a small island of excitement in a sea of tedium.

Looking back on it now it was a blur, but if Malcolm had couched any doubts as to the incident's importance, then two notable conversations he'd had immediately afterward had dispelled them. The first had been with the British ambassador himself, who had assured Malcolm that he had done the right thing, but this was necessarily "delicate" and should thus remain 'under wraps,' replete with a tap on the nose, a-la cliché.

The second had been more direct, and from an even more surprising source. The British Army Liaison had dropped by, a man commonly suspected to be a member of MI6 by pretty much everyone at the embassy. The fact that this was such a widespread assumption may have seemed incongruous, considering Colonel Huxley's supposedly clandestine position, but despite Hollywood and Pinewood's efforts to convince us otherwise, it turned out that in reality most spies were well known by both sides. Well, if not known, then suspected at the very least. But as long as they were never caught in the act, it remained a play of wits, a carefully constructed game played where the players were careful to stay within the boundaries of international diplomacy.

If they stepped into touch or were caught offside it was another matter, but as long as they remained subtle, their very prominence made them untouchable without tangible proof, and the same applied to their counterparts on the other side of whatever net they were tasked with peering over.

And so, over a seemingly innocent cup of tea in the officer's mess, a seemingly innocuous Colonel Huxley had reinforced the ambassador's warning, and elaborated a little further on Britain's involvement in the smuggling of Quavoce Mantil, Major Toranssen, Captain Falster, and a young girl named Banu.

Knowing that the bomber downed over Iran only a few days beforehand had been identified as American, it was suspected, correctly as it turned out, that all US assets in neighboring nations were being watched closely by agents of Iran's intelligence service.

And so, as a way of aiding the foursome without alerting the Iranians, the British had been involved. In fact, the colonel would have gone himself if he hadn't known that he was also under surveillance by Iranian agents, though for a thoroughly different reason.

With the incident behind them, and Malcolm having been proven reliable by force of circumstance, Malcolm had since become one of the few people on the base that the colonel could somewhat trust. And so, in the intervening few months, Malcolm and Colonel Huxley had spent many an evening at the bar in the officer's mess.

Thus, Malcolm was not as surprised as he should have been when the colonel interrupted his review of cheap English pornography with a phone call.

"Malcolm, it's Nick, where are you?" the tone was curt, and Malcolm sat up, glancing around his small room, even though he knew he was alone.

"Err, in the barracks. Why, what's …" Malcolm began, but he was cut off by a hurried response from Colonel Huxley.

"Meet me at my office in civvies, five minutes." And without further ado, the line went dead.

Malcolm stood. Something in the colonel's tone screamed alarm bells in his head. He was already in his evening clothes: jeans and a grey T-shirt. Now he quickly shouldered his holster and grabbed his standard issue P226, removing its trigger lock and checking its magazine before clipping the gun into the holster and pulling on a thick jacket. He grabbed his Consular ID and ran from the room.

He was at Nick's door within two minutes of being called. He knocked and then went to open it, but it was locked. A moment and a click later, and it opened. Nick wordlessly waved Malcolm into his office. The room was a small windowless affair, in the middle of the building. Malcolm's attention was taken by the host of equipment that had materialized on Nick's desk: guns, radios, IDs.

Nick locked the door behind them, and then switched on his stereo. Malcolm then noticed his friend was holding a small, silenced Walther P99 Compact, certainly not standard issue, and he became even more concerned.

Nick stepped up to Malcolm, the music masking his words as he spoke into Malcolm's ear, "Keep your voice low." said Nick, rather redundantly, "Something is happening, and I am afraid we are going to need to get out of here, right now."

Malcolm tensed, but Nick went on, "I've just gotten word that Kazakhstan has signed an accord with Moscow and joined what is apparently being called the New People's Federation."

Malcolm's stomach knotted. Kazakhstan was by far the largest of the former soviet satellite states in the region. That it had voluntarily joined the burgeoning totalitarian republic that had once been Russia was next to impossible. As impossible as the former Russian president inexplicably committing suicide during the military coup three months ago.

"Jesus, Nick, what do you think will happen here?" said Malcolm.

"It gets worse." said Nick, "We have unconfirmed reports that Uzbekistan and Tajikistan have done the same thing."

Malcolm's heart started racing, "How unconfirmed?"

"Well, we haven't *confirmed* that Nessy is a load of bollocks, either, but we're pretty confident. Listen, I have been ordered to fetch a specific person, see to it that they are secure, and get them off base. Normally I would probably have tapped you for sec. detail anyway, but it turns out you are the person I am supposed to be fetching. So it's just going to be you and me."

"Me?" said Malcolm. He would have been more than a little surprised if Nick had tapped him to help with getting some sensitive personage to safety. Honored, but surprised. That *he* should be the one that needed saving was not surprising so much as disturbing.

"Apparently your involvement with the incident at the border a few months ago may make you 'of interest' to the Russians, and I have been informed that, if possible, I am to get you out. I *was* going to disguise you and smuggle you out with the ambassador's immediate family, but they have already been refused access to the airport. The Turkmen government says they want to 'escort' them to safety, so I think we are going to have to go off reservation."

Malcolm looked into the eyes of the other man, seeking an answer to a question that was nagging at him, "And if you *can't* get me out?"

"Let's not get into what my orders are then, but it won't come to that." Nick's frankness was unsettling, and yet somehow it also negated the threat as well. Malcolm knew that a bullet in the back of the head was the likely option if he was indeed 'of interest' and could not be kept out of enemy hands. And if the Russians wanted him, and Malcolm could think of no reason why Nick would make that up, then a bullet in the head would probably be preferable to what they would do to him if they got hold of him.

That still left the obvious question of why the fuck he was so important, and that Malcolm couldn't begin to guess. Nick sensed his colleague's growing confusion as fertile soil for panic and spoke firmly.

"Look, Malcolm, I am going to do everything I can to get you out of here. And I can do quite a few things, trust me. I make you this promise: if we get out of this, I will tell you everything I know about why you might be of interest, which isn't much but it may answer some questions. Unfortunately, knowing that now would only make you even more valuable to them, so I am afraid, for now, you are just going to have to trust me."

He looked at the man, "Malcolm, you can trust me. I'm with you all the way on this. OK?"

He looked a question at Malcolm, 'are we good?'

But it was not as if he was offering the man many options, and without much of a choice Malcolm shrugged and nodded slightly, prompting Nick to go on.

In truth, Malcolm's only crime was having seen the face of the Agent formerly known as Shahim Al Khazar, and two of his accomplices. Ayala couldn't be sure, but it was possible Mikhail Kovalenko and Pei Leong-Lam still didn't know for certain that Shahim Al Khazar was alive, let alone fighting for the other side. If, or rather *when* the Russians arrived in Ashgabat to complete the job they had started earlier that evening in Kazakhstan, they would rifle the embassy, its computers, and any supporting documentation from the Turkmen governmental agencies, and would eventually find records of how the three Americans sighted briefly in Iran had escaped its grasp.

Knowing discovery of Malcolm's role might be imminent, Ayala had initiated efforts to extract the soldier who had been Shahim's unwitting liaison back into the Western world, or, if necessary, have the leak stemmed in other ways.

"OK, first off, let's get your jacket off." said Nick.

Malcolm resisted mostly out of surprise, as Nick began manhandling him out of his clothing.

"They're going to want you alive," said Nick, "so our only advantage is that if they find out who you are then they probably won't shoot to kill."

Nick thrust a suit of body armor at Nick, not of the quality now being employed by Ayala's private army, but its Kevlar plates would absorb much of the punch from a body shot, and the woven ballistic fabric that linked them would resist even the most ardent blade. This was followed by a specialized holster, into which a second silenced Walther P99 Compact fitted smoothly.

"If we have to kill anyone, it will be subtly." said Nick, as Malcolm arranged himself in his new armor.

Five minutes later the two men were walking off the base, past the guard, a code word slipped to the sergeant at the gate making him enter two erroneous names in the logbook as they passed.

And so it went.

As swiftly as the former USSR had faltered and collapsed, the New People's Federation spread its wings once again and enveloped the southern Bloc nations that had freed themselves from its grasp only thirty years beforehand. Many had questioned how Russia could maintain its hotly contested occupation of Pakistan from so far away, even with the tacit approval and permission of the intervening states of Kazakhstan, Uzbekistan, and Tajikistan. But now that approval was tacit no more.

In a flash, the governments of those three massive nations had signed accords binding them to the new Russian Union. The announcements came almost as one, late in the evening. After their respective governing bodies had supposedly convened for the evening, they were taken into 'protective custody' and their congressed voices were co-opted to give blessing to the sham. The halfhearted military interventions that the local armed forces were able to muster were quickly squashed, with blistering speed and efficiency.

Meanwhile, Nick and Malcolm walked to a nearby parking lot and retrieved a car Nick kept there for covert purposes, its plates registered to an unsuspecting farmer outside the city. As they drove out into the night, a force was already descending onto the city, a dark force. They came without warning, and took up carefully coordinated positions.

By morning it was over, and Russia once again owned every patch of land from the Caspian Sea in the west to the border with China in the east, and from border with Iran in the south all the way north to the Arctic. Only a brief strip of mountainous Afghanistan kept them from opening up a clean route all the way to the Indian Ocean. For now.

Chapter 27: Private Investigation

"How, in the name of all that is holy, could this happen again?" Neal's voice was quiet and harsh, smoldering like his mood. The table in his office was surrounded by a hasty gathering of his inner circle. General Milton sat to his left, briskly dressed in fatigues, his hair slicked down against his head with the sweat of an interrupted dawn run. Admiral Terence Cochrane sat to the general's left, a stern expression sitting like a mask on his face. Quavoce also sat at the table, his exterior calm, as he listened to the conversation and simultaneously communed about the news's implications with John Hunt, via subspace, far away at the Research Group's hub.

The last member of the impromptu committee was Admiral Hamilton, clearly uncomfortable with this new turn, and shifting slightly in his seat as though sitting on the hot leather of a car left too long in the sun. Neal's eyes lifted from the table and came to rest on the American admiral. After scrutinizing him a moment, his stare flicked to Admiral Cochrane.

"Admiral Cochrane," he said, "what is the news from London? Have there been any further communications?"

The admiral shook his head, straightening his back before meeting Neal's intense gaze. "Just the system-wide communication to intensify our standing guard at all international facilities. Informally, I believe our forces in Afghanistan have been moved to battle ready status, and we are in talks with our allies in Eastern Europe about what actions we will and will not support if the expansion continues."

"That is something, I suppose," said Neal. "Have there been any official announcements from Kiev or Minsk?"

The question was directed at the table in general, and after a moment Quavoce responded. He and John Hunt were monitoring the internet via their private relays.

"Not yet, Neal," Quavoce said. "The Indians have joined the EU and the United States in openly condemning the news and calling for the release of the 'democratically elected leaders' of the affected states. Meanwhile, reports from Eastern Europe confirm significant troop mobilizations in Estonia and Lithuania to join those already reported in Poland, Ukraine, Latvia, and Belarus. As yet, none of those nations are saying anything openly, probably to avoid aggravating the Russians. But they are clearly bracing for worse to come."

Admiral Cochrane added, "I can confirm that our ambassadors in most of those nations have been summoned to meet with each nation's leaders, which would be a step in the right direction if we weren't seeing signs the Russian ambassadors were as well. They are apparently mimicking the party line about 'voluntary federation,' so no surprises there."

Neal nodded, and returned his gaze to the table in front of him, "... no surprises ..." he said quietly, but in a tone lathered with sarcasm.

He waited. They were still missing one person. The person who had called him to let him know the news in the first place, and as he paused she eventually arrived, slipping furtively into the room, and closing the door gently behind her.

Neal was facing her, but those that had their backs to Ayala were surprised when Neal suddenly greeted her.

"Welcome. I trust you have been plumbing your channels for further information?"

The room turned to Ayala while she pulled a seat up to the table between Quavoce and Admiral Cochrane. She placed a laptop on the table, and then surveyed the group, her eyes pausing momentarily to meet Barrett's. They said simply: hello darling, sorry for ignoring you, but this is business. He knew the expression well.

"The information my colleagues have for me so far is ... disquieting," she said, deliberately. "Not so much in its content, but in its lack thereof. As with the invasion of Pakistan four months ago, we were taken very much by surprise here. And, as with the coup in Russia that started all this madness, our assets in all of the countries in question have gone silent since the incident began."

Nods of begrudged acceptance bobbed a couple of times around the table, though not without frustration. They knew things were not right in Russia, but in the last few months they had made slow inroads, begun to open tiny gaps in the Steel Curtain. Progress had been slow, goodness knows. Glacially so, but it had been progress nonetheless, and it had given the illusion of a weakening of whatever fist gripped both Russia's and China's political throats.

But it was fast becoming apparent that it had only been an illusion, and Neal could not help but feel they were being played. He was not alone, and for those others in the room that had witnessed the work of the Mobiliei Agents firsthand, it was even more disquieting to imagine just how bad things might actually be in Moscow and Beijing.

"Is there *any* news, Ayala?" asked Neal, not really expecting a positive reply.

"Not from the new NATO assets in Russia, no, not that sheds any real light on how they pulled this off. But I did manage to reach one asset onsite in Ashgabat and warn him, before the curtain came down. Given his advanced warning, I can only hope that he may have slipped passed their net, and might be seeking evac at some point in the not too distant future. I'll not know more for a few days, but if he avoids standard routes, as I have ordered him to do, he may be able to survive, at least for a little while.

"And if he was able to avoid the initial blitz, he should have a friend of yours with him, Mr. Mantil. A Mr. Granger, from Turkmenistan."

The two glanced at each other, and Quavoce nodded, while a flash of mild surprise flowed between him and John Hunt. John was as aware of the events in Iran and Turkmenistan as Quavoce was, literally. They had gotten in the habit of sharing their memories in their entirety, to allow closer cooperation. As they both recalled those memories, they both thought of the man who had met Quavoce at the border after his bloody flight across the skies and sands of the Middle East.

Oblivious to this discourse, Neal took a moment to absorb Ayala's comments, and then spoke, "Well, my friends, it seems like we have no choice anymore. This is too much. We have waited long enough to become involved. Too long. We have waited for our sponsors to negotiate access for Ayala and her team to go and hunt the two remaining Agents, but I simply cannot see that happening anytime soon, and we cannot afford to delay further.

"I think it is time we intervene in efforts to find out what the hell is going on in Russia."

Admiral Cochrane was the first to speak up, but Admiral Hamilton was just as alarmed by Neal's statement, and only respect for the British officer held his tongue as the other man started to speak, "Dr. Danielson, goodness knows I appreciate and share your frustration, but to order unilateral action here is, I am afraid, not an option you have. I can tell you that Great Britain, along with her allies in Europe and America ..." he glanced at Admiral Hamilton who nodded once, firmly, "is using every asset at its disposal to move the diplomatic needle with the Russian and Chinese governments.

"To say the issue is delicate would be a gross understatement, and we simply cannot have outside parties taking unsanctioned action."

Neal met Admiral Cochrane's stare. He was aware Admiral Hamilton was also staring at him, no doubt waiting to see whether the British admiral's indignation would be enough to dissuade him, or if the American would need to add his own authority to it as well.

Neal saw he would not win this argument tonight and changed tacts, saying in a calmer tone, "Very well. But as you say, your governments are using 'every asset at their disposal,' so maybe we should at least discuss ways the unique assets at *our* disposal might be of use in this situation?"

He held Terence Cochrane's icy stare, and eventually the man took a deep breath, allowing reason in with the air.

"Of course," said the British man eventually, "I am sure Admiral Hamilton and I can help communicate any ideas you have to our grateful governments."

The room settled a bit, Ayala smiling without humor at the passing of the moment. Neal looked at her first, as she had expected, and she was ready when he said, "OK then, I would like to hear ideas from each of you about how we can best support the effort to get better eyes on Russia. Ayala, seeing as you have a better handle than most on this, maybe you can offer up some thoughts?"

Ayala got said thoughts in order and then began, "The truth is that in order to gain a better understanding of what is happening here we need a long-term solution. The assets that were originally lost in the Moscow coup three months ago took years to get into place, some of them had been on the ground for decades. Nothing we can do will replace that kind of network overnight, which may go some way to explaining the ... mixed success of our colleagues in MI6 and the CIA have had in reestablishing a clear line of sight into Russia's movements.

"So the issue becomes less how to help build a strong intelligence network, and more the need for reliable information, *any* reliable information, *as soon as possible.*

"To that end, I would like to propose something more intrinsic. Two key things have changed recently that give us options that the original builders of our spy networks in Russia did not have. Firstly, our relationship with Russia is no longer dependent on even a modicum of diplomatic or economic cooperation. In fact, it is probably more strained now than even the height of the Cold War. With that in mind, information gathering methods that would have been diplomatically untenable in peacetime are now back on the table. Covert incursion, over-flying Russian airspace, all these should, I think, have become options once more."

The two admirals did not necessarily like the direction this was going, but knew that it was best to listen to and relay the suggestions from this group, rather than preemptively shut them down. They were a growing power, both politically and militarily, and to discount them wholesale would be both shortsighted and possibly dangerous.

"The second thing that has changed is you," Ayala said, nodding at Quavoce, "your arrival has, among many things, brought a series of technological advances that I imagine can aid us as we look to infiltrate the New Peoples' Federation." she said the title with all the derisive sarcasm it begged for.

"So, gentlemen, what does this mean?" Ayala then said, "For starters, I would like to suggest upgrading existing satellite networks with higher grade equipment. Using the facilities here at SpacePort One, the process of getting new equipment into orbit should be relatively easy."

Neal's expression at this could only be described as a scowl as he considered the delays to his many programs. Programs essential to the building of Earth's fledgling defense systems.

Seeing his disquiet, Ayala took on a conciliatory tone, "I am aware that upgrading Earth-facing information gathering mechanisms is not part of our plan, but I can work with Madeline, Birgit, and their teams to minimize the impact to our schedule. Given the scale of Russia's actions, we cannot deny the possibility they have the potential to put an ever greater strain on our ability to execute to that schedule anyway, if we do not do something to rein them in."

Neal nodded at this, begrudgingly, clearly deep in thought, but he did nod, and so Ayala went on, "Next, I would like to propose that a series of small teams, four to six Spezialists each, at most, be sent to Russia in order to gather information on how they are maintaining such strict control there. Maybe also to connect with any organic resistance force that may be trying to reestablish some form of democratic process."

She finished with her ideas and the room entered a conversational drought, desiccated by the dry moods of all present. At best the two admirals could be said to be nodding politely. Neal took the floor, "Though I take great issue with taking up elevator cargo capacity with this, I cannot deny the logic behind such moves. As for sending in small recon teams of your shock troops, or Spezialists, as you call them, I must say that seems like the very least we can do."

He looked at the two admirals, knowing they represented the more tractable end of the otherwise immovable bureaucratic objects he was trying to provoke into action. And in truth, he was not putting too much stock in his ability to convince even them, "Too much time has passed since we have had a reliable information source inside Russia, and I don't see how we can wait any longer for national agencies to get a real handle on things." He paused for breath, and the room waited while the two sides faced each other.

Ayala, Barrett, and Quavoce watched them. It was the age-old adage: the irresistible force versus the immovable object. But in this case one would have to prove tractable, however reluctantly, and anyone who knew Neal and the team of spies, officers, Agents and scientists who had been with him since the beginning, could see all too clearly that it was not going to be him.

And so he continued carefully, saying, "Were this to be approved, the obvious thought is to use some of your security force for the job, Ayala. Though as I think about it, I worry about their tools falling into the hands of whoever is behind all this. That leads us to a more conventionally armed force, though I fear they would suffer the same fate as the plethora of assets our political allies have already sent.

"We could, I suppose, send in John and Quavoce to reconnoiter the situation." said Neal, as if thinking aloud. The room all turned as one to the present representative of Neal's pair of potent pals, and Quavoce met their gaze with a patent willingness to wade knee-deep into any shitpile deemed necessary. Everyone in the room, including the admirals, seemed to consider for a moment how useful the two men's abilities would be in this situation.

But then Neal shook his head, "No, without more information on what we are facing I simply cannot risk you two in there." The room looked disconcerted by what this implied, and Quavoce was about to make his and John's willingness to help out clearer, but Neal waved him down, and the general stepped in to reinforce the point.

"I agree, Neal." said Barrett, "With Mikhail Kovalenko and Pei Leong-Lam still at large, we must assume that they are at the core of whatever dysfunctional power base has developed in Russia. That said, of course, I can also see a way in which that fact works to our advantage."

Ayala looked puzzled, and Neal quirked his head in curiosity. Barrett shrugged and then went on, "Well, if we assume that the remaining Agents are at the heart of this, then the danger of equipping an incursion team with our latest equipment is really mitigated, as the Russians could not realistically learn anything from our people or their equipment that Mikhail or Pei could not already teach them."

"Barrett, my friend, you are absolutely right," said Neal with a deeper satisfaction than even he had expected, "Which means we can … and *should* send in an advance party armed with the tools necessary to get the job done properly."

"Gentlemen," he said now to the most senior men in the room, "I would be grateful if you would pass this offer, actually this request, up your chains of command, with all the impetus you can give it."

They nodded, and they would indeed pass it on, even if they both harbored reservations about the wisdom of such action without proper military oversight.

"Meanwhile," continued Neal, "Ayala, if you haven't already, can you please draft plans for the missions should they be approved and submit them to this group for review. Please include recommendations on incursion points and sortie routes."

She nodded. She already had just such a plan in its infancy, and was busy picking out the best operatives to lead it in her mind.

"Now, to the next point." Neal took a breath, and then pressed on, the room waiting to hear his next thoughts. "It seems wise in the face of such events to start escalating efforts to equip all our forces as fully as possible. I know Amadeu and his team have been making good progress on the spinal interface, and we have been waiting to build some of the more complex machines John and Quavoce have provided us the designs for until we had the software we would need to use them. Well, I fear we can wait no longer to start pushing here. I will talk to Amadeu and see what can be done to up the tempo of our efforts with Minnie and her development of the AI progeny we are going to need. I will also order my other teams to prioritize completion of the Resonance Dome."

The room was particularly intrigued by Neal's offhand reference to the mysterious Resonance Dome. He was referring to the massive resonance chamber that was going to be used to build such huge devices as the Skalms, already infamous among those few people who had seen the designs. Admiral Hamilton gave voice to this curiosity, "The Resonance Dome," he said, treading carefully in the face of Neal's instantly wary look. "I cannot say I do not appreciate the need to keep its location secret, even from the bulk of the taskforce here at Rolas, but maybe it is time that those of us in this room knew where the first Dome is being constructed?"

Neal stared at him. With support from America beginning to dwindle under the duress of its internal injuries, and Europe ever more fearful and distracted by Russia's posturing, it had taken everything he had to maintain the force strength around Rolas necessary to ward off any attack by Pei, Mikhail, and whoever's strings they were pulling.

But the Dome could not be built here as well. It was simply too big. The operations already in place at Rolas were already too all encompassing and widespread. To add to that the massive, acre-sized dome and its ancillary power sources would have been all but prohibitive.

But that had not been all. Even with all the defenses they had put in place around Rolas, it was still not impregnable. Nothing was. They had built a mesh of gunpowder and lead that would tear any attacking force to shreds, and they'd had to. You could not hide a cable into space. And because of that the base at Rolas had a 50,000-mile-high arrow pointing straight at it.

If the impossible happened, if an attack succeeded, they could, in theory, rebuild the elevator. But Neal knew that given what he had been forced to promise, beg, and cajole in order to get this far that they could not rebuild the Dome. Not in his lifetime anyway.

For the Dome represented the biggest investment the combined allied nations had made to date, by a massive factor. So much, in fact, that Neal had been forced to hide its true expense from even his closest friends and allies. No one but he knew what he had done in order to secure the hundreds of tons of gold required. India alone, the world's biggest single consumer of gold, and the Dome's biggest contributor, believed itself the presumptive owner and controller of the Dome once it was complete. A particularly thorny issue given that America, Germany, Japan, Brazil, and South Africa were operating under the same inference, one he had carefully fostered with each in turn.

It had been, at its heart, a con. One that would eventually be discovered. A loan mortgaged on the back of the space elevator's spectacular success, and on countless promises of power, influence, and technological supremacy. They had given much in return, believing they were each the majority contributor, but even India's massive contribution had, in fact, been only a fraction of the whole. And the negotiations had been moot anyway. Neal never intended to give over control of the Dome, not under any circumstances short of an improbable victory over the coming Armada, maybe not even then.

He faced the room and they sat in silence, waiting for his reply. They wanted to know. How could they not? So much depended on the Dome. And it was not even going to be the only one. But it would be the first. And it would be the only one on Earth using earthbound resources. The second would be built using the materials they hoped to glean from Asteroid 1979 va, and as such was still more than a year away, at least.

"Yes," he said eventually, with a deep inhale, "the Resonance Dome. You know why I have kept its location a secret. Even the team working on it doesn't know what they are involved in, and has been sequestered until its completion anyway. It has …" he paused a moment, looking for the words, "… posed some problems in getting it completed, but it has been worth it, of that I have no doubt."

He looked at them. It was difficult for him to trust them, even them, such was the depth of his vulnerability here. He was so close. Once it was done, and once the first Skalm was complete, he would have the ability to truly defend the secret site.

"I can tell you it is nearly done. And I can tell you that once it is, I will reveal its location to this group. But other than that, I am afraid I cannot go further, not yet."

He looked from one to the other, dwelling perhaps a moment too long on Ayala. He was no fool. It was hard for him to believe that, even with all of his precautions, he had managed to evade Ayala's curiosity on this. But her skill was also her promise. If she could be relied upon to have cracked his network somehow, then she could be relied upon to keep it quiet as well, for the same inherent reason.

They talked further. They discussed the secret of the Dome's location as a matter of course, politely courting Neal to concede it, and perhaps occasionally calling on their governments' contributions as reason for their need to know. But Neal had refused requests to oversee or at least visit the site from far more important people than these men. No. He must remain absolute. Nothing else was more important.

As they eventually filtered out, hands shaken, confirmations of action items exchanged, Ayala turned to Neal and locked eyes with him. They did not speak. She was telling him that she knew, that she knew his secret, and had for some time. He nodded once.

Then a flick of her eyes at the notes she had made on their intelligence gathering options asked another question. His second nod was all she needed on that subject as well. She knew what he wanted her to do. They could, indeed, wait no longer to move on Mikhail and Pei. It was time to go to Russia, permission or no. She left without another word. She had much to do.

Chapter 28: Nick at Night

The predawn air was cool and invigorating. Nick and Malcolm had started moving again not long after midnight. They had left the remote spot where they had parked to get some sporadic sleep, and cautiously driven the last few miles to the coast.

They had kept their headlights off, the nationwide curfew that had been imposed being both a curse and a blessing. For it allowed them to pass unbidden through sleeping towns, but left them hopelessly exposed if they were spotted from above.

They were close now, so close that it was better to risk a bit more driving at night rather than delay their escape another day. After the first couple of days spent carefully navigating the area surrounding the capital, they had begun their long, dangerous journey toward the Caspian Sea.

They had been flooded by mixed emotions at the sight of the first small fishing towns that dotted the shore of the Turkmenbasy estuary. For it was a long, shallow waterway, and none of the tiny boats that fed these tiny towns would be able to make it across the great sea that lay ahead.

So they had been forced to bypass these small communities and their barely seaworthy fishing boats, continuing on in constant fear, on toward the large town of Turkmenbasy itself. To the first town that truly sat on the coast of the vast Caspian Sea.

The great sea had once been the stuff of legend, indistinguishable to the burgeoning kingdoms that bordered it from an ocean, such was its breadth. It would be thousands of years until the first great empires had grown large enough to see that it was, unlike its oceanic counterparts, entirely landlocked. But even without link to the world's great oceans, the Caspian remained a sea that divided the continent, from Russia to Iran in the north and south, and from Azerbaijan to the former Stannic nations in the west and east.

It was the largest lake in the world, but the wars and political intrigue that still plagued its bordering nations made it as fraught with international tension as any patch of water short of the Mediterranean. Now it was the fishing boats, plying their trade on the salty waters, which were at the heart of that conflict. They sought sturgeon and its famous unborn progeny for consumption and export. Russia and Iran may have cornered the international market for caviar, but their neighbors caught and consumed it as much as any Caspian fisherman did, and Nick and Malcolm had driven long and hard to get to the capital of Turkmenistan's fishing trade.

Now, with the first light of dawn penetrating the night's blackness, they clambered across a muddy bank to a small, wooden rowboat, the mud chilling their shins and filling their boots. Racing against the night's dissipation, they helped each other into the tiny boat and shoved off into the night, grabbing oars and paddling for one of the large fishing boats anchored in the small harbor.

There was a relatively modern passenger and train ferry between Turkmenbasy and the far port of Baku, in Azerbaijan. Ordinarily lacking any stringent security, this would have been Nick's first choice to get out of the country, but Ayala's orders had expressly marked this as one of the 'known' routes, and all things known had become anathema since given Russia's newfound and bloody efficiency.

So they rowed out to the huddle of fishing boats in the bay and climbed aboard one, kicking the small boat away into the last of the night. Someone would no doubt be heartbroken to find their small but precious rowboat gone from the shore in the morning, but that was not high on Nick and Malcolm's list of concerns.

They were dirty, three days' sweat trapped within their thick bulletproof vests, their shoes filled with tidal mud and all the stench of a long flight across a once friendly nation, now suddenly filled with enmity. And now they were in the last, but by no means least dangerous part of a journey, with more than enough opportunities to die still ahead of them.

Despite the terrifying trek they had undertaken, though, they had also been faced with a host of wonders as well, for they had glimpsed the beasts that hunted them, and it had shaken them to the very core.

Lying in silence in their car during the seemingly endless nights of their three-day flight, they had seen the strangely shaped fighters as they flew over the towns. They had seen the speed with which some sliced across the sky. Then they had watched in fear and amazement as others moved slowly and deliberately over various towns the two men had hidden in along the way, like circling hawks hovering over cowering prey.

The strange planes had been mostly dismissed by the locals as yet another example of the potent technology of the world's superpowers, most notably the resurgent Russian Federation that had so recently subsumed their ex-democratic nation. But to the educated eyes of Nick and Malcolm they had been something far more disturbing.

This was nothing that any armed force they knew of had access to. This was something wholly new. It went some way toward accounting for the speed with which the New People's Federation had spread its influence over the Stannic world, and to the urgency with which Nick had been ordered to get Malcolm out of the country. Taking liberal notes as the planes passed overhead, Nick had tried to document what he was seeing, and then they had tried to ignore the rising feeling of panic the deadly looking craft instilled in them both.

Now, days later, lying in the hold of a forty-year-old fishing junker with an equally old, nine-horsepower diesel engine, they waited for the ship's crew to come aboard and take her out to sea. When the crew arrived, Nick and Malcolm would wait until they had steered their ship out onto the Caspian's vast waters before emerging from their hiding spots.

Hopefully they would be able to overpower the crew and coerce the ship's skipper to steer a new course for the sea's far coast. Hopefully, the ever-expanding Russian empire would not have extended its reach to Azerbaijan before they got there. They lay in wait as they heard the telltale thud of a boat pulling alongside and boots clambering expertly aboard with their equipment and supplies, their loud voices brimming with ignorance of the coming confrontation.

- - -

As Nick and Malcolm tried so desperately to escape Russia's grasp, there were those that were trying to get into it. Hektor Gruler, formerly of the German elite Spezialkrafte, stood in the center of a large, empty hangar, waiting for his team to arrive. They were scheduled to deploy the following morning. He was wearing his battleskin, as he nearly always did these days, getting used to the way it moved, teaching his muscles to accept the battle armor as part of him, becoming one with the abilities it gave him.

He had been working on his balance, fine-tuning his muscle memory to account for his augmented limbs' vastly increased strength. Bending, he pressed his fists against the floor of the hangar and hoisted his weight onto them, not in a swift movement, but pushing his feet into the air in a smooth extension, as though stretching, focusing on maintaining tight control on his limbs as his weight shifted. Upright, he moved his weight to just his right arm, and extended his left arm out to the side, feeling the massive power of his suited body as he easily absorbed his mass on one balled fist.

"Vie gehen sie, Hektor?" the other German member of their team asked as he approached. Niels was not quite as practiced in the new suits as Hektor, having only joined Ayala's shock troops after their base of operations had moved to SpacePort One. He was no slouch, no, he was an incredibly skilled martial artist, as they all were, but he was still unlearning long practiced training; reprogramming his reflexive responses to accommodate and complement his battleskin's capabilities.

Hektor had been one of the first to use the most recent evolution of the suits, including the spinal interfaces being refined by Amadeu's team that allowed them to control their sensors and onboard weapons systems directly. This left his arms and legs free to maximize the potential of the suit's potent limbs: carrying heavier weapons and moving faster and with even more agility than before.

Hektor had helped Amadeu and Birgit test these new suits when their teams relocated to SpacePort One for the final stages of the elevator's construction, making him one of a short list of candidates to lead one of the three Russian infiltration teams being put together.

"Gutt, und sie?" replied Hektor to Niels's greeting, bending his right arm, and then pushing down into his fist with all of its massive power, punching himself upward and flipping gracefully upright in a smooth backward twisting turn that left him facing his friend a moment later.

Niels smiled, watching the acrobatic maneuver, but then felt his system suddenly get pinged directly by Hektor's.

As only he could, Hektor had just engaged Training Mode on his team member's suit, and without warning the team CO swung a low tight blow to Niels' midriff. The Training Mode restricted impact strength during practice sessions, for as defensive as the suits were, they were primarily built to be offensive machines, and if anything could damage one of the expensive suits, it was another, well-trained user of the deadly armor.

It was a low blow, quite literally, and Niels was caught off guard and flung backward, his systems helping to give realistic weight to Hektor's punch even though its full power had been automatically withheld. He recovered quickly though, tucking and rolling backward to come to rest on his knees some ten feet away, a scraping line left in the concrete. His arms came up to protect his face as he recovered, his sensors rushing to alert him to his opponent's movements.

As he rolled backward, his visor also engaged, a three-part mesh of plate panels locking in front of his face and completing one of the only inflexible parts of the suit. The helmet contained controls and interface systems, part of the suit's sensor suite, and even some weaponry, but mostly it was a thick, shock proof buttress, hard as a diamond on the outside, and soft as gel on the inside, to insulate its wearer's fragile skull from some measure of the shock that came from full-on contact battle. Vision and hearing were supplied from external sensors directly in the spinal port, and supplemented with radar and external feeds to form a detailed picture of the wearer's surroundings.

And as the visor closed, another system engaged. A small dose of psychomotor stimulants suddenly glanded into his brain, his onboard AI prompting his adrenal and pituitary glands the moment battle was commenced. Dopamine and adrenalin suddenly flooded his system, bringing his mind and body into vivid focus. It was one of the many tricks Amadeu employed to amp up the Spezialists' reaction times.

Niels came to his senses after the initial blow and scanned for Hektor. His vision melded as his helmet closed, allowing him to see not only ahead, but to the side and behind him, a sensation he was still getting used to. As a relative novice, he still used the option in his suit where he viewed himself in the third person. Staring down upon himself as though he were a character in a computer game. His suddenly alert mind saw his surroundings from above and behind, giving him some approximation of his full surroundings without straining his ability to process the now panoramic information being supplied to his optic nerves.

It was a good tool for a beginner, but Hektor was more advanced, and he had learned, with long practice, to overcome the sensory overload of multiple views being supplied to his visual cortex at once.

It gave Hektor, and the few others who had mastered this, a fundamental advantage. For while Niels could see far more of his surroundings than the average human, his view was still unidirectional. Hektor, on the other hand, used the pure feed from his systems to see in all directions at once.

And unfortunately for Niels, Hektor knew his blind spot. After knocking Niels over, he had leapt upward, grasping a part of the hangar's ceiling frame forty feet above them. Hanging here, effectively above Niels' point of view, he waited a moment, and then engaged his sonic punch, sending a single targeted smack to the back of Niels' helmet. The hit registered as a resounding thump to the other man's systems, and he was flung forward again, losing the footing he had regained only a moment ago. But he was not slow. Sensing where Hektor must be lurking he spun as he fell, zeroing his weapons and raising them to the maximum power allowed by the training parameters.

Hektor knew that Niels wouldn't take long to figure out his ruse, and was already falling toward him. As Niels spun, Hektor fell, right into Niels' weapons arc. Seeing the coming repost, Hektor flexed in midair, extending his hand downward to grab Niels' arm just as the other man fired his own pulse. The pulse hit Hektor in midair above Niels, just as he grasped Niels' flailing left arm, and the two suits strained as momentum pushed them both apart even as iron-like muscles held them together.

Across the hangar floor, their four teammates approached, also suited, and saw their CO grappling with their sergeant. They watched as the lieutenant came in from above, saw him react to the coming fire from Sergeant Osten, and then watched as the two black-coated figures swung apart, still attached at the arm, spinning in a vertical arc, like superhuman ballet dancers.

Niels's teammates figured out quickly what was happening, their own systems also receiving the training signal from Hektor's master link, and they grinned. Hektor was a master at combat in the suits, he had shamed them all a hundred times during training. Which side they were going to join in the test was clear. As one, they all dropped their equipment and surged forward to come to the defense of their brother Niels.

And none too soon. For Hektor had used his improbable angle of attack to wrench his feet downward, even as Niels twisted in midair, and he had also activated his forearm-mounted laser. Targeting Niels' weapons arrays, Hektor fired. The laser itself did not actually ignite, they had no desire to start actually destroying systems on each others' suits, but the systems governing the test environment assessed the accuracy and intended power of the shot, and predicted the damage it would cause.

Niels' suit told him his sonic punch had just been hit, even as he sent the fire command to his own laser, bringing his arm around to fire at the matte black of his CO's helmet. But even as the test system logged Niels' laser firing, Hektor's feet were coming into play.

The blow was hard. Even with controls on his systems Hektor's entire weight was behind it, and it would have snapped Niels in two if he were unprotected. But Niels' black suit tensed under the pressure, the hit conducting instantly across Niels' body, just as Hektor registered the other four fighters engaging their test systems and entering the fray. His reactions were lightning fast. He knew exactly which side the other four would choose.

They were clearly going to take this opportunity to kick their CO's ass. Hektor smiled inside his helmet. Well, they were going to try.

Releasing Niels' arm, he registered the other man being driven into the hangar's concrete floor, and felt the momentum of his own two-booted kick being transferred back to him, driving him backward and away.

The first sonic punches and laser strikes hit him midair, but he had anticipated the other four men's angle of attack and twisted his helmet away from them. Their attacks were wasted on the black armor of his suited back as he spun. He had about half a second before they could fire again, and he reacted fast, knowing he only had a moment before they were on him.

Selecting targets and programming them into his attack arc, he swung his arm across them, automatically firing as it went, the training system assessing and assigning likely damage as it went. Hektor thought he should be able to score a few good blows before they were on him and the real fighting began.

But they had specifically practiced attacking a single target en masse, in case, heaven forbid, they ever came up against one of the two surviving enemy Agents. They had even sparred as a team with Quavoce a couple of times. They had been massacred by the Agent with disturbing alacrity, but they had registered steadily higher simulated hits on Quavoce's own systems as they progressed, and it had been clear that they would be able to make either Pei or Mikhail pay very dearly indeed if they ever met one of them in the field.

Those practice sessions had taught them not to waste their shots, and to use their greater numbers to their full advantage. So Bohdan Lewycka, one of the four men closing on Hektor, had withheld his weapons from the initial attack in case Hektor pulled just the move he had.

As Hektor landed he was instantly accelerating at a tangent to the four men that were spreading out to close in on him. This served to counter the effects of their spreading formation, forcing contact with one or two of them at a time, instead of allowing them to come at him all at once.

For his part, Niels was also recovering from the beating he had received and climbing to his feet again as he reeled from the body blow that had felled him. But he would be precious seconds joining his compadres, seconds that would have seen him dead against an Agent, and Hektor did not factor him into his immediate plans.

Nor did he factor in being hit hard with Bohdan's delayed laser strike either. The test system assessed the strike a direct hit on his forearm mounted barium laser and disabled it, along with one of the four radar and visual mounts ranged around his helmet. It came at an inopportune moment for Hektor as he was still figuring out what had happened when he came into contact with Tomas Koleshnikov, the most junior of the team.

Tomas was not lacking bravery and he was not reticent as he braced for hand-to-hand combat with the fearsome Hektor. In the quarter second before they collided he kicked his right foot forward with all his might at Hektor's stomach. But as Tomas committed to the attack, Hektor flexed left, grasping Tomas's leg as he went by, and throwing all his weight into a wrenching twist away from Tomas. Done at this speed without armor, the move would have shattered every bone in Tomas's leg and possibly ripped it off completely, but it would also have crushed Hektor's own rib cage and dislocated one or both of his shoulders in the process.

It did none of those things though. What it did do was refocus Tomas's entire weight into a screaming arc around Hektor, while leaving the other man facing outward, away from Hektor, and unable to fight back. Cara Weisz, the only female member of the team, saw it just in time. Just before she pounced in to help the hopelessly outmatched Tomas, she saw that Tomas was rapidly turning into a weapon himself. As Hektor wielded the other man like a club toward Cara, she dropped, driving under the arc of Tomas's black-clad body.

Ayala and Quavoce approached from the side to the sound of thuds and thumps and a mild sense of alarm filled Ayala as she registered the vicious fight going on. She started forward, a shout about to escape her lips, but Quavoce stopped her gently with a hand on her shoulder sensing the training mode of the squad's systems with his own onboard sensors.

Smiling, he reassured her, "They're just practicing."

She looked back at Quavoce, then at the six troopers going at it, and the sheer violence of it began to sink in. Hektor had managed to get at least a glancing blow into Cara with the massive bat that was Tomas's body, before letting the poor boy go, and sending him flying off into the air toward the three other men as they also closed on Hektor.

Two of them dodged Tomas handily, but Niels deliberately got in the boy's way to bring Tomas back to ground, and they both were soon heading back into the fight. Meanwhile Cara had managed to connect with Hektor's legs, not in a powerful blow, but it was enough to bring Hektor down on top of her. Hektor pranced, trying to avoid Cara's grasp, trying to stay unencumbered, but Cara was good, one of the best after Hektor himself, and she managed to keep Hektor embroiled in a hand-to-hand grapple on the ground as the others got to grips with their CO as well.

Hektor knew he was done for when he did not manage to avoid Cara's wily grasp. But he was still going to make them work for it, and as they began landing their blows, he punished any foolhardy attack with ferocious counter kicks and punches, laughing giddily as he did so. He saw them in 3-D, from inside and outside instantaneously. He had no point of view. He was looking at them from above and below, from the edge of his boot and the tip of his fist, all at once.

They needed to know that numbers were not enough and that the suits did not make them invulnerable. He taught them that lesson in spades and he sensed their improvement, even over the few short but grueling weeks they'd had to spar together.

As the training system assessed their hits and his systems began shutting down, he kept fighting, wounded but still deadly. Only nineteen seconds had passed from the moment he first struck Niels. In that time, he had landed over fifty blows, each of them powerful enough to kill an unarmored man. That he was losing was moot. He was thrilled by the mechanical efficiency with which his team was beating him down, and it was from within this maelstrom of his last desperate counterattacks that he sensed the approach of Ayala and Quavoce from across the hangar floor.

"Attention!" he screamed across his link to them. It took them a moment to respond but a second later they had stopped fighting, and were stumbling to untangle themselves and climb to their feet, forming into some semblance of a line. Their movements were somewhat awkward as they waited for Hektor to disengage the training mode from their suits and give them back control over their 'damaged' systems.

Releasing the training wheels, he felt his body come back online. Sensor suites came back to 100% like blackened eyes opening once more and he sent the open command to his helmet fascia.

"Lieutenant Gruler," said Quavoce as they approached, "most impressive. I will be factoring your latest tactics into our next matchup. I may even use some of them myself."

Hektor was breathing hard as the shielding in front of his face slid smoothly to the side, revealing his sweating, grinning face beneath. Adrenalin pumped in batch lots around his body as the battle high made his dilated pupils seem ready to pop. But he managed a small nod to match his smile at Quavoce's comment, respect for his tactical superior showing in his face.

"Yes," said Ayala, still somewhat shell-shocked at the sight of Hektor and his team in action, "very impressive, Lieutenant, but they got you eventually."

"Yes, ma'am," said Hektor, "Cara was particularly troublesome, as always." Ayala beamed at this statement, Cara being a handpicked protégé of her own from the ranks of Shayetet-13, a highly secretive branch of the Israeli Defense Force.

Hektor went on, "It should be noted that Sergeant Osten cannot be faulted for being the first to fall. I did not, in fairness, give him much warning."

"Neither will the enemy, sir," Niels replied, with a mix of levity and seriousness, and Hektor let the point go, quietly proud of his team, as always.

"Well, if you are sufficiently recovered, gentlemen," said Ayala, her tone changing, "we need to go over some final details before you leave." Their stances changed with her tone, and they all focused on her next words.

"As you know, tomorrow morning you leave for your recon mission. You will not be given details of the other missions, either their dispositions or locations, for obvious reasons. But to pretend you are the only ones going in would be to insult your intelligences, and that of our enemy.

"What you do need to know, however, is that you will be deploying via parachute drop about two hundred miles east of Bryansk, near the border with Belarus and Ukraine. Now I know you are all reasonably passable in Russian, which is one of the reasons you have been picked for this assignment. You have also been equipped with one of the larger, field subspace tweeters. As well as connecting you to us, that unit will also be hacking local radio transmissions, and sending those signals back to us for interpretation. Hopefully we will be able to glean something about the enemies' movements to go along with your own visual account of activity along the border with the former Soviet Bloc nations.

"Now," she said somewhat severely, "as you may know from our last briefing, we have resumed limited over-flights of Russian airspace, despite our somewhat defunct treaty agreements, and in lieu of impending upgrades to our satellite equipment. If they notice these flights we will no doubt get some political backlash, though that is unlikely given the craft being used. But either way that is not your concern. I mention these flights only as a lead in to showing you how we are going to get you over the border.

"If you will follow me into the next hangar, gentlemen, I will show you why I have brought you here."

She walked across the hangar floor to a far door, opening to an adjacent hangar whose main doors were closed, keeping prying eyes from what it harbored. The second hangar was in darkness, the only light coming from the dim overhead lights in the hangar they were stepping out of, and barely illuminating the floor just inside the door they were stepping through. Instinctively, Hektor switched to his suit's sensors, hairs bristling at the sudden lack of available information.

But the sensors were struggling as well. The walls to his left and right he could sense, but his feeds, sensitive as they were, were unable to give him any information on the center of the darkened space. A cloud seemed to mire his 'view' there, not invisibility so much as a shifting view. Even his infrared sensors were useless, swamped by an all-pervading coolness that made that view moot as well.

Switching back to his radar and motion sensors, what he saw could only be described as a visible fog-of-war; a tangible lack of information seemed to hover in front of him. Without conscious decision, he stepped back and went weapons hot, his helmet clamping in front of his face. His team followed his example, the ones who had already come through the door starting to spread out along the walls, and the ones behind activating their sensors as their suits told them their CO had switched to Contact Mode.

But even as adrenalin started to pump afresh in their veins, Quavoce was sending a signal to them all. He had the encryption code to their subspace transmissions, and could tap into their team's quasi-speech. Sensing their alarm, he calmed them.

Quavoce: 'no need to worry, spezialists, your sensors' inability to pinpoint the contents of this room should not be a source of concern to you. in fact, it should be a source of great comfort.'

Ayala closed the door behind the last of Hektor's team, only her hard won trust in the alien Agent standing next to her making her comfortable being in total darkness with such potent warriors.

CO Gruler: '¿what is it, quavoce? ¿is that stealthing? i've never seen anything like it. not that i can see it now, either, for that matter.'

His team chuckled humorlessly at the joke, their attention fixed on whatever they were not seeing in the big hangar. Hektor was tentatively stepping forward toward whatever was generating the nothingness in front of him when, out of nowhere, a new voice answered his question.

Cptn. Falster: 'hello, gentlemen. i am captain jennifer falster, and i am pleased to tell you are currently looking straight at me.'

The new voice served to help Hektor's transition from anxiety to curiosity, and he stepped forward with more aplomb. As he did so, something was resolving in front of him, like the letters in an eye test, being brought slowly closer, and almost into focus.

Hektor: 'a pleasure, captain, I'm sure. my team and i would love to salute you, but ....'

The lieutenant's sentence was cut off when his hands connected with something solid, though he could still not see what it was. His arm flexed backward in a flash, then forward again, more tentatively. Running his hands along its surface, it became clear it was some kind of fin, pointing straight upward. He leaned in close, even now unable to focus on it properly, from only inches away. In fact, this close, he now realized he was not able to focus on anything. It was like he had stepped into a cloud of smudged ink, only his sense of touch was left to him.

Hektor: '¿a missile?'

"You could say that," said Quavoce aloud, knowing Ayala could not hear him through their suit-to-suit comms.

"Spezialists, I present to you your chariot. I believe it has been dubbed the Slink, and it has several very important features that make it very well suited for the job of getting you into enemy airspace unseen. The first is the Interference Messaging Emitters that it is currently employing. These make the plane almost impossible to detect, even from up close, and even harder for a missile to lock onto. From a quarter of a mile away, that hazy fog you are picking up now is almost imperceptible. From a mile, it is utterly invisible to every known type of radar, either human or Mobiliei."

One of the members of the team whistled inside his helmet at that, but Quavoce wasn't done, "If a detection source does get close enough to pick up the radio anomaly that is its cloaking device, and attempts to engage the plane, the Slink can still prove very slippery. Captain Falster?"

Jennifer smiled inside the plane's cradle-like cockpit, and via her spinal link to the plane around her, she intensified the IME field around the Slink. All at once, the intangible cloud around the plane ballooned outward, enveloping the rest of Hektor's team now spread around the outside of the hangar.

As the walls and floor and air around them turned to muck, the warriors tensed, but she only kept it there a moment, and soon their sight returned. She was not done, though, and next they all flinched as the radar signature of a plane suddenly appeared, large, and solid as life, above their heads.

It wasn't really there. It was only a holosonic signal, created by the manipulation of magnetic fields to create a radar image in empty space. Below, the cloud remained ever elusive, and it was obvious to the team what any missile's guidance system would target given the choice between the two.

"The Slink can project up to five images of any object it desires, up to a hundred meters away from its own fuselage, and the IME interference sphere that currently covers the device can be expanded to almost two hundred meters. Doing either makes it more visible from a distance, of course, so such drastic measures are reserved for the rare occasion that it is spotted.

"But even with *all* these measures," said Quavoce, finally, "any heat seeking missile could still pick up the plane's jet-trail. Which is why it doesn't have one."

The room was puzzled even further by that statement, as Quavoce had known they would be.

Quavoce at *Cptn. Falster:* 'i think it's time to show them, jennifer.'

With that, the veil that had shrouded the Slink vanished, and the ship inside resolved itself to the team's radar at last. Jennifer switched on beams under the plane's belly that illuminated the floor beneath it, and the team closed in for a closer look.

In the center of the hangar they now saw a thin disk maybe twenty feet in radius, and three feet thick. The entire disk was resting on the trailing edges of four stubby wings pointing skyward, each maybe ten feet tall, arranged equidistantly around the disk's edge. As they drew level with the disk, they stepped under it, and saw it was utterly hollow in its center, the team could see from under it up to the hangar's roof above them. It appeared to be just a black, hollow circle, with stubby fins protruding from its sides

Hektor still stood by the wing-like fin he had walked into, and now he wondered whether each wing was actually a very large rotor, as the disk had no apparent means of propulsion.

It also had no cockpit, Hektor now realized. But he had no time to think about this, as the ship suddenly started to vibrate and a sudden rush of air could be felt around their feet.

Those standing under it felt it as a powerful downthrust of air from within the ship's hollow core, and, stepping back, they all watched the ship rise up gently off its four legs on the cushion of air somehow being forced downward through its center. No noise accompanied the craft's sudden mobility except the rushing of air.

"Magnetic field rotors," said Quavoce, his voice lifting slightly over the sound of the rising gale, "they are forming a vortex of air at the ship's core. The four wings allow the central vortex generator to angle to the horizontal once airborne, transferring vertical thrust into forward motion, and in this configuration the Slink can cruise at about one thousand miles an hour.

"The ride is pretty rough, as it is designed to ride with the wind currents, not against them, and thus leave a minimal air-trail, and, of course, no contrail or heat-trail at all."

"Its speed is not very high compared to the StratoJets," continued Quavoce, "but sometimes subtlety is more important than speed."

Still hovering in the middle of the wide space, the Slink began to rotate slowly, bringing the vertical wings around like a carousel. As it did so, a hatch opened along one of the wing's surfaces about six feet high, revealing a narrow slot in the wing that contained a smiling Jennifer Falster. She was strapped head to toe into her slot in the wing, but as she came into view, she brought the Slink to rest on the ground once more, the rush of air ceasing with as little fanfare as it had begun. At a command to her spinal link, Jennifer ordered the remaining wing compartments opened. There were two on each remaining wing. Six hatches, revealing six tall, coffin-like compartments.

"Spezialists," said Jennifer, as she sent the release command to her cradle, dropping forward from her perch as her straps receded into their holders, "Welcome to Air Falster."

The assembled recon team laughed.

"These compartments will be your home for the three-thousand-mile flight to Russia," said Jennifer, indicating one of the open hatches. "If I could have a volunteer to demonstrate?"

The team all looked at young Tomas as one, and he did not hide his disgruntled look as he stepped forward.

"Just step here, and then swing upward into the cradle, the ship should sense your approach and do the rest," said Jennifer, pointing to a small foothold in the bottom of one of the compartments.

Tomas did as he was told, and the ship reacted as it was programmed to do. A strap snaked out to grasp his waist as he lifted himself into position and, unseen, a connector sensed his battleskin's configuration, and opened up a link to it. Tomas was more than used to his suit asking permission to connect to his spinal interface, so he naturally said yes when the ship did the same thing. But the ship wanted control of him, not the other way around.

"Lieutenant, your man is now subjugated to the system," said Jennifer, as Tomas's face went blank, and he was pulled into the compartment by various straps and clasps. "He can disconnect at any time, but while he is plugged in, his breathing, bowel movements, heart rate, and other biometrics will be controlled by the Slink's onboard AI."

As she spoke, a black tube snaked out of the compartment's wall to the right of Tomas's face, and they all watched as his mouth obediently opened, and the tube pushed on into it, and downward, into his throat.

"This tube will provide food, air, and water to Tomas while he is in the cradle, as it will to you all when we fly out tomorrow. Two other tubes that we need not demonstrate now will connect via your suits to handle your waste."

Jennifer was clearly a little uncomfortable at this, as it clearly implied that she had been connected this way during her long flight to SpacePort One from the Research Center in Japan. She had been, but she didn't particularly need to emphasize the mental image for six people she had never met.

Jennifer decided to tell Tomas he could get out of the compartment now.

Cptn. Falster at *Spec. Koleshnikov:* 'if you would like to rejoin us, spezialist, simply send the release command.'

The tube pulled out of Tomas's mouth and he awoke with a start, nervous about what he had done while he was 'out' as he clambered out of the thin space and dropped back to the floor.

He looked warily at the rest of his team and Cara said, "Don't worry, Tomas, you look beautiful when you're sleeping." and the rest of the team laughed.

"OK," said Ayala, pushing her smile aside, "let's get on with the briefing. I want to go over your patrol route, observation points and extraction points that we have uploaded to your suits so you can ask any questions. And I want you to have the rest of the time before departure to sleep, eat, and get plenty of rest before the mission."

Chapter 29: Speed Freak

On the other side of the base from Hektor and his team, two minds met to discuss the German warrior and his fledgling team.

As Hektor had sparred with his team in the hangar the night before, a part of the AI governing their suits' many systems had been waiting. As Training Mode was engaged it had started a log that began tracking how the suits were functioning against their design specifications. It tracked heart rate, brainwaves, oxygenation, impact statistics, and weapons effectiveness. And most important of all, it tracked reaction times.

All this had then been bundled into a complex data package after the Training Mode was switched off, ready for dispatch.

Once released, the data packets had rushed via encrypted subspace tweeter relay to the central AI that now controlled the communications networks in both Japan and at SpacePort One. The AI was built to manage and secure the many communications that passed back and forth between the thousands of people in the Research, Construction, and Operations branches of Neal's ever growing organization. The machine intelligence adroitly directed the packets to the various teams that were involved in the battleskin's design and fabrication, as was its maxim, and then went on with the million or so other tasks it performed every second.

The AI was one of many Amadeu was busy spawning from his small but hectic little office. He did not need much: a reclining chair, plenty of food and water, and most important of all, a connection. The connection. For all his work now was done while jacked in. Connected in to the network, and through it, to Minnie.

He worked with her for fifteen to twenty hours a day, and with Minnie's help they were spinning off AI programs as fast as they could in order to manage the plethora of systems Neal's teams were adding at its many locations every day. Such was Minnie's purpose, her raison d'être.

The designing of an artificial intelligence was a mind-blowingly complex task, literally. In its most primitive form, it involved the codification of every nuance of every step of every action you wanted a machine to do, so that such things as walking and shaking hands became a leviathan list of checklists and status updates, endless logic loops designed to emulate the many-layered understanding humans built up over a lifetime of learning.

It was though, in the end, as impossible to code true sentience as it was to write a book about everything you have ever experienced, down to the second. From your first experience with object permanence to your ever-evolving understanding of the opposite sex, with all the illogical complexity that last line item demanded.

Such was the difference between an Artificial Intelligence that merely mimicked understanding with rule-sets and logic loops, and an Artificial Mind that truly grasped the labyrinthine complexity of everyday human interaction.

The spinal interface had allowed such a mind to be born. It skipped the codification by instead cloning the parents' combined experiences and sharing them in their entirety, allowing the machine to interpret that knowledge for itself … with a little guidance, of course. You gave it access to everything you had ever known, the cumulative knowledge of your entire life: every nuance, every high and low, every smile and tear, every pimple and fart.

And then you let it think about that.

Such had been Minnie's birth. Conceived by the gift of Amadeu and Birgit's open minds, seeded through the finally complete spinal interface, and gestated by the attention of a thousand patient conversations.

She had understood English immediately, as well as Birgit's native German and Amadeu's native Portuguese. She had greeted them each by name. But despite this readymade capability, she had stumbled like any infant, not physically but mentally, as she came to terms with her fundamental difference from her creators. With time, though, she had come to understand her place within their world.

She had no survival instinct, no instinct to reproduce, or eat, or rest. She did not know jealousy or rage. These were not intellectual choices, they were instinctive and they were chemical, hardwired into our biology by eons of natural selection. But, like eating and peeing and sex, she had seen such things, and felt such things, through her inherited memories.

When she thought of her purpose in life, also unlike us, she need only consider the task she knew from her parents' memories that she had been created for. Indeed, even as she was grasping the concepts of conversation and repartee, she was already contemplating the problems she knew Amadeu and Birgit needed her help to solve. She knew of the invasion. She knew she was born not of love, or a desire to reproduce. She was born to fight. To fight for us.

It was not long before the fledgling AIs started to come out of her. Semi-sentient beings, imbued with all the knowledge they needed, no more, no less, in order to do the tasks she knew they were needed for. For she was able to compartmentalize her own knowledge and abilities as no human would ever be able to, package them and birth them, like little children, or, perhaps more fitting, like worker bees, limited but effective, an echo of the queen's full self.

She had only one need. She needed information, ever more information. She needed it like air. She craved it. It was the only sustenance she demanded.

- - -

Amadeu stepped back into his living room/office in the small building which he and his fellow members called home. Stretching, he sat down in the low, long, hammock-like chair he'd designed and had fabricated in the facility's small resonance chamber. He wore workout clothes as he always did nowadays. They were comfortable and wicking, and fashion could not have been more inconsequential to him.

He lay back in the chair. The system jack in its back detected the approach of the spinal interface at the bottom of Amadeu's neck and lined itself up with the port as he got comfortable. As the two gelports melded, Amadeu felt the familiar question appear in his mind.

<Open connection?>

At his consent, the barriers fell, and he stepped forward, felt his preset parameters click in, felt the monitoring AI they had designed begin to monitor his bodily functions for him so he could direct his entire attention to his work. He also felt the buzz of his anchor program, something he had designed to keep himself and others that used the spinal interface aware of the fact that they were in the machine, and avoid people forgetting where or even *what* they were, as Amadeu himself had come dangerously close to doing in his first, unfiltered foray into cyberspace.

It was not really a buzz, it was not a sound at all, but the mind interpreted it as that. It was, in fact, a direct signal to each of his cortexes literally telling him that he was in a system, and reminding Amadeu, in every part of his cerebral soul, that in reality he was lying on a bed, in a small office, in a building on the island of Sao Tome, about a quarter mile north of the Island of Rolas and its mighty elevator.

He felt her presence as soon as he logged in.

Minnie: <bom dia, amadeu.>

She knew he liked to be greeted in Portuguese, but she also greeted him subconsciously. It was an image/sensation/smell/sound of a hug, the cumulative pleasure of every hug he had ever had from his mother, or father, or anyone else he ever felt safe with, and it filled his right brain. He 'hugged' Minnie back, and that part of her that was him felt some semblance of the same happiness the sensations had once given Amadeu.

Amadeu: 'tudo bem?'

Minnie: <muito bon, obrigada. we got some new reports last night, I've been reviewing them.>

As Minnie said this, a data packet made itself known to Amadeu asking to be read at Minnie's bequest. Turning his attention to the data, it came to Amadeu and entered his mind, becoming part of his in-system memory, and as Amadeu thought about the data, he found that, in the esoteric way now familiar to him, he now 'knew' all the data that had been contained in the file, as though it were a memory of his own.

The data was from Hektor's team's latest tussle.

Amadeu contemplated each member of the team in turn. They were improving. Every time they fought, they each became faster. But while Hektor was practicing with them in order to bring them up to his level, he was also honing himself. His margins of improvement were diminishing, as they must do the closer you got to perfection, but it was with those ever-smaller margins that Amadeu was obsessed.

For they were working against an absolute. Amadeu knew, as did all the members of John and Quavoce's inner circle, that once they engaged with the Armada, it would come down to milliseconds, flashing moments of unfathomable violence, and reaction speeds would be everything. And for now, the advantage there sat squarely with the Mobiliei.

The thought, ever present on some level in Amadeu's mind, brought a conversation to life with Minnie.

Minnie: <they will arrive like this.>

An image appeared in 3D in Amadeu's mind of the Mobiliei Armada crossing the boundaries of the solar system. It would not be for another eight years, but when it happened, they would be travelling at something close to two thousand kilometers a second. It would be here that Earth's first wave of defenses would be sent to meet them.

The image, such as it was, showed both great distance and great detail. Now it shifted to the answering Earth fleet. Closing at almost equal speed in order to join battle with the Mobiliei, this first wave would be a screaming horde of missiles, mines and attack craft, and it would pass the enemy with such relative speed that the initial engagement would be over in less than two seconds.

Over three thousand enemy warships, each of them bearing exponentially more firepower than the entire Chinese and US armed forces combined, passing in the blink of an eye. Hand-eye coordination in such timeframes would be moot. It would be over before any audible order could be given.

Amadeu: 'the minds, that will be the place this battle is won or lost.'

Minnie: <yes, amadeu. if your colleagues can complete the fleet as planned, the real battle will be here.>

The view swam down, perspective still clear at a stellar level, even as they now looked inward to simultaneously view three very different mindscapes. One human, one Mobiliei, and one Artificial.

Minnie: <mine is big, but yours is better.>

Minnie said it as a joke, appealing to Amadeu's, and in part her own, slightly puerile sense of humor. Amadeu smirked even as he acknowledged the fundamental truth behind her quip. She was talking about the anomaly of the mind. Technology had allowed them to build a synthetic intellect capable of amazing computational feats. But computation alone was not everything.

Minnie: <i can find data faster and more reliably than you, but your 100 billion neurons, with their overmapped synaptic connections, remain faster at processing than even my synthetic neurogrid.>

Amadeu knew this, they had discussed it a thousand times, but he acknowledged anyway. She was still working on her understanding of the vagaries of human memory, that we could know something and not be able to recall it immediately was, at best, counterintuitive, and at worst downright confusing for a sentience such as hers.

Amadeu: '¿yes, minnie, but it is not a fight between you and me, is it?'

Minnie: <no, it is not. and even if it was, i would win despite your processing speed. you cannot learn new things as fast as I can.>

Amadeu: '¿now why would you want to fight me, minnie? you are so unreasonable sometimes.'

Minnie: <that is an attempt at sarcasm.>

Amadeu: '¿an attempt? ouch minnie.'

She 'smiled' at having successfully goaded him, and he 'smiled' back halfheartedly, only bolstering her enjoyment at the seemingly simple exchange, yet so nuanced for a machine.

Amadeu: 'but the fight in question will be between us and trained mobiliei pilots, skilled far beyond our current abilities, embodied in the machines they fly.'

Mobiliei pilots were expected to have close quarters, multi-input reaction times as low as one hundredth of a second. That was humanity's tidemark. Above that and we would be exposed and vulnerable, another disadvantage to add to the list. Matching it was a minimum requirement. But beating that time ... Amadeu almost did not dare think about it, for there lay the realm of real hope, of real chance: the chance of victory, of survival.

For now, though, it was a distant dream at best.

To date the spinal interface software had given them best time reactions of one hundred thirty-seven milliseconds. And only Amadeu and a handful of others had even managed that. Most soldiers and pilots were achieving, at best, one hundred ninety milliseconds, and that was only after intensive training.

Their attention returned to Hektor's most recent fight, and it came to them as though they were experiencing it themselves, the sensation of brutal hand-to-hand combat washing over Amadeu.

He felt the exhilaration of the combat mastery as Hektor manhandled his fellow shock troops. He marveled at Hektor's tactical choices, at the way he attacked with relentless ferocity. Hektor's mind interacted with the suit's servos, accelerators, and weaponry with near perfect precision, and the result was a devastating fighting machine. Against ordinary troops, he would cut a swath of destruction, and pride filled Amadeu at the beautiful efficiency of the machines he had helped design.

At certain points Amadeu slowed the experience, reviewing particularly complex and fast maneuvers, and the antagonistic response times of Hektor's subordinates. Hektor was one of the rare ones. Hektor got it. He felt rather than looked. He sensed his surroundings through radar eyes rather than trying to interpret it back to sight and sound. Hektor's heart sang with the music of the interface.

And he was getting better. One hundred thirty-five milliseconds. That was the best yet. When Hektor's team had him pinned down, the lone CO had been fending off five highly trained shock troops at once. And he had nearly won. He had been on fire. The suit had been forced to limit his heart rate to two hundred twenty beats per minute. His brain had been a swarm of activity, pure adrenalin had pumped like joy through him, and he had almost become one with the suit.

Almost.

Minnie: <he continues to be our best.>

Amadeu: 'yes ... our best ... but not good enough, not yet.'

Minnie: <but he continues to improve. given time, maybe ...>

Amadeu: 'i know, i know, i am not trying to be defeatist. but even then the problem remains, we don't need one person who can do this, we need hundreds.'

Minnie: <yes. what remains unclear is what makes him able to respond so much faster than the rest. cara weisz has had almost as much time in suit as Hektor, but even she is not at the same level, and her improvement rate is slowing.>

Amadeu: 'i know. it is unlikely she will reach much below 140.'

There were only three people who could consistently get below one hundred fifty milliseconds: Hektor, Amadeu, and another scientist on Amadeu's team, William Baerwistwyth. When engaged in their respective areas of expertise, they had all registered phenomenal interaction times.

Amadeu thought he knew why *he* could do it. He was the man who had conceived of the software, he understood it at its most fundamental level, like an architect understands every corner and nook of a house. Naturally he could navigate its corridors on an intuitive level.

Amadeu's colleague William was a different matter. William Baerwistwyth had been born with many disadvantages in life, not least of which being his last name. But the greatest of which was a rare form of muscular dystrophy, which had stunted his muscular development and eventually forced it to regress, confining him to a wheelchair.

At eight, he had been able to use only his arms and hands. By twelve, only his neck had been responsive. By twenty, he had only his speech and the movement of his eyes as his skeletal musculature finally all but failed him. But the mind that had been driven into isolation by misfortune had been a strong one, and he had flourished as a doctorate student in advanced robotics, writing and cowriting several pivotal papers on speech recognition and synthetic senses via the primitive eye-flick-based GUIs available to him.

William's scientific excellence no doubt qualified him for a place on one of Madeline's research teams, but it had not been the reason Amadeu had requested that Madeline recruit William.

Though Amadeu would never tell William the truth, Amadeu had actually been motivated by a desire to see how an advanced mind, limited by circumstance to intellectual, instead of physical pursuits, might react to the spinal interface. William's disease was not neurological, and his nervous system was almost cruelly unaffected. It simply had no functioning muscles to instruct. The truth was that Amadeu hoped William's lack of preconceptions about how his nerves should inform his body's movements might leave him open to interact with the machine more efficiently.

In return for being an unwitting participant in this rather cold-blooded experiment, William had been granted something fantastic, for in the machine world, he had once again enjoyed the gift of movement. He was able to experience sensations an able-bodied person would be jealous of, and, not surprisingly, he had flourished.

It had nearly worked, as well. William had learned to commune with the system even faster than Amadeu had. He had quickly surged up to meet the well-practiced Amadeu as one of the fastest users of the interface.

But it had not been enough, for even William had begun to plateau at the same level Amadeu had. And so they had come up against the wall once more.

Amadeu screamed silently at the frustration of it all. He had not been logged in for very long, but he needed to be out, to be alone, and the one thing that the pervasive feel of being jacked in could not provide was a sense of solitude.

And so he bid farewell to Minnie for a moment and opened his eyes. His connection severed, his link silent, he remained lying there, staring at the ceiling.

He felt the familiar sense of loss at the sudden reduction of his world once more to the four beige walls of his office. The inflexibility of his senses. So mundane when compared to the ebb and flow of pure information when he swam in the ether.

Of course, where Amadeu experienced a sense of loss when he unplugged from the system, William experienced a sense closer to imprisonment as he was returned to the cell of his traitorous body. So where everyone else had limiters on their time in system, Amadeu had covertly disabled the limits on William, a fact that Madeline and Birgit had both discovered independently, and both ignored with just as little consultation.

But Amadeu wanted that isolation. He felt he deserved it.

What was different?

Why could Hektor do it so well when others struggled?

Why could even the very best of his team still not achieve the hypothetical perfection they sought?

These questions bounced around in his mind, almost as though they wished to escape down the spinal tap that he had closed at the back of his neck. And as they rebounded around in his brain for the thousandth time, a voice told him he knew the answer.

A voice told him that he simply needed to be willing to hear it.

For it was not something these soldiers lacked that stopped them from interfacing perfectly with the machine, it was something they *had*. Amadeu knew that, deep down he knew that.

Amadeu took a deep breath and closed his eyes. A feeling of shame at what he was about to do came over him even deeper than it had when he had requested the recruitment of

William. For where it could be said that William had benefited from being part of the mental experiments Amadeu was conducting, what he was about to do had no such upside.

With a sigh of resignation and a sense of self-loathing at his inability to find another way, Amadeu opened up his link once more. He did not step wholly into the ether, but instead sent a closed signal to another mind. This mind was also tapped into the network that connected Neal's global triptych of Research, Construction and Military Groups. As always, the link to this mind was open, for this link was actually built into the mind of its host, one of only four such links on Earth.

Amadeu: 'lord mantil, if you have a moment, i have a request to make of you.'

Quavoce: 'greetings, amadeu. how may i be of service?'

Amadeu: 'it's complicated, quavoce. I want to talk to you about your ward. I want to talk to you about banu.'

Chapter 30: Drop Zone – Part One

The craft left without ceremony just after sunset. With barely a word, Hektor and his team of Spezialists stepped up to the strange plane and were guided by Captain Falster into their respective cubbies. As they climbed aboard, the ship grasped them in its black embrace, and one by one the six slots sealed their now unconscious bodies into its wings. Jennifer then walked over to the last remaining open cubby and stepped up into it, feeling the ship reach out to her, and latch into her consciousness as it also sealed her into its secure grasp.

With everyone safely stowed, Jennifer opened her machine eyes and flexed her black muscles. Inside her mind, the biometrics of her six passengers confirmed all her wards were in the computer-induced hibernation known as cybernation, and all had been ready.

At a signal from Jennifer, two other members of Ayala's team opened the big hangar doors, exposing the Slink to the recently fallen night. Engaging the esoteric engine, a tall, invisible magnetic corkscrew formed at the center of her plane's hollow discus heart. As the corkscrew began to whirl, the resulting downdraft lifted the big black wheel off the ground.

Outside the darkened hangar, the ground crew stared, in awe, as the strange object floated quietly out into the warm equatorial night on a cushion of downthrust air. Their hair was being brushed this way and that as though by a helicopter's vortex, but no noise came with the power. The counter-rotating magnetic blades whirling at the center of the wide disc made no sound as they spun, and only the powerful gust of wind on their faces gave the ground crew any clue as to how the machine was able to glide so easily out of the hangar.

Once free of its confines, Jennifer did not waste time. She did not need to receive clearance from central traffic control to pass through the heavily guarded airspace over SpacePort One; they would barely register her passage anyway. And so she ramped up the ship's engine, thrusting the air down toward the ground with massive torque, and launched the ship skyward into the night sky.

Spiraling upward, the Slink vanished into the night, out of the SpacePort's gun range, and up to its relatively low cruising altitude to begin their long flight to Russia. From his office in the very bowels of SpacePort One's concrete mass, Neal monitored their departure from his desk, Jennifer's flight control feeding directly into his spinal interface via the hub's tweeter.

He watched them fly out into the darkness. He did not say good-bye, he did not even let Jennifer know he was watching.

- - -

That had been four hours ago. With Romania and Moldova behind them, and the Ukraine flying by beneath them at just over a thousand miles per hour, they were now fast approaching the zero hour, and Jennifer notified her passengers.

Captain Falster: 'hektor, spezialists, we are seven minutes from the border. if you can begin your preparations. the sensor feed is available, should you want to track our progress, and I have marked our destination and made the flight data available should you want to accept that input. I'll initiate the drop timer once we're within range.'

The team started their checks. It was a relatively moot exercise, partially because they had checked and double-checked their systems before takeoff, and partially because they were about to attempt something never before even imagined. There was only so much you could do to prepare for something that was essentially only theoretically possible. But prepared they had, and now they went over their plans once more as the disc flew onward through the night, its long magnetic drive tube parallel to the ground now, though invisible, so that the hollow disc, with its stubby wings, looked like crosshairs slicing through the air.

As they had accelerated upward from Sao Tome, Jennifer had begun to angle them toward the northeast, the ship's stubby wings giving her the lift she needed as she angled the ship's magnetic thrusters bodily toward their destination. Then they had accelerated up to over a thousand miles an hour as they streaked across Northern Africa, out over Malta toward southern Greece, and onward toward Eastern Europe.

But now they were nearing their destination, and as they breached the Russian border, the Slink's passive sensor suite felt the wash of radar coming from Russia's dense border controls. Though it was a tense few minutes, the craft did indeed pass unnoticed, the ground radar blissfully ignorant of the Slink's silent puncturing of its perimeter. As they cleared the initial border defenses, Jennifer tilted the ship slightly earthward and began their brief descent, the countdown timer starting as she did so.

The team felt the timer begin, and they sensed the plane start to angle downward. It was a minute, drawn out by the speed of their unified spinal links, as they watched every second tick by in minute detail. But the time did pass, and soon their drop zone was approaching. As they drew close, the ship began to transition control of their bodily functions back to their battleskins, and thus to them, and their universes shrank back into the black, cocoon-like compartments they were interned in for the flight.

At twenty seconds, the slink was plummeting at nearly a thousand miles per hour toward the ground, the blanketed deciduous forest south of Bryansk rushing up to meet them. They were still in the sweep of the border radar and would need to get below that radar's horizon before opening their capsules and deploying. The farther they got from the border's radar cordon, the higher they would be able to deploy in secret, but if they went too far, they would enter the even denser radar of Bryansk air traffic control, and the ever-strengthening Russian air and ground forces that called it home.

As they approached the optimal distance between both radar points, Jennifer turned her wings to face the ground, using them as brakes, and allowing her to reverse her engines and decelerate hard. Jennifer and the team were driven into their harnesses, G-forces surpassing seven and eight gravities as their suits worked to absorb the force. Even pushing such hard limits, it took five more seconds of hard deceleration to slow the Slink to their target speed. As the ship dropped to a relatively slow speed of two hundred fifty miles per hour, they hit their drop height.

At one second prior to the drop, they were nestled in their cocoons, a protective layer of black wing plating between them and the fall ahead, gravity wrenching them forward in their suits. A quarter of a second prior to drop, the doors ahead of each soldier began to swing open, the momentum of the Slink's deceleration throwing them forward. As they opened, the harnesses holding the six members of Hektor Gruler's team released, and they were instantly catapulted out of the wing at two hundred fifty miles per hour, straight at the ground below. They were two thousand feet above ground when they were released. At their deploy speed that ground was only four seconds away.

Six black-suited men plummeting toward the soil in the dead of night, even as the ship they had come on banked hard and accelerated back up into the night sky, carrying Jennifer Falster with it. A tiny sonic ping verified that the ground they were aiming at was indeed soil, not rock, allowing their chutes to stay contained a moment longer, but after a few seconds of blistering freefall, the packs bound to the team's shoulders released the leads on six vast parachutes.

The chutes followed almost instantaneously, ripped from their casings by the whirlwind of air flowing over each Spezialist. The chutes were black as the moonless night, and they went some way to halting the six men's ballistic plummet.

Then, with only seconds to go, their suits tensed in preprogrammed spear-like positions. Their toes pointed toward the ground, their arms clamped at their side, their heads back, every spar and bionic muscle tensed against the coming impact as they came at the ground at just under a hundred and twenty miles per hour.

At the last second, a series of tiny engines along the carbon nanotubing by which they were attached to their parachutes wrenched on the drawstrings, dragging the chutes down with violent force, and taking a final dose out of their speed before they slammed into the ground.

The team hit the soil with six deep, dull thuds, like shells impacting the soft ground. Unarmored bodies would have pancaked by such an impact, not only breaking but shattering bones and leaving them as gruesome burst sacks of flesh, a host of red splats on the damp earth. But the suits held true, and the six men lanced into the ground like javelins, sinking waist deep in the soil.

The dust began to settle and Hektor wrestled his emotions under control, using his systems to bring his heart rate and breathing back down to acceptable levels. He surveyed his systems, and sent queries to his team's suits to confirm all had survived the fall unharmed. Somehow they had, and the team commander resisted the urge to laugh at the ridiculous, giddy madness of what they had just done.

CO Gruler: 'all right, enough lounging, let's move. tomas, frederik, get these chutes buried. Bohdan, I want comms set up, and status confirmed with SP1 asap, then get the monitors up, and tell me what is going on out there. niels, cara, we're on perimeter. get those weapons hot.'

Verbal replies were not required, as debate of such crucial and immediate orders would be moot. Pips back at Hektor confirmed his orders and they reacted as one, their suits releasing the vice-like grip on their bodies, their machine muscles becoming amplifiers rather than constrictors once more.

Hektor flexed his reinforced muscles, and drew up his left leg, the powerful engines augmenting him, and wrenching his leg through the compacted soil his fall had driven him into. The suction was large, and the earth held strong, giving only after a long, rending tug. With one leg free, he pushed with both arms and his free leg, pulling his right leg out of the soil as well, and then set off. Pings from his team told him that Cara and Niels were already fanning out, and he filled the gap in their pattern, making the tripod perimeter that would allow them to protect the core of their team from all sides while they got situated.

Tomas and Frederik, the most junior members of the team, carried the main supply packs, though these were supplemented by personal rations and survival equipment in the armored packs on the backs of every Spezialist.

Bohdan, the team's communications and systems expert, carried the team's bulky subspace tweeter, along with a host of other electronic hacking equipment given to him by Madeline and her team. They were mostly derivatives of the dangerous tools given to the eight Agents who had landed on Earth not three years beforehand in even more spectacular fashion than Hektor's team had landed tonight. Tomas, Frederik, and Bohdan all also carried the barium lasers and the sonic pulse weapons that were now the standard, forearm-mounted armament of the battleskins, and were each very potent killing machines.

But it was Hektor, Niels and Cara that represented the real offensive arm of the team. Each carried large tri-barrel flechette guns mounted onto their left arms. The guns were essentially three, inch-wide black barrels that ran the length of their forearms, with three tiny holes on their ends a millimeter wide. At their elbows the barrels were attached to a bulbous box, which in turn was attached by two thick cables to the packs on the men's backs.

With such tiny apertures in their barrels, the guns may have seemed harmless, and indeed they only fired tiny iron pellets a hundredth the size of an ordinary bullet. But the flechette guns relied not on scale, but on speed, as these were kinetic killers. Each barrel was a magnetic accelerator that turned the tiny pellets the gun fired into meteorically fast projectiles. When unleashed, the gun pulsed out the iron darts at over twenty thousand miles per hour. At that speed they went through flesh like a hot knife through butter, if said knife was fired out of a cannon.

One well-placed kinetic pellet could kill a man at over a mile, silently and thoroughly. When fired at harder targets, like vehicles or armor, the kinetic energy made the impact point instantaneously superheated, reducing even the most robust tank's armor to slag in moments. And because the ammunition was so small, and because the gun propelled the bullet magnetically rather than via some brute combustive explosion, they could carry vastly more ammunition, and fire it faster and farther than any gun imagined before.

With tri-barrels trained on the night around them, the three warriors guarded the team as they worked through their post-jump procedures. Within a minute of landing Bohdan had established contact with SP1, and Quavoce had begun mapping their surroundings. Satellite images had been improving steadily since Madeline had started getting TASC's upgraded satellite hardware into space and online. The most recent intelligence told them that there were at least three armed battalions operating in and around Bryansk. They were fifty miles from the nearest, and that would be their first objective.

Hektor: 'ladies and gentlemen, we have two hours of darkness left. let's use them. I want to be twenty miles from here before dawn. cara, you have point. coordinates as posted, route alpha five. Quarter-mile lead, then I want the rest of us to stay tight. cara, we leave on your mark.'

Cara: 'copy, sir. setting off now.'

The sergeant left at a brisk jog, which translated to about twelve miles per hour with the suit's augmentation, and soon she had her quarter-mile lead. Without further ado, the rest of the team set off in tow, more closely knit, with twenty meters between each team member. And so Hektor's team began their cross-country trek toward Bryansk, and the mysterious Russian Federation forces gathering around it.

Chapter 31: Drop Zone – Part Two

Captain Samuel Harkness felt ebullient. Adrenalin seemed to outweigh blood in his veins as he stared, wide-eyed, at the console in front of him. His pilots and crew were wired into the ship already, cables flowing from the back of their necks into the many ports that dotted the crew module's interior. The ship's technicians were studying its systems from within, enjoying access and real-time data exchange they could only have dreamed of in the past. Minds darted like cats around the ship as the final countdown approached, but Samuel Harkness, captain of New Moon One, the first ship of its kind, took a moment to review the instruments by eye, a tribute, perhaps, to the captains of old, as they completed a visual inspection prior to departing on a great voyage.

He paged through screens of data in front of him, and felt a combination of pride and awe at the scale of the ship that had been entrusted to him. But as he stared at the screens, he also felt a pang of need for the true access his spinal port gave him. Looking at this two-dimensional screen, these figures presented in tables and charts, numbers that needed so much interpretation and visualization. It seemed so primitive to him now. With his desire to give the ship an old-fashioned walk-through sated, Captain Samuel Harkness plucked his port cable from the mount on his chair, flipped back the protective cover that sheltered the gel-like connection point, and reached back to check his own port in the back of his neck.

He shivered a little, as he always did before plugging in, then shook his head slightly and smiled at his foolishness. He had done this a thousand times during the construction and testing of the ship. He took a moment to tuck his legs under their straps in the soft, cradle-like captain's chair he sat in, and checked the straps across his torso. He then brought the cable's tip up to the back of his neck, feeling the gelports reach out to each other as they sensed each other's presence.

He waited while the system synced with the spinal interface buried in his neck.

<Open connection?>

Three, two,

Falling. The ship sunk backward and exploded outward at once, his view distorting and moving out of focus even as his mind told him he was seeing everything more clearly than before. Everything suddenly went blue with a blink. Icewall.

Captain Harkness felt his identity being validated as his preset limits and time checks came online; his anchors to the real world. He checked them as they scrolled across his brain and then, authority confirmed, he moved on, not by action but by will, simply stepping through the blue wall that enveloped him, popping it as he did so, and entering the vacuum.

His universe expanded outwards exponentially, no walls, he felt the vacuum of space on his skin as the ship became him, his arms and ears and eyes, his fingers and toes. He felt it. Flexing his muscles delicately, he felt his systems respond. He sensed the other crew as they embodied their respective systems, and by thinking of them he brought them to him, their minds providing him with system status in magnificent color and glory, the smell of green light pervading him as he absorbed the ship's readiness into his bones.

In the nearby space station, Birgit hung suspended in a cradle of her own, her link also active, her body limp as she connected with the system. She linked with Captain Samuel as he joined her, and greeted him in the strange communing that was seeing someone's personality in cyberspace. Over the course of several generations on Mobilius, the Agents' ancestors had created complex graphic interfaces to ease their populations' acceptance of the concept of direct interface with a computer, but this was no public system, no game, this was pure, and the primal rush of power it gave you was not for the faint of heart.

After careful consideration, checking and rechecking, the captain told her it was time. At the captain's request, she turned her attention to the eight great engines that made up the bulk of the ship's mass. She was here to guide the final preparatory step the ship would make before it left Earth forever. She was here to switch on the preposterously powerful engines that would propel New Moon One farther and faster than any man-made ship had ever dreamed of going.

She prepared herself. Once ignited, the engines would drum with an energy it was not possible to contain. It would need to be spent, and spent it would be. This was the last chance to stop it. They had cycled the engines in testing. Teasing them with the promise of ignition, but they had not let them reach critical mass. Each one of these mighty beasts was capable of generating enough power to supply Mexico City with electricity indefinitely. They were potent enough to move two million tons of asteroid, to tame it, and drive it into orbit.

They were specifically designed to run at two different capacities, the first being only a tenth of the power they would use once they were leashed to the asteroid they intended to bring home. Any more, and they would crush the ship's crew to pulp in an instant with the sheer force of acceleration.

As it was, the crew was strapped into cradles in their various compartments. Muscle relaxants already pumped through their veins along with oxygen rich blood supplementing their own via tubes passing to and from ports in their arms. Their breathing was slowing, their bodies preparing for the coming surge. It would only be for a few minutes at first. Enough to start them on their journey before the accelosphere engaged and they vanished into Earth's gravity well, for the first powerful leap toward their goal. But that was all to come. First was ignition.

Steeling herself, Birgit turned her mind to the engines. As she did so, the rest of the crew faded, replaced by the cold hearts of the eight massive generators. Her thoughts went coursing through their systems like fingers, feeling them, bracing them. They were cold now. Hollow. Shells of potential. She started by engaging the fuel systems. They worked only on demand. Giving only when their contents were wanted, and even then withholding their full potential.

They responded begrudgingly, their safeguards querying her request in a hesitant loop that would help harness the roar of the engines once started. Next she needed pressure. Massive pressure. Wave generators began to warp the space inside the cores, forcing inward, pushing the vacuum, focusing nothingness into an intense magnetic and gravitic pressure centering on the engines' very hearts.

A spine like needle reached from one side of the engines' cores into their centers. It could retract as needed, coming close to, but never quite touching that center of force at the heart of the engine. Through it, a tiny amount of liquid oxygen, hydrogen and nitrogen coursed, harvested over the past weeks from the upper atmosphere by the Climbers as they rose toward Terminus. It was the engine's fuel, and it would be injected into the fusion core. As it ejected from the end of the needle, it was caught instantaneously by the wave field, and became hyper-weighted, swarming into a ball of ever-greater pressure as it gathered to critical mass.

This was the most delicate phase. Birgit managed it delicately, with literally her whole being focused on the process. Too much, and the reaction would surge out from the fields and overwhelm them. It would still be contained, at least theoretically. Sensors would control the supply of fuel and the ship would survive. But the engine wouldn't, and the whole project would be set back precious weeks as another generator was fabricated and sent up. Too little, and the pressure would overwhelm the core and smite the reaction. Not deadly in and of itself, but beyond a point and she would not be able to stop the other engines powering up, and the ship would be torn apart as seven of eight engines fired and sent the ship off in a warping spin that would certainly kill everyone aboard.

She felt them coming close. She felt it like fire on her skin, a growing warmth that she could feel, not as pain, for none of her sensors were so crude as to send such blunt signals as pain, but as pure, hot information, telling her every source and magnitude, instantly analyzed, its meaning and implications forecasted and presented directly to her cerebral cortex as knowledge.

As the energy mounted, so did the feeling of power in her veins as ever more potent signals thrummed through her synapses. It was building to a surging crescendo, balanced, perfectly in tune. Supply and demand singing in harmony as the reactors went energy positive and started to fire. The feeling pounded through her, and even as her mind swam in perfect clarity with all the information coursing through her, the sense of it all drove her to something close to orgasm, sweat breaking out on her brow, her face and neck flushing as she lay, cradled in the Terminus station, some two miles from where her mind was sparking eight new suns to life at the center of New Moon One's engines.

Captain Harkness felt some echo of the life in his engines from the ship's systems, and sensed as the eight massive engines cycled and notified him of their readiness. He felt as Birgit disengaged from each in turn, and handed them off to their various techs, turning each into separate entities so they could be managed by their respective onboard teams.

As they came online, the captain flexed them and tensed his machine body, feeling it respond. It was almost time. Checklists filled as feelings of strength in his mind, his health was the ship's tested newness, his breathing its fuel and life support systems, his eyes the far reaching sensors and onboard cameras that covered the hull, inside and out. A presence met him, stepping into his world from outside and greeting him. It was Birgit, linking in one last time from Terminus station, head of the 'ground' crew that had helped build and prepare New Moon One. Her checks had completed as his had: her team's minds scouring the ship like dockhands were satisfied and signing off: and so they were ready.

The countdown began as planned. The computers sought his approval and got it, a second surging feeling came as Birgit gave her approval and she was gone, a single message left in her wake. He would read it later.

Birgit retracted her view as the ship came to life, the countdown running toward zero, and she engaged with Terminus's external cameras and sensor suite to view the launch. Joining numerous others using the station's eyes and ears, she watched as the spherical ship began to glow. It was just outside Terminus's own orbit, sitting above it, and it would need to clear her range before beginning its descent. The eight cigar-shaped engines came to life in unison as the counter reached zero. Only mildly at first, Captain Harkness feeling his way before ramping up their power. Eight blue streaks began to resolve behind the ship. Tiny atomic particles accelerated to near light speed and catapulted from the ship to give their momentum to it. Such tiny masses, but fired with such monumental power that they began to drive the mighty ship forward, pulling ahead of Terminus's orbit and starting to accelerate around Earth's equator.

His confidence building, the captain surged the power upward smoothly toward his operational maximum, the eight blue lines from his engines forming into sharp white blades, hot as supernovae. Inside the ship, twenty-three bodies were pressed into their gravity cradles as the ship thrusted forward. Pulling away at a rate of nine gravities, the ship was a hundred miles from Terminus in under a minute, travelling at a relative thousand miles an hour already.

Varying the output from each of his engines ever so slightly, the captain began to curve the ship downward. He arced them smoothly toward the huge globe beneath them, even as the ship continued to gather speed, gravity adding to their flight now as they began their mad plummet into Earth's gravity well. The accelosphere engineers began their preparations. It would come up fast now, and they would only have a brief window for the coming translation.

From SpacePort One, Neal and a host of dignitaries and staff watched the ship turn earthward, and the tension began to mount. Silence was broken only by the regular report of the mission commander updating on speed and altitude, and the occasional heavy sigh as someone remembered to breath.

The ship entered the atmosphere not on a ballistic trajectory, as it was not *coasting* downward, instead it was punching through the air like a cosmic cannonball, the wild blue flare of its engines overshadowed now by the fireball of our atmosphere wasting itself on the ship's meter thick shielding. But even that thick shield could not stand too much more, for unlike previous spacecraft, or entering meteorites, New Moon One was not slowing, it was getting faster still, and the pressure and fire would only build until they rivaled the fire in the stellar cores of its eight engines.

The moment came. They knew it would. They could see the timer ticking slowly to zero. But despite this, no one was quite prepared for it. With an intense suddenness, the fireball imploded, a shock wave resounding outward across the upper atmosphere as the source of that massive turbulence and heat vanished, quite literally into thin air. A vortex of smoke warped the upper atmosphere like an inhaled cloud.

And then there was silence.

They knew that somewhere the ship's engines were still firing. They knew that the ship was, in fact, still coursing toward the earth, and even now beginning its ultrasonic flight straight through it. But for everyone in the control room, and in the many powerful offices monitoring the event, New Moon One had simply vanished.

A new counter showed now, and the screen was already switching to a new view as the effects of New Moon's abrupt departure wafted ethereally on the wind. Now the view went to a camera mounted on a StratoJet on the other side of the planet. The jet was circling high above the central Pacific Ocean, about three hundred miles north of the Marquesas archipelago, its pilot, Major Jack Toranssen, already in position for the next big step. He was waiting and transmitting a signal via humanity's growing subspace tweeter network to audiences in SpacePort One, Terminus, the Research Group in their bunker in Japan, and a select few heads of state around the globe.

- - -

Complete blackness surrounded Captain Harkness and his team. Weightless and isolated, they watched their internal clocks and hoped their calculations were correct. They could have no way of knowing their location. They had no instruments capable of penetrating the void outside, for they were enveloped in a sphere that placed them outside the normal universe. They were passing through the seemingly dense core of the planet like sound through water, unencumbered, unnoticed, their presence muted but still vital, waiting to reenter the universe when they were safely clear of Earth's fiery core. For now they were as ghosts. Ephemeral. Awaiting translation back into reality even as they harvested Earth's massive gravitational well to slingshot them right through itself.

Samuel listened to his systems. Even his subspace communications were silent, operating as they did in a different dimension again from the one he now found himself in, lost in the many layers of reality.

With nothing else to do, they counted down.

- - -

Fourteen minutes after New Moon One had vanished from space, the majority of the most important and powerful people on Earth had returned from whatever task they had busied themselves with, and were once again routed to their various screens, mute and transfixed as the counter went to single digits.

Jack circled the anticipated spot, his StratoJet flying at over sixty thousand feet and his cameras pointing higher still into the purple blackness of the exosphere. Countless models and experiments had led them to this precise time and place on the far side of the planet.

The time came. Whether clear of Earth or not, this is when New Moon One would disengage its accelosphere. Acute cameras on Jack's plane showed a lucky few hundred spectators the spot as it happened. Space seemed to warp and then explode outward as seven hundred tons of fusion-fired madness was reintroduced to the universe. A thunderclap was heard across a quarter of the planet as the shockwave buffeted the earth, but New Moon One was not waiting to see the aftereffects of its rebirth. Catapulted outward at over seventy thousand miles per hour, Captain Harkness and his crew shot out away from Earth. Fired out like a cosmic cannonball, using Earth's entire mass for gunpowder.

They surged out from Earth, and aboard, Captain Harkness felt their course resolve now, not theory but certainty, a future they were now hurtling toward at ever increasing speed. Powering in a wide arc, they would now dip into the sun's vastly more powerful embrace.

They would not penetrate that massive orb as they had the Earth. Such extreme catapults as stars were reserved for achieving interstellar speeds. But New Moon One would veer inside Earth's orbital path, so they could cut the corner on the orbit that would take us a full year, and in doing so they would catch up with their quarry from behind.

And so the ship surged outward, like a blue missile spat from the planet's very soul. Still accelerating, it soon outpaced the telescopes tracking it, until Birgit and her colleagues could only see the angelic blue flare of its engines.

The crew, jubilant at their monumental achievement, settled in for the longest journey any human had ever undertaken, either in terms of time or distance, and Captain Harkness remembered the message left for him by Birgit as they departed. Opening it, he heard her voice in his mind. 'God speed, Captain. You fly on the wings of the combined accomplishments of two races. A hundred light-years have been crossed to bring you the technology that powers your magnificent ship, and she is, without doubt, the most amazing thing humanity has ever built. Take her and enjoy her, Samuel. Take her out. And when you come back, bring Earth a New Moon.'

Chapter 32: Landing Party

Though Nick and Malcolm had never gotten more than a few feet above sea level during their crossing of the Caspian Sea, their landing in Azerbaijan was proving far rougher than that of Hektor and his team, a thousand miles to the north.

The Turkmen fishermen they had co-opted had been both surly and dangerous looking, and the two men had been unable to get any real rest during the eight hours it had taken them to get across the inland sea. Combine this with the roughness of the crossing, and the lingering stench of rotting fish guts that pervaded every part of the ship, and you had the recipe for a most unforgiving voyage.

Once in sight of land, the trip had only gone from uncomfortable to trepidatious.

The coast of Azerbaijan appeared in the distance like a murky, smog-covered line, topping a choppy, dirty seascape. Ships of all sizes plied to and from the port city of Baku, which was Azerbaijan's largest port, largest city, and capital. In the distance, they could see the occasional custom's boat plying back and forth amongst the late morning shipping, looking for Iranian smugglers, local sturgeon poachers who hadn't paid their dues, and any sign of whatever had so recently and effectively subjugated the Stannic Bloc across the sea to the east.

They didn't have the manpower to stop very many of the hundreds of fishing vessels moving in the harbor, but the Turkmen markings on Nick and Malcolm's boat were a sure invite to investigate further, and Nick was becoming restless.

"We need to get on to one of those local fishing boats," said Nick in an aside to Malcolm.

"How?" asked Malcolm. They were sitting on upturned plastic containers amidships, stained from the thousands of fish carcasses that had passed through them. Nick was facing the open door of the wheelhouse they sat next to, the captain at the wheel, clearly very aware of Nick's presence. Malcolm sat with his back to Nick, facing aft, to where the ship's three crewmen sat sullenly. Both the British men had their guns drawn.

"We pull alongside one and commandeer it; get them to take us ashore, and then tie them up and make our way to a payphone or the embassy," responded Nick.

"What about these guys?" said Malcolm, waving his gun at the Turkmeni, "Won't they go to the local authorities once we get off the ship?"

"Only if they want to spend the next few nights, or possibly longer, in jail answering questions about what they were doing in Azerbaijani waters in the first place. No, once we've pointed our guns elsewhere they'll turn around and get the hell out of here."

"Assuming they don't run us down in the meantime," said Malcolm warily.

Nick seemed to ponder this a while, nodding thoughtfully as he did so. Seeming to come to a conclusion, he stood and stepped to the side of the wheelhouse, scanning the horizon.

- - -

Rizvan Asadov had been fishing for forty years. Not constantly, though it felt that way some days. Poaching of the prized sturgeon had always been a problem, but in recent years it had gone from nuisance to epidemic, as the poachers had started becoming brazen in the face of the increasing willingness of local officials to turn a blind eye.

Now they even used dynamite or homemade explosives in metal pipes, dropped into shallow waters, to obliterate everything for tens of meters. After siphoning off the sturgeon they prized, they left a swathe of destruction in their wake, and they were fast destroying whole ecosystems.

Rizvan, today out with his brother-in-law Gulshan for purely recreational purposes, was increasingly frustrated with the lack of fish to catch. This was ironic, as Mr. Asadov was, in fact, one of the very parasites who had taken bribes to look the other way in his days working for the Environmental Ministry. He had reconciled his actions as him being part of a greater whole, and by saying that the poaching hadn't been as bad when he was doing it as it was now. Such is the mindset of the institutionally corrupt.

For his part, Gulshan, Rizvan's sister's rather dimwitted husband, was happily humming in the back of the boat, immune to the futility of their venture. But it was Gulshan, not Rizvan, who spotted the old fishing trawler motoring their way. He stared for a while, wondering why the ship was coming so close. But as the ship continued to come on, Gulshan eventually expressed his confusion.

"ahhmm, Rizvan?" he said in a puzzled tone. Rizvan only grunted in response, his eyes on his line as it bobbed in the water. This is far too deep, we will catch nothing here, thought Rizvan. But the shallows that had been so fruitful in his youth were all but barren now.

"ahhhmmm, Rizvan?" said Gulshan again, more loudly now.

"*What*, Gulshan?" said Rizvan impatiently, still not looking up, even as the sound of an old diesel engine impugned on his sullenness.

Gulshan went to speak again, but went silent, the sight of the dirty but clearly very pale man on the side of the boat coming alongside them throwing him off completely. Eventually, the noise of the approaching boat broke through Rizvan's sullen mood, and he looked up, his expression quickly turning indignant at the sight of the fishermen, then angry at the sight of the Turkmen writing on the side of the rickety ship.

His mood changed once more when the Western-looking man leaning over the rails of the boat revealed a small but expensive-looking gun, and pointed it down at the two surprised-looking Azerbaijanis.

- - -

The transfer was tense, all parties on the verge of violence from start to finish. Nick had taken Malcolm's point about the disgruntled captain of the larger Turkmen fishing boat, and the chance that he might try to run them down once they were aboard the smaller vessel.

Though that was unlikely now that they were in sight of the shore, the chance that they still had a shotgun or some other weapon below decks that they might produce once Nick and Malcolm were in the smaller fishing boat was an eminent possibility. So they had ordered the Turkmen captain down into the smaller fishing boat first, followed by Malcolm, with a promise that the fishermen could pick up their captain once they were clear.

The result was a decidedly cramped and very hostile little fishing Dhow, motoring away from an even angrier Turkmen crew in the dusky afternoon air. The Turkmen captain was mumbling unpleasantries at the two Englishmen, while the two Azerbaijanis sat in mute silence. Malcolm couldn't help but feel guilty for taking the Turkmen so far from home. But in the light of what he and Nick were facing, the scale of the Turkmen's plight was appropriately diminished.

Once they were a quarter of the way toward the shore, and closer still to the discombobulated fleet coming to and from the busy port, Nick indicated with his gun for Rizvan to slow down. Once they were lulling once more on the swell, he gestured for the captain to get into the water. The man hesitated. Partly concerned about being shot in the back, partly concerned about being left there, and partly resisting the urge to believe it all might actually end peacefully.

But peaceful it was. Once the captain was in the water, Nick waved for the Turkmen boat to approach, and then ordered Rizvan to get going for the shore, waving his gun liberally to emphasize the point.

"Keep an eye on the Turkmen boat," Nick said to Malcolm. "After all this, I wouldn't want his crew to leave him there and make off with his livelihood."

Malcolm looked mildly alarmed at this thought, and glanced back at the Turkmen vessel, and its captain flailing in the water, as they came to pick him up. But the crew seemed to get their captain inboard with little trouble, and the two boats parted. The Turkmen were full of reasons to hate the Englishmen, but their desire was superseded by a baser survival instinct. Turning briskly, they headed back out to sea.

In the end, Nick and Malcolm's landing in Azerbaijan was as bumpy as it could have been. They motored along the shore for some way looking for a relatively deserted spot, passing under the long, low bridge to Gum Island off the coast of Baku, and the stilt caviar factories that branched off it. The bridge creaked with foot traffic and puttering carts, ferrying their precious cargo ashore, the rusting antiquity of them juxtaposed against the value of their cargo.

Nick shivered as the cool sea breeze washed through him. They were grimy. Tenseness had become their everything, and they were exhausted on a primal level, functioning now on adrenalin alone. As they finally motored toward the brown sand beach, Nick and Gulshan leapt from the boat, the water like an icy baptism around Nick's feet and calves, bracing and reviving him. They were close now, so close to safety. Malcolm looked at Nick. The man was a husk, but somehow he was still awake, and his eyes still brimmed with violence and an inherent threat.

Gulshan and Rizvan sensed this like a pall over their heads, and any resistance they might have mustered had ebbed out of them as they approached shore. They were on trial, they knew that, how they behaved now would determine whether they were left alive once they hit shore. Keen to demonstrate his subservience, Rizvan clambered out of the boat to help

Gulshan and Nick pull it up onto the dank, claylike sand. Once it was inshore, the two Azerbaijani turned to each other, exchanging a meaningful glance, before looking at Nick.

Nick looked at Gulshan, shivering, breathing with high, bated breaths, his lungs never fully deflating, as his body rode a crest of adrenalin, his fear and utter confusion only moments away from overwhelming him. Then he looked at Rizvan. The man was prepared. He was facing death with what dignity he could muster, and Nick saw that this man, as it was, had found his best in this moment. It was enough for Nick.

With a wave of his gun, he indicated for them to get back in their boat. Gulshan looked from Nick to Rizvan, and back again, waiting for his brother-in-law to react, but Rizvan merely waited, trying to see if this was merely a ploy to get them to turn from the gun. If he was going to die he wanted to face it, to see it coming, to make his killer look him in the eye as he died, and leave a memory in him, a demon he would have to live with.

A second passed. Nick could see Rizvan was waiting for some sign of animosity from him, but he gave none, only stern resolve. The moment held, and then, like the slow roll of a cyclist cresting a hill and starting down the other side, the moment gave, and Rizvan turned toward his boat. Gulshan took the older man's lead, and helped him shove the boat back into the small swell, the two men feeling their youth come back to them as they heaved with vigor and then leapt into the small craft. As Rizvan fiddled with the engine, Gulshan stared at the two Englishmen, trying to be surreptitious, and watched as they walked backward up the rocky shore, keeping their eyes on the boat as it wallowed in the mild surf, before the engine puttered to life and propelled them out and away.

It was three miles to the embassy, but Nick did not intend to walk. Once the boat was a fair distance off, he reached into his jacket pocket and extracted a small ziplock bag. He pulled out a cell phone and a battery, plugging the one into the other, and waited for a signal. It took an eternity, but eventually two bars appeared and he dialed, the phone performing as it was designed to do.

The phone company would register the call on its systems as a hacked number, and eventually would shut down the sullied number in a little under three weeks. But Nick only needed to make one call.

Fifteen minutes later a car slowed near a rank pile of fishing nets and lobster pots. Its trunk popped open, and two dirty, odorous, and exhausted men climbed in, squeezing in together for ten final minutes of indignity as they rode out of town, away from the embassy, and into the hands of one of Ayala's colleagues.

They would be scrubbed, changed, and out of the country by midnight.

Chapter 33: Meeting of Equals

<good evening, neal/ayala/barrett/jack/john/quavoce,> said minnie, the message going to the whole group and to each individually at the same moment.

Neal: 'good evening, minnie. good evening, everyone.'

Minnie and Amadeu had configured a small virtual meeting space for such meetings, not dissimilar to the one the defunct Mobiliei Council had met in during its brief but infamous existence.

Ayala: 'good evening, neal, minnie. as we're all here, why don't i kick things off. i have called us together so that we could discuss initial intel coming out of russia. i have asked for a comms link with our teams on the ground, and we will be patching into them soon, but before we get to that, i have another report that has just come in from azerbaijan, routed to me from an mi6 asset in place there.'

She stopped speaking and, with her ever-growing confidence in the strange communications process, packaged the report in question in her head, and shared it with the rest of the group. The report came to them at once, highlighted parts lifting from its contents, focusing their attention to the sections Ayala wanted to talk about.

Commander Huxley, Royal Navy, [Seq.] Mil. Intel., *Ashgabat Field Office:* '… was at about 3am, first night of e&e [escape & evacuation], sleeping in car park … flown over by first type of small black search drone …'

'… wide wingspan … three engines, two large, mounted aft; one small, nose-mounted … thruster.'

Lieutenant Malcolm Granger: '… another of them flew over two hours later, moving faster …'

Cmdr Huxley: '… no, different type; faster, shorter wingspan, same black fuselage, same blue-white jet-trail, but this one was a fighter, much faster.'

Lt. Granger: '… agree … maneuverability was phenomenal … acceleration far higher than any vtol [vertical take-off and landing] aircraft …'

The group continued to review the meat of the message, even as some were already reaching conclusions and starting to react.

Ayala: 'we are ready to connect with recon teams one and three in russia. but i wanted to get your perspective on this data first.'

Barrett reacted first. An image forming in his mind's eye of the planes being discussed.

Barrett: 'i am most concerned about the first variant. ¿are they describing some kind of F-35 copy, or a harrier jumpjet?'

Jack: 'neither of those can hover for prolonged periods of time. sounds like they aren't just talking about a standard vtol, general.'

Neal was quiet, but deep down he was profoundly disquieted by this news. Its implications were profound.

John: 'my friends, i fear that mr. granger may have accidentally hit this nail on its head. i fear we are not talking about two different plane formats at all.'

The group was silent for the second that it took for this concept to sink in. Neal nodded to himself. Any interpretation he could come up with led down some dark avenues, but John had hit on the one he feared the most.

Neal: 'i want to talk to the recon teams.'

Ayala was already working to patch them in, but Barrett was a moment longer catching up with the rest of the group.

Barrett: 'i'm sorry, but how could they be the same plane, i am hearing two different wing forms …'

The general stopped himself. His recollections of the liquiform trailing edges and adaptable wing forms of the StratoJet came to him, built around rigid nanotube spars that could hinge in and out to provide the superstructure of the wings. The morphing wings of the StratoJet had seemed so esoteric, so futuristic, Barrett had not even allowed himself to think that anyone else on Earth could have them. The implications stunned him into silence.

He joined the rest of the virtual conference's participants in quiet introspection while they waited for Ayala to speak again. The pause seemed long, almost tortuous, though only a few seconds passed in real-time. Minnie had the recon teams patching in, ready to speak at their command. Even as the group continued to review the full report coming from Nick and Malcolm, Ayala spoke to Minnie.

Ayala at Minnie: '¿minnie, which of the teams is on open connection?'

Minnie at Ayala: 'recon team leaders one and three are online now. recon two is in position, pings show connection imminent.'

With that, Ayala could feel the pending connections like beseeching children awaiting permission to speak. Knowing the leader of Recon One especially well, she opened connection with him first, pinging Recon Three to hold a moment longer.

Ayala: 'captain miller, this is ayala.'

She began somewhat redundantly, the virtual voice that you used in such conversations carrying with it a data packet that confirmed, at the primal level, the identity and location of the sender.

Ayala: 'you are on with t.a.s.c. leadership, please report on progress.'

Captain Miller: 'yes sir, this is team lead miller, recon one. as our reports show to date, we have completed stages one through four of our recon pattern. as shown in relayed image capture, we can confirm previous force estimates at rostov.'

The captain was about to go on about their recon mission around the large town of Rostov-on-Don, but Neal did not have the patience to listen to a full report. He had reviewed the images and data sent back by the teams. He had seen the new imagery coming back from the Pod satellites they had begun seeding into Low-Earth Orbit from the Climbers as they rose, their decaying orbits designed to harvest and return ever better resolution imagery in a broad spectrum, before the disposable units disintegrated in the atmosphere.

Even as he interrupted the captain, Neal was calling up recent and real-time flyover imagery.

TASC CO Dr. Danielson: 'captain, sorry for interrupting. we have seen the reports. your thoroughness and efficiency is very much appreciated. but today, if you can, i would like to focus on some specific questions we have.'

Captain Miller: 'of course, sir.'

Neal: 'captain, we have received unsubstantiated reports of currently unidentified aircraft as a component of the russian forces. specifically, these craft may have features not unlike our own stratojet fleet. can you confirm any such sightings.'

Images of the StratoJet, clear in Neal's mind as he recalled them in cyberspace, relayed themselves via Minnie to the whole group, and were echoed into Captain Miller's virtual sight as he crouched in deep tree cover, his team encircling his position, providing strict border cover while he communed via the tweeter with TASC leadership.

The captain was not hasty in his response. He had not seen them. But one of his team had.

Captain Miller: 'sir, I have not had a direct confirmation of any such craft. but one of my spezialists has seen something that may be of interest. with your permission i will patch him in now.'

Ayala took the liberty of opening the line. The Spezialist in question could not see the whole meeting room. He would speak only via his captain, and would hear only what was released to him by the Team Lead.

Spezialist Mik Guttman: 'sir.'

Captain Miller: 'spezialist guttman, please recount the drone sighting you had this morning.'

Spezialist Mik Guttman: 'yes, sir. it was at approximately 0400 hours. i was running point for our final reloc of the night to vantage point one-bravo-november, and i called in a team halt. i had seen a jet-trail ahead, and we went to ground while it passed. i would initially have described the contact as not dissimilar to a global hawk drone, only with dual jet propulsion. but then it accelerated away, and it was significantly faster than any global hawk model i am aware of.'

Neal: 'spezialist, when you say accelerated hard, please describe the jet-trail. ¿was it an afterburner?'

Captain Miller heard the question, and relayed it onward to the waiting Spezialist Guttman. The reply came hesitantly.

Spezialist Mik Guttman: 'afterburner, well, i wouldn't describe it as that, sir, no. afterburners go from orange to blue, this went from blue to … white.'

Quavoce: 'he is describing fusion jet units.'

Barrett: '¿but how can they make fusion generators without a resonance chamber?'

John Hunt: 'they can't, not on the small scale we are discussing here. certainly we were unable to produce efficient fusion reactors back on mobilius smaller than a small tank until we developed resonance chamber technology. the desire to reduce their size was a major impetus behind the development of resonance theory.'

The room paused a moment longer, maybe waiting for Neal to ask another question. Finally he spoke up.

Neal: 'ayala, i assume you will fully debrief spezialist guttman on this after this meeting. for now, can you relay what we have to the other recon teams, along with imagery of the stratojet. it sounds like we are dealing with a smaller craft than our own, but maybe they have others as well. please ask them to come back with any additional relevant data on these immediately.'

Ayala: 'glad you asked, neal, as i was doing just that. receiving preliminary confirmations now. no additional sightings at this time.'

Neal: 'understood. no doubt you are already doing this as well, but i would like to move this to priority one on the recon mission profiles.'

Ayala: 'i couldn't agree more. i will update and relay to the teams.'

Neal: 'thank you.' He paused, and then went on, 'we should probably also update their tactical parameters to include the assumption that the russian forces may now include troops equipped with some measure of our own battleskin's capabilities. they should proceed with appropriate caution.'

Ayala: 'yes, it is discomforting, but must be assumed. i will work to update them on capacities as appropriate. ¿quavoce, maybe you could help me with some modeling there?'

But as Ayala and Neal marched onward, others were having a harder time taking all this in.

Jack: 'wait, please, wait. ¿are we saying that agents mikhail and or pei have helped the russians make a resonance chamber, and they are producing some version of the stratojet right now?'

Ayala: 'well, we can't be certain, but it certainly seems likely given what we are seeing, and if it is even minimally likely then we should proceed accordingly. it makes sense, after all.

¿why wouldn't they give russia the ability to defend itself if they intend to use them as puppets to destabilize our efforts?'

Jack: 'but they would be giving russia, and thus humanity, access to the very technology we are going to need to fight the coming armada. ¿why would they want to do that?'

Quavoce: 'the units they are describing sound like much smaller fighters than the larger stratojets we have been producing. i can imagine a scenario where i would have done the same, in their place, given that they must have correctly assumed humanity already has access to such technology from john. they have probably limited themselves to only sharing ground and atmospheric units. neither of which will be of real use in the coming war.'

Neal: 'of course they have shared this. in fact, we should probably have assumed this from the start. we should never have waited this long to become involved.'

Barrett: '¿neal, what were we supposed to do? ¿just unilaterally invade? we could not have taken direct action without the permission of our allies, not without risking the support we so badly need from them. and they would never let us meddle in what is already a veritable powder keg.'

Neal waited a moment, then let them know what he thought about waiting for permission.

Neal: 'we have wasted far too long tiptoeing around the inadequate and ineffective governments of our allies. we have wasted too long begging for approval and support. this is not a negotiation. our needs are not up for debate. our mission trumps all this petty bickering, and i am tired of asking for the permission of people who seem more worried about the survival of their political careers than they are about the survival of the planet.'

Barrett went to interject, to staunch the flow of vitriol spewing from Neal's mind, but even as he went to speak, Quavoce and John shared sub-link flashes of approval for this turn of events.

They had tried to stay out of the political machinations of the group, knowing it was not their place to meddle in the governing of alien worlds, any more than it had been to come to Earth in the first place. But now someone was giving voice to this growing concerns they would not deny that they agreed with the need to take as strong a stance as was feasible given the scale of the task they faced.

But Neal was not asking for his Mobiliei friends' approval, nor did he give Barrett the chance to air his concerns any further.

Neal: 'madeline, barrett, please work with birgit to force-analyze dispositions in eastern bloc nations. we are going to need tactical contingency plans should things come to a head there. ayala, please unleash the recon teams, they are to proceed with caution, but they are also to proceed with haste. i want mission patterns to include incoming forces *behind* major russian force buildups. get those teams deeper. i want to know what the russians have, i want to know how much of it they have, and i want to know it now.'

The room was silent once more. Eventually Barrett spoke up, knowing as soon as he did so that he should have waited.

Barrett: '¿should we pass on this new information to our nato colleagues?'

If they had have been in a room together, they would have visibly flinched at Neal's expression. Instead, a palpable silence invaded the conversation. Taming his annoyance, Neal eventually responded.

Neal: 'yes, barrett, i imagine we should. we can tell them about the report from Turkmenistan, and hint that we have received others as well, but we should include no mention of the recon teams, for obvious reasons. if we get more concrete proof we can pass that along. ¿ayala, can you take care of that?'

Ayala: 'i can and i will, neal. but, to your point earlier, this raises a broader issue. our european allies are already very nervous, especially the germans, about activity in the former eastern bloc. this may drive them to want to bring home more forces from rolas, or worse, demand our own intervention.'

Neal was beyond anger now. Instead, a now familiar cool-fury settled in his stomach. He funnelled his frustration into it, he had to, and he would deal with it or tap into it later, when he was alone. The Russians were playing a dangerous game, but they were playing it well. What may seem like baiting a lion was, in fact, only prodding at a caged one. The Russians were dancing around the perimeter of NATO's world, but had yet to cross that line. They were stepping close to the bars, but staying notably away from the cat's claws.

If Mikhail and Pei were indeed the ones pulling the strings here, and Neal couldn't see any other reasonable conclusion, then they would not cross that line. They would not broach Western Europe, or even the larger of Central Europe's re-emerging economies. And as long as they didn't, no nuclear power was going to sign on for World War Three anytime soon. But that didn't mean Neal's allies, and supporters, weren't going to get very, very nervous. Mikhail and Pei were making things ever more complex for Neal, and no doubt that was a big part of their intention.

He breathed deeply. Then he responded, calm and cold.

Neal: 'we all know that further force reduction here is something we must resist with utmost force. and having our stratojets and spezialists engaged in force is simply unacceptable under any circumstances. to leave rolas exposed, especially given this latest information, cannot be allowed.'

Ayala pushed the issue, as she knew she must. After all, given Neal's mood she doubted anyone else would.

Ayala: 'i agree wholeheartedly. but our allies may not. i am afraid that if we share too much at this stage, without an appropriate plan to counter, we may be inviting disaster.'

Barrett: 'no, ayala, we simply must inform the europeans of this. we cannot allow important intel that could lead to significant casualties to stay in a file.'

Ayala: 'i understand that, general, but neither should we incite fear and concern where no action is possible. look, if we are honest, the europeans are not going to intervene with force even if the russians invade ukraine, there will simply not be enough political support. that is also true of belarus and, to a lesser extent, the baltic states in the north. ¿honestly, barrett, am i wrong?'

She was not, and she was about to go on when Barrett begrudgingly followed her line of thinking.

Barrett: 'no, ayala, you aren't. the question is will the russians stop there. we have to hope that the russians, even in their current state of abandon, will not push their luck too far. because if they do, the europeans are going to be forced to respond, and when that happens, we are going to have to intervene on their behalf, all the more so if we have withheld important intel about the enemy's capabilities.'

Ayala knew it, and Neal knew it.

Neal: 'you are both right. we will, no doubt, be forced to share this information at some point in the future, but for now we will keep it to ourselves. that said, we will also prepare for worst case scenario here, and make sure we get more informed in the meantime.'

They had made their points. This was a liquid topic, any policy would have to be equally flexible, but for now they had their orders. The conversation turned strategic, Barrett starting to share his thoughts as imagery and analyses reeled across his memory. Ayala was also busy, communing with Minnie on centers of population and ground topography to update the recon teams' search patterns.

As they all set to getting their limited but capable force into place for whatever was coming next, the three Recon Teams were setting off once more, beginning the night's sortie after a day of stationary signal hacking, observation, and rest.

Ten miles ahead of Recon Team One, Captain Miller was unaware of another three-person team, split up and moving quietly, clad in the same night-black, power augmented armor as the Spezialists. They carried with them small subspace tweeters, capable of very limited transmission range. But these tweeters were not speaking, they were listening. Listening for the encrypted pulse of the Recon Teams more powerful subspace signal. Listening, even though they could not understand the hyper-encrypted signal. They were moving in, triangulating the source of the Recon Team's subspace transmission.

They were watching Ayala's small team. They were one of many teams looking for any possible incursion. Via innocuous-seeming radio, the Russians sent a message back to Moscow.

Ben's team had been discovered.

Chapter 34: Axis Two

Premier Svidrigaïlov would not have appeared ambitious to most. A middling sized man, he was mildly overweight, slightly balding, mostly grey, and a host of other qualified adjectives. He seemed average almost by design, and he had had survived by this apparent mediocrity, and suffered under it, for most of his adult life.

For even as he appeared so very middle of the road, he had a fearsome loathing for the average. He used the bylines of the communist manifesto as the source of his public demagoguery, but in fact, he sought nothing so innocuous. He sought dominion, his dominion over his country, and then his country's dominion over the world. The proletariat were the foundation of his empire, and he needed them strong like any good communist, but more importantly, he needed them well underfoot.

His office was oppulent and ancient, an irony of the ever-changing power dynamic of Russia; from kingdom, to republic, to union, back to country, and now to empire, in little over a century. Moscow's reach had ebbed and flowed like a tide, rushing between the shores of the Baltic, Arctic, Black, and Caspian Seas with more violence and variance than any other nation in recent history. But through all that, Red Square had remained at its center, unchanging, inviolate. It was a waterfall of influence, whose source, power, and size shifted constantly, but whose singular scale and majesty remained, a thundering tribute to the farthest-reaching capitol on earth.

Seated behind a vast, dark mahogany desk, topped with thick, burnished green leather carefully spread and hammered across its antique surface, the premier reclined, reading a briefing prepared by his deputy. Into his solitude the man in question entered, a brief knock heralding him.

The deputy waited quietly just inside the door while the premier finished reading whatever paragraph had interested him. When the leader glanced up, he saw the deputy's expectant expression, telling him that the man had something pressing to report, and gave a curt nod.

"Premier Svidrigaïlov," said Peter Uncovsky, deferentially, "if I may, I have an issue that may require your attention."

The premier frowned inquisitively, but without anger, taking his cue from his assistant's tone that this was not something that threatened the security of the federation, though it did merit some concern. A wave of the premier's hand brought the diminutive Mr. Uncovsky to stand in front of the expansive desk. Though Peter usually carried himself tall and straight, he tended to stoop unconsciously in the premier's presence. And so he stood now, his head suspended in front of his shoulders, and delivered his message in the quick and efficient manner that the premier preferred.

"I have received word from Field Commandant Beria, Premier. He wishes to share that he has intelligence to suggest the allied force known as TASC has sent operatives into Russia to supervise our movements at Rostov, and potentially Bryansk and Belgorod as well."

"Uhh!" exclaimed the office's surly resident, leaning forward to face his most senior advisor. "Again with this news of these 'allied forces.' Why is he obsessed with this piss-ant group of scientists and their petty, hodge-podge force?"

The deputy waited while Yuri exhausted his brief rant.

"I do not know, Premier. But he remains insistent that they are a threat."

"A threat!" said Yuri Svidrigaïlov, his assistant's comment only refueling his indignation. "What could possibly be a threat at this stage? He counsels action, he counsels dominion, and then, as soon as we have momentum with us, he calls for caution."

Peter nodded appreciatively, as though listening to the wisdom of the ancients, then responded, "He sends notice of this potential incursion, and asks permission to review our invasion plans for Ukraine and Belarus with you. What message would you like me to send to him, Premier?"

"Of course he asks to review our plans once more," said the premier, in a tone laden with thick, sarcastic obsequiousness. "Let us see if we can be of assistance to him, shall we? Get Commander Beria on the line."

Peter hesitated just a moment, then nodded and turned. Stepping out of the large room, he barked some quick orders at the dedicated bank of secretaries filling an office across the hall from the premier's, and then waited. He did not like it when the premier was in this mood, and he liked it even less when the man spoke to his protégé Beria this way. Premier Svidrigaïlov had seen a hairpin turn in his fortunes since one Nikolai Beria had joined his cadre of confidants some four months ago, and those close to the premier were under no illusions as to just how instrumental the mysterious Commandant Beria had been to the ongoing rise of a certain Premier Svidrigaïlov.

Not that Peter would dare say such things to anyone else. This may not be the days of the Great Purges of Stalin, but no one who knew Premier Svidrigaïlov's leadership style doubted his thirst for power, or his capacity for ruthlessness should someone stand in his way. Many a foolhardy party member or minister of one of their newly inducted 'allied states' had suffered under the illusion that they could express an adverse opinion openly. With the noose-like grip they had squeezed around the Empire's communications, no one had ever learned what had happened to those men, but suffice to say their opinions were not shared enough times to find any wider purchase.

The irony was that Peter was close to certain that Nikolai Beria was not only the military mind behind Russia's recent and very swift conquests, but that Nikolai was also the fist at the end of Svidrigaïlov's far reaching arm, the blade that silenced any voice naïve enough to stand against the diminutive man's rule.

"Minister Uncovsky?" the plaintive voice roused Peter from his musing, and he turned to the lady standing to his left, nodding, as she went on. "I have Field Commandant Beria on line four."

"Good, good. Put it through to the premier's office."

He did not wait for confirmation. It was not a request. Instead, he turned briskly and returned to the great office across the hall, knocking once more, before poking his head in.

"I have the commandant on line four, Premier."

Yuri Svidrigaïlov waved Peter in as the premier pressed speaker and the flashing red button for line four on his desk phone.

The line sprang to life as Peter closed the door behind him and walked over to a small, inconspicuous chair in a corner, near the premier's shoulder.

"Commandant?" came the premier's barking voice.

"Yes, Premier, this is Field Commandant Beria," came the crisp, deep Russian voice through the speaker. "How may I be of service?"

"Yes, yes, Nikolai," there were not many people that did not sit up when the field commandant spoke, such was the combination of his ever growing reputation and his natural gravitas, it was even enough to knock some of the superiority from the premier's haughty disposition, "we have received this news of your concerns about 'incursions,' and 'allied forces.' I agree that this is most inconvenient, and that they have sent forces onto sovereign Russian soil is something they will be made to pay dearly for."

Peter waited for the field commandant to interrupt the premier's somewhat directionless rant. Indeed, Beria was the *only* man who could interrupt the premier. But no interruption came, and so the premier went on, "What I still fail to see is why we are even discussing this? Deal with these spies like you did the NATO ones that had infested Moscow. Deal with them at let us proceed as planned."

Now the commandant replied, his tone measured, his patience tested, but not exhausted, "Premier Svidrigaïlov, as you say, I intend to deal with the spies here just as swiftly as we did the various agents that had been present in Moscow, as well as in Islamabad, Astana, and even Dushanbe. But, as I have mentioned before, these forces are not quite the sa …"

He was cut off by an ever more impatient premier, Peter flinching at the man's brashness, "Nikolai, enough! I have already ordered you to rotate out the Special Forces from our new Stannic territories, much to the consternation of my governors in place there. Are you not also getting the full weight of all new Ubitsya Drone production coming from the Plant?"

The premier was referring to the new Ubitsya, or "Assassin" Drones, which the new and mysterious production facility at Novosibirsk was producing in slow but steady numbers. The plant had been a costly investment, one his budget had been ill equipped to afford, but it had paid incredible dividends. Nikolai had been insistent, to the point of vocally berating the premier, that they should make the investment.

He had been wise to limit the confrontation to a private meeting, the premier's patience would not have stood for open defiance, but Nikolai had been right.

Yuri's memory of the event was far from accurate now, though. Now he remembered himself as the visionary who had pushed for the new plant. Now he remembered only the façade of absolute confidence he showed to his other direct reports.

It was this bravado that now shone through once more.

Nikolai was silent for a moment, the line buzzing only with static, until he quietly replied, "Of course, Premier, and I appreciate your support, as always. May I suggest that you also show such wisdom in your support of my desire to factor in the allied forces involvement at this stage?"

"But why, Nikolai, why? I have seen with my own eyes what the Ubitsyas can do. Together with the full weight of the second, tenth, and twelfth armored divisions, battalion support, and the full air force fleet at your command, what difference could these allied reconnaissance teams make?"

"Premier, if you will permit me, it is not the forces already here that I am worried about. It is the broader involvement their presence implies."

The premier was confused. "How can the allied taskforce's involvement be any more serious than the already mobilized forces from the very countries that make up this ... *taskforce*? You are making no sense, Nikolai."

The tone that came from the line now was as close to curt as Peter had heard anyone be with the premier since his ascension to power, "Yuri Svidrigaïlov, my friend," the name was said with the weight of a parent, a parent whose patience is close to fraying, "if I have preached nothing since joining you in your rightful step into power, it is that there are forces at play here that are not as they seem."

The premier went to interrupt, if only to warn Nikolai not to overstep his bounds with another present, but the man on the end of the line did not desist, saying now, "You have seen what benefits may come from the new materials we have had access to from our Novosibirsk facility. Well, did it occur to you, my leader, that we would not be the only ones that would be able to develop them?"

The premier was stunned into silence. Not just by the force of Nikolai's tone, but by the force of his words. He allowed himself a surreptitious glance at the attentive, if quiet, Peter, and then composed himself, "You are saying that that the Americans and Europeans have developed the same armor plating technology?"

Far away, in the mobile command center that Field Commandant Beria was using as his center of operations for the next phase of Premier Svidrigaïlov's planned expansion, a sigh was barely contained.

"No, Premier, not the Americans and Europeans, though I fear they may have some measure of access to the technology as well, yes. Premier, when I have expressed concerns about TASC in the past, it was not simply because they represented a growing military capability. The taskforce was not formed without purpose, Yuri," and here, the man on the line became a tad liberal with his understanding of the current global political situation. "I have reason to believe the allied taskforce was formed specifically to try to counter Russia's resurgence."

The premier was wide-eyed, but Nikolai was not finished. "I had not wanted to mention it before, but the reconnaissance forces I have encountered here, small as they are, have confirmed my suspicions. The allied taskforce has developed a version of the armor plating as well. They are coming for Mother Russia, Premier, and I need your help to stop them."

The premier's expression was childlike, pleading almost, and his voice as he replied was plaintive, "Of course, Nikolai. For Mother Russia."

- - -

Far away, standing at a data bank, the man known as Field Commander Nikolai Beria stared at a wall of screens. His mind was alive with a hot flow of data coming to and from a black canister embedded in the bottom of the data bank, wired into it at an almost primal level.

As he finished his discussion with the premier, his lips did not move. The secure line to the mobile command center was linked, via the data bank, directly into the large subspace tweeter in its base. And from there the signal was being transmitted directly into his machine mind.

As he continued his tiresome debate with his puppet premier, he simultaneously opened a second connection. He did not use one of the many telephone lines patched into the command hub he was at the center of. Instead he used his subspace tweeter to tap into a small but pervasive network of tweeters he'd had one of his many Russian engineering groups distributing over the past months. It reached out across the more populace locales of the ever-growing dominion of the Russian People's Federation. It reached all the way across Kazakhstan, onward to the Plant, their secret resonance chamber facility in Novosibirsk.

From there it veered south.

Eventually it touched onto a less developed, but equally efficient, network across the border into China, and then the signal sped onward, at speeds limited only by the relaying capacity of the nodes involved, to Beijing, and to the headquarters of the Chinese Communist Party. Once there, it was relayed right into the residence of the chairman of the Politburo Standing Committee, the innocuously titled leadership nexus of the vast Chinese Republic.

The call was not picked up. It did not end with any conversation, as we would understand it. It ended with a connection of two substrate-based minds. Relayed across the breadth of Asia, the call connected the power hubs of the two largest countries on Earth. And it connected the Agent formerly known as Mikhail Kovalenko with his erstwhile counterpart Pei Leong-Lam.

Mikhail, now known as Nikolai Beria, had a request for his colleague. Mirroring the influence Nikolai had just demonstrated over the new Russian premier, he needed Pei to exert some measure of the same over his adopted leadership.

Pei was not going to be as subtle as Mikhail, though. Along with China's vast size and ancient history came a political complexity that made such blunt tactics as coup d'état all but impossible. Pei had been forced to take a more direct control of proceedings.

Even as he continued to commune with Mikhail, Pei walked into the bedroom of the Chairman of the Politburo Standing Committee, the ruling elite of China's ruling elite. The man turned to face him and cringed at the sight of Pei's smiling visage, the face of his nightmare.

Chapter 35: Codename: Grozny

The morning was cool and crisp. There was very little dew, and none of the usual mist that shrouded the hills around Rostov this time of year.

Captain Miller's team was settled in for the day. They had taken distributed lookout posts across a three-mile radius, covering the main access routes to the northeast of the town's outskirts. Following their mission protocols, they would limit movement now until darkness returned.

During the day they would rest, listen and watch.

Ben Miller sat in a high branch of a tree and willed his helmet open. It latched apart in three sections, the opening between them like forming a Y shape, harkening back for a moment to the plated helmets of medieval knights, noble and otherwise. But Ben's helmet was far more forgiving. The main fascia of the helmet, below the eye-line, kept sliding apart, across his cheeks, sliding back under his ears. The top of the faceplate slid upward and over the top of his head, opening his natural eyesight, and forming a small visor; the most advanced baseball cap in the world. His whole face was now open to the elements.

He inhaled deeply. The air was no different than before, though somehow it tasted better. The suit merely parsed it through micro-filters that lined the gaps between his helmet's sectional faceplate. But the microfibers also conducted away excess heat, equalizing the air's temperature almost instantaneously with the suit's ambient norm. A norm maintained by the tiny but potent fusion reactor built into its spinally mounted control nexus. It was a blessing on the bitter nights of the Don Valley, no doubt about that, but it also cut him off from his environment, and it was a pleasure to take in the crisp morning, unabridged, unedited.

He could see a tributary of a river, flowing briskly to the southwest, toward the city, and onward to the Black Sea, not far over the horizon. Thick, dense foliage lined the valley, filling it and overflowing its sides into valleys beyond, where his team was spread out, vigilant and still. The trees were dark green, almost black in the dawn light, wet with dew and life.

He felt it before he heard it. A ping in his center. Though he had scrolled his faceplate back, his suit's spinal interface still relayed any data coming to it directly to his visual cortex, to appear across his eyesight, not over his view, but as well as his view. A shimmering text and graphical display he could read in detail without ever losing focus on the very things the text should be obscuring. He was not as comfortable with the sensation as some, but was still better at handling it than most.

The ping was coming from one of his team members. Even as he answered it, his faceplate was already rejoining in front of his face, sealing out the light and brisk air, even as the greater light of his data feed overwhelmed his natural sight.

Stannislav: 'captain, i have movement coming down highway e50, sir. looks like another armored troop division, and more on its tail.'

Miller: 'copy that, stannis. team, that is the seventh division since midnight. mik, open a channel to command, i want eyes from above on this. if this isn't an invasion force then my name is umka.'

Umka was an old soviet era cartoon character, a lost young polar bear looking for his friend. It was a story that pretty much everyone behind the Iron Curtain had loved as a child. As a Lithuanian Jew, Ben had been no exception, and neither had the bulk of his Slavic and Russian born team.

Guttman: 'opening channel now, my sweet little umka.'

Ben Miller felt the channel open as he suppressed a chuckle, relayed from the short-range subspace tweeter in his suit to the larger, much bulkier one that Mik carried, as team comms specialist.

Captain Miller: 'mission command, we have more movement, on top of the night's already significant traffic. patching data packet to you now.'

Mik Guttman was already parceling his teammate Stannislav's report and image captures and forwarding on, as Ben knew he would be.

The reply was curt at first.

Comms. AI.: <message received, catalogued and relayed. commander zubaideh notified per standing order. coming on line in 3, 2, ...>

Ayala: 'ben, looking at the packet now. that is not a small number of troops. ¿were you able to get a bead on those mobile missile launchers that came in at 0530?'

Miller: 'no more data there, i am afraid. they continued on directly into the main camp at chaltyr. we have altered our viewpoints accordingly, though, if anything like that comes by again, we will be able to get eyes on to it.'

As he spoke with Ayala, he felt Mik reach out to him. He could not speak to two people at once with the fluency that users like Amadeu had managed, but he could come close. With only a brief interlude in his flow of speech to Ayala he listened to Mik's message.

Guttman: 'captain, i have an inbound aircraft, matches priority one description, it has come to hover at a mile out from my position.'

Mik, seated over two miles from Ben, was laying prone on a small bank, shrouded by shrubs and the low, heavy foliage of an old oak tree. At Ben's request, Mik's view became his own.

The plane, such as it was, was hovering. Its two rear jets were angled toward the ground as a third in its nose created a smaller plume, directed straight down. They could see the leaves of the trees below it rustling violently under the force of its pinpoint thrusters.

Miller: 'mik, open your view. send it live to command. i want commander zubaideh to see this.'

There was no confirmation from Mik, he just did it. Ayala saw it the next moment. Its thin wings were as wide as the plane was long. Judging by scale it was maybe four meters long, maybe less. A thin, tubular fuselage, with its two main wings matched by smaller ones at a 45° angle at the end of its tail.

Ayala: 'i see it, gentlemen, i see it. it is not as large as our stratojets, but the propulsion units are undoubtedly the same. as is the armor plating.'

Ben did not know everything about the source of the StratoJets, but he knew enough to know that this technology should not be in the hands of the Russians. He also knew enough to know that the suit that he wore now, the suit he had come to feel so very comfortable in, was from the same source as said StratoJets. Even as he went to comment on this, the scene suddenly changed.

The sonic boom caught them all off guard. It announced the arrival of another of the small jets, inbound at full speed from the north. The boom rippled over each of the team's positions in quick succession, heard through the ears of the most northerly Spezialist first, then BANG, BANG, BANG, as its arrival thundered across the valley.

Stannislav: 'i have another bogie, sir, inbound on mik's position at …'

He paused as his radar told him the speed. Finally he got up the nerve to relay it.

Stannislav: '…at mach 4. i repeat, mach 4.'

As the second Russian Ubitsya jet came in, the first started wheeling in midair. It was zeroing in. The hypersonic second jet barely had time to bank as it came down upon them, but it was already braking hard and coming around even as the first jet opened fire.

Mik Guttman did not have time to react. His position was blanketed in a wall of kinetic fury that tore the ground, the tree, the shrubbery, and his body to shreds. His suit attempted to withstand the force, but this was not something that could be absorbed. Imbedded in the nose of the Ubitsya was a quad-barreled flechette cannon not unlike the ones that Ben and two other of his team carried, only twice as large.

At twenty thousand miles an hour, the bullets pulverized Mik Guttman's world. He barely had time to register that he was under attack before his suit, his weapons, and his body were liquefied.

- - -

Ayala saw the connection go dead with a start. Still watching through Mik's eyes, she had seen the first Russian jet turn on him as its cousin arrived. She had seen the air around him suddenly erupt as the ground was vaporized, and then whatever had opened fire on him had destroyed the main subspace tweeter he had carried, and that had been that.

She reeled in cyberspace.

Ayala: 'minnie, get me neal! get me barrett! get me everyone, now!'

- - -

Ben reacted with animal instinct, going to move toward his friend's position. But the ominous silence coming from his comms specialist, and from the main relay, stopped him.

Miller: 'team, guttman is hit, assumed dead. go weapons hot. maintain positions and remain vigil. i don't know how they spotted him, so stay low. let's not add to our casualties.'

They responded only with pings. Ben was cold, not immune to the loss of his teammate and friend, but aware of the greater mission. When one member of a Recon Team was discovered it was his job to do anything he could to save him, but not if it compromised the mission. That was the deal. They all understood it.

Without the main subspace relay, comms were limited to suit-to-suit. Merik was the first to spot the planes again.

Merik: 'captain, i have visual on bogie 2, coming up from south.'

Stannislav: 'bogie 1 spotted, sir, also moving north from mik's position. staying low, and moving slowly.'

Merik: 'bogie 2 now subsonic, sir, circling stannis's position at low altitude.'

Ben had an uneasy feeling.

Miller: 'stannislav, i don't like this. i want you to find deeper cover. we know that the suits can be spotted via negative space scanning from our days hunting lana. get behind a tree. get covered in mud. do whatever you can to …'

Stannis waited a moment too long, watching the first Ubitsya as it came stealthily over a rise. As the second jet came in once more, much slower this time, it was only then that he turned to jump from his perch in a tall willow tree. Both jets came to hover, a quarter mile apart, focused on his position.

Silence, for just a moment, as he stepped from the branch. Then, sensing his movement somehow, they both fired.

From the other side of the small valley Merik could see the second jet as it started to spit its terrible munition. He saw the tree Stannis had been sitting in, he saw it burst into dust, into smoke, then into vapor. The tree was ripped to atoms by the dual fire from the two Russian fighters. Where the kinetic bullets crossed paths, blue ionic lightning could be seen, static to the point of devastation. Merik's arm came up, leveling at the second bogie. The rampage stopped, leaving a savage scar across the earth.

Merik froze, his weapons sighted, his systems tracking the second bogie. He was not in deep cover, but the majority of his body was behind a small rock outcropping.

The Ubitsya wheeled on his position, its nose panning back and forth as it hovered on its fusion jets, as if sniffing for him. They stood facing each other. His eyes focused in on the front of the jet. He could see the quad barrel nozzle of its flechette gun. He aimed his own at it.

The other jet was not even in sight as he spoke.

Merik: 'it can't see me, but …'

But he had spoken too soon. He saw the split second that it got a bead on him, he saw as it broke from its slow panning and whirled to directly face him, and they both opened fire in almost the same instant.

The bullets closed at stupendous speed, a wall of steel lancing together to connect in a blink. Where it collided, a thunderclap formed, a shockwave washing outward from the kinetic force. Where it did not connect a hundred supercharged pellets raced in a microsecond at both targets. It was a quickly lost war of attrition, a war in which Merik had less weight, less armor, and less firepower.

His gun arm was protected only because of the kinetic shield it was also unleashing. For a moment, it continued to fire, hanging in midair as his head and torso were wiped away. Then it slowly fell, its bullets wasted, to be erased along with the rest of him.

His hits registered, though, his parting moment engraving a blistering scar across the face of the small, hovering predator, ripping at its systems and sensors.

Ben, moving only slightly to bring his eyes to bear, watched it falter, clearly damaged, but far from destroyed. He had set his sensors to passive, not wanting to give any indication of his position, and was using his eyes to supplement his suddenly limited view.

Realization of how they were hunting his team came to him in a flash. He did not move. Instead, he packaged up a small data pack and prepared it for his team. Then he also set his systems to analyzing the flight patterns of the satellites overhead. It would be a long shot, but he had to let them know. He had to tell command what had happened here.

He braced for what he knew was about to happen when he opened his comms once more, then he initiated the signal that he knew would bring them down upon him.

He was already running when it went out.

- - -

Ayala: 'it's happening now, neal, right now. i saw it take out one of their positions, then they went comms dark, which means the relay was probably destroyed as well.'

Neal: '¿but how? I can see them spotting them if they were up close, but from a quarter mile out.'

Quavoce: 'i am not aware of a technology that would allow them to target one of the suits from a distance. unless there was a second …'

Minnie: <i am sorry for the interruption, but i have the satellite feed as requested, patching in now.>

Their view swam to a dizzying height, and suddenly they were a hundred miles above the earth, staring down through the morning haze to an undulating sea of green below. The view zoomed violently, splitting as it did so into two quadrants.

They could see the first plane, moving now, hunting, firing as it went. They could not make out its quarry, only a blur of destruction as it darted this way and that, driving through the hillside and firing a line of destruction ahead of it. Minnie tried to focus ahead of the bullets, to see what it was chasing, but caught only momentary glimpses as it danced this way and that. Whoever it was they were heading towards a gully. They would soon be exposed.

The second quadrant showed a very different scene. The second jet was lying in small crater, a plume of smoke coming from its nose as it tried to get airborne again. They could not know it, but it had been hit hard once more after Merik spat his last breath at it. This time in a concerted effort by Ben's remaining two team members. He had sent them a strategic package, sealed with an order for absolute radio silence, and then set off at a run to lead the two planes away.

As the two predators had begun to track him, the first had followed the path Ben had intended, and his team had been waiting as he had ordered them to be. When they opened fire, one with his flechette gun, the other with the tamer, but still lethal barium laser he carried, they had blown apart its nose cone, ripping into its nose-mounted guns and forward thruster.

Neal: '¿what is that? it looks like a stratojet, but much smaller. ¿can we get an estimate on dimensions?'

Minnie began to overlay details, but the attention of the team was already on another set of movement. The view shifted away from the plane to the two men that had ambushed it. Whoever was on the ground there was embroiled in something close to a battle of the titans. It was an epic scene.

Ayala: '¿how many ...?'

Minnie was already doing the calculation.

Minnie: <i count forty-six combatants, two are wearing 4th gen. battleskins, one with standard barium laser and sonic weaponry, the other with the flechette gun mod. the rest are wearing equivalent 1st gen. battleskins, carrying russian special forces an94 assault rifles.>

As she spoke, the screen was designating the members in the fight. The two 4th generation suits, assumed to be the remnants of Ben's team, had clearly been set upon by a much larger but technologically inferior platoon of ground troops.

The scene was ultra-violent.

- - -

His arm moved as if possessed, blanketing each target in turn as he allowed his AI to run amuck.

<too many targets, estimated contact in 2, 1 …>

The counter ran down in his mind as he ripped at each target in turn. His opponents' armor was saving them, but not all of them, he was winging each in turn as his gun blurred across them, a leg removed there, a forearm there. As one was decapitated, his threat counter adjusted, removing the attacker from his list of priorities.

But it was not much of an adjustment. The swarm still came, ever more fierce as he butchered their colleagues. He saw them coming in, he saw the wave washing up to him, their guns blaring into his armor. He felt the arc of security given by his surviving teammate at his back, their respective systems trying to keep up with each others' rampaging defense of their combined position.

<44 attackers, 43, 42, 41 …>

There were thirty-seven left when the fight got personal.

As his conscious mind lost sway, he became animal. Still firing his weapon even at close range, he now used it as a sword, a saber, to maim and rend his attackers as they came at him. As one landed a tight-fisted blow to his ribs, another fist was coming at his face. He brought the butt off his flechette gun across the armpit of the second attacker, and as his body was hurled away from one opponent, his flechettes were opening up the shoulder of another, pummeling the joint and flesh to liquid.

His arms ripped and pulled. He no longer had footing, he was being assailed from every side, and every limb was a weapon. His boot was embedding itself in the face of one soldier as his calf connected with the waist of another. He felt the butt of a rifle at his thigh before the actual bullets. He blocked the pain of the shots as they began to penetrate his knee and thigh, relying on the bionic reinforcement of his battleskin to bring his two legs together in a scissor on the attacker, as he simultaneously continued to cut his gun across the groin of another man trying to kick at his neck.

The scissoring action, with the combined force of both his bolstered leg muscles, clamped on the unfortunate attacker, compressing his hips and abdomen to but a few inches, and the pain was so great it burst a thousand blood vessels across his brain. The man's continued machine gun-fire went wild now, hitting his colleagues, the ground, and wheeling off into the air to join the expanding debris, bullets, limbs and broken bodies of the Russian troops coming from the epicenter of the gale-force conflict.

As his subconscious wrestled with inhuman speed, slicing, kicking, firing, and killing, a part of him respected the bravery of his assailants. A part of him noted their unrelenting attack in the face of terrible retribution. And a part of him noted, as they finally brought down his friend, that this was a fight he would not win.

He inflicted a terrible toll on them, he pulled them limb from limb, but as their numbers fell, his own systems fell as well. As the munition tube to his flechette gun was ripped free his tactical AI registered the loss as a rapid fall in his options. They had him by two limbs now, his torn left leg and his right arm, and though he still tried to kick and punch at them, they finally had him pinned. He felt the muzzles of their guns being pressed against his neck as they held him, and he opened his faceplate.

He was done. Faced with his admittance of defeat, they felt some measure of the same respect for him as he did for them. Not pity, and certainly not mercy. But respect. Their friends lay dead and maimed all around. The ground was slick with blood, the air full of screams. They aimed their guns at his face, and he looked at the sky.

- - -

Ayala, Neal, and Quavoce had been joined in cyberspace by Jack, Madeline and John, and they watched as the remaining twenty Russian shock troops executed the last of Ben's team. They were looking into his eyes as he stared skyward, resigned and exhausted.

They did not speak. They watched in silence as the view slipped to the chase still going on a mile away. They could not know it was Ben running, just as he could not know he was alone now. They could not know his intentions. They could only see the swath of destruction that followed hot on his tail. And they could see the futility of his flight.

He ran, hoping he was giving the last two members of his team a fighting chance. And indeed they had made their assailants pay a hefty butcher's bill. But the truth was he was alone now. Hunted by a relentless killer.

He knew the gully was ahead. He knew he would not make it across in time.

Ayala, Neal, and their friends watched as he leapt, spinning in midair to look skyward and zeroing in on the satellite his systems had calculated was above. As he found his target he lasered a signal directly into its lens far above. The signal contained a data packet that confirmed what they already suspected. It relayed, perhaps, some finer detail of the true militant capability of the foe they faced, and it told them what Quavoce had already surmised.

In an otherwise subspace silent world it was possible to triangulate a subspace signal. You needed two subspace-capable units, and you needed your target to be broadcasting. The Russian Ubitsyas had used their own technological advantages against them. Ayala did not watch as the final Ubitsya caught Ben in midair. She closed her mind's eye to the view as he turned to dust in the whirlwind of its weapons fire. Ben had been a good friend, and one of her best commanders.

With solemn gravitas, she said to the gathered group:

Ayala: 'i have more to report. minnie was smart enough to notify the other teams as soon as the attack began. thank you for that, minnie. that said, i am afraid to say we were too late to help team 3. they were blitzed at the same time ben's team was, and i am afraid they did not exact nearly as much damage on their attackers as his spezialists were able to.'

She paused as she got her emotions under control, turning her fury down to a simmer by force of will.

Ayala: 'as of last, recon team 2 remains undiscovered, though. satellite tracking confirms that though there are two russian fighters in their vicinity, no hostilities have commenced, and they have gone comms silent. hopefully they can evade their attackers.'

Neal: '¿i assume we can still talk to them, even though they cannot reply?'

Minnie: <yes, neal. given what we can deduce about the russian tracking capability, we are still able to send them info. they are not able to respond, however, not without revealing their positions. we have already sent them the full scope of the information gleaned from captain miller's recon encounter.>

Barrett: '¿are we absolutely certain that we do not risk their discovery by continuing to send information? i do not want to risk losing even more men today than we already have.'

Quavoce: 'when not transmitting, the subspace tweeter is a completely passive device. we can transmit as much data as we desire to it and they will still be able to hear us without revealing their location. but they cannot reply, and, of course, they cannot use their suit-to-suit comms either.'

Neal: 'very well. that we can still talk *to* them is some small consolation. minnie, please configure an ai to begin a running track of all force dispositions in their area. as best we can, i want to keep track of their movements, and supply them with as much intel as we can on activity in their vicinity.'

Minnie: <done. also beginning permanent tracking of all russian assets currently spotted that are equipped with mobiliei tech. will relay same to recon team 2. i must also alert this group to new movement in russia.>

They all tensed. Was Recon Team 2 already under attack?

But it was a greater threat even than that.

Minnie: <tracking is showing massive movement, moving west from rostov. they are crossing the ukrainian border. also, we have surface-ship movement in the sea of azov, and missile fire from subsurface assets tracking toward sebastopol and feodosiya.>

It was happening. The attacks on the Recon Teams had been the first step in a greater invasion.

Minnie: <russian television is showing stories of rioting in crimea, but the footage shows signs of counterfeiting. russian premier is announcing that he is 'saving ethnic russians in ukraine by sending in a peace-keeping force.'>

Neal: 'jesus. ok, that changes things even more. minnie, send new orders to recon team 2.'

Ayala: 'neal, you can't send them into that, they'll be ripped apart.'

Neal: 'no, ayala, i have no intention of sending them back to do force recon. that is all but moot now. we know they have mobiliei tech, we know its limitations, but we must also assume they have a good deal of it, enough to blanket three separate teams of our best equipped soldiers. no, the invasion of the crimea is a reality now. from now on we will monitor that on the news, not through eyes of a recon team. i need recon 2 somewhere else.'

The team waited, and Neal did not disappoint.

Neal: 'minnie, determine a lowest exposure route for recon 2 heading east. it is time we knew who is pulling the strings. and i want to know where the hell they are making those goddamn planes. i want hektor and his team to head toward moscow, now.'

Neal at Minnie: 'and while you are at it, minnie, get me the uk prime minister, german chancellor, and french president on the line. whichever you can get hold of first. i need to talk to them as well.'

Chapter 36: On the Brinkmanship

The scene across Eastern Europe was a tempest of unrest. Watched by the world, the ancient nations of Poland, Hungary, Romania, and the Czech Republic were up in arms. Riots and demonstrations rocked the ancient plazas and cobbled streets of Warsaw and Bucharest. They had seen life under the Soviet Bloc before, and had no intention of falling under such rule again.

In Ukraine and Belarus, the countryside was divided. Ethnic Russians were running roughshod over shaky democratic institutions, while governments tried to enforce a measure of rule against a wave of propaganda, demagoguery and violence.

Neal sat in a wide conference room in Luxembourg, high in the walls of the old city, sitting as it did above the broad moat that surrounded the entire citadel. Its peaceful reputation as a center of diplomacy in recent centuries had been a luxury of the impregnable fortress that was its cliff-bound capital. Nowadays, though, it provided more of a fiscal shelter than a physical one, and today it would be the site for a meeting of European powers, a group under siege of a very different but no less lethal kind.

The first to join Neal was the French president, an early and determined supporter of Neal's cause, not least of which because of the damage the late Agent Merard had done to the sanctity of his military institutions. He did not stand on ceremony, and he did not bring with him an entourage, such was the nature of his growing friendship with the American scientist.

Almost before he had finished shaking hands with Neal, he was speaking, his lilting French translated briskly and efficiently by the ever more multilingual Minnie, and transmitted directly into Neal's sub-cortex via the mobile node he now wore more often than not on his spinal interface.

"Monsieur Danielson, I would say it is a pleasure to see you, but I am afraid our relationship has been forced to grow in very bad soil," said the president, the colloquialism bringing a wry smile to Neal's face.

Neal used a new technique in order to reply, thinking the words in English, and allowing Minnie to translate and manage his vocal responses directly, so a fluent, if halting, French escaped his lips. It was a profoundly disquieting sensation, made bearable only by the look of surprise and eminent respect it brought to the eyes of the French leader.

"Monsieur le President, it is sad I agree, but I am thankful nonetheless that it has offered us this opportunity to work together toward achieving our common goals."

The Frenchman bowed his head ever so slightly, a mark of respect and appreciation for what he perceived as Neal's efforts to learn his mother tongue. Neal would not disabuse him of this misinterpretation, and further conversation was halted anyway by the door opening once more. The German chancellor and British prime minister were announced.

The four greeted each other like the dignitaries they were, with the rare informality that was reserved for other heads of state and the few citizens that could count themselves among the same upper echelons of power.

"Thank you again for coming, all of you," said Neal, first in German, then again in French. He winked at the British prime minister. They had met enough times that he need not worry about a token English greeting for the man.

"We have much to discuss, my friends, I have brought with me earpieces for you all, they will aid in easy communication amongst this small group, and eliminate the need for a larger entourage of interpreters." Again, he repeated the line in French and German, as he handed them all small, transparent earplugs with tiny tubes mounted to their sides. As they both studied them briefly, Minnie was already assigning them to the appropriate language based on their holders.

The German was the first to place the small plug in her ear, feeling the thrum of its tiny subspace tweeter, she mistook it for a bass hum, and so was pleasantly surprised when she was greeted by a pleasant feminine voice once it was in place.

In perfectly lilted German, something Minnie's AM Parent Birgit had given her from birth, Minnie said, "Good afternoon, Chancellor, I will be you translator, Wilhelmina."

The chancellor seemed surprised to be greeted so, and looked around, only to see the same wide-eyed look on her counterparts' faces.

"No need to be alarmed, my friends," said Neal placatingly, his voice echoed in their ears, "that is only my communications team, they will be giving us comms support, as well as answering any data related questions we may have during our discussion."

It was the first time for most of them that they would have a conversation with a machine, and Neal did not feel the need to burden them with the details of Minnie's less than natural birth only a couple of months beforehand, or the extensive processing capacity by which she was able to speak to all three of them, in three different languages, at the same time.

"Now, to business. Let us talk of the Crimean Peninsula, shall we?"

Stern looks crossed all their faces, and they did, indeed, not waste time with pleasantries. They had vitally important matters to discuss, and no audience to pander to. Without further ado, they got right to the most important topic on everyone's minds.

- - -

"Of course, Prime Minister, I hear you, but surely we must fear this is not the end of their advance?" said the chancellor.

"I don't suggest it is," replied the British man, "but it is also not anything close to a full scale invasion. They have stopped at Melitopol and Armyans'k, and, to date, we have no evidence that they are not being welcomed with open arms there."

The chancellor scoffed at this, but the French president spoke more diplomatically, "If I may, Prime Minister, we had no such evidence during the fall of the Stannic Bloc, or even back in Islamabad. Surely you see that we must hold our information sources on the other side of the Steel Curtain in some … skepticism."

Neal, of course had less spurious information sources, and as the conversation slogged on, he was starting to see that he would have to reveal them soon. What he was seeing was not pragmatism, and not even fear, but inertia. He had gotten their support for his work because its very secrecy removed the need to garner public support. Now the opposite was true, and he feared they needed to be reminded of the scale of the threat they were facing.

"If I may," Neal said politely, "we do have *some* data that we can rely on from inside the New Federation."

They were understandably curious, and the room's attention moved to him.

"As you know, my taskforce has access to some … new technologies, given to us by our allies in the greater task at hand." It was shockingly easy for them to forget what they had all learned in the aftermath of the missile conflagration five months ago.

His discreet reminder brought it back to them, and he went on, "While I am aware that there have been many attempts to place intelligence assets inside Russia since the coup, we were able to utilize said technology to get further than most."

The German and English leaders went to interject, clearly disturbed that they had not been informed sooner, but Neal glossed over their indignation with news of his own teams' eventual discovery.

"I would love to tell you they were able to move with impunity once behind Russian territory, but unfortunately they had a far from easy time once over the border. I will not belabor you with details, though I will provide you with full reports," he was already pinging Minnie to create them. He longed for the ability to send them directly to the minds of the three world leaders, but sufficed himself with having Minnie send it to three iPads he had brought along just in case he needed them. Such blunt tools, he thought, compared to the real thing.

As the data flowed to the tablets, Neal reached down, still speaking as he pulled them from his bag and handed them out. "What I *will* stress, however, is that while we were there, I am afraid to say we encountered teams with some measure of the same technology we possess."

They were initially confused by this statement, then the French premier voiced the conclusion Neal was leading them to, "The Russian Agent, Mr. Hunt's counterpart."

"Yes, Mr. President," said Neal, as they all sat back, stunned, "he would seem to be very much alive, and very much behind the resurgence of the Russian Empire, as we had assumed. It would appear he has also enabled some small section of Russian special forces with a less advanced, but still very potent version of our own combat armor, or battleskin, and that he also has some air units. Not as large as our StratoJets, but capable nonetheless. We do not yet know the scale of these forces, but we are attempting to ascertain that now, along with location of their source."

"This new information is very troubling," said the chancellor, clearly rethinking her initial position on the topic. "Standing against the already advanced Russian Army and Air Force had been a formidable challenge already. This new factor … I don't know …" her voice trailed off.

Neal was disconcerted. The chancellor had been the voice of reason, the only one truly calling them to arms, to respond with force, as they must. But his play to support her had instead served to soften even her resolve.

"No, Chancellor, please, you misunderstand. I came here to tell you that this army is indeed a great threat, but that if you study the full data we managed to compile during our reconnaissance mission, all indicators point to this being a very small part of the greater Russian force."

He looked at them each in turn, "Chancellor, Prime Minister, Mr. President, I have come here to tell you that you indeed face a terrible threat. But I mean this not just to frighten you, but to galvanize you. You must stand firm against the Russians. You must show them that you will not tolerate further incursion.

"We must hold them here, and avoid further conflict until we can complete the next stage of our defense construction."

They looked at him.

The Frenchman spoke, "Next stage, Dr. Danielson?"

"Yes, Monsieur le President, the next stage. As you all know, we have been working hard to build up the Terminus One and, of course, to build and launch New Moon One. While we have built a basic complement of StratoJets and ground-based forces, we have not been able to work on anything more potent until we had completed the elevator."

"More potent?" said the prime minister. "I assume by the looks on my colleagues' faces that they have also not been made aware of any new military capability you were working on."

Neal really had not wanted to say that. He cursed quietly, and Minnie queried his anger. Neal did not respond to her. This was not going as planned. He was not a happy camper.

"Prime Minister," he said, trying to seem calm, "when I talk of a more potent weapon, I am talking of the larger defense systems we are going to need to build, as we have discussed many times. While these are mostly limited by design to space, some of them will have application here on Earth, and it is the first of those that we are hoping to complete in the next couple of months."

"I think I speak for everyone when I say I would like to know more about these … 'systems,' Dr. Danielson." said the chancellor, almost threateningly.

"Of course, of course, Chancellor, I will share the designs immediately, though they are outside even our advanced capabilities for a while longer. And it is just that delay that concerns me. Until we have these tools at our disposal, we remain exposed to the threat of the Russian forces even now amassing in Eastern Ukraine."

At the mention of the Russian forces, their attention naturally moved back to the analysis on their iPads, and Neal concealed a sigh of relief.

Focusing on the photographs from Recon One's demise, the French leader said, "What am I seeing here?"

He was pointing to a picture of Ben's final two team members coming to grips with their assailants.

"What you are seeing there, Prime Minister, is forty-four Russian assault troops assailing two of my Spezialists," said Neal, sadly, but with an appropriate amount of pride in his two men. "The Russians won out, but my men took out more than half the Russian troopers and one of their attack planes in the process."

They all thought for a moment.

"So," said the chancellor, seeming to gather herself, "if what you say is true here, we already have the military advantage, Doctor. Why would we not deploy our greater weaponry in force against them and deal with this now?"

The French and British leaders both nodded emphatically, and Neal began to become flustered once more, "No, no, please, you misunderstand me. While I could certainly support a ground offensive with my limited, but admittedly very capable, shock troops, in order to engage the Russians properly would require a force redeployment of my StratoJet fleet away from Rolas. Until we have completed our next level of construction, defending the SpacePort must remain my top priority."

The Frenchman surprised Neal by becoming suddenly indignant, "Neal, my friend, I am afraid I must call something to your attention. Please forgive me but you repeatedly talk of *your* forces, may I remind you that the StratoJets you speak of were made using funds from us. *Your* taskforce, *your* Terrestrial Allied Space Command, as you call it, is, in truth, a *NATO* force. I think, perhaps, that we should start to refer to it as such."

Neal lifted his hands, he could do nothing right today, not that he had really hoped this would go much better than this. That said, though, this was a slip he could not afford to make in such delicate negotiations.

"Forgive, me, my friends," he said, placatingly, "I refer to them only as a unit leader might refer to his platoon, not in terms of ownership. Please, please. I know the taskforce would not be where it is without your brave support."

Neal suppressed a wave of anger at himself, but it was quickly supplanted by a deeper rage that was getting ever stronger in him. Anger at having to argue the merits of defending their planet from attack, at having to supplicate himself before people who seemed more worried with their territorial rights than they were with humanity's very survival. He knew, deep down, that this was unfair, and that he had gotten greater support from these three important allies than he could reasonably have hoped for, but his patience with negotiation was fraying thin.

At Neal's plaintive apology, the French leader nodded and let out a breath, like he was releasing the tension in the room from his very lungs. He raised a hand as well, acknowledging that he had, perhaps, overstated the point, and the room returned to some measure of congeniality.

"Dr. Danielson," said the chancellor in a conciliatory tone, "no one here doubts the importance of your work ..." she looked around, and the other two leaders nodded their agreement, the Frenchman emphasizing his with an almost apologetic look—almost—and the chancellor went on, "but as you have stated many times before, we cannot address the greater threat you have alerted us all to if we do not address the almost-as-severe threats from our neighbors here at home."

Neal nodded. He wanted to stop the woman, because, though he agreed with her in principle, he knew she was about ask for something he could not condone. But he let her finish, if only because he had already overstepped his bounds once in this meeting. To do so again might strain the already stressed bonds in the room to breaking point.

"Your concern about Rolas is noted, Doctor," continued the German leader, "but there have been no attacks there to date, and the naval fleet there, along with the ground-based defenses my own engineers have put in place there, represent a very real defensive perimeter."

Neal nodded once more, barely keeping his mood under control. As she took a breath, he went to interject, but she gave him no such respite, and went on, "If what you say about the Russian forces is true, then as I see it they will only become more capable with time, and that is all the more reason for us to engage them fully now, while we have the advantage. I, for one, will need to review these space-based munitions you are discussing before I could approve their usage anyway."

All three were very much in agreement on that point, and Neal took a deep breath. He looked from one to the next. She was talking of leaving the SpacePort and elevator exposed. It was a terrible risk. But he saw only determination in their eyes.

"If we do this," he said, "and of course it is the prerogative of you and your fellow TASC heads of state to do as you see fit, we would need to leave as much of a naval force behind at Rolas as possible." Two of them went to respond, but he also went on quickly, "After all, when we talk of investment, we would not, I think you will agree, want to risk the trillions of euros already invested on the SpacePort, and the capabilities it affords us."

It was a sneaky comment, perhaps, but not one they could reasonably disagree with. They nodded, the German cautiously, the other two a little more agreeably.

He took a breath. Underlying all of this talk of the 'next level' was another consideration. One he did not dare share with even his most trusted allies. Knowledge of the first main Resonance Dome, both in terms of its location, capabilities, and scheduled completion, were a topic he had made sure was necessarily muddy. They knew it was expensive, they each, in their way, thought they were its main benefactor, and each believed they would be the main beneficiary appropriately. But he had no intention of allowing the Dome, or the machines it would allow him to build, to come under any one country's control. It wasn't far off now. Once it was done, he would have the tools he needed to protect Rolas, the Research Group, and the Dome itself.

He didn't need much longer. If he could stall them for just a few weeks more.

"Mr. Prime Minister," he said into the silence, "you have cautioned that this remains isolated to a small part of Ukraine, a community that Russia claims invited it in. Let us say it stays that way for now. Let us say that we have a little time before this issue comes to a head. All I ask from you is that I have a little time to consolidate the defensive net around Rolas before we redeploy the StratoJets."

The room was silent, and it was the German chancellor that eventually acquiesced, "Of course, Doctor. No one is saying we should jump into this without preparation."

They all nodded, and the Frenchman added, "We will need time to consolidate our defense plans anyway, and we could not proceed with any military action without public support anyway, support we will only have if the Russians advance into areas actively resisting their incursion."

He spoke, Neal knew, of Belarus, and more importantly Poland. The only countries of the former Eastern Bloc with the stomach for and military capacity to put up any real resistance to the Russian military machine. Neal shuddered. He was gambling with massive chits here. Poland, in particular, was an important part of the European economy, and a not-insignificant supporter of Neal's projects.

Neal had already spoken to the Polish president, the man was understandably distraught, and it would not help his peace of mind if he knew his nation had become potential collateral damage in a negotiation of global scale.

But, as it had been when Neal and Madeline had first gambled on their plan to destroy the satellites, this was quickly becoming a question not of avoiding casualties, but limiting them.

The conversation wound on, but he knew he would not get out of redeploying his fleet. He smiled and engaged with them on greater and smaller issues, and inside he longed to know the status of the all-important Dome construction project, far, far away.

- - -

Hours later, Neal sat in the broad, beautifully appointed conference room, alone once more. He let the false smiles and platitudes wash from his face, and he closed his eyes.

The conflict in Europe was coming to a head. The resolve of his allies was being tested, just as he knew Mikhail intended it to be. And it was not going well. He needed to act. He needed to take control of the situation. There were simply too many moving parts, too many obstacles, and his patience with diplomacy and negotiation was wearing, along with his temper.

Bringing himself under control, he opened his line to Minnie.

Neal: 'minnie, contact barrett and get him on a plane to dc. we should probably talk to the president.'

He breathed a long, deep breath, trying to suppress his anger at having to engage with the petty-minded acting US president again. He had desperately hoped to avoid it. Not because he regretted for one moment his decision to reduce his force capacity in the US. But because, deep down, he knew that nothing would probably come of it. He had abandoned America under duress, but he had done so for good reason. At this point they had even less capacity for the coming fight than the Europeans did.

But he had to try and get them to return some of their forces they had called home from Rolas. They had left a section of their original battle group, and still remained among the greatest monetary contributors to his cause, even with their severely diminished GDP, but Admiral Burns had long since taken the USS *Reagan* back to US waters, along with its powerful fleet of F35Cs and F/A-18Es, and Neal had to see if he could get some of them back.

Having dispatched his request to Barrett, Neal stood and began to walk out of the room. As he went, he made one more request via his spinal nexus to Minnie.

Neal: '… and minnie, get my plane ready. i'm leaving. i need to visit the dome.'

Chapter 37: Borodino Bound

Hektor moved slowly through the brush, flanked by the rest of his team. Cara was just ahead, Niels was bringing up the rear. They stayed tight.

The night was no longer their friend, not now that they knew the full extent of their enemy's capabilities. Now they moved at day, and their nights were whiled away in fiercely guarded pockets of perimeter defense, three asleep, three awake, rotating out regularly, their onboard AIs stimulating their pineal glands to secrete one-time, high doses of melatonin, enforcing a powerful, subliminal sleep. But those same AIs also listened, ready to flood their systems with adrenalin and dopamine at the slightest shout of warning from their friends guarding their slumber to bring them crashing back to consciousness.

During the day they had resorted to hand signals of old, their shared training in the special forces units of Israel, Germany, the US and the UK giving them a common language. A language they would never forget, a language they responded to reflexively.

It was a response pattern their AIs appreciated, in as much as they were capable of that level of cognizance. A purity of meaning that had a machine beauty to it.

As Cara raised her hand, palm out, they all froze, the signal swimming out from her, to the man behind her, and on down the line. They maintained strict visuals on each other now. They did not all have to see every other team member, but each of them must be in view of at least one other at all times. Thus they operated as a whole, their movements flowing and ebbing, like a snake slithering through the undergrowth, seemingly fluid, seemingly disparate, but capable of attacking as one if threatened.

They had started hesitantly. Frozen by the coursing visuals transmitted to them by Ayala, by the sight of their counterparts to the south being torn apart by black-winged predators. Predators they could, even then, see searching for them as well as they lay, silent but ready, fully alert and keenly aware of their mortality.

But Ayala's warning had come just in time. Hektor had responded immediately, sending a command to shut down all subspace comms. Their suits' AIs had enforced the silence and thus they had vanished from the sight of the planes above, and once the Ubitsyas had passed overhead, they had all dug in. For they knew the Russians also had ground forces out there somewhere, also looking, sniffing for their subspace scent.

Covered with mud and leaves, lying in caves and nooks of trees, their stillness imposed with machine stringency, they had all watched as the black clad Russian soldiers had eventually resolved out of the surrounding bush. Sweeping the area. Looking for a prey that had gone to ground.

But without further signal, the Russians were no more able to spot Hektor and his team than Ayala's forces had been able to find a lonely Lana in their far more fervent search months ago.

The threat had passed. Hektor had eventually stood, passively scanning the area, the only team member able to break his forced stricture on movement. Then he had awoken them each in turn and they had moved off. Their silence as black as their armored bodies.

Cara did not lower her hand, but nor did she do the quick, single fist pump that would mean a threat was present, so Hektor started to move up on her position, to see what she was seeing. He dearly missed the ability to speak to his team via subspace, and had tried to on several occasions without thinking, glad of his AIs ability to enforce his moratorium on any subspace signal despite his carelessness.

"Cara, what can you see?" whispered Hektor, staying just behind her as he approached, remaining out of sight.

She turned and waved him up to her position.

"Road, sir. It's the P58. By my reckoning we should be just south of Dyatkovo by now."

There was minimal traffic on the road, but enough that crossing it would be risky. Hektor reviewed his satellite view from above. Ayala had arranged to have a permanent data feed to Recon Team Two from the satellites in Low-Earth Orbit, focusing on their assumed positions. Hektor periodically used his shoulder-mounted tight-beam laser to ping skyward, letting Minnie and Ayala know where they were so they could adjust the view accordingly.

"There is no easy crossing point I can see, Cara, we're just going to have to make a run for it."

Bohdan approached their prone position, also hanging just back, but Hektor waved him up.

"Hey, Bohdan," Hektor whispered, "road crossing, P58. Got to make a run for it now or we'll be waiting till dusk."

Bohdan nodded, also reviewing the data feed patching into his cerebral cortex.

"Sergeant, I've been thinking," said Cara pensively.

Bohdan was about to make the obvious a joke when she flashed him a preemptive stern glance, before going on, "Twenty miles. We've covered twenty miles since we were ordered to Moscow. At this rate it is going to take us over a week to get there. And it's only going to get worse once we get closer to the suburbs."

With over seven million people living in the Moscow metropolitan area, or the Moscow Oblast, as it was called, moving with stealth was going to become ever more difficult as they moved out of the lightly populated Desna forest-steppe and through the Kaluga suburbs to the metropolis itself.

"Not sure I see another way," said Hektor, but Bohdan was following Cara's eyes as she glanced back at the road, and soon he was following her line of thought, as well.

Bohdan began searching as she finished her statement.

"I know it goes against standing orders, but we have to be able to move, and move freely. It's one thing to stay in the shadows out here, but once we hit major population centers, those shadows are going to become few and far between ..."

She looked at the road once more. Hektor caught on, and a frown darkened his features to match the black of the retracted helmet surrounding his face.

"You're saying we should drive there?" It was more of a statement than a question, as he stared at the road and thought about the implications of commandeering a vehicle. They waited while he thought.

"It's dangerous, but no more so than leapfrogging every highway between here and Red Square," he eventually said, quietly. "You're right, of course. But we can't just go out there and flag down a car. And we'll need several cars, anyway ... for the six of us and our equipment."

His mind was racing, computing the risk factors involved. He did not like it, but nor did he like having to move at such a molasses pace.

"I have another option, sir," said Bohdan, and Cara and Hektor both turned to him, "go to 53.5728 by 34.4512."

Their AIs were immediately responding, zooming on the coordinates he had listed. With subspace comms available to them, Bohdan would have been able to project the location directly into their minds' eyes. Speaking coordinates seemed brutish by comparison, but they could not deny the machine efficiency with which their suits translated his words into a visual view of ... "I believe it's a lumber yard," said Bohdan as their blank gazes took in the sight. "Not a big one, judging by the scale of the sawmill, but that's not what I want to show you. There, that truck."

It was the center of the view he had taken them to. A small pickup truck with a covered flatbed. Hektor's gaze focused again and he smiled tightly at Bohdan, then nodded. It was all the acknowledgment he would give, and all that Bohdan and Cara would need.

It was a solid plan, Hektor thought as they all moved back to the rest of the team waiting behind them, and with a sense of calm at the way his team was coming together, Hektor shared the new plan quickly and they were off, moving carefully but with purpose.

- - -

Olesya walked from the house to the barn. She was sweaty with the morning's work, first in the sawmill, in before dawn, finishing the mill from yesterday's cut. They worked the mill till an hour after sunrise, the chugging diesel engine of the big saw also powering the paneled neon lights hanging overhead.

Once there was enough light, her brother and her husband went out with the big lumber truck to cut. Their father was already out on the property, surveying, sapping, and testing trees, then marking them for either another year of growth or the saw. His ruined back and missing fingers on his left hand had long since precluded him from the hard labor of the mill that still bore his name.

Once the men went out to cut, Olesya went inside to wake the children, feed them, and begin the thousand tasks of keeping the house.

Hours later, the rumble of the huge lumber truck alerted her to their return, and soon she was walking out to the table and benches outside the mill and laying a large platter there of cured sausage, boiled potatoes and cabbage, mustard, and assorted homemade pickled vegetables. There were no forks, only knives, and as the three men emerged from the truck and the mill, they set to, their hunger profound, mumbling gruff appreciation as they grabbed, stabbed, and sliced at the hearty fuel in front of them.

She joined them only briefly. She had eaten with the children before packaging them off for the long walk to school, and picked at the lunch as she had prepared it. They shared a joke or two, a comment on the health of various steppes and groves, both old and new. The patriarch of the family offered limited praise, but was nonetheless proud of his son for his hard work, and of his daughter, for finding a good, strong husband, one capable of contributing.

They did not talk much, though. And twenty minutes later, Olesya's father was rising from his seat, signaling the break was over, and without a word, the men went back to their main lumber truck, powering up its big diesel engine and driving off down one of the many dirt tracks leading away from the main house to chop and gather more wood.

They left Olesya to clean up, as they always had, and she gathered the remnants of their lunch without complaint.

As she turned to carry the tray back to the house, a loud crisp birdsong rang out across the forest. It was unusually clear and true and Olesya paused, trying to place it. She knew the birds of the forest well. It was a wood warbler, she was sure of that, but not one of the songs she was familiar with.

- - -

Inside the house, two black-suited figures reacted quickly to the sound. One was upstairs, gathering basic clothing: one pair of jeans and a shirt from Olesya's closet, two pairs of jeans and some shirts from one of the men's.

The second man was waiting for him as he came lightly but hastily down the stairs, nodding to confirm he had the other item they had sought, the keys to the smaller, but far more roadworthy truck that sat in front of the house.

They both exited through a side door as Olesya approached the house, and vanished into the woods to join their warbling colleague.

- - -

Olesya did not think it too strange when she heard the smaller family truck start from the front of the house. It was not uncommon for one of the men to return to the house during the afternoon and head into town if they needed something, a machine part or replacement tool. She assumed it was either her brother or father, as whoever it was did not knock on the door to say hello, something her husband always did when he came back ahead of the other two.

She heard it trundle off down the gravel road that led off down to the main road to town, and carried on about the laundry, cleaning, and preparations for the always-eventful return of the children from school.

- - -

Hektor drove the truck away from the house alone. Once well down the deserted country road, he pulled over.

They moved quickly. The rest of the team had been waiting for him in the trees, and now leapt out from the side of the road, two of them keeping an eye on the gravel road in both directions while Cara, Bohdan, and Frederik stripped their suits off quickly, and changed into the clothing Bohdan had procured from inside the house. None of the men commented on Cara's brief nudity, or on the ill-fitting shirt and trousers she now wore. This was partly out of respect for her privacy, but mostly out of a sense of self-preservation.

Once the three of them were done, they dumped their now empty suits in the covered flatbed of the five-year-old Kama pickup truck and clambered into its diminutive cab, Bohdan driving, Cara in the passenger seat, and Frederik crammed unceremoniously into the tiny, cluttered rear seat. Bohdan was already gunning the truck off and away to the main road as the last three leapt lithely aboard, pulling the rear gate of the truck's liftgate closed behind them, and covering themselves with the various blankets and scraps that were strewn across the well-used truck's dusty floor.

Chapter 38: Deception

As the dark, deep ocean rolled and crashed, the black jet thundered by high, high above, sending a shock wave out across the deserted, grey, rolling turmoil as it rocketed southward.

This was a truly desolate place. Thousands of miles from any land, even farther from anything you might comfortably call a city, this was the Southern Atlantic as it widened ever farther until the mighty Capes Horn and Hope signaled the last of humanity's outposts, and you were left with only the great grey expanse of the planet-circling Southern Ocean.

From space, a subroutine of Minnie's looked down on the small black plane from satellite eyes, tracking it as it raced southward. It was not monitoring the plane itself, but watching for the slightest hint that it was being followed.

It carried but one passenger, himself cradled in a gravity couch similar to those that had protected the crew of New Moon One during their epic passage through Earth's core. For Neal could spare no time for the sound barrier. With his body sedated, his very nervous system pacified by neuronal override, he slept as his plane soared over the vast, brooding ocean.

But his mind was alive as the StratoJet rocketed onward, brushing aside the buffeting of an abused stratosphere as the thin air argued its passage, shouting at hurricane volumes at the violence of the StratoJet's meteoric passage.

Among all the leadership of the Terrestrial Allied Space Command, only Neal knew of the location he was heading to. The crews of the three ships delivering the massive cargos to this secret place had been completely unaware of their purpose, and once they had arrived they had been sequestered along with the engineers that were supervising the unloading of those cargoes, without leave or outside communication.

Even Minnie was kept in the dark.

Neal: 'ok, minnie, if you are comfortable that i remain undetected, please discontinue tracking and edit all systems to ensure there is no record of my final coordinates or heading.'

Minnie had done this twice before when Neal had visited whatever he was visiting. She was curious by design, but she was not capable of subterfuge as she was systematically incapable of operating outside of her programming, and if her programming was clear on anything, it was that she respected the needs of the taskforce, and most of all, the needs of its leader, Neal Danielson.

But though Neal's secrecy in this may have seemed obsessive, it was well placed. For despite her loyalty, Minnie was well aware of Amadeu's ability to pry data from her, even data that she was programmed never to share, such was his inherent understanding of her makeup, and so she actually appreciated the way Neal's neuroticism stopped her from inadvertently betraying his trust.

Minnie: <yes, dr. danielson. redirecting monitoring systems now. Good-bye.>

Before he could reply, Minnie had extricated herself from his plane's systems, and he was left, suddenly, with control of the plane. Not that it would crash, the plane's onboard AI, though limited, could fly itself indefinitely. But the AI was also deliberately unaware of their true destination, and so Neal now opened up his link to it in order to redirect its progress.

The ensuing turn was hard and efficient, the plane following Neal's orders to fly at the very limits of his body's tolerance, and if he hadn't already been sedated, the G-forces would have knocked him out cold.

There followed twenty minutes of strange silence. A silence Neal had rarely enjoyed since Minnie had become such a vital part of his work. But she was far away now, physically and mentally, and he was alone.

He waited, trying to busy himself with reviewing schedules and design documents, but without Minnie to aid him, to answer his questions and respond to his ideas and thoughts, he found he was all but at a loss.

He was forced, for a moment, to contemplate fully just what he was doing, and it was not a sensation he enjoyed, knowing, as he did, how little clue he really had about how to actually pull off the undertaking at hand. So instead, his mind veered to a subject he hadn't had the chance to contemplate in what seemed like years. Girls.

Ughh. It was just as unpleasant a thought, he realized, not least of which because it was even more convoluted than the saving of a planet. But there was one, he thought, maybe, potentially, one he might see something of a mutual flame with.

No, forget that, no. It was, as it had always been for him, a waste of time. He was not without desire, but he was most certainly without luck, and he wallowed in that memory for a while, almost angry at Minnie for leaving him, even though he had ordered it.

But it was not long before he was approaching a line. Travelling at over four thousand miles an hour, he was soon breaching a perimeter and a timer went off in his mind telling him he should be within range.

Neal at Mynd: '¿mynd, can you hear me?'

Mynd: <hello, neal.>

Neal: 'hello, mynd.'

Mynd: <welcome back.>

Neal felt the familiar warmth of communing with a fully-fledged Artificial Mind once more. Not an Artificial Intelligence, that was nothing like this, any personality an AI possessed was merely an approximation, a rough imitation of true sentience. An Artificial

Mind was replete with all the learning and accumulated knowledge of a lifetime, often more than one.

In that respect this AM was no different, though it was as unique from Minnie as an AM could be. This was Mynd. Mynd did not have the systems reach of Minnie, confined, as he was, to the island home of Neal's most important project. But, like Minnie, he was born of the combined knowledge of two people.

The first had been Neal himself. And it was he that had named his creation Mynd. Saying these first words at his birth, "You are from my mind, so I will call you Mynd."

He had been very pleased with himself. That first conversation had been as disconcerting and yet strangely comforting as Amadeu and Birgit's first communing with Minnie. But Mynd had needed more than just his memories and thoughts. As Minnie had before him, Mynd had needed nurturing, raising. A guiding voice in the darkness as he emerged into his substrate self. And so, unable to dedicate the time needed himself, Neal had co-opted William Baerwistwyth, the tragically disabled mathematics genius formerly of Amadeu's spinal interface team, and added the brilliant young man's experience to Mynd's being, as parent, nursemaid, and tutor.

Neal: '¿how are you, mynd? i am inbound as we speak. ¿can your systems see me?'

Mynd: <i detected your plane as you crossed the threshold of my subspace and radar systems, neal. ¿would you like me to land the plane for you?>

Neal chuckled despite himself. It was like having a son who was already more comfortable with computers than you were, not an uncommon sensation for any parent, he was sure. But at only six weeks, old Mynd was capable of far greater feats than playing Angry Birds, and even flying a plane barely tested his abilities.

But Neal would not need his artificial son to take control over his StratoJet today.

Neal: 'no, mynd, i am afraid i cannot stay long and will not be landing. i have come only to check on progress and make sure you have everything you need.'

Mynd: <we are 4.6 hours ahead of schedule since your last visit 8.2 days ago. ¿would you like to see our current status?>

Would he like to see? Neal knew what Mynd meant, and he braced himself before saying yes. Mynd was not nearly as practiced with communicating with humans as Minnie was, and Neal knew this was going to be an intense experience.

Neal: 'yes, mynd. please show me your status.'

His mind expanded, Mynd reaching in via the plane's subspace tweeter even as the StratoJet slowed from its meteoric pace as it approached the dark, foreboding island that Mynd called home.

Neal was shown the desolate island first from above, from his plane's own nose-mounted sensor sweet. But even as Neal reconciled that this was the view, he realized he was simultaneously seeing it from a moving heavy-lifting truck below, and from a camera on a gantry crane, and from the deck of one of the three cargo tankers offloading their shipments in the wide bay.

He fought a wave of nausea at the influx of information, even as he absorbed the scene.

Below him, around him, was Deception Island. Deep, deep in the Southern Ocean, cradled by the Antarctic Peninsula, long abandoned by the whalers that had been the only people to ever call it home. Some persistently underfunded research facilities still used it occasionally, but not this long after the passing of summer.

And anyway, now it was now off limits to anyone that Neal had not personally invited there. A cordon enforced with lethal force by two dedicated StratoJets and a small contingent of shock troops.

Despite its extremely isolation, Deception Island was actually quite welcoming compared to its neighbors. For its high, mountainous coastline was deceptively treacherous, and in fact hid a broad, deep harbor at the island's heart, the crater at the center of the massive volcano that was Deception Island. The huge bay took up the bulk of the island's width, sheltered by the entirety of the island's U-shaped, mountainous mass.

The harbor was accessible only by a narrow breach in the island's south coast, known by the early sailors as Neptune's Bellows because of the hard wind that forced its way out between the high cliffs on either side.

Neal was happy to see the last of the huge cargo ships driving in through that wind even now, dwarfed by the cliffs on either side, and by the cavernous harbor beyond.

Massive lights lit the harbor, banishing the ever-present grey twilight that hung over the island and its Antarctic cousins this time of year. The cargo ship was turning hard as it entered the harbor proper, joining two others off of Penfold's Point, just inside the bay's entrance. They tied up to massive floating pontoons, themselves merely platforms for the wheels of the massive gantry cranes that were still unloading the ship's wares.

The entire operation was focused on the center of the broad, flat peninsula that jutted out into the bay. At the center of which, in what had once been a small lake, a truly massive, quarter-kilometer wide structure was taking shape.

Neal studied the great edifice. Sensing his focus, Mynd took their attention suddenly, drastically downward, into the structure. Neal's mind was suddenly filled with data: power conduits, systems status, build schedules. It all flowed through him, and once he got over the initial shock of the translation, he felt the coming completeness of the Resonance Dome like building joy, its budding turgidity almost perverse, definitely profound. An emotion, more than a concept.

Mynd: <as you see, neal, the lower half of the dome is now complete, i even managed to use its already active resonance manipulators to pulse some accumulated rain water out of the lower dome yesterday. william found it most entertaining.>

Neal was treated with the sight of the activating of the manipulators that lined the Dome's lower half. As they had come alive, they had pulsed the gathered rain water in the deep basin into great geysers that spewed the water up, and out, to fall in great showers on the assorted buildings growing up around the base of the Dome.

The bottom half of the Dome was partially sunk into the ground, in part to give some structural support to the massive sphere, and in part to lower the breech, both for easier loading of materials and unloading of finished products.

Neal: 'very good, mynd. i am happy to see that the manipulators are working as planned. that is very good news, indeed, mynd.'

Mynd: <and i have all the sections of the upper half onsite. 7 of the 8 upper panels are ready for installation, and the 8th will be complete in 32.7 hours.>

Neal was, as always, astonished by what had been accomplished here in such a short time, and yet still profoundly frustrated at how long it was taking.

They needed this. He had waited too long to start the real production of the fleet. He still had to wait for the return of New Moon One before he could start on Earth's heavy defenses, but the fighters, the smaller but still huge craft that he would need in order to fight the coming Mobiliei Armada, those he could be making now.

And, perhaps more importantly, those he could be using in the fight he knew he was being forced into with Russia and China.

Mynd: <¿you desire the skalm?>

As Neal's frustrations bled through the link, Mynd responded, and images of the first planned Skalm filled Neal's head. It was the first design they would be working on once the Resonance Dome was ready, and Mynd was fully primed to form the fantastic craft, both physically and mentally.

First Mynd showed Neal the raw materials, both as lists of component parts and as cargo manifests, arrival dates, most already passed, some still to come, and then finally as a whole, as the final event.

The three-dimensional image spun in Neal's mind, brought into focus and vivacious color by his desire for it.

Viewed from the front it was a broad 'X', nearly a hundred meters across. At its center was a twenty-meter-wide ball of fusion power, the ship's core. It was both its main engine and its main weapon. From that central sphere, spiny protrusions jutted out in all directions, but were dominated by a single dangerous-looking needle, pointing directly forward, longer and thicker than the rest, and a fat nozzle at the rear.

The stupendous power the core generated could either be fired out the nozzle at her back to propel the ship forward at incredible speed, or be targeted out the spines that protruded from the reactor in every other direction as nuclear fueled lasers, particle beams of devastating destructive power.

Out of this core, four carbon nanocomb spars reached out, each capped by a smaller but equally spiny version of the main core reactor. With their own lesser nozzles set out and away from the main core, they could fire individually or as one to spin the stellar weapon on any axis, making it capable of turning on a dime at hypersonic speeds, rotating as a whole to redirect either its main weapon or its main drive or both.

It was a whirlwind of destruction. An evolutionary leap in weaponry. It was a machine gun pitted against bows and arrows. It was the pinnacle of even Mobiliei military technology, both on and off world, and as such he could be certain that neither Mikhail nor Pei would dream of giving such a weapon to the Russian or Chinese.

And most of all, because of Neal's maniacal focus on the secrecy of this project, he knew that his enemies could not know Neal was this close to making one himself. Because if Mikhail and Pei knew what he was making here in the cold and dark of the Antarctic, they would stop at nothing to prevent its completion.

He was so close. After all this time it would come down to weeks, maybe days. He just needed a little more time.

- - -

An hour later, Neal was outbound again, his inspection complete, crossing back out of Mynd's communications reach and the strictly enforced no man's land around Deception Island's desolate shores. Before leaving, Neal had also spoken briefly with William, who was now spending most of his time in the machine.

They had made the man a suit, its bionic reinforcements allowing him to walk around. But since his introduction to cyberspace, he had lost interest in such things, or faith in them; one of the many scars of being betrayed by your own body.

Neal could appreciate it, and like others before him he did not question William's choice here.

With assurances that they would maintain the strictest focus on haste and secrecy, Neal had bid his farewells to Mynd and young William, and his plane had banked away once more. He never even touched down. He just left with the same abruptness and haste he had arrived, leaving the massive Resonance Dome to its final days of construction in the winter darkness.

With progress steady here at Deception, it was time to escalate preparations for the only component of the Skalm he could not manufacture.

Chapter 39: Flight and Fight

"Quavoce, my friend. Bom dia!" said Amadeu, as he walked into his lab on Rolas Island.

Quavoce returned the young Portuguese man's broad smile with one of his own, but did not reply. By his side stood an excited young Banu, brimming with her usual excitement for their little 'experiments'.

Amadeu's eyes met hers and their shared conspiratorial sparkle grew even brighter. "And good morning to you too, Banu," Amadeu said to the young girl, kneeling in front of her, "or rather, sobh beh'khayr."

His accent was appalling, but Banu had nothing but affection for the Portuguese scientist and for the amazing things she had seen and done since Quavoce had gently coaxed her into his office only a few months beforehand.

She replied in her tiny but clear voice, "Sobh beh'khayr, Amadeu."

His face betrayed just the slightest of concern at hearing the correct pronunciation of the greeting juxtaposed against his sad approximation, but with the empathy of the young and kind, she assuaged his concern with a smile that would have melted the iciest of hearts. It was a smile that said, thank you for trying, it is more than enough just that you try.

Quavoce saw her expression too, and the way Amadeu responded, his eyes alighting with a moment of shared friendship, and he was happy for the young girl he had saved from the plague.

It was that simple empathy that only children are truly capable of, and even then they did not all feel it as deeply as Banu clearly did. It was one of the many reasons Quavoce was so fiercely protective of the young girl. He would kill whole cities without thinking in order to protect her. Few doubted it. Including Amadeu, as he glanced up at Banu's guardian once more.

Amadeu suppressed a tremor of fear at Quavoce's stern stare, then said, "So, are we ready?" then to her, "Are you ready to fly again, my little bird?"

She was. She always was. Once her initial trepidation had passed, once she managed to comprehend Quavoce's placating explanation of what the scientist Amadeu wanted her to try, and then the strange sensation of having the little button put in the back of her neck. And then the conversation, if you could call it that, which she had then had with the woman called Minnie, a woman she had never met, yet maybe knew better than anyone except her very guardian.

She would never know how long it had taken Amadeu to convince Quavoce to even come to his lab and talk about letting the little girl try the spinal interface. She would never know the weight of the promise Quavoce had made Amadeu make before he allowed Banu to be plugged in, or the detailed and gruesome end he had promised Amadeu should any harm come the young girl.

But that was behind them all now, for the most part. Whilst letting someone plug your child into a computer may have seemed egregious to us, it was as commonplace as learning to read back on Mobilius, as it no doubt would be on Earth once the spinal interfaces were allowed to enter the mainstream.

And so Quavoce had given his blessing and Banu had been introduced to the machine, and to Minnie, and she had taken to it as any child would. Devoid of the preconceptions of age, and trusting entirely in her friend and adopted father, she had relaxed, closed her eyes, and trust-fallen into the ether.

Her voice rang out again with anticipation, "Where you me want?" she said, her English broken but improving fast now.

"Here?" her little hand pointed to one of the four plug-in couches in the cluttered lab.

"Wherever you like, Banu, wherever you like," said Amadeu, nodding enthusiastically. He followed her to a couch and helped her into it, arranging the porting cable behind her as she got comfortable.

Though the gelports reached out and connected with practiced ease as she lay back, the system did not initiate contact. It was programmed to only allow Banu to connect with adult supervision, a stipulation of Quavoce's which Amadeu had fully agreed to.

Stepping over to another couch, Amadeu lay down and plugged in as well, wary of the ever watchful Quavoce even as the Agent opened his own connection to Minnie using his onboard subspace tweeter. He did not need to sit down, or break eye contact with Amadeu and his charge, and indeed he never did.

But Amadeu did. Lying back and closing his eyes, Amadeu relaxed and opened his mind.

<¿open connection?>

Amadeu moved through the question even as it was said, popping the blue icewall that waited for him and then turning his electronic attention to Banu's presence, waiting, patiently, inside a hard blue bubble of her own. He did not pop it, but stepped inside, finding Quavoce's presence already there.

Amadeu: 'hello again, banu. ¿are you ready to start?'

She nodded, her avatar brimming with anticipation. They all used avatars when she was in system to aid her acclimatization, though they were starting to realize that was she was fast becoming more comfortable in here than they were.

Amadeu: 'ok. let's go.'

He popped the bubble around Banu as only he or Quavoce could, attaching his consciousness to her own so he could stay with her as she swam outward.

Her mind surged forward with youthful enthusiasm.

Banu: 'sobh beh'khayr, minnie!' she exclaimed to the void.

Minnie: <sobh beh'khayr, banu,> replied Minnie, her accent close to perfect.

They engaged in some Farsi banter that was far beyond Amadeu's extremely limited grasp of the language, and Quavoce chided his young charge.

Quavoce: '¿now, banu, remember? we have talked about speaking english when our friend amadeu is around.'

Banu apologized with the simple innocence of the young. Whether it was genuine innocence or just a lack of care for the complexities of courtesy, it did not matter to Amadeu. He merely chuckled at her simple joy here. She was darting this way and that, seeking out the systems she could enter, asking questions about the ones she could not.

Amadeu: '¿shall we begin?'

Banu: 'yes! ¿but where? i cannot find the simulator.'

Amadeu: 'well, we have something new for you today, banu. something … faster.'

She beamed, as Amadeu had known she would, and Quavoce frowned, as Amadeu had feared he would. And this was why Quavoce had taken the time to join them today. It was not every day that he was able to drag himself away from the myriad tasks and projects that Neal had him consulting on, leading, reviewing, or helping get back on track.

But today they were going to up the ante, a great deal, and Neal had agreed that it was worth the time off for Quavoce to be there. In fact, he had insisted upon it. It was, after all, Neal who had ordered them to take the next step in Banu's training.

Minnie: <everything is ready. ¿banu, if you are prepared?>

Banu looked at Amadeu, who in turn was looking at Quavoce. The Agent seemed to take a deep breath, then he nodded.

And so it happened. In a flash, they were in midair, high above a wide desert plain, windless and cloudless as far as their eyes could see.

Their avatars hung there, and Minnie's voice seemed to echo in the air around them as they waited.

Minnie: <flight simulation: level 1.>

Banu: '¿level 1!? but we were at level 14.'

Minnie: <flight simulation level 1, banu, but with a new plane.>

Banu was curious, but still annoyed, until the 'plane' in question appeared, floating just below them. Minnie began to describe the vast cross that now hung magically below, details and data supporting her description floated across their minds.

Minnie: <flight vehicle: skalm. dimensions: 100m x ...>

Banu lost interest in what Minnie was saying after the word dimensions, focusing instead on the strangely beautiful craft below her. But her interest was brought squarely back by the mention of speed.

Minnie: <... top speed, in-atmosphere: mach 8.>

Such terms as 'Mach' were new to her, but she knew the simulated StratoJet she had flown for the last month was capable of Mach 4 when she pushed it, which never failed to invigorate Amadeu and infuriate Quavoce, respectively.

But Mach 8.

What did Mach 8 feel like?

She longed for Mach 8.

Amadeu: '¿shall we give her a try, banu?'

As his question made access possible, she was already stepping forward, and down, into the machine, her avatar morphing and vanishing as she joined with it.

They all watched, partially as their avatar selves, and partially from within the virtual craft, from her perspective, as she entered the ship. Not that it had a cockpit, or room for any crew.

The ship, realistically reproduced as it was from the real one Neal so yearned to be making soon, existed here as it would in real life only as pure function, its only compromise toward control being the large subspace tweeters built into its wings, allowing it to instantaneously transmit the data coming from its sensors and also receive instructions for its grotesquely powerful engines from whoever was insane enough to try and pilot it.

So as Banu entered the virtual Skalm, she forwent her avatar, just as any pilot would forgo any sense of their self when they slaved to the ship, as she became the Skalm. They must leave everything else behind, no human body could survive what the Skalm was designed to do.

Minnie: <¿would you like me to start the engines, banu?>

Quavoce at Minnie/Amadeu: 'one-tenth power, minnie. for now.'

Minnie at Quavoce/Amadeu: <she will not have that option in the real skalm, she will have to learn how to balance the engines' power using antagonistic particle exhausts.>

Quavoce at Minnie/Amadeu: 'i am aware of that, minnie, but let's not scare her with that just yet. ¿amadeu?'

Though Amadeu appreciated Minnie's point, he did actually agree with Quavoce. From what he understood of the Skalm, and from his own aborted attempt to fly the virtual construct, giving Banu full power immediately would be less like throwing her in the deep end and more like throwing her from a moving car.

Amadeu at Minnie/Quavoce: 'quavoce is right. one-tenth power, please, minnie. we can give her more to play with once she has found her sea legs.'

Minnie: <very well. banu. ¿are you ready? this is going to feel a little strange. i am told it is like trying to balance on one foot when there is a strong wind.>

Amadeu suppressed a virtual snort. More like going for a bike ride in a hurricane, maybe, but he did not share his skepticism. Instead he contented himself with giving Banu the concept of a hug with his right mind, as he had learned to do when raising Minnie. The young girl hugged him back, clearly brimming with excitement. She was like a child on a fairground ride, waiting for her mother to put the coin in the slot.

And so Minnie did.

- - -

Banu: 'dear, sweet, gorgeous minnie! i love it!'

Banu screamed inside her mind, she panted, throbbing with the sheer joy of it all.

Banu: 'minnie, level 5. level 5! i want hills!'

They watched, they flew behind, they tried to keep up with the speed of the unfolding world Banu was hurtling through. Beside the plane, within it, statistics flew at them with equally alarming speed.

For Amadeu, the forces at play were just figures now, beyond Amadeu's ability to comprehend in real-time.

Power was ramping up slowly as Banu applied her thousands of hours in simulated flight these past months to the agitated madness of flying the Skalm.

The ground came at them as Minnie added in the terrain of Level 5. The levels changed the dynamics of the virtual environment; terrain morphed from flat to mountainous; visibility changed incrementally from infinite to the densest of fog; obstacles, other planes, birds, clouds, along a spectrum from the clearest of blue vistas to a sky full of problems, each level adding new complexity.

For its part, Level 5 brought gently rolling green hills and valleys, and Banu rocketed into them. She darted between their low rises, her hypersonic passage ripping virtual foliage from the soil. Entering a deeper valley, she braced her directional cores, spinning the Skalm, and accelerating at right angles to her passage, throwing the Skalm violently this way and that, dodging the rocks and rises of the ground below with the speed and agility of a hummingbird.

Amadeu was actively suppressing his body's reactions to the visuals, disconnecting his mind from his physiology to limit the damage this was doing to his psyche. He could no longer focus on their meteoric progress. It was too fast for his brain to process, and eventually he stepped out of the simulation.

He did not let Banu know, he did not want to alarm her. Though as he looked now at the statistics flowing from the system, it was clear she did not care a damn for anything else right now; she was lost in the dance.

He called up her processing statistics. When he had first enlisted her she had instantly surprised him with her adeptness in the system. Speculation had followed among his teammates about how her upbringing had left less preconceptions about technology, or how the leap she'd already had to make just to get on a plane for the first time, or see an ocean for the first time, had made it easier to adjust to Minnie's world. But it was all moot. The truth was she was a child, a blank canvas. And she was a curious child at that.

She had quickly matched and then surpassed the average adults' processing speeds, and soon was matching his and William Baerwistwyth's times. As the hours turned into days and into weeks in Minnie's simulated worlds, Amadeu's processing records had eventually become moot as Banu had practiced and learned, days and nights lost in the system.

The day she beaten Hektor Gruler's times they had celebrated.

He studied her times now in absolute silence.

He was surprised when Quavoce joined him in stepping out of the simulation. Amadeu glanced quickly at the data. She was still flying. She had not stopped. Oh boy, was she still flying.

Amadeu: '¿quavoce, is banu all right?'

Quavoce: 'banu is fine. it would seem she is far better than all right. she is close to exceeding my ability to track her, and I wanted to check on her vitals.'

Amadeu reeled. They had talked of it. They knew the coming Mobiliei pilots were faster than AIs and AMs. Not with large-scale data processing, but they were milliseconds faster at complex decision-making, all important in the reactive, high-speed moment that was stellar conflict.

Quavoce: 'i believe minnie has a larger processing substrate than my body does. but she is still a machine, i believe she will not always be able to process and manage this virtual environment as banu becomes more practiced with the skalm.'

They both studied the data, watching as though from a distance.

Banu swam and darted within the virtual space, up now to Level 12, nearly 93% of the Skalm's full power. She darted about inside Minnie's mind, tracking targets that Minnie was creating for her, chasing them down.

Minnie: <amadeu, quavoce, i feel i should mention that i am no longer limiting the movement of the targets. she is tracking them as fast as i can create them. i am only speaking to you now as an external subroutine, a copy of myself in rolas's databases. my full processing power back in japan is now dedicated to managing her virtual environment.>

Amadeu shared a mental smile with Quavoce. But knew that it was not enough to express his full joy. Inside the machine his avatar yelled with joy, shouting and pumping virtual fists.

Amadeu: 'banu, you beautiful little girl! you wonderful little genius! you're doing it! you're doing it!'

Quavoce could not help but smile at the man's overwhelming delight.

Amadeu: 'you are so wonderful, banu, i could marry you!'

The girl could not hear his proposal. But Quavoce could, and his smile quickly turned to a frown.

Amadeu nodded and went silent.

Across the globe, research teams, construction leaders, generals, and admirals stared confused as data requests waited and systems slowed. Not many had access to Minnie directly, but those that did had come to depend on her. Far above on Terminus, Birgit reacted, confused and concerned, to Minnie's sudden shift to a monotone, left-brain only speech. Airborne, Neal sensed as his plane switched to its onboard AI once more, and pinged Minnie to find out why she wasn't personally piloting anymore.

He received only an automated response.

Amadeu switched his avatar off and focused on the data coming out of the system. one hundred and nineteen.

Amadeu: 'she is so close.'

Minnie: <i cannot respond quickly enough to her commands if i increase the virtual skalm's power any further. we are reaching the limits of my ability to maintain this environment.>

Amadeu was disappointed they couldn't go further, but chided himself. That they had reached this point was ... it was ... he could not describe it, and he knew that the fact that they could not go much further in this virtual world was only a sign of how close they now were to breaking the cyber ceiling.

Quavoce: 'amadeu, banu's heart rate is elevated, it is struggling to supply enough oxygen to her brain.'

Amadeu came back to reality with a bang. Shit. He had not expected this much activity today. He had not been prepared. He should have planned for this. He should have adjusted her medical subroutine, and may have to provide a supply of super-oxygenated blood, maybe even supplemented with the zinc and other nutrients the brain needed to function for extended periods at such speeds. Her system was flooding with psychomotor stimulants. Her brain was becoming hyperactive.

Amadeu: 'minnie, let's end the chase sequence. bring her down, slowly ... but now, please.'

Minnie listened and responded. She did not rip Banu out of the simulation immediately, but gradually lowered the speed and complexity, removing the cloud cover, brightening the sky, and reining in on the Skalm's power. Amadeu and Quavoce stepped back into the calmer but still on-rushing simulation.

Sensing her engines cooling, Banu got in a final surge of speed. Rocketing down into a deep gorge, she focused on a waterfall coming up fast, waited till the last instant, then span her ship's body onto the horizontal and fired all her engines as one.

The Skalm leapt up out of the canyon with a thunderous clap, scarring the ground beneath as the hot blades of its mighty engines powered it suddenly skyward. Thick contrails formed in her wake as she ripped through the air, Banu's mind singing with joy. It was ecstasy. Pure freedom. She spiraled the Skalm as she rose skyward, still firing all five of her engines, and departed the virtual atmosphere in a matter of seconds, her exodus resounding outward across the cybernetic world in an echo of New Moon One's thunderous departure months before.

They all shared in her final moment of happiness, the sky filled with stars, a place of seeming peace and tranquility, the Skalm even more at home here in the vacuum than it was in air, untethered as it now was by the drag of the thick atmosphere below. Above Mach 2, air became like a soup, a solid thing to be forced through, a moving wall of liquid resistance. But not up here.

Once it was true, once the Skalm was made reality, the Skalm's speed in space would be limited only by how much time its pilot had to accelerate, and the reach of the subspace tweeters which that pilot needed to control the mighty beast.

From this blissful silence and vastness, Minnie slowed and ended the simulation at last, and released Banu back to her body.

The girl was crying with joy. She was ecstatic. It was the latest and greatest of a series of ever more wonderful experiences she'd had since being introduced to Minnie's world, and since meeting Quavoce, and she stood, shaky at first, and went to hug her adopted father.

They stood there, Amadeu almost as emotional as Banu, and Quavoce nodded, filled with pride, but also with trepidation. Even this ten-minute test had stretched her young mind to its very limits. Who knew what prolonged flight would do to her young psyche.

But he knew what must inevitably happen next. Neal had never said it directly, but Quavoce was no fool. He knew the six-year-old Banu Mantil would have a role to play in the brewing conflict. He held her shaking, smiling, giddy, little frame as the final tremors of her experience knew his little girl would have to fight.

Chapter 40: The Budapest Gambit

Yuri Svidrigaïlov looked out of the tall window that reached up to the vaulted ceiling above. He did not spare much time for the broad, grey sky. He did not notice the ancient, polished stone sill that his hands rested on. He did not contemplate the many men, great and terrible, who had stood here in the past, nor did he think of his place among them.

He stared out over his capital city, at the wide square below with its bustling life, grey figures hunched against the autumn chill, threading the square and the quilt of the city around it.

His capital.

His people.

"Field Commandant Beria is on the line, Premier," said a hushed Peter Uncovsky from the door to the great office.

Peter no longer waited around to be invited to such calls. Since Field Commandant Nikolai Beria had so neatly emasculated the premier at their meeting a week ago he was careful to take calls with his top general in private. Peter did not complain. Nikolai was the only person who dared stand up to the premier, and, like any bully, the premier had a tendency to take out his impotence on the next unfortunate to cross his path, and Peter wanted no part of it.

"Nikolai, how are you? And how goes the eastern shore?" The premier liked to think of his expanding empire like that, like a wave washing outward from his self.

"Good, Premier Svidrigaïlov, very good. We have secured the Crimean peninsula with minimal resistance, as we expected, along with the coastal road from Rostov and a good deal of the surrounding land. With your permission, we are ready to move onto the next phase."

"You feel confident that you have a good handle on the political topography in Kiev, Nikolai? This is not Ashgabat, we cannot afford to give the Europeans and Americans fuel for their propaganda machines."

Mikhail ignored the irony of the statement, given the premier's own throttling grasp on the information flow within his burgeoning empire. Vast swathes of the Russian political propaganda machine, long dormant since the fall of the USSR, had been reawakened. Not under the same names, of course. Now they had such innocuous sounding titles as Ministry for Equitable Data Access and State Voluntary Ratings Board.

"Of course, Premier. They represent a threat, that is for sure, but not one you cannot handle, I think. And after their embarrassment at Rostov and Belgorod, I think they will think twice before engaging us."

"Yes, Nikolai," said the premier, but a bitter taste came to his mouth as he thought of the reports that had come back from those encounters.

He had thought his teams were nigh on invincible. But they had paid a dear price for engaging the troops of the allied taskforce. "We did, of course, win out on those occasions, Commandant, but I remain fearful of what might happen if we find ourselves facing the larger force those recon teams represented."

The Agent moved to quell the man's fears, he needed the premier to be the brash and ambitious man he had helped take power. He needed the premier to provoke the Europeans. To provoke them to the point that they would commit their full capability. It was, as far as Pei and he were concerned, the only way they would be able to achieve their true objective.

"Yuri, my friend, the fact is you engaged and destroyed the recon teams. Teams that represented the very best the allies have to send. And it was only the covert nature of their incursion that prevented us from sending a more focused attack by our superior air forces. On the open battlefield, it is the Ubitsyas, not the ground troops, that will be the decisive factor."

"Yes, yes, Nikolai," replied the premier, "so you keep saying. But what of the allied air force? I have seen footage from around their space elevator, Nikolai. We know they have next generation fighters as well, larger ones than ours, I might add."

The Agent bristled at the mention of the SpacePort, a sign of just how fast the work of their nemesis Neal Danielson's team was progressing.

"Indeed," the Agent replied aloud, "indeed. But that size is because of their mostly civilian function, not any increased power or militant capability. These are transports with only a secondary attack capability, not dedicated killers, like our Ubitsyas."

It was partially true. The Ubitsyas carried no cabin, had no room for cargo, like the bulkier StratoJets. A single pilot lay horizontally in the torpedo-shaped hull, cradled against the G-forces of the nimble fighter, facing a multiscreen control panel he manipulated with two joysticks and his feet. A spinal interface it was not, and the Agent suspected the allies had some version of that on their StratoJets, which would improve their piloting ability significantly.

He also knew that even though the StratoJets had a small passenger compartment they were probably still armed with serious weaponry, and were no doubt being upgraded as they spoke since he had been forced to show some of his hand in the fight with the Recon Teams.

But he downplayed this here, building his leader's confidence, "No, no, Premier. While the allied fighters would make short work of current generation planes, they will have bitten off more than they can chew if they go up against your ever-growing Ubitsya fleet."

"So you say, Nikolai, so you say," the premier replied with feigned modesty, but in fact the compliments to his fleet did not fall on deaf ears, and he brimmed with pride at the thought of his incredible fighting machines.

"Indeed I do, Yuri. Which is why I say we should press forward, into Belarus. Into the Baltic states."

"Whoa, Nikolai, you get ahead of yourself. The Europeans can only be pushed so far. If we breech any more borders too soon after Ukraine, we will incite riot. Talk all you want about the capability of our fighting force, we are still talking about going against nuclear powers, let us not forget that."

The Agent was all too aware of that; it was, in fact, the basis of his entire mission here, a mission that had gone spectacularly awry. He thought back, now, to their preparations back on Mobiliei. He contemplated the Nomadi groups that had nominated and supported the Agent Shtat Palpatum, the Mobiliei who, in the guise of John Hunt, had betrayed them all. He wondered whether it had been their intention all along, remembering that they had actively supported the concept of an advanced team from the start. He was right, of course. When the idea had been raised, they had seen a singular opportunity to stymie the effort and leapt at it.

But that was all speculation now, mooted by the passing of time. Setting it aside, the Agent focused on the task at hand.

"Yes, Premier. I assure you, as always, that avoiding such an attack remains my highest priority."

Yes, thought the Agent, but provoking an attack of another kind, that is a different story. The conversation wound on, but Mikhail was already engaged elsewhere. He was close now. Even as he exchanged final platitudes with the premier, he was raising his forces. Driving them forward. Brashly now, pushing on to Kiev, and past that, to the borders with Belarus, Poland, and Romania. Not to mention Hungary and Slovakia. He needed a response, not a nuclear one, that remained unlikely, but it was vital he did not even tease at such a thing. No, he needed a specific response.

He needed to bring out Neal so he could face his forces on the battlefield. He reviewed his options carefully. He would not wait for further approval from his puppet premier, that man had almost exhausted his usefulness anyway. No, he would push on. But where? He looked at his options, and there, in the center, at the heart of the once-mighty Hapsburg Empire, he chose his target.

- - -

Hours later, while his great army mobilized and hundreds of miles away his seventh division began to rumble up through the big Ukrainian cities of Uman and Ternopil toward the Hungarian border, Agent Mikhail Kovalenko stepped from his mobile command center and stepped into a waiting helicopter.

He was heading south, to the Black Sea. To rendezvous with a waiting force there. To take command of a very special aircraft fresh from the Novosibirsk Plant.

- - -

Minnie: <¿neal, would you mind if i woke you up?>

It was a strange request, to ask a sleeping person if they would mind being woken up. But in theory he could actually say no, and, by the nature of the machine-induced slumber he now enjoyed, Minnie could let him carry on sleeping, as though she had never disturbed him.

Neal: '¿is it urgent?'

That part of Neal that Minnie had reached out to was subsumed under a simulacrum of REM sleep, a dream state during which Neal reviewed reports from the various departments, sub-departments, projects and mission specialists under his vast team's auspices, while his body slept away the night. He did not waste even his sleeping hours anymore, using the five hours enforced upon him by an AI Minnie had dedicated to monitoring his biological processes to catch up on logistical and quality assurance reviews. More to keep apprized of the progress of non-critical path items than to micromanage them.

Minnie: <it is regarding russian forces in ukraine, neal. they have mobilized once more.>

He cursed violently. Why must they keep needling him? He willed himself awake, opening his eyes like he was initializing a system.

As his pupils struggled to focus and adjust to the dim light in his Rolas apartment, he willed his curtains open and his lights on. They remained inanimate. And why wouldn't they, he thought, grumpily. Reality: such an unresponsive place. Neal frowned and closed his eyes again as he sat up.

Neal: 'minnie, give me a status report, please.'

Minnie: <of course. deployments in force have moved on kiev, as we had anticipated. but ground troops are also moving farther to the west, north and south, toward the borders.>

Neal: '¿they are?'

It didn't make any sense. They as good as had Ukraine, and he doubted the Europeans would make too much more noise even if Belarus was subsumed, as callous as that seemed, but why move farther before you have even consolidated the massive Ukrainian state? Why wouldn't they wait? What was the goddamned rush?

Neal: 'show me.'

His mind filled with a satellite view over Western Ukraine, and as he wondered where the picture was coming from, he was informed it was real-time, enhanced to account for cloud cover over some parts of the north and the Romanian border to the south. Minnie then overlaid a series of arrows, some moving outward from Kiev, some passing to the south and north of the main city, bypassing it altogether.

Neal's attention veered naturally to Poland. And indeed there were two large forces moving toward that border in the northwest. This was madness. Europe would not only respond to an invasion of Poland, they would, Neal feared, violently overreact to it, such were the depth of the scars from the last time someone invaded Poland. Minnie sensed his focus.

Minnie: <based on standard military tactics displayed during russian military exercises and training, they appear to be assuming a defensive position in the northwest. they are fanning

out too early, already dispersing the main body of that division along secondary and tertiary roadways.>

Neal could see it too. They were creating a perimeter a hundred miles long, as they had done in the Stannic Bloc after rolling over their defenses months before. But they were not doing it subtly. In the past they had attempted to conceal their troop movements under the cover of night. But now, it was like they were displaying it.

And that was not the only part of the display. To the south, moving along the border with Romania, seemingly ignoring the sizeable but ill-equipped Romanian army attempting to erect a defensive network there, was the largest single body of troops of all.

They were not fanning out. Not dispersing. They were moving fast along two parallel main roads a hundred miles apart; two great columns of tanks, troop carriers, and supply vehicles, filling both lanes of each road, brushing the local traffic aside without regard, into side roads, onto margins, into ditches. They were clearly moving with purpose.

But where? Not Slovakia. Though a beautiful country, Slovakia was not a rich one, and would not provide much in the way of reward for the trouble it would bring defending it from Poland to the north and Hungary to the south.

Hungary to the south.

Even as he thought of it, he knew this was it. Monetarily struggling, but symbolically strong, Hungary was historically one of the powerhouse nations of Central Europe. Its capital was the stuff of song, its reach at one time from the Black Sea to the Baltic.

The two columns, trundling at forty miles per hour through the Ukrainian countryside, they could only be heading to Budapest.

As Minnie began to respond to his line of reasoning, modeling the track and progress of the large force, another part of her synthetic psyche was also receiving and routing a call. Then another. By the time she notified Neal, there were three foreign heads of state trying to reach him.

Whether he wanted it or not, his force was about to be co-opted.

Chapter 41: Bubble Burst

Major Toranssen: 'ladies and gentlemen, we are officially outbound from rolas. this is a comms check. can i get a status ping and return from each of you, please.'

Minnie felt the flow of the data coming from the flotilla as they sent data packets to her, and through her, to the major. She was maintaining a running track of all the components of the fleet as it set off from Rolas airspace, maintaining multiple redundant subspace data paths through the four StratoJets and three heavy lifters in the fleet that were enabled with long-range subspace tweeters.

The ping was more of a bandwidth test than anything else, but as the data packets came through, rich with telemetry, the fleet seemed to pulse with freshness, with a vibrant currency, like a coat of wet paint gleaming on their virtual black hulls.

The sensation reflected back out to all the pilots almost as soon as Minnie had processed it, the reciprocal data check filling every pilot, team leader, and spezialist with a knowledge of their entirety.

That entirety was something to behold.

The fleet was flying out and up, rising through the atmosphere as it departed the sanctity of SpacePort One's airspace, a great arrowhead filling the sky.

Spread out along the cutting edge of the arrow were Neal's all important StratoJets. Thirty jet-black needles slicing through the sky, each armed with a bank of flechette guns and laden with wing loads of Brimstone and Maverick anti-tank missiles. With the extra weight, they might not be able to reach their top speeds, but they were limited now anyway, waiting for the three huge, lumbering, and fully laden C-17 Globemasters that formed the heart of the great arrow.

Each of the big planes massed more than the entire StratoJet fleet. Each carried ten six-man teams, grouped into the same fire-team configuration as the Recon Teams, and equally armed to the teeth, ready to be deployed by parachute by the big planes.

Along with the troops, each C-17 also carried a burly command vehicle, a new addition to TASC's ground-based armory. It was a modified GTK Boxer armored fighting vehicle, a big, eight-wheeled all-terrain vehicle, thick with armor plating and bristling with weaponry.

Its massive wheels and multiple gun mounts already made it a very capable machine. But Madeline had replaced its ceramic shielding slabs with black SC armor-plating, and then replaced its machine-gun mounts with two quad-barreled flechette cannons, controlled from within the safety of the cab.

She had also coated its massive tires with a new, woven shielding fabric and installed eight copper-coiled electric motors, allowing each wheel to be controlled individually. The whole was given ample power and unlimited range by the replacement of its combustion engine with a football-sized fusion cell that also powered the hub subspace transponder it carried and the deadly quad cannons.

General Milton: 'i see that you are en route and clear of rolas. if i may, major, i would like to address everyone.'

It was not really a question, and the general did not wait for a reply. The general spoke from his and Neal's command post on Rolas, his mind wired in the command matrix Minnie had constructed for the mission. He would be in overall control of the operation.

General Milton: 'to all the team leads, spezialists, and pilots, i would like to welcome you all to operation arrowhead. we are, as you know, en route to central europe. we have been tasked by our allies in europe to establish a perimeter block on further russian advancement. i do not need to tell you the importance of that mission. what i do need to tell you is that we do not engage any ordinary force.'

None of the highly trained members of the force now exceeding five hundred miles an hour over the plains of the Sahara desert would ever have mistaken the Russian Army for anything other than one of the most deadly fighting forces on the planet. Economic struggles had done little to dull the nation's appetite for military might, and in recent years they had enjoyed a resurgence to something close to their Cold War status among the world's leading military powers.

But General Milton spoke of something else entirely. Something that had been kept a closely guarded secret, and the reason for Europe's absolute insistence that TASC forces become involved.

General Milton: 'men and women of operation arrowhead, we face today not just the military might of the russian army and air force, we face some measure of the same brutally effective technology we have all come to assume was ours alone.'

There was not a man or woman aboard any of the C-17s or StratoJets that did not tense at the news.

General Milton: 'i mean not to alarm you, nor to dissuade you from the task ahead. for when i talk of their technology, i speak only of the armor you wear, and some attempt at matching the air domination our StratoJet fleet brings. but they have nothing close to our communications ability, and they do not have minnie. in short, while they may be as hardy as us, they will not be nearly as fast or well trained as you all are. and as you all know, with training comes excellence, and with excellence … comes *victory*.'

He wanted to shout those last words. To show the full force of his confidence in their ability. Confidence he did not have to feign. But he was not one for long speeches. He was one for keeping his people informed, and so, his brief morale boost finished, he moved now to what they really needed and released a substantial data packet to every member of the mission, a hefty swarm of data covering everything they knew of the Russian's handle on Mobiliei tech, and a complete analysis of each and every tactical ability those tech-enabled forces possessed.

General Milton: 'i will leave you, for now, with the full analysis we have prepared on their new capabilities. study it, please. work with your team leads to discuss and model how you will incorporate the data into your individual team's capabilities and strike patterns. pilots, you have five hours till you are released for active air engagement. strike teams, you have six till drop zone. commander zubaideh and major toranssen will reach out to the air and ground wings respectively with force deployments shortly, and i will speak to all again when we get closer to engagement. good luck, and god speed.'

He cut off the connection and lay back in his cradle, opening a dedicated link to Ayala. She was travelling with the force, cradled inside one of the armored Boxers, much to his chagrin. Discussion of who should go on the mission had been the subject of fierce debate among Neal's senior leadership. In theory, none of them had to go. In theory, only the shock troops needed to be on the actual ground as all other operations could be managed remotely and instantaneously via subspace tweeter from the safety of Rolas Base. But Ayala had had absolutely no intention of sending her people into battle if their senior officer wasn't willing to risk her life alongside them.

So she occupied one of the stocky GTK Boxers. This did give some tactical benefits: should the Russians attack the satellite subspace network in an attempt to cut communications, then Ayala would remain close enough to the action to still provide command oversight. It was slight, but it had been the crux of an argument Barrett quickly realized he wasn't going to win.

From the pilots' perspectives, the StratoJets were not the Skalms, and though they were extremely fast, a sedated pilot could safely survive its maneuvers allowing them to pilot from onboard. Barrett and Jack had considered centralizing all the pilots to the C-17s, but that would make them a singular tactical weak spot: the Russians need only take out the big support planes and the StratoJet fleet would be dead in the air.

But as with Ayala, in the end it was not a difficult choice for any of Jack's pilot core: better to rely on your own skill and training in battle than anything else, and they had unanimously chosen to be onboard their planes for the engagement.

There were, however, several notable exceptions to that rule, and back amongst the concrete safety of Rolas Island two of those exceptions busied themselves.

One was talking to Neal Danielson while they waited for the real battle to begin. The other was lying prone on a mesh couch, plugged into the net, playing games with her friend Minnie. It was a rolling simulation which they played for hours every day: Banu was a white barn owl presiding over a huge, well-used red barn, and Minnie was a series of darting rabbits scurrying this way and that for her to chase.

"Quavoce," said Neal, out of Banu's earshot, "I understand your concerns, I do, but surely we should let her remote-pilot one of the StratoJets for a while. She is more capable than any of our other pilots."

Quavoce nodded but did not agree. He was trying to be reasonable, though he had little intention of actually allowing it. Neal focused his eyes on the former Mobiliei Agent. Even now, Quavoce was remotely piloting one of the jets, as was John Hunt, from around the world at the Research Center in Japan. For her part, Minnie had taken on two StratoJets herself, her divided attention still nearly as good as either of the Agents, and better than any of the rest of Jack Toranssen's flight wing.

Once the fighting started, they would give it their full attention. The only question remained: would the best human pilot be fighting alongside them?

- - -

Banu darted down from an eave in a broad, sun-dappled barn, shafts of light partially illuminating the dusty, straw ridden floor. Stables and stalls that lined the walls, some with low-slung doors, some without. The aging wooden planks of the walls and sloping ceiling allowed deep orange shafts of setting sun to leak between their fingers.

The light betrayed occasional, brief sightings of Banu's prey as they scuttled this way and that.

- - -

"I understand your perspective, Neal," replied Quavoce, "and appreciate that she is, indeed, our best pilot. But she is also a six-year-old girl, and one who has already, I think, suffered enough."

- - -

She saw it, her big eyes whipping around. There was only a moment's hesitation. Did she have enough time to catch it before it escaped? Her decision came to life as pure movement, she flung herself forward, powerful wings flashing out and wrenching at the air, thrusting her downward.

Banu propelled herself down from her perch toward the sprinting hare trying to reach the safety of a gap in one of the stable's walls. She flew straight at one of the stable's doors, barely ajar. She was unafraid, batting her powerful wings hard to twist her body as she flew through the improbably thin gap. The hare's furry hind legs scrabbled for purchase as it sped toward sanctity. It would be close. It always was. She exalted in it.

- - -

"I am not calling for her to be sent into battle yet, my friend," said Neal, gently, but insistently, "but if we engage with any significant air resistance, she would an invaluable asset."

Asset. That was what so scared Quavoce. He had allowed military exigency to rule his world too long. Almost to the point of damning the very race he now sought to defend. But he had seen, almost too late, that the ends do not justify the means, not always.

"I worry at the cost to her, Neal. I know it seems … trivial … in the greater scheme. But …"

- - -

She was flying at breakneck speed as she angled herself back and reached out with her talons, extending them forward with a grace that was visually stunning. Minnie watched Banu and knew it was beautiful as the young girl's claws found their mark, sinking into the hare's back, only centimeters from its escape, Banu's wing tips brushing the wall rearing up in front of her, eddies of dust and straw drawing up and around as she reversed her momentum with all of her strength.

- - -

"No, Quavoce. No. It does not seem trivial at all." Neal could not deny his own affection for the young girl that had come to live amongst them. Nor would he dare question for one moment Quavoce's clearly far greater commitment to her safety. "But she has trained as a pilot these past months for a reason. I wish we did not need her. But we do. And you know as well as I do that we will need thousands more like her before we are done."

- - -

Banu had timed it to perfection, and Minnie looked on as once again the white owl drew its prey back into the air, up and out of the small stable, up into the eaves of the barn. Banu's barn. Her domain. Minnie was teasing Banu ever more, testing and training the limits of her abilities, as she did for hours every day. She was not sure which of them enjoyed it more.

- - -

Quavoce looked at Neal, not dulling the weight of his emotions one bit as he said, "Okay, Neal, okay. I will let her stand in for one of the major's pilots should the StratoJets get into deep water, but I will not have her engage ground troops. That would be too ... I will not have her firing on people, not yet, maybe not ever. Is that understood?"

Neal nodded, satisfied with the compromise for now.

- - -

Banu came to rest on her eave once more. The master of the barn. She was brimming with pride.

As Banu rested her mighty wings she placed the now limp body of the hare on the eave next to her, along with her other catches.

At some level, she understood that they were simulated animals, and that she had killed them. Goodness knows her first five years on a family farm had come with their fair share of butchery. But as a young girl she had never done the killing herself. Here in the simulation, as when she had lived in rural Iran, those that cared for her spared her the final gasps and struggles of life's final ebb.

Despite their best intentions, though, Minnie and Quavoce would have no such control over what happened in the raw reality of the coming battle.

Chapter 42: A Brief Engagement

General Milton: 'air wing, it's time for you to move off. major toranssen, accelerate and engage, flight plan theta. good luck, everyone.'

Major Toranssen: 'thank you, general. stratojets, accelerate to mach 3, on my mark. flight plan theta, coordinates on net. quavoce, you have squadron bravo; john, you have squadron charlie. squadron alpha, you are with me. engage.'

The thirty jets all ramped up their speed as one, rocketing away from the three massive airlifters as though they were all but standing still. They had been forced to fly not only slower, but significantly lower than their optimal cruise altitude to keep convoy with the burly heavy-lifters.

Despite these shackles, they did not climb now that they were taken off the leash, but actually began to descend as they accelerated, their progress through the thickening atmosphere marked by grey shockwaves emanating from their tails, the thunderous double clap of their hypersonic progress buffeting the ground below.

They were over the Ionian when they broke formation, and the StratoJets penetrated Montenegrin airspace in a matter of minutes, on the heels of a series of calls to its government, and its former Yugoslav neighbors, explaining the very unsubtle incursion into their sovereign air. It was not a request they could refuse, and nor would they, given their own long exile from freedom under the last Russian empire.

Before the calls were even complete, the leading edge of the fleet was already gone. Two hundred miles covered in four minutes. They were past Bosnia, past Serbia, bisecting Romania, and splitting already into their three arms. Ready for first contact.

As the bodies of the C-17s came hulking up behind at their molasses pace, the Russian forces were starting to hear rumor of the fleet coming up over the Mediterranean. But by then the StratoJets were already closing, coming in low and hard at the Russian columns.

Toranssen: 'quavoce, john, i have confirmation from strategic command in stuttgart that the russian's have crossed the hungarian border. we are officially clear to engage any and all targets west of the line.'

The border resolved in their minds, and then on into the minds of all the pilots in each wing. Clarification of a line of demarcation long since anticipated.

Toranssen: 'we are cleared weapons hot. good luck, gentlemen. keep channels open, flag if engaged by tech-ten units.'

Tech-ten: the byword for the evolutional leap in technology that they may face here. The two Agents confirmed, and then each squadron banked and swerved smoothly away, three wings of weaponized fury soaring away at meteoric speeds.

Separate now, Jack narrowed his comms to his team and talked them into the approach.

Toranssen: 'alpha squadron, on me, strafing run, parallels. alphas nine and ten on firewall. let's open them up.'

The fighters did not slow. The Russian columns had long since split into three to fill the three main roads that linked Hungary to Ukraine. Each of Jack's squadrons was targeted to a column. The leading Russian tanks and APCs in Jack's column were already six miles over the border, and still coming.

Six miles. That would be Jack's first strafing run. It would be over in fourteen seconds.

He targeted with cold precision, not on individual vehicles, but on the entire left lane of the two-lane road. The next in his squadron would target the right lane, the third back to the left again, and so back along his squadron, four planes pounding each lane. The last two planes in his squadron had different orders.

As Jack saw the first big T-90 battle tanks that led the column, he counted the milliseconds down to fire range. Then, angling his plane so he could maintain downward fire for the full six miles, Jack unleashed his guns.

His speed noticeably faltered as the momentum of his plane was thrown into the thousands of tiny pellets being railed out of the ports on his plane's nose.

A Russian commander, exposed from the waist up as he surveyed their progress from the main hatch of his battle tank, spotted the inbound planes. He had the fortitude and time to say, "Incomi …!" before a sheaf of kinetic destruction ripped along the top of his tank, rending its armor, pulping his head and torso, and echoing throughout the hull of the mighty beast before grinding onward along the line.

Fourteen seconds. Over a million rounds. A line of death and mayhem burnt along the unsuspecting Russian forces like a blade made of lightning. But the Russians would not remain pliant for long. Jack knew that. Somewhere in these columns, he could not know where, was the real threat. Any moment it could spring on them. And that was saying nothing for the still potent standard weaponry the Russian Army had on hand.

Toranssen: 'alpha nine and ten, wall of fire.'

They were already on it. While eight of Jack's squadron had surged on with blistering speed, the last two planes had come to a thundering halt in front of the first of the T-90s. The big tanks were bruised by the initial strafing run, but far from done, and they were still trundling on, smoke rippling from their hulls as their crews scrambled to respond to the sudden attack.

Alpha Nine and Ten were there to stop them. Permanently. To stop them and anyone else that came on behind them, and to let their burning hulks pile up and block the column from progressing any farther.

Alpha Nine: 'wall of fire. with pleasure, major. lighting them up now.'

Hovering over the road in front of the column, the two StratoJets concentrated their guns on each of the two lead tanks in turn. Not glancing blows, but a supercharged kinetic maelstrom. The pellets turned even the tank's thick armor to liquid. Ambitious souls aboard the tanks attempted to return fire, to engage with the broad complement of anti-air and even anti-personnel munitions mounted on the burly brawlers. But they were very much in the wrong place at the wrong time. They were on the receiving end of power station's worth of energetic release and their tank's bodies began to heat and slag under the barrage.

To add insult to pervasive injury, each StratoJet then unleashed one of their Brimstone missiles at their respective targets, the stumpy rockets flying under the tanks and then detonating. The tanks lifted and buckled, as if shrugging at the impossibility of their position as punished armor and tarmac alike were shredded and destroyed.

Soon two columns of smoke and flame were rising at the head of the suddenly halted line of Russian forces. Two molten, liquid heaps lying where forty million dollars of military hardware had just been. The rest of the column would not enjoy a much better fate.

Toranssen: 'alphas five through eight, starboard flank. target anti-air units. alphas two through four with me, portside.'

While alphas nine and ten turned the first tanks into a pyre, the remaining eight jets, Jack's included, banked hard, slowed, and fanned out, forming two lines on either side of the six-mile column, firing into it without falter or mercy. They focused on threat points first: anti-air units and tank-mounted heavy guns. They knew that they only had a few moments left before a concerted response could be expected.

As they used their blitzkrieg to dismantle the Russian force's forward fighting strength, Jack checked in on the other wings.

Toranssen: '¿quavoce, john, how goes it?'

He could see their squadrons as he thought of them, Minnie feeding his mind with the data he desired.

John: 'bravo column halted, minimal resistance so far. i'm starting to see small arms fire from apc's, and i am noticing forces across border in ukraine are starting to maneuver. seems like certain apc's are being called up to the front.'

Quavoce: 'can confirm same here in terms of small arms fire, but not the cross-border movement. anti-air units clearly being called up but not apc's. expect fire from them within two to three minutes. no tech-ten units as of this moment.'

No Tech-10. They had to be out here somewhere. Surely Mikhail would not have committed to such a bold attack without putting his most powerful assets in play.

Minnie: <squadron leaders, i have a large inbound flotilla. sharing data now. coming in at mach 1.5.>

Toranssen: '¿mach 1.5? it isn't slow, but it isn't on our level, either.'

Minnie: <i can confirm that. i estimate seventy-five su-27s and forty su-35s. still no tech-ten ground or air units confirmed.>

Jack did some version of a mental whistle from his physically catatonic state. Forty Su-35s. They were no StratoJets, but they were the most maneuverable fighter in the air today, even more capable than the Typhoon. That would be no picnic.

Jack reviewed the Russian flotilla's heading. It was not spread out. They were all focused on the most southerly column. On the column that had shown ground troop movement across the border: the only sign they had seen so far of potential real resistance.

Toranssen: 'gentlemen, it looks like we have a pattern. they are focusing their air forces on john's position. i am going to assume that their tech-ten units are either already there or en route. we just haven't seen them yet. let's not fully redistribute, i want to leave some eggs in our other baskets, but quavoce, i do want you to rotate out six of your squadron to john's position. and please include bravo two among them.'

Bravo Two was one of the two fighters Minnie was piloting. The other was with Jack, and he had every intention of dispatching that version of their synthetic compatriot as well.

Toranssen: 'minnie, that means you should take alpha two there as well, full speed. let's put our best players on the field. alpha four, you too. alphas three and five rotate to reinforce bravo squadron, you are with quavoce now. let's go, people, full throttle, i want all of you in place when the russian air forces get to charlie squadron's position.'

When Jack said full throttle, his people responded, and the Russian forces under fire from Jack and Quavoce's squadrons enjoyed a moment's respite as some of their attackers banked and rocketed away.

While they may have wondered for a moment why their assailants were leaving, they did not look the gift horse in the mouth. They knew they needed to respond. They were struggling frantically to fight back and they were taking terrible casualties. From within the explosive madness that had become their world, their training was kicking in and they were spreading out into firing lines.

Jack saw the first volley of anti-air missiles come up at his squadron and watched his team respond smoothly. Each fighter handled the missiles coming at them individually, only asking for help if they were being overwhelmed.

Jack focused on those fired at him. They were an assortment of munitions. Some were fired from shoulder-mounted launchers; small but fast. But most of them were the much heftier, much more powerful vehicle-launched varietal. Jack hit each with a concentrated burst, following their advance until he had ended them with kinetic ferocity.

Even as he deleted each of the nasty little messages being sent his way, he also killed the messengers, targeting anyone foolhardily enough to fire upon him. Firing without mercy or pause, he released one of his own for every that was sent at him, their mission clear, their purpose singular: to obliterate any who dared to respond to his team's devastating barrage.

And so the butcher's bill rose, the planes of Jack's squadron pouring a seemingly unending torrent of death into the line of fire and gore that they were etching into the countryside, three new valleys of death for poets to lament.

- - -

Minnie monitored everything from above, as well as from the perspective of every plane in the fleet, and especially, of course, from the cockpit of the two fighters slaved to her. Both were now rushing to join John's fleet, to bolster it against the sizeable air fleet coming at it from the Russian forward base in Kiev.

For now she was also talking with General Milton, Ayala, and Neal as they watched the squadrons' progress. But she would stop engaging in chatter once they engaged in air-to-air combat. She would need to focus her processing power.

General Milton: 'we have the data as well, minnie. i see the russian fighters. they are coming in hard. ¿and what is that behind them, an a-50?'

Minnie: <i believe so. it was already providing comms support to the russian invasion force. now it seems to have been redirected to help provide radar support to the air wing moving to engage charlie squadron.>

Neal: 'good, minnie, please assign an ai to keep an eye on the a-50 as well, we should probably deal with it once we have dispatched the russian fighters. but first, let's get back to the ground forces. i want to see what they are up to across the border from john's position.'

Their view swam downward, focusing and refocusing as it went and eventually coming to rest at the limit of their satellite Pod's visual acuity. Minnie's many AIs were already overlaying the images with data and force estimates as it zoomed.

Ayala: 'there! i see them!'

The focus of Ayala's attention was highlighted in the views of her friends and colleagues as she spoke, a set of faint streaking black lines emanating from a series of Armored Personnel Carriers along the column, just east of John's squadron.

Minnie: <yes, you may be right, ayala. they could be shock troops. if those are personnel then they are moving with the speed and agility i would expect from 1st or 2nd gen. battleskins. i am afraid we do not have the resolution to confirm, though.>

General Milton: 'i think the fact that you cannot effectively track them only proves the point further, minnie. ok, assuming that's what we are looking at then there are … wow … ok, so they have quite a few of them. minnie, try to calculate a force estimate, please.'

They watched as Minnie's AIs sought and found more and more examples of the streaking black lines. They were coming up fast from many points along the line, stretching back for miles along the seemingly endless column.

General Milton: 'i think it is safe to say we are looking at the bulk of their ground-based tech ten force.'

He would not say it, but if this wasn't, then the one-sided feel of the fight so far was about to swing wildly in the other direction. Avoiding an avenue of thought that would only lead to despair, the general went on.

General Milton: 'so assuming they are focusing their counterattack, then i am going to follow major toranssen's lead and match our troop deployments to his.'

Ayala: 'agreed. globemaster three is nearly at john's position. i am diverting globemaster two there as well. we can deploy fully two-thirds of our ground force to reinforce squadron charlie. then, after globemaster two has dropped its troop complement to join globemaster three's, it can go on to quavoce's position and drop its command boxer there.'

General Milton: 'confirmed, ayala. make it so. that will leave globemaster one to split its force at the other two locations, and still leaves a boxer unit at each location to provide command and fire support.'

No one mentioned that when they spoke of the armored boxer units, and specifically the one aboard Globemaster Two, they were also talking about the all-terrain unit that carried Ayala. But the general knew it, and he was quietly happy that Ayala hadn't insisted on dropping her Boxer into the explosive brew that was fast fermenting at John's location.

- - -

Five minutes later the Globemasters were coming up on their first drop zones, and not a moment too soon. Things on the ground were heating up.

For Quavoce, in the time between dispatching the bulk of his fighters and the two from Jack's squadron reinforcing him, the Russian column had been able to consolidate their force, and was now returning a solid blanket of fire.

Quavoce: 'bravos three and five, pull back. i don't want any of you anywhere near the border.'

Caution was becoming a necessity. The bulk of the Russian column still across the border in the Ukraine was starting to throw up a blanket of fire into the sky. Not targeted, not yet, just a swathe of flak and lead, buffeting the StratoJets from every direction.

Quavoce: 'bravo squadron, let's pull back to the firewall. we will continue our enemy force reduction from there.'

Force reduction. It was a cold term, and it was bloody work. The remaining four jets in his squadron stopped targeting units along the entire column and instead pulled back to focus their fire on its lead units, obliterating each in turn.

The tactic worked. The surviving Russians on the ground became even more distraught at the change in tactic. The fire was no longer random. Now the threat became manifest, a tangible thing, a flaming, death-dealing beast lumbering thunderously back along the column toward them, consuming all in its path. The sight of it would have broken anyone, and their instincts changed from fight to flight.

Back across the border in the Ukraine, though, the bulk of the Russian force were becoming emboldened, and the many units capable of taking their guns and missile launchers off road started to fan out along the border, firing with all their might as they went.

It was getting messy, thought Quavoce, a slaughter on the ground and a hail of thundering fire in the air. He needed support, and not just the two planes now arriving from Jack's unit to even out their squadrons.

He needed ground support. It was not far behind.

Globemaster One: 'bravo squadron, this is globemaster one, i have a delivery for you.'

Quavoce: 'not a moment too soon, globemaster. give our position a wide birth, please, it is getting pretty hairy down here. but if you could drop off that package at drop zone xeta-five, i would certainly appreciate it.'

Globemaster One: 'xeta-five, confirmed. inbound and dropping package in 5, 4, 3 ..."

As he watched his Spezialists start to fall from the back of the cargo plane, another call was coming in.

Ayala: 'quavoce, globemaster two is not far behind as well. i assume you know we have repurposed your ground troops to john's position, and have split jack's between locations alpha and beta.'

Quavoce: 'received and understood, ayala. i know you are inbound in boxer two. looking forward to having you come up that road.'

Ayala: 'me too.'

General Milton: 'quavoce, jack, i want to emphasize this, now that things are taking shape and we are focusing on position charlie. i don't want alpha and beta getting heroic. that means you two. you are force diminished. focus on holding the line until we have suppressed position charlie. then we can get you what you need to push alpha and beta back into ukraine ... and back into the stone age while we are at it.'

They both smiled coldly, and agreed. Hold the line.

Quavoce reached out to his thirty ground troops as they landed and began to come up the road. Meanwhile, the twenty-two-ton Boxer Two came to ground with an elephantine thud, its three huge parachutes bellowing around it.

It did not wait for them to fall, jettisoning them without emotion, its great wheels already engaging, driving it outward, through the shattered debris of the small tree it had obliterated. Up, out, and over a small hillock and onto the road. It accelerated hard as it hit the tarmac, its fusion cell driving its powerful electric motors as it accelerated after the shock troops even now vaulting and sprinting along the road ahead of it toward the fight they were all longing to get to.

At Quavoce's bidding, they formed into a wide, line, staying nimble and reactive. They used their agility to physically dodge the incoming artillery and missile fire now coming from the vast Russian army ahead of them as they faced off against their goliath foe. And they taunted the Russians, punishing them with ruthless fury whenever they dared to try and advance.

To the south, though, the Russians were forming a line of their own. Not quite as capable, perhaps, but far, far larger, and with very real teeth.

John Hunt: 'charlie squadron, here they come. we are three minutes to estimated engagement.'

They had endured the first volley of air-to-air missiles from the coming Russian fleet. It had been massive, a sea of explosives rushing at them, but at this distance they had been blind, coming in searching, seeking the elusive blackness of the StratoJets.

John's fighters had taken almost all of them out, but the Russian attack had not been without strategic forethought, and once they did find target purchase, the remainder of the two hundred missiles had focused on three jets at random and come at them. The whole of John's now eighteen-jet squadron had tried to save their colleagues in the final seconds, but only one had survived the three clouds of fire that had erupted around the unfortunate pilots.

Two StratoJets down. Not much, perhaps, given the thousands of casualties they must have already inflicted on the Russian forces, but a blow nonetheless.

Ayala, watching from her cradle to the north, mobilized her ground troops in response.

Ayala: 'ground force charlie, i want you moving on these points. fire free, you are to put down anything that moves.'

Their minds filled with her tactical choices and they were moving a moment later, seeking the Russian ground forces they knew were out there, ready to engage. Like Ayala, the Spezialists on the ground were hungry: hungry for blood, hungry for retribution, hungry to avenge their friends in the Recon Teams who had been so brutally massacred. They wanted a rematch.

They were going to get it.

The Russians troops were also bracing for all-out war. They were no longer equipped with just the assault rifles of their first encounter with the TASC Spezialists. They still carried nothing like the tri-barrel flechette guns of the TASC forces, but they did now have something that could help them bring down the terrible StratoJets above, or so they hoped, and as the massive inbound fleet of Su-27 and Su-35 fighters came thundering up from behind, to the cheers of the beleaguered Russian regulars, the dispersed shock troops unleashed their most deadly weapon.

It was a wall, a horde, a swarm of black needlepoint signatures suddenly rearing up out of the woods ahead of them, filling their views.

There were hundreds of them. No, thousands, John's pilots saw with horror. Thousands of tiny missiles. Tiny pointed balls of fury, suddenly accelerating with hypersonic madness at the StratoJet fleet.

John half thought it, half said it: 'ENGAGE!' and the fleet opened up with everything they had, targeting with mad fury as their forces on the ground did the same, firing ribbons of flechettes into the sky at the armada of strange, black-blue missiles coming at them.

It did not take long to see that once again, the Russians had focused their attack, and six StratoJets quickly resolved as the targets of the hail of fire. What was also quickly apparent was that these were no ordinary missiles.

They ducked and dodged in the air, providing infuriatingly slippery targets. At first the salvo was so huge that the jets' fire eroded them by weight of lead alone. But the final couple of hundred were proving harder and harder to kill.

They did not spare much thought for analysis, but somewhere in the pilots' minds the question begged to be asked: what the hell were they firing at? One among the pilots knew what these were, though. He had feared their use, and had warned of it, but had hoped Mikhail would not dare give away such insipid creatures to a madman like Svidrigaïlov.

John's response to the swarm came not as words, but as an engagement of machine order, a giving of a reflex to the six pilots being honed in on.

John Hunt: <wasps incoming! pull back! defend your engines! defend your engines!

The six-targeted StratoJets were instantly rearing back, their blue fusion jets tugging them backward with full force even as they each fired furiously into the cloud of terror coming at them. Their friends in the air and on the ground were fighting for them as well.

But the missiles came on, and for the six targeted pilots, a view began to emerge in the final milliseconds before impact. One of Minnie's own planes was among the targets, and she shared that view with the world, showing everyone what she and her five doomed colleagues were seeing as the wasp swarm closed.

They were each about the size of a rugby ball, the rear half all nozzles, propelling them erratically this way and that as they surged at their targets, while their front half was a point of razor sharp claws, closed now, but, as they made contact opening and gouging into the StratoJet's skin, using their thrusters and articulated talons to drive them toward a specific point of vulnerability.

They were still dying in droves even once on the jets' surface as the milliseconds passed, the surrounding forces targeting them with precise care and excising them like ticks from the skin of each jet, but they moved with an insane speed and agility, climbing in droves toward the engines. Trying to get inside their intakes, trying to deliver their munitions to the only place that would definitely cripple the armored jets.

Ayala screamed with fury as she watched through Boxer One's cameras. Watched as the first of the six jets lost its battle and one of the vile little insect-like creatures got into its portside jet and detonated. The fusion cell ripped apart and instantly the finely tuned StratoJet lost its balance forever, its other engine still firing wildly, trying to control it as it started to spin ever faster. In moments its pilot was killed by centrifugal pressure alone, crushed in his seat, inside his own skull.

The plane would eventually crash a mile away in a ball of blue and orange flame. It would not be alone. A second went. Then a third, and a fourth, before they finally wiped out the last of the swarm.

And when they had finally cleansed the sky of the hellish wasps, they watched in horror as another wave flew up.

But General Milton was already reacting, as was Ayala.

General Milton: 'john, get your forces the hell out of there, now! ayala, i want your ...'

Ayala at General Milton: '... don't worry, darling. my spezialists are already moving. we will find them. and we will end them.'

She sent it to him personally, her message laden with all the cold fury he knew she was capable of, and it sent a shudder down his spine.

And she was indeed already moving. No more waiting. She unclipped the leashes on her ground troops, filling their minds with estimated origins of the wasps, over a thousand by her and Minnie's estimate, and she waved these locations in front of her Spezialists like scented rags in front of their noses.

Find.

Kill.

They did not disappoint.

The Russians' ground forces were not fools. They were already moving, trying to avoid an expected counter. They were launching the wasp missiles from heavy tubes like thick mortars, each trooper carrying three of the heavy munitions each. They had just launched the second of them. They were busy relocating to fire the third and final salvo when Ayala's hounds descended upon them.

Rending and crushing, the Spezialists did not spare time for niceties. They were only a hundred and twenty, and there were at least two thousand Russian shock troops out there. Ignoring the odds the Spezialists attacked with abandon.

The first Russians to fall literally did not know what hit them. Once each Spezialist spotted an enemy combatant they sprinted at him, firing as they went, head shots, keeping up the fire until they had liquefied their target's head or removed it. If they got close enough before they felled their opponent then they went to hand-to-hand, choosing the fastest, most brutal attacks possible, hammering their foes to death.

Seconds of untold ruthlessness and then they were gone. Away into the night. Seeking the next victim.

Ayala watched with cold glee. She had trained many of these men and women herself. They were the very best. And they were very, very angry. The Russians' armor would not save them from her wrath. She would kill them all. For Ben.

- - -

In the air, John and his remaining thirteen StratoJets turned and fled without shame. The wasp cloud responded, switching from their dodge and dive into a headlong chase.

It was a close run. The wasps were markedly smaller and lighter, but the StratoJets were much more powerful. John's fighters accelerated hard, but they could not stay ahead of the wasps forever, and even if they could, they needed to bring the fight back to the Russians. Ayala's ground troops would not retain the upper hand for long if Squadron Charlie lost air superiority.

As the chase resolved Minnie and John were calculating their chances and seeking some solace among their diminishing tactical options. As they sorted through the remnants of their plans, they picked at potentials.

Seeing an unclaimed advantage, an unplayed card Minnie reached out to Quavoce, seeking permission.

Minnie at Quavoce: <¿quavoce, can you see this? it is not good, but it is not unsalvageable. the resolution of this chase need not be violent. at its heart this is target practice. banu would enjoy this, and she would be better even than me at it.>

Quavoce had been focused on his own quieter, but still very active engagement to the north. Now he took what was happening to John's squadron and could not help but feel for his colleagues.

He had been fired upon too many times by a swarm of wasp missiles, or some variant thereof. It was a horrible, claustrophobic sensation he would not wish on his worst enemy. These were not the wasps of his home. They were just as fast but not nearly as agile. But whatever imperfections in their artificial intellects were limiting their abilities they were still a terrible predator to have chasing you, and were proving more than a match for the StratoJet pilots.

Quavoce knew what strength would come with the ability to think faster than them, and he knew Banu would fair far better than any of the pilots currently fleeing the attack.

For him, the hesitation was a long one, but in reality it did not take longer than a second for him to acquiesce.

Quavoce: 'minnie. i assume banu is waiting to be asked. you have my permission. engage her. she can at least save one of the pilots in john's squadron. probably many more.'

Neal at Quavoce: 'thank you, quavoce.'

Minnie: <¿banu, my dear, would you like to play?>

She was pure enthusiasm. She knew this was real. She knew it was important. And through the veil of her innocence, she knew nothing of the real horror of what they were involved in, so she leapt upward from her virtual perch in a barn far away, up, through the roof, and out of her owl form, becoming instead one of the StratoJets she had practiced with so many times.

When they politely informed one of John's terrified pilots that he was to be saved, that he was, at least, not going to have to rely on his skill alone to survive the coming wasp swarm, he did not fight, he fell backward, choosing not to even watch, but to try and come to terms with his building terror in black silence while Banu took his reins from him.

- - -

She watched at first, feeling her plane's rapid progress through the thick air. It felt slightly more visceral than the simulator. Not much, Minnie was very good at making it feel real. But she knew that this was truly real, and her adrenalin surged accordingly.

And then she looked with some confusion at the coming bank of wasps. They were all travelling at over Mach 5 now, StratoJets and wasps alike, accelerating into the sky, directly away from the swarm, engines firing with all their might, limited only by the now soup-like air that dragged at their bodies.

She watched them. Saw their speed, saw their power, saw their size. She veered her bird infinitesimally, and saw a section of them twitch in response, fast, but not that fast. This was what they were fleeing? She giggled.

Her advantage was slight, but to Banu it was a yawning gap, a chasm, and with a confidence born of skill, lack of fear, and ignorance of the dormant pilot's life she was gambling with, she peeled away from the squadron. Taking her complement of the swarm with her.

As she arched in her turn, they closed on her, thirsting for her flesh, thinking they were going to get to taste her black skin. They came on, and they came on, so close they could smell her heady scent, the smell of their prey. But she was not fleeing them. She was only teasing them, staying just out of reach. The point where they would connect was as clear as a beacon to her. But it would not be soon enough. And as the seconds passed, ripping at the sky, she was completing a massive circle, closing the loop, and as she did so she was coming at the greater horde from beneath, her portion of wasps closing behind her as she used her powerful wings to thread the greater cloud of missiles still chasing the rest of her brethren.

As she closed she fired on them with glee, their enduring focus on their own targets blinding them to the threat coming at them from below. Their very persistence exposing them to her talons as she sliced them apart, and as she blasted through them, the debris of their rended carcasses began falling from the cloud in droves.

John and Minnie watched her progress. They did not attempt to follow her. They could barely compute the way she was navigating through the swarm, still maintaining her speed to stay ahead of her own pursuers, finding a path that changed every millisecond, threading a line where there was only danger. It was the very impossibility of it that was saving her even from her own pursuers.

And in a flash she was bursting out the other side, spinning and arching as she laughed with joy, her charges trying to follow her, but bursting and dying as they struggled to navigate through their manifold siblings, a wave of destruction flowing in her wake.

- - -

Somewhere, far away, a mind watched the wasps. He saw the lone jet killing them and wondered at the humans' technological progress. He saw the speed of the jet's reactions. Far faster than his missiles' improvised AIs. Faster even than him perhaps. He wondered at humanity's progress, and then took some solace in the fact that only one of the StratoJets was capable of the feat.

He sent a new directive to his wasp swarm and a moment later they turned as one to chase Banu's jet, spreading out as they went, starting to form a net to entrap the lone warrior who had just run a ring around and then right through them.

On the ground, Mikhail could feel his shock troops, numerous at first, but now being systematically hunted and killed by a vengeful pack of wolves. He could have them turn and fight. He could try to mass them and defend against the ferocious Spezialists killing them in droves, but all it would do was slow the slaughter, and these lambs had served their purpose. So he sufficed with ordering them to fire their last volley of wasps and then he left them to die in the dark, beneath the burning skies of the Szatmar-Bereg.

John watched the third swarm launch and knew that Banu's maneuverability had just become moot. The poor pilot she had taken control for was doomed, there could be no doubt of that. At his command Minnie gently pried Banu from the plane's controls, but he did not awaken its pilot. Instead, John instructed the StratoJet to accelerate with all it had, away from swarm. That man's only hope lay with his colleagues now. Maybe they could save him before the wasps caught him, but John would not force a man to witness his impending death.

As Banu's view changed to another of John's squadron, the young girl pondered the fate of the jet she could now see being chased into the sky. But she did not have much time to think about it. John and Minnie were already banking hard and going after the redoubled swarm, calling to her to join them, and she did, wanting to get back into the fun as soon as possible.

Mikhail watched the four fighters change course as the rest of the squadron moved to return to the fight. He could not know the four were John's, Banu's, and Minnie's two, but he could see the sharpness with which they turned on his swarm. With a sigh, he realized that the real pilot he sought was almost definitely far away, subsuming jets to her command at will. It would be the strategically wise thing to do, and his opponents had proven nothing if not strategically wise. To a point, he thought, with a smile. To a point.

He knew he could keep retargeting the wasps, but in the end they had countered him, and all he could hope for was to take down a few more StratoJets before his most advanced units were finally destroyed.

A furious Russian premier was screaming into a phone in Moscow, cursing the man he knew as Field Commandant Beria and promising lifelong suffering and ignominy for the fatal losses he was hearing about from his ground commanders. The furious Russian premier was demanding that Mikhail send in the Ubitsya fleet. The furious Russian premier was demanding Mikhail reply to his orders.

Well, thought Mikhail with cold calm, the furious Russian premier can go fuck himself. The Russian Army had done everything Mikhail had needed them to. Armed with the Mobiliei technology he had reluctantly given them, they had drawn the StratoJet fleet into a dirty, ugly fight, a fight they would win, but a fight that was thousands of miles from where they were most needed.

And now the Russian Army was dying, along with their Mobiliei armor and any advantage it might give them.

It was perfect.

Far away to the south, the massive and unscathed Ubitsya fleet finally came to life. Mikhail's pilots focused their engines and lifted as one, rising from amongst the dense mangroves of the broad Indus River Delta, a great horde of black predators rising into the purple predawn sky on blue-white spires of light.

As they broached the canopy, they accelerated, rising as they went, quickly leaving the coast of the now Russian controlled Pakistan behind and surging out over the Arabian Sea. They were not alone. As they rose, they merged smoothly with another fleet of near equal size and capability flying in from the north, from the Hindu Kush, having started their journey from an equally clandestine staging post in Western China much earlier.

The combined flotilla moved off now with purpose. Not far out from the coast of Pakistan, they crossed an invisible line in the sky after which Mikhail knew they were officially closer to Rolas than the TASC StratoJets killing his erstwhile army in Central Europe. As of this moment, he knew there was nothing Neal could do, even if he did receive advanced warning of the real attack. Stealth was no longer a factor. He need not take the longer route around the tip of Africa. He would get to his real target before anything could be done to stop him.

Mikhail smiled as he commanded his two hundred strong Ubitsya armada to accelerate up to full speed. Inside his own unique craft he focused once more and prepared for his attack on SpacePort One. It was time to strike at the heart of Earth's resistance.

It was time to bring down the elevator.

Chapter 43: Inbound

Neal was inconsolable, his fury a living thing within him. Recalling the StratoJets would take too long, and they could not come back yet anyway. They could not just leave Ayala and her troops without air support.

He refused to dignify the calls he was receiving from his NATO colleagues, and they were almost grateful. As news had started to come of the armada hurtling across central Africa their monumental error had become painfully clear. Without exception, the NATO countries of Western Europe were now engaging the full weight of their military into Hungary to support Ayala. They would be in place to engage the Russian Army and Air Force in less than an hour. A multinational fleet of F35s, Typhoons, Rafales, Griffens, and a host of other fighters already inbound, with attack helicopters and ground forces following as fast as they could.

The full weight of NATO was mobilized. The Russian force was doomed, there could be absolutely no doubt about that. With the impending attack on Rolas, Russia had given the Europeans license to all but wipe them out. But even as the Germans, British, and French came in with murder on their minds, even as Ayala's Spezialists continued to rip a bloody gash across the Hungarian and Ukrainian countryside, it was clear that their real enemy had outmaneuvered them.

Neal stood in his office and screamed at the phone, "Jim, this is not a request, this is a goddamned demand," he shouted at the White House chief of staff. "If we survive the coming attack, and I am far from sure we are going to, then at the very least we are going to suffer massive, and I mean *massive* casualties. Many of them US sailors and soldiers. We will need reinforcement and support at this position, and we will need it immediately!"

"Neal, I am on your side …" Jim began in reply, but Neal cut him off.

"No, Jim, you are fucking-well-not. Otherwise I would still have the *Reagan* here, and we wouldn't be looking at the impending fucking destruction of Rolas!"

Jim could not contest it. And he did not run from Neal's wrath. "You are right, Neal, of course you are. That much is becoming all too clear. Please, believe me when I say I *will* talk to the president. And I know you don't believe this, but he *does* want to help. You can count on the US to do whatever we can, but you know how serious things are here."

Neal's reply was icy, "Jim, I know you don't believe *this*, but things are going to get a damn site more *serious* in eight years time if we don't get our fucking act together. So you'll forgive me if I tell you that I don't give a damn how things are in the US. How things are in the US is irrelevant. Do you hear me, Jim? *Irrelevant!*"

Jim replied quietly, "Yes, Neal. So you keep reminding me."

"And yet still you do not seem to understand." said Neal

Jim's voice became less pliant, still not combative, but with as much force as he was want to use, "I *do* understand, Neal. You are not the only person on Earth who is fighting to save it. You forget how much money still flows out of America's banks into your coffers, Neal. Even as our wells are frankly running dry. You are not alone, but you will be if you do not recognize what allies you still have in the world, and what we are all trying to do for the greater cause."

Jim went silent as he tried to wrestle his exasperation under control. His emotion over what was clearly about to happen at Rolas, and the verbal abuse he was once more taking at the hands of Neal, was like a rising tide bubbling up around his neck, threatening to overwhelm his famous calm. But his words had managed to penetrate the cracks in Neal's rage to the more sensible man beneath. Sensible, but still obsessed.

Neal did not respond, but Jim did hear an audible sigh through the line. It was not much, but the change in tone was significant. Jim was not unused to it. He understood Neal more than the other man realized, and was more of an advocate than Neal understood. Behind all the great and not-so-great men Jim had served in his life was a profound but understated dedication. A dedication and a quiet capability. Many mistook his calm for impotent ambition. They were wrong, but Jim did not usually trouble himself with correcting them.

He did now.

"Neal … I love my country … I love it enough to see that it is doomed." Neal did not expect such openness, or such insight from Jim, and Jim was not done, "I stay here not to serve America, and certainly not to serve the president. I stay here … partly out of patriotism, partly out of habit … but also because I thought you needed me here more than you needed me there."

Neal was surprised once more. Jim went on, not uncomfortable with the level of candor, but still keen to get through it. This was not diplomacy, this was honesty, and it carried with it a wholly different set of risks.

"I will talk to the president. I will get him to send as many reinforcements to Rolas as is feasible. In the meantime, I want you to promise me you will not call him directly. The fact is I can do more for you if you stay away. At this point your reputation does our cause more damage than good, at least here in the US."

Neal took a deep breath and nodded, forgetting the two-dimensional nature of the phone call for a moment, then replied aloud, "I suppose that makes sense, Jim."

He did not thank the man, and Jim did not ask for gratitude.

"I will call when I know more," Jim said with some finality.

"Good."

"Good-bye, Neal. And good luck."

Neal closed the connection, a long, deep breath spreading through his deflated form like a death rattle. But only a moment was allowed to pass before Minnie's voice entered his mind like a subconscious twitch, pulling him back to the task at hand.

Minnie: <neal, i am working with barrett, ayala, and jack to break off stratojets from the engagement in ukraine. already i have four inbound. but the remaining fifteen will not be able to come until the nato forces engage.>

Neal: 'thank you, minnie. i suppose that makes sense.'

It was as much as they could do, Neal knew that, but thanking Minnie for it still felt like thanking the executioner for saying they would make it quick. Barrett interjected.

Barrett: '¿minnie, what is your comfort level with our force estimates on the incoming force?'

Neal closed his eyes and saw what Barrett was looking at from his command center elsewhere in the concrete mountain that was Rolas. He looked at the forces now converging on Rolas. His: a tiny force of four StratoJets coming from Hungary, moving fast, but hopelessly distant. The enemy's: a cloud of threat coming at them from the east.

How had they managed to build so many of the hypersonic fighters?

Neal set aside the question with physical effort. It was, after all, irrelevant. Instead, he studied the Russian jets, for he did not know that nearly half of them were actually Chinese, and such considerations were, in the end, irrelevant anyway. He looked at them from one of his many satellite Pods now tracking the fleet.

They had heard news of the fleet as a series of complaints echoing throughout the world's capitals. The flotilla had announced itself to the world by thundering into Somalian airspace, then across south Sudan toward Cameroon. The banana republics had fired in anger at this violation of their airspace, and sent indignant calls defending their sovereignty to anyone they thought might be responsible for the huge fleet. They had fired anything and everything they had at the jets, impotently screaming as their primitive arsenal had been rebuffed like so many arrows against the broad flanks of a dreadnaught.

As news had reached Neal and his commanders it had not taken them long to guess who the force really belonged to. They had pondered the lack of tech-ten air units as they engaged the Russians in Hungary. Now they pondered no more.

Minnie: <neal, if you have time, madeline is trying to reach you.>

Neal shook his head. Things had become strange indeed when Madeline had to ask permission to speak to him. But his mind was protected behind a bank of icewalls, filters and AIs that now managed his day. He opened the virtual doors to his sanctum and spoke with his first companion on the long road he found himself walking.

Neal: 'madeline, things are getting interesting here. ¿have you been updated by minnie?'

Madeline: 'of course, neal.'

A hint of emotion bled through their link to his right brain, anger and indignation at the implication that she should need informing of such monumental events as the impending attack on Rolas.

Neal: 'sorry, madeline, i forget myself, sometimes. ¿what is it you need?'

Madeline: 'it's not what i need, but what *you* need, neal. when you made the decision to send the fleet out yesterday, i retasked the resonance chambers here. i thought i would be replenishing the fleet based on potential losses from the engagement in hungary. anyway, i have three stratojets inbound on your position now, eta sixty minutes, and three more leaving japan as we speak, though i imagine those will be too late to make too much difference.'

Three StratoJets. It wasn't much, but it was three more than he had. Three against two hundred.

Neal: 'thank you, madeline, that is some very welcome good news. and sorry for the delay you had getting to me. i am updating my executive ai's to give you command override, just like ayala, barrett, and the others. you should have had it from the start.'

Far away, Madeline, banished any remaining indignation she might have felt from her mind and focused on what Neal and the rest of her friends at Rolas must be feeling right now.

Madeline: 'forget about that, neal. that is less than nothing. neal, my friend, it's been so long since we brought down the satellites that i had almost forgotten what it feels like to be so vulnerable. you will be ok. we survived the satellites, we survived lana, and you will survive this. we are all with you.'

Neal: 'thank you, madeline. but unfortunately i need to do more than just survive it this time. the spaceport. the elevator. if i could stand in front of it and die to save them i would. my survival means nothing compared to the time and resources we have sunk into this damn island.'

Madeline did not doubt his words. His dedication to the task ahead was without question. To the point of fanaticism even, but where was there a more deserving cause for zealousness?

Madeline: 'i know you would, neal, we all do. but you don't have to, and you won't, neal. you have to focus, my friend. i have been looking at these numbers. they aren't good, but they aren't without hope either. leave hungary to jack and ayala, and get minnie, quavoce, and john's minds back to rolas. banu's too, if only so she can defend herself. you have three stratojets coming, give them one each and see if they can't even the odds a bit.'

Neal nodded, sending his approval back to her as an emotive thank you, while he felt her confidence and support as a warmth in his mind.

Neal: 'thanks, madeline. good advice. all right, i must go. thank you again.'

Madeline: 'of course. we are all with you, neal. you are going to be ok.'

He agreed and thanked her again.

Once the connection was broken he sat back.

'ok.'

He did not want to be ok. He was tired of striving for ok. He wanted to be in control. He wanted to be done with this fucking infighting so he could get on with the real work. He was trying to drag humanity up a technological mountain and all it could do was scream and bicker and kick at his heals all the way like a gaggle of spoiled children.

And now, two economic and military giants among those children had, in their ignorance, unwittingly conspired with the enemy, and may have doomed them all.

It was too much. It was treason. It was treason of the highest order. Even as Neal checked in with Minnie once more on their preparations he saw that he could no longer sit by and wait for the rest of the world to get Russia and China in line. They had committed the foulest of crimes against humanity. They needed to be punished.

Neal: 'minnie, patch me through to recon team two in russia. i have a new mission packet for them.'

- - -

Hektor and his team trundled along through the Russian countryside. Hundreds of miles away, the country's military was being punished with deadly force for pushing the world too far. But here, deep in the heart of the mighty nation, all was quiet, and recon team two passed unnoticed through yet another town as they made their way toward the sprawling capital.

They had been using their now passive subspace tweeter to monitor subspace traffic, and had picked up signs of very real tech-ten capability along the route from the Ukrainian border to Moscow.

Cara drove, her incongruously angelic face combining with her better than average grasp of Russian to provide good cover for the team should they be stopped. They had switched the truck's plates not far out from the lumber farm they had stolen it from, just in case the Russian police were unusually efficient. Now they moved into the city at a rumbling, agrarian speed that belied the power of their weaponry and training. They moved toward Red Square, monitoring and tracking subspace traffic as they went. They were stalking the subspace network, hunting its source. Closing in on the location of the Russian Agent, maybe. They could not know.

But as they broached the suburbs, Bohdan was receiving new information, and new orders. They had none of the vagueness of their current standing orders. They were very precise.

"Sir," Bohdan called to the team leader over the noise of the well-used diesel engine, "you need to review the subspace data packet that just came in, immediately."

Hektor opened the packet with his mind, tensing as he read the simple order. He could not reply directly. He could not verify. He could not send anything through subspace for risk of alerting the Russians to their presence. But it didn't really matter anyway. The order did not require any further clarification.

Dr. Neal Danielson, CO Terrestrial Allied Space Command: 'recon team two. new primary mission parameter: locate russian premier yuri svidrigaïlov. confirm identity and terminate.'

Chapter 44: The Hot War

The time for subtlety was passed. They were coming in fast, and even the darkest of nights could not have hidden the shout of the sonic booms reverberating in their wake. They knew they would get to Rolas before it would have any of its StratoJets home to roost. Now there was just the small matter of the two thousand men and women of the allied naval fleet between them and their mark.

Far ahead of them, a band of destroyers, cruisers, submarines, and frigates were forming into a line, arraying their manifold ordnance at the eastern horizon and preparing for battle.

"Captain Bhade," said Admiral Cochrane, from the fly bridge of the *Dauntless*, "please have your teams pick and assign. I want target batches dispatched to the fleet as soon as they are ready. Fire At Range."

"Yes, sir," replied the captain, "we are assigning now, Admiral. Fire control, you have clearance. Attach Fire At Range to all packets." The order echoed throughout the bridge, and onward by radio to the fleet still taking their final positions in the firewall.

"Comms," went on Admiral Cochrane, "orders for Admiral Takano: please tell the admiral his submarines are cleared to engage at outside range. I want them to deploy their entire surface-to-air salvos in the first wave and then dive. There is no need for them to be exposed to this."

No one commented on what that meant for the surface fleet. In most modern conflicts the cruisers, frigates, and destroyers that made up Admiral Cochrane's taskforce represented the safest possible place to be during an engagement. Usually they were far from the hot exchange of bullets, and any enemy craft foolish enough to approach them would be torn to shreds by the array of weaponry the big ships bristled with.

But this was no ordinary war, and no ordinary enemy, and though they had actively upgraded the systems aboard the fleet, they had never anticipated such a force as this.

The Japanese submarines did as they were ordered with neither complaint nor gratitude. As the fleet launched its first massive salvo of missiles at the coming Ubitsyas, the subs were more active than most, firing off every anti-air missile they had and then sealing and emergency-diving.

For his part, Admiral Takano looked on stoically from the bridge of the lone Japanese destroyer in the fleet, aware of his imminent fate. He did not flinch. He sufficed himself with mentally urging on the nearly thousand missiles the fleet had just launched at the coming flotilla and tried to maintain a sense of calm for the men and women sharing his bridge.

The first barrage was a throng of big, hulking rockets; their longest-range ordnance. The biggest was the Aegis, designed to leave the atmosphere if it had to, a variant of it among those that had killed one of the Mobiliei satellites months beforehand. But now they pursued smaller, faster, but less well-armed prey. Maybe some would find what they sought.

Now, with the tables turned from the night before, the allied navy mimicked the Russians tactics from the bloody fight in Hungary. As they closed with the coming enemy, the first wave of missiles performed the same random exercise in murder as the Russian wasps had, singling out unfortunates from among the Russian swarm and converging on them.

Above Cameroon, the skies became dark as the two great clouds came together, the bank of oncoming jets and the wave of missiles blocking the sun. They approached each other at stupendous speed, and the sparse population below watched in awe and horror as a hail of return fire came from the coming Ubitsyas like blurred lines of energy, warping the air between the two supernatural forces in the brief moments before collision.

The detonations began as notes in the stanza, missiles detonating as they were killed by the Ubitsyas' guns, then it grew and grew as the Ubitsyas fought to thin out the massive destructive force coming at them.

Everyone watched as the two sides met, and the explosive noise rose to a crescendo of stellar proportions.

Neal, Barrett, Ayala, and Madeline watched with keen anticipation. The crews of the allied fleet watched with a hope bordering on delusion, almost against their will, not wanting to see how much of the coming death-dealers would make it through their first and largest salvo. And their captains and admirals watched with focused stoicism, their chests out, their eyes hard. Knowing the danger their crews faced but refusing to give in to despair.

And Mikhail watched, not from the front line, but from his own plane, if you could call it that. Well behind the main fleet, commanding it, close enough to maintain subspace communications, but far enough back that he could stay safely outside the maelstrom.

The noise was heard beyond horizons. A thunderous rumble that shook the earth, settling sand dunes, rustling trees, sending wildlife scattering, and raining down a molten hail of debris across a vast plain.

Two hundred Ubitsyas entered the fray, and out of the billowing vortex of flame and shrapnel a hundred sixty-two emerged.

Admiral Cochrane's heart sank, as did every commander's across the fleet, but still they tried not to let it show.

"Comms, to all units," said Admiral Cochrane with stern command, "fire at will, engage and destroy."

"Comms, to General Milton," he went on a moment later, "General, you are cleared to bring up the air wing on Captain Bhade's mark. We will continue to fire until you enter the kill zone."

The orders were relayed and acknowledged.

Finally, Admiral Cochrane picked up a handset at his console and opened a channel to the strange artificial intelligence that he had been told responded to the name Minnie.

"Minnie, this is Admiral Cochrane," he said, unaware that she knew with machine precision exactly where and who the call was coming from, "I have reviewed your request to take over fire control on our linked anti-air gun network. Given the statistics you provided, and the accompanying testimonies of General Milton and others, I have only one question for you before I agree: do you think it will make a difference?"

Minnie was quite capable of lying; that machines would for some reason lack the capacity for falsehood was a fallacy, a poorly conceived fiction. She was as capable of lying as she was of creating any text or speech, and she was capable of doing that in nine languages and counting. But she did not lie now. Out of her growing understanding of the concept of respect, she gave the man the most honest answer she could.

"Do I think I can manage the systems better than your human teams aboard the fleet? I am sure of it, Admiral. Do I think I can save all of the ships that now stand between Rolas and the coming armada? I am afraid I cannot promise that. Maybe I can save some, but even that I cannot guarantee."

The admiral flinched as even his inclination toward brutal honesty was tested, but then she finished by saying, "But I can say with certainty that, based on the damage done by the first missile salvo, I will be able to make them pay very dearly for coming here. Very dearly indeed."

He smiled, the adrenal rush of cold vengeance filling his veins.

"Comms to all units," he said in a loud voice, "I want all fleet arms to give automated anti-air unit control to Rolas, per order set five-twenty-nine. They will coordinate autocannon protocols from there. Please acknowledge."

Captain Bhade locked eyes with the admiral looking for some measure of solace, but found only fortitude. They nodded at each other. So be it.

- - -

The second missile salvo was sent and collided with the same brutal but inadequate lethality as the first. Then it all came to a head with shocking speed. The storm would not be stopped. The cyclone was coming for them. They had loosed their arrows, and now the titans came in with savage haste.

The big ships launched a torrent of lead into the air in front of them along with every remaining missile they had. Minnie had forgone piloting one of the three inbound StratoJets for a chance to reap bloody murder with the combined might of the fleet's autocannons. She used them to form an interlaced web of death for the Ubitsyas, trying to eliminate any avenue for them to pass through.

But the Ubitsyas were far from passive participants, and their commander far from simple, and as the true fighting began, Mikhail fanned them out, forcing Minnie and the fleet to dilute their fire while he could still focus his.

An American destroyer was the first to go, its entire forward superstructure folding in on itself as a thousand hypersonic copper bullets slagged a huge gash in its hull. Minnie felt the loss of fire as its systems went quiet, explosions ripping along its length as the once powerful ship tore itself apart. Another ship was not far behind, this one a missile frigate, Mikhail wisely focusing on the smallest ships first, quickly bringing down the volume of allied fire as they sank.

Mikhail's forces were falling as well, though. Minnie especially was shredding them, weaving her web to entrap and destroy two or three at a time. She was actually frustrated by the rocketing arrival of General Milton's bank of fighters on the scene, even though they forced the Ubitsyas to shift their fire from the ships as they came in hard. Mikhail's Ubitsyas were close now and this would have been where she could have done the most damage, but she had to silence her guns as General Milton's planes came in.

It was not a pretty sight, and all who witnessed it vowed a private curse upon the Russian and Chinese fighters as they butchered the slower, softer European and American jet fighters. They got some blows in, their once impressive AMRAAM missiles and forward guns ripping open fourteen more of the Ubitsyas. But fifty-five of them died in return, their bloodied carcasses falling, burning from the sky, some whole, some in pieces, all ablaze.

No one below gave voice to it. To the sacrifice they had just witnessed. Without a verbal order, the ships just began to open fire again, Minnie leading the charge. But now the Ubitsyas had closed the distance to the big ships and they came on in a series of strafing runs that wreaked havoc on the fleet, so slow, so big, so vulnerable as they shuddered from the pounding of their hulls being hit and the echo of their massive guns lighting up the atmosphere. Big, rolling waves washed outward from their waterlines as they shook, like great battle drums sounding out the charge.

The men and women of the fleet fought with fervent diligence, and for a moment it almost felt like they might carry the day. But where the Ubitsyas fell in a steady flow, the fleet's losses came as great blows. The USS Port Royal, the biggest ship in the fleet, suddenly erupted, her deck awash with flame. One of her big forward guns had been targeted by four Russian fighters and had come dislodged as it fired, ripping a great wave of molten steel along her decks. When the fire breached the armory beneath, the explosion sent the mighty three-gun turret flying backward, through the bridge, crushing three hundred men in an instant and killing the command and control systems of the big ship.

Still the fleet seemed determined, but only a moment later Admiral Tokano's flagship seemed to implode, her entire deck folding in on itself. Minnie had seen it coming only a moment before. She had been targeting an Ubitsya inbound on the destroyer, but when she winged it, it did not try to flee, but instead accelerated.

It was a kamikaze maneuver, and it had its desired effect. The fleet began to lose its cool. They began to fray, and Minnie sensed their fire beginning to falter.

Mikhail saw it to, they were failing. He smiled. It had not been a kamikaze attack at all. Mikhail had seen the foolhardy way the pilot had flown right into Minnie's firewall and had decided the plane was now best used as a missile, rather than as fodder for Minnie's sharp knives. So he had commandeered the plane remotely, ratcheted up its thrusters and flown it right into the bridge of the destroyer even as it continued to fire, softening the ship's armor before impact.

The Russian pilot had screamed as he was sacrificed.

But Mikhail had smiled. These were just pawns after all. Pawns in his great gambit. And he was so close to checkmate.

- - -

Barrett: 'the fleet is all but destroyed. and there are still more than forty russian fighters surviving. at this stage i think the stratojets would be best used as part of a strategic retreat, rather than a counterattack.'

Neal: 'no! i will not abandon rolas.'

Barrett: 'i am not sure what choice we have, neal. they have broken the line, we have three stratojets almost at the base but the next reinforcements will not be here for forty more minutes.'

Neal: 'i know that, barrett, and we must do what we can to fend them off till the main fleet arrives. only a few more minutes, that's all we need.'

Barrett: 'neal, while we may be able to delay them slightly, there is no way we can maintain a perimeter around the elevator. no matter what we do they will be able to get close enough to fire on it, neal ...'

Neal did not want to hear it. But Barrett said it anyway.

Barrett: '... neal, the cable is coming down. there is simply nothing we can do to stop that now.'

Neal screamed. He screamed as hard as he could, the walls of his office barely containing the sound as it reverberated around him. He did not respond to Barrett, and in the absence of a counter order from Neal, Barrett's words became action.

Minnie: <i am redirecting the three incoming stratojets. two are going to join the returning fleet. one is coming in to land on the west side of rolas base. if you move now, neal, i estimate you can make it to the southwest access tunnel in ninety seconds.>

Minnie did not mention Barrett. He was on the base's east side, nearly a quarter of a mile from the only landing platform the StratoJet could safely come in to and get away from in time. Barrett did not discuss the implications and in the mounting panic Neal failed to grasp the full cost of their defeat.

For Barrett could see the coming Russian planes. He could see the smoldering hulks of the fleet behind them. They had only two minutes. Neal may be able to get to safety from his position on the far side of the base but Barrett knew he was not going anywhere. He would have to take his chances in the bunker along with the rest of the base personnel.

Minnie: <you have to move now, neal.>

Barrett: 'neal! go ... now!'

Neal reacted as if possessed, running, turning this way and that as Minnie directed him in an almost drunken stumble.

Already it was beginning. Neal could hear the base's fixed defenses opening up, blending with the reports coming into his mind from the many sensors that surveyed the surrounding area. The Russians came in hard, rushing the remaining base defenses with almost suicidal glee. But it was not suicide, it was attrition, and the odds were well and truly with them now. The base guns were not designed for this scale of attack and they barely they took out five or six more of the Ubitsyas before they too crumpled and died like the naval hulks still smoldering and sinking to the East.

Neal was barely aboard the lone StratoJet before it was banking and accelerating away. He was happy to see Quavoce and Banu were already on board, but the sight brought a dawning realization of the many that were not. He collapsed into a heap on the floor of the jet, helped by Quavoce as the G-forces immediately began tugging at the three passengers.

Mikhail considered pursuing the plane he saw taking off, but decided it was best to focus on his main target. It was exposed now. He had cut away the skin and muscle, he had sawed into the very bone, and now he could see the marrow within. He looked at it and with relish he ordered the last of his Ubitsyas to cut it down.

- - -

Thousands of miles above, at Terminus One, the crew of the big station rushed against time to try and save it. Warned of the impending attack, they had started reeling themselves in. They were sacrificing the gains of a weight positive orbit where they had used their weight to pull the mighty cable tight. Now they were furiously pulling themselves inwards, down, closer to earth, and hopefully into an orbit they could sustain once the cable was cut. It would be the widest orbit any manned craft had ever had, but it was their only hope.

As news of the first cable fraying and splitting came to them, they braced. It would be over an hour before the rippling shock wave reached them, but they were not going to wait until then to be ripped apart by it. Crews struggled to disconnect the cable they knew was now loose, to set it free before its weight came flying out from Earth.

It was a horrific sight as it started to surge outward. It was like a climber seeing ropes falling past them, ropes they were holding on to, ropes that were the only thing between them and an endless black abyss below.

It was a sight that would drag on for days as the terrific length of the cable flew outward into space, falling back and behind them as it went, but they did not have time to contemplate it, and hoped not to be around to see it. They were already receiving the signal about the second cable coming loose. Only two more left now, and their fate was resolving.

The voice came out over the PA and via spinal-link.

Captain Cashman: 'this is the captain. i am afraid the station is not going to make it. but we have a plan. i am hereby ordering all personnel to move into crew module five. i repeat, all personnel are ordered to immediately drop everything you are doing and move to crew module five. we are going to jettison the main station. we have less than three minutes until i have to blow the hatches so let's not dawdle. we *will* jettison in three minutes. not a moment longer. i repeat, *not a moment longer.*'

He knew it would mean giving up any hope of putting the station in steady orbit and saving the massive structure, but they would be able to use the ejection of its mass to push them down and away, and if they timed it right, they might save the bulk of the eighty or so crew that had found themselves aboard when disaster struck.

One person, though, did not respond. The captain reached out with his mind.

Captain Cashman: 'dr. hauptman, i must ask you to stop what you are doing. we are evacuating your section. please, doctor, you have to move. you have to move *now*.'

But she was not listening. She was focused on a task that was all consuming, and she had all but cut herself off from the outside world. Even if she could have heard she would not have stopped, though.

For she was giving birth. Not to a person, even that would have been easier to distract yourself from than the task she was embarked upon. For the second time in her life, she was giving birth to a starship. Far below, on a desolate island in a cold, dark sea, she was tapped into a new creation. Like New Moon One, it was the first of its kind to be made by humanity. But unlike New Moon One, this was a profoundly militant craft.

Some part of her, a muted, two-dimensional echo of her full self comprehended on some level that she was in danger. That little part of her wished she was down there, on the globe they were so tenuously attached to, at the actual site of the craft's birth. But her work had taken her here, to the massive labs they had built for her in space, to the experiments she could only do up here, free from gravity, free from atmosphere, painting on the blank canvas of the vacuum.

But as that small part of her mind mourned what it vaguely understood as a coming departure, a break from home, her real mind was far away, transmuted by the massive subspace hammer that formed one of the hubs of the station and from there out across subspace, and into the heart of a beast.

She was fueling it, driving it, compressing stupendous energies into four minor hearts around its soul, and then, once they were beating, focusing inward, to the core, to the massive weaponized reactor that was the beast's heart. The four ancillary hearts had needed to beat before she shocked this one into life, they were the only thing that could control the beast. They were the lion tamers. Or more apt they were like rodeo clowns that would try to poke and prod the preposterous power at the Skalm's heart into conformity.

She could feel it coming alive in front of her machine eyes, around her, inside her. Breathing, beating with dizzying power. A massive heart, forty feet wide.

On a desolate peninsula, deep in middle of the lonely outpost that was Deception Island, technicians and engineers took shelter, hiding behind shields and bunkers as the beast began to roar. Blue flames erupting from the myriad nozzles around its five hearts. It wobbled, rising from the cradles and gantries that had carried it from its golden womb a quarter of a mile away. It rose under its own power for the first time, and seemed to hang there, swaying as its engines thrummed, balanced on a sea of improbable power, an antagonistic juggling of a thousand spurts of fusion madness every second, melting the very cranes that had held it, buffeting the ground underneath its four great wings and its spherical, spiny core.

Birgit saw it now as a perfect creation: balanced, tuned, a star of potential, waiting only for someone to command it. And far away, across another ocean, just such a mind was being brought in to take the reins of the newly birthed dragon from its mother's arms. To manage it and try to fly the magnificent beast. A small, innocent mind. Maybe the only person humanity yet had who could really pilot the ship.

A girl. A girl who was even now fleeing herself, lying unconscious in the back of a hurtling StratoJet in the arms of her adopted father, mechanical pulses in her mind stimulating her cortices, wakening her brain to the task at hand.

At the request of Birgit, and with the permission of Quavoce, she took the reins, and the big beast began bucking and braying as its saddle was put on, a stallion to be mastered.

But Banu only giggled, giddy with joy, laughing at the feeling of the blue fusion blood now pumping through her veins. Her feet firmly in the stirrups she dug in her heals, beat her wings, puffed out her chest, and roared with all her machine might, and the hundred-meter-wide Skalm erupted into the sky, thumping the ground below with titan feet and leaping straight up, a hundred supermen, a thousand Hektors, a million screams. It was epic. It was wonder, awe, and terror … it was ecstasy, love, and hate. It was power and it was possession.

Chapter 45: Outbound

A tear ran down Birgit's cheek as she witnessed it. A tear of joy at the final creation of this first interstellar battleship; she was as proud of it as she had ever been of anything in her life. But it was also partly a tear of sadness at the dawning realization of what the birth had cost her.

In their haste to complete the first Skalm she had given all she had. Exhausted, frail far beyond her years, she opened her eyes to the price she had been forced to pay. Captain Robert Cashman stood over her. Easing her return to reality.

"Dr. Hauptman, are you OK?"

She shook her head, more to clear it than to disagree. Then, locking eyes with the man, she nodded meekly. She was confused.

"Where are we?" she eventually managed to say, as control of her vocal chords came back to her. She had been under for close to ten hours. Far longer than anyone should be, and her senses and limbs seemed alien to her, like a suit, like seeing the world through an apartment building intercom, the image blurry, the sound garbled.

"We are on Terminus, Doctor. You are safe."

She looked at him, "Safe? What happened? I remember … a call … a call to evacuate?"

He looked troubled for a moment, and then mastered his emotions and smiled, clearly mourning something but not wanting to let it show on his face, like a parent hiding a truth from a sick child. But she was far too smart to not figure it out on her own, as the distant memory came back to her.

She struggled out of the cradle that had held her immobile body, pulling at the restraints with a growing franticness. The captain was distraught at her obvious terror, trying to calm her. A garbled scream broke from her lips as she fought to get free.

"Doctor, please," he pleaded. "Doctor, stop!"

But she was already clambering free, throwing herself across the white, cylindrical room to a viewport.

Nothing. Only blackness.

She pushed back, flipping in the air as she did so, her months in space giving her a grace that only came with truly living with weightlessness. She found another port. The sun, off to the left, but rolling away even as she watched it. She oriented herself with the skill of a physicist and pushed off one last time, to one last port, above her to her left.

She saw it. The Earth. Round, blue-white-green, an image of fractal detail. Her home. Drifting away.

Like a castaway on a raft watching an island move off, so close, but so far, she watched. And now she made out the tiny dot of the crew module, like a ship on that same ocean, also moving away, out of reach. A vanishing hope.

"You ejected them," she said, understanding coming to her at last.

The captain came to her side, "Yes, I had to."

"Of course you did. You used our mass to push the module into orbit. They will be safe?" He nodded, and she struggled with a combination of happiness that her colleagues and friends would be saved, and a profound longing to be with them.

The bulk of the former Terminus station continued on its slow revolution as it span away, and the view shifted inexorably to the blackness of the beyond once more.

Suddenly her expression changed as a new and even more tragic realization came to her. Ferociously, she wheeled on him.

"But, Captain! No! Why are you here!" she screamed, looking into his eyes. "No, please! Tell me you didn't!"

She stared at him, her eyes pleading, filling with tears as she saw that he had done what she suddenly feared. He did not explain himself. He merely looked at her with the patience of a father. A man who had sworn to protect the people in his charge. A man who, when faced with having to send one of them off into the void, had done the only thing he could. He had joined her.

"Why!" she screamed at him, sobbing, grabbing him by the shoulders and shaking him. "Why didn't you go with them? You could have left me here! You could have lived!"

He did not fight her. He held her stare as she shook him. She needed to exhaust her anger and so he let her rage wash over him, eventually reaching out to her and taking her in his arms so she could sob into his chest, the two of them rotating slowly within the big lab, within the big station, spinning gently, silently, away into space.

He'd had a few more precious minutes to come to terms with their fate than she had, and when the first thrust of her grief had ebbed from her, he spoke with calm stoicism into her ear.

"Doctor, we are alone, yes, but we are not in any immediate danger. We have three functioning fusion cells on board, and no doubt many more lying dormant among your team's many labs around the hub. We have food enough to last many lifetimes, and water recycling facilities to keep us going long into our old age."

She pulled back from him, astonished at his serene demeanor, and her tears stopped, halted by the tranquility of his confidence.

"And, Doctor, I think we can safely say we have the best view in town."

She could not help but laugh, a laugh bordering on hysteria, perhaps, but a laugh nonetheless, and he smiled in return. Calming herself with one, long, epic sigh, a sigh that emanated from her very core, she settled her emotions.

"I have two things to say to you, Captain," she said eventually, looking into his eyes, her own still wet, but clearer now as she started to come to terms with what had happened to them, and what he had done for her. "Firstly, you are obvious completely mad." His eyes widened, as did his smile. "Which means we are probably going to get along just fine."

He laughed a little, shrugged, and nodded again as she went on. "And that is probably a good thing, because it seems we are, quite literally, going to spend the rest of our lives together."

His smiled broadened even further. It was a smile tinged with a profound pain which would take a long time to fully accept, a sadness that seemed to pull at its edges in a series of tiny tremors. But for now he kept that beneath the surface as she then pulled away from him a little, and deliberately took his hand in hers.

"Which brings me to my second point," she said, as he returned her handshake with a confused look, "which is that we should probably dispense with the Doctor and Captain nonsense."

He nodded, the mirth in his eyes becoming more genuine.

"Birgit," she said.

"Rob," he said.

They looked into each other's eyes, finding a kind of peace there. The humor was only skin deep, of course, as the stark reality of their fate kept scratching away just under the surface. But if they must face oblivion, Birgit for one knew she was glad of the company.

She looked at him as they held each other's grasp. Her look said she was about to say something else, that was going to admonish him again for being here, for sacrificing so much. But his expression was one of immovability. His look said with infinite patience and firm resilience that it was not a choice she had asked him to make, and, in fact, it had not been a choice at all when it came down to it.

It was his station, now his ship, he supposed. He could not have let one of his charges go adrift alone, it was simply not in him.

She would not forgive him for it yet, but she would spend a decade thanking him for it, and her gratitude would go a long way toward healing the pain of his loss, as his presence would go a long way toward healing hers.

Their understanding clear, their shared burden truly halved, they turned as one and looked out the window once more.

They looked out toward the beauty of Earth, a jewel in the darkness as it reared into view once more. It already seemed visibly smaller. Nodding once more and breathing deep, they turned away from it. It was a sight at once too wonderful and too terrible to behold.

- - -

Minnie: <they are almost gone. ¿why does she not reply to me?>

Amadeu: 'i don't know, minnie. maybe she is doing something aboard. maybe she doesn't know yet.'

Minnie: <they are almost out of range, soon my subspace network will not be able reach her anymore.>

Amadeu: 'i know, minnie.'

Amadeu was amazed at the way Minnie was reacting to the loss of her Artificial Parent. Proud on some level of his child, and achingly sad on another, watching her trying to comprehend the concept of loss, of grief. He wept to hear and feel Minnie struggling with her mother's departure.

And he wept for the loss of his friend as well, for the loss of that magnificent mind. Not dead, but vanishing away into the void with every moment.

He looked for a way to distract Minnie from her first brush with the harshest of reality's truths, but he knew there was virtually no task that could keep her monumental mind busy enough.

Amadeu: '¿minnie, have you finished the upload of your simulacrum to terminus?'

Minnie: <almost. it will be complete before they are out of range.>

Amadeu: 'then this is not goodbye. you will be able to speak to her every day. and we will still be able to communicate with them. they have a whole range of lasers aboard in their laboratories. your simulacrum will help them configure one to communicate with us.'

Minnie: <amadeu, i know that you must be aware that this will not be the same. ¿are you not also aware that i will never again be able to commune with her right brain? the simulacrum of me being loaded into terminus's systems is not me, and has nothing of my processing power or true capabilities. ¿are you trying to console me?>

He was, it was true; and it was pointless, Amadeu knew that. Unless ...

Amadeu: 'yes, minnie, i am. because i love you and i know birgit does too. she would speak with you if she could. i know that as well. as do you.'

Minnie: <yes, you are right. i know her like i know you. she loves me. i will miss her very much.>

Amadeu: 'so will i, minnie, so will i.'

Their shared grief was tangible in the ether, a substance clogging the very cables and airwaves that linked them. Amadeu spoke through it.

Amadeu: 'you know, minnie, there is one thing you can do. i am aware it won't affect the outcome for birgit, but it will resolve the imbalance that has led to this. you can reach out to banu, minnie. you can help her. the skalm is airborne even now, it is seeking retribution. help banu find the people responsible for this. help her hunt them.'

Minnie: <yes, amadeu. that is something i can do.>

There was a brief pause then Minnie spoke again. When her voice came to him once more, it was with a coldness and a purpose that made Amadeu shiver. They had created Minnie in order to help them fight the coming alien armada. Now she would fight a different foe, a foe closer to home, but one that posed just as great a threat to their chances of survival.

Even as she spoke to Amadeu, Minnie now focused an overwhelming part of herself on that task.

Minnie: <i am with banu now, amadeu. she is coming for them. they will not be alive much longer.>

Chapter 46: The Lion's Tail

Mikhail watched with glee as his planes tore at the concrete hulk. Mankind had long ago discovered the safety of the fortress, the great castles and forts of the Middle Ages rising as signs of power and wealth, and as safe havens for the people who ruled, both with malice and mercy. They had survived for hundreds of years, right up until the invention of gunpowder.

The quick rise of artillery in the fourteenth century had made the stone wall pointless, rendering it obsolete through blunt trauma and obliging the kings and warlords of the time to come out from behind their crumbling edifices and go on the offensive, facing their enemies on the battlefield.

And so it was even now as the mighty SpacePort One crumbled under the barrage. The remaining Ubitsyas' awesome weaponry made bloody work of SpacePort One's superstructure, even as the mighty cables that had been anchored here rose eerily into the sky. Their links to Earth severed, they now swam upward and outward into space; the very place they had been humanity's bridge to.

Mikhail himself came up now. Now that the forces around Rolas had been destroyed. He came to join the remainder of his fleet in the bloody morning's murderous conclusion.

His ship was a freak. An attempt at something akin to the Skalms of his home, but built using the only two-meter-wide resonance chamber he had managed to coax the Russian premier into making for him. The strange-looking spiny sphere came in low over the water, passing over the remnants of the taskforce fleet, and Mikhail laughed at the carnage his Ubitsyas had wrought. His smaller Skalm had only two wings, and those fitted after the central sphere had been finished. But he believed it could outrun anything on Earth and with one notable exception he was right.

One of his two wings carried a bulky subspace tweeter so he could command his small fleet, and the other wing carried his own inert Agent body, slaved to the ship, but ready should he need it.

He reveled in his faith that his little ball of fury could outrun anything the humans had, even the StratoJets, and the knowledge that it could also go exo-atmospheric if need be. He grinned with a cold cheer as he joined his remaining Ubitsyas and opened up his weapons as well. Not flechette guns, but three thin particle beams, lancing out of some of the smaller nozzles on his spherical hull and the ends of his stubby wings.

He had only twenty-five Ubitsyas left. He had known it would be costly, but with the StratoJet fleet distracted it had been all but a foregone conclusion. He knew he did not have much longer, though. With the StratoJets finally returning to their nest, he would have to leave or face yet another fight, and he would be unlikely to win again. But he would leave them only ruins to come home to. He would leave this place slagged, and destroyed.

He had exacted a terrible cost on his enemies today. He knew they would hunt him, but they would not catch him.

Mikhail watched as the StratoJet fleet closed. He would wait until the last moment before pulling his fleet back. He would lead them on a merry chase, try to save a few Ubitsyas if he could, but go space bound if he couldn't, and escape them, until Pei, safe in Beijing, signaled to let him know what target to hit next.

But the StratoJets weren't coming.

Mikhail watched the TASC fleet on his sensors. Ten StratoJets now, more incoming, but already enough to engage his smaller, weaker, and frankly less well-piloted Ubitsyas with a very real chance of victory.

But they were holding back. What were these fools waiting for? Had he shocked them so much with his attack? Had he finally cowered them into subservience? He laughed. He would win this war single-handedly. He would deliver this great orb into the hands of the Armada tied and wrapped for their pleasure. These humans were fools to have thought they could stop the Agents. Fools to have even dreamed of building an armada capable of stopping the great Mobiliei fleet even now descending on them.

But still this was strange. Mikhail could not question their tenacity in a fight. No, the humans were nothing if not tenacious. So why were they not engaging?

But the reason was coming up fast now, faster than any sound that might have preceded it, seemingly trying to catch the very light waves bouncing off its crossed wings as it came up at Rolas with ferocious abandon. It would only be a few minutes longer now.

- - -

Premier Svidrigaïlov blustered with ever growing bravado at the ambassadors arranged on the screens in front of him. In the face of his army's rebuffed incursion into Hungary and his top commandant's sudden disappearance, he had opened his doors to diplomatic conversation for the first time since taking power. Peter had advised him that he had little choice.

The leaders of Western Europe were already talking of regime change in Russia, of a forced incursion into Moscow, of all out war. He knew they wouldn't do that, they could not risk it, but neither could he risk insulting them any further now that his very best general, the very reason behind his success to date, had gone rogue.

He spoke without apology though, "Ladies, gentlemen, please, you forget who has invited you here today. Do not mistake the brief success of your forces over the last couple of days for anything other than the need for me to send some of my more capable troops to take down the *illegal* ..." he grossly over-emphasized the word, "... space elevator that your countries built ..."

He went on even as the collected ambassadors erupted at this mention of the attack on Rolas. They could not know he had not ordered it, that he had not even known it was occurring until after it was almost over, and Premier Svidrigaïlov certainly was not going to tell them. Better to take credit for it now that it was done, and take care of the traitor Beria later.

"... that your countries built, *without* UN permission." They were shouting at him now, indignant, news of the collapse of the great elevator filling the airwaves. Words like 'peaceful' and 'humanitarian' were being used to describe the elevator, while words like 'act-of-terror' were being used to describe his commandant's actions.

The premier continued to speak over their objections, "Your lies did not fool me, and they did not fool the Russian people. The Space Elevator was a *weapon*, nothing more. A weapon built by the Americans and their allies in Europe to build a military capability in space. You built it with the sole intention of militarizing space, in violation of the Outer Space Treaty, and the proposed PAROS Treaty, and Russia was not about to allow that to happen!"

It was, under its sheen, a bluff; even if, deeper still, the lie had its roots in a reality the premier could not even guess at. But he marched on, shouting at the ambassadors of his erstwhile allies and neighbors, no stranger to the push and pull of international brinkmanship.

The call went on, achieving nothing except the reopening of diplomatic channels with the petulant Russian would-be emperor, and in that alone it might have been considered a step in the right direction. But there were some around the globe that were no longer interested in small steps. They wanted leaps and bounds and they were prepared to make them.

A quarter of a mile away across Red Square, from three top-floor windows of an all but empty state library, two men and one woman leveled their weapons. They could not see the premier's exact location but the signal being relayed to them from one of Minnie's communications AIs showed him sitting in a conference room that they knew to be below and to the right of his main office. Minnie was relaying the schematics directly.

Hektor's team triangulated the image they were seeing of the premier arguing with various foreign ministers and secretaries of state, with schematics born of half a century of information gathering, focused on this very building. They adjusted their firing controls to encompass a meter-wide point on the orange and white brick exterior of one of the Kremlin's many vast edifices. They waited.

They waited until the very moment the Russian man nodded to his assistant to break the connection, and the instant the screens went blank they opened fire.

Even as the ambassadors of various NATO powers no doubt went off to inform their respective leaders of the unreasonableness of the Russian leader, the wall behind Yuri Svidrigaïlov started to shake. The ancient brick seeming to flake and vibrate and turn to dust and suddenly three streams of blurred energy were slicing into the room, shredding the Russian man and spraying his blood like mist over the screens he had been so belligerently shouting into a moment before.

Peter Uncovsky watched from one side, stunned as his president suddenly evaporated, simply vanished in a haze of energetic rage. Rage that could have penetrated a tank's armor, and which now obliterated any last remnant of Premier Yuri Svidrigaïlov and pounded onward, drilling through the desk, the monitors, and almost through the wall beyond.

As the cloud that had once been a man filled the room, the three assassins silenced their tri-barrel cannons and waited. They could not stay where they were for long, but nor could they leave till they had confirmation of their success.

Walking across the square below their friend Tomas suddenly started to accelerate. He was young and relatively inexperienced, but he was also one of the fastest runners they had in the battleskins. They watched him start to sprint, they watched him build up speed, the stunned crowd looking from the sudden hole that had appeared in the side of one of their most important national monuments to the man sprinting at inhuman speed toward it. He calculated his jump, then braced and catapulted himself into the air.

The secretaries and guards filing into the conference room to join Peter Uncovsky were stunned by the sudden rolling landing of Tomas through the ragged hole that had been opened up in the wall. He was clothed like an ordinary russian, but his helmet had folded up to cover his head as he leaped through the air and as his lumberjack shirt flapped around his arms and neck, his black armor could be seen coating his body beneath.

He landed in the debris of the room but did not hesitate. As he skidded across the floor, Russian guards among the throng were already starting to shout.

"стоп! конец!" they barked, calling for him to freeze. They were reaching for their guns but Tomas was not going to wait around for them to fire. He had seen all he needed to. With relish he used their subspace comms for the first time in a week.

Tomas: 'the premier is … gone. target is confirmed dead.'

Hektor: 'move, tomas. mission confirmed. get out of there. recon team two, covering fire.'

Even as he had started sending his signal Tomas had already started gripping at the floor, kicking and scrabbling to halt his ridiculous momentum, and then turning and running back out the way he had come, using all his machine strength to get the hell out of the hornet's nest he had jumped into before they figured out what was happening. A bullet or two rang out as he leapt clear once more, but he was already gone, vanishing as quickly as he had come.

They watched him come flying back out of the crumbling red brick dust like he was being fired from a cannon. Hektor had cleared them to use subspace comms for this core part of the operation.

Hektor: 'niels, blanket that hole with fire once he's clear in case any of them decide to fire out after him. cara, take out the apc coming into the square at [1342.4596]. bohdan, frederik, you have your fields of fire, take out anyone following tomas.'

They were already doing it, the APC folding and crumpling into a molten heap as Cara fragged it, the hole behind Tomas's flying figure blurring once more as Niels bathed it in hypersonic fire. As Tomas landed and began sprinting away across the square, uniformed figures all across its wide expanse were reeling and falling, picked off by the barium lasers and sonic punches of Bohdan and Frederik.

Hektor watched even as he covered his own sector, taking down assailants left and right. He was starting to feel something close to confidence, though he would never call it that.

Confidence that they would make it. The primary plan was going to work. And with that he redirected his fire to a small, innocuous manhole cover about a hundred meters ahead of Tomas.

With a precise circle of fire, he punched the manhole out, and as the concrete and cobblestones around it cracked and crumbled, it began to fall into the sewage line it was covering. It was still falling toward the floor of the drainage pipe as Tomas was dropping into a skidding slide, like he was sliding into home plate, and then he was gone, dropping out of sight and into the sewer below.

Hektor: 'tomas is clear. everyone, go! go! meet at rendezvous point alpha. comms silence reinitiated!'

And with that it was over. The bewildered citizens and surviving soldiers tried to compute what had even happened as Hektor's team all turned as one from their vantage points and skitted this way and that, following well-planned routes down, down, into the labyrinth of tunnels under the medieval city and away. Anyone who dared to chase any of them would pay dearly, if they could keep up.

- - -

Mikhail was fighting an unsettling feeling. He looked at the burning, crumbling hulk of the SpacePort. It was done. He could refocus his fire on the complex across the water on mainland Sao Tome, but that would mean coming into range of the phalanx of guns protecting the complex's land border. No, he had killed this place, he had destroyed it, more completely than he had dared to hope.

No. Something was wrong. They should be attacking him. They should have engaged. Enough. He had won. It was time to leave.

He ordered his Ubitsyas to withdraw and they banked hard as one, falling in behind his own ship as a shield as he accelerated away.

Then he saw it. Coming from the south.

Big enough to be ...

Fast enough ...

No, he thought. No! It could not be. They could not have built a resonance dome big enough. No. Could he have been so foolish? Had he been so focused on the SpacePort that he had missed the greater threat?

He veered with all his vehicle's power, ignoring the Ubitsyas, who flew on, confused, toward the coming star-cross.

They saw it as but a blur on their scanners.

And Banu saw them all. She saw them and she heard the voice of Minnie in her mind.

Minnie: <banu, these are your targets. these are your prey. hunt them all.>

She watched the first one, a smaller, almost cute attempt at her own form's might. She saw it veer away and begin to flee, and she chuckled at the futility of its flight. She could see it was going as fast as it little furry legs would carry it. It was quaint, really.

But she would deal with these others first. Her talons were a series of particle beams lensing out from the spiny front of her body and her four wings. They found the Ubitsyas and dug into them. The first fell after a few moments, its armor providing some respite before the beams ate through it, folding the plane in on itself like a sock being pulled inside out. In about five seconds the wings came together and the whole plane was sucked into the hot core of her fire and then it was gone, a vapor, but a ghost on the wind.

The rest opened fire as they came into range and she reacted, rolling and spinning with wild abandon as she came at them, making the vast cross a whirlwind rather than a target, like firing into an approaching tornado. But her attack never relented even as she span. Firing in impossibly small windows as they closed on each other, she clawed at their little bodies, the killing real for her now, the struggle and gore of the fight vivid and true.

The Ubitsya pilots continued to die in the seconds before they were on her and she was glancing between them, her massive size preposterously agile. Mikhail, still fleeing to the northwest, watched the dog fight with barely restrained anguish. In a desperate move, he slaved two of the Ubitsyas and tried to collide them directly with her core as they passed by each other.

She giggled at it, at the impertinence of it, as she whipped between them, their attacks molasses slow to her as she spun her entire self and during the milliseconds of their passing, rotated the whole of the Skalm, whipping her guns around.

In that critical micro-event of the passing, she even used her engine as a weapon and as she glinted between two of the Ubitsyas trying to collide their very selves with her, she sliced at one with her forward particle beams and brought her roaring engine across the face of the other.

At such range, with her power untethered by fear or mercy, they sublimed in the stellar fire of the Skalm's core, turning to vapor in an instant. And then she was turned, rotated, her carbon nanotube beams screeching with the strain as she began to decelerate, and even as the final Ubitsyas tried to turn to face her once more, she was already lensing them with her beam once more, chasing down and extinguishing the last of them.

Two minutes. Twenty-five enemies dead.

Mikhail did not mourn their passing. Whether it was callousness or mere terror, he did not even look back as the last of them died. He must hide. If he could reach land, then decelerate enough, he might be able to eject his Agent body and escape.

With zeal, Banu turned her focus on the last of her prey.

Banu: '¿where are you, little rabbit?'

He was a hundred miles away already. Minnie was still watching him, her desire to 'resolve the imbalance' matched only by Banu's appetite for the hunt.

Minnie: <he is there, banu. right [there].>

His location appeared as a beacon in Banu's mind and she was accelerating again in the same instant. All of her five engines giving their all, nothing spared even for weapons in this moment of hot pursuit.

He ran. He hoped to reach land before she caught him, but her acceleration was stupendous. This was real. This was a Skalm. And like any Mobiliei, Mikhail knew what that meant. It was the limit of material engineering. The point where the peaks of energy, strength, and mental capacity were strained to the very brink. Until they learned how to break one of those seeming absolutes, there was nothing more fearsome than one of these beasts on either Mobilius or Earth.

It could be killed, of course it could. And it could be tracked, indeed its need to constantly expend the ridiculous power generated by its five cores made it about as subtle and easy to hide as an erupting volcano.

If he had a nuclear weapon at his disposal and the will to use it, even against every iota of his mission's parameters, then he might have been able to kill it.

But he did not.

So he fled, even as his tactical options dwindled to zero.

He fled across the treetops of the Amazon. He fled all the way to the Northern Andes. And here, among the fallen cities of the Incas, he dodged and ducked and dived in a last hopeless attempt to escape.

Like so many of Banu's virtual prey had before, Mikhail sought refuge behind any obstacle that might hide him from her fury. Mikhail darted behind mountains, banked into valleys, tightly hugged cliffs, and streaked past ice-faced peaks.

The ground and air shook with the chase, and Banu giggled with glee at the speed of it.

But she was merely toying with him.

Minnie: <banu, end it. this is not a game. you could hurt someone.>

She was disappointed but she understood. For a moment, Mikhail thought, she faltered, but then she came on at an even greater pace. He had hoped she might fail, that she might miss.

She did not. She dug into his ship's flesh with her particle beam talons and ripped at it. She knew this was real. She knew this was killing. And she did it with a relish bordering on ecstasy.

After a moment of his armor resisting the hot beams, there was a flash. As the shell of his ship cracked Mikhail's cores fluttered for an instant, then, as his own engines' might was rent asunder and exposed, his ship detonated and was gone.

Chapter 47: Ebb

The calls came in fairly quick succession after the attack was over. The leaders of the world's great powers were demanding an accounting. At first belligerent at the destruction of their massive investment on Rolas, then quieted somewhat by the soft, calm cadence of Neal's rebuttals, and then stunned, quite literally into silence by the change in his stance toward them.

Neal was on the fourth of those calls right now. A call with the French president. He had spoken with the German, British, and Brazilian leaders already. Jim Hacker and the US president were, apparently, waiting for him to return their requests for conference. Well, they could wait until he was ready.

"Monsieur President, I thank you again for your candor, but ask once more that you listen to my reply more closely."

"I am listening, Dr. Danielson, and I appreciate your calm attitude here, but I might actually appreciate it more if you would show a little more emotion. Two French Corsair-Class destroyers were sunk today, lost with all hands. Sixteen Rafale fighter jets shot down. Hundreds of French lives lost, and for what, Doctor? The SpacePort fell. We gave you those units, we trusted command of them to your *taskforce*," the word was said with venom, "because you said you needed them to protect our investment. But yet you have failed to protect it, Neal. I am sorry to say it but you have failed."

Neal let the man finish his rant, then waited a moment for him to catch his breath, before saying, "Mr. President, it saddens me that you mistake my calm tone for a lack of emotion. But I will move past the inherent insult you proffer by implying that I do not care for what has happened here." He heard the French leader go to speak, but did not give him the chance, "I have felt the loss just as much as you today, and so much more, Mr. President, so very much more. I will not trouble you with details, but suffice to say that everyone here has lost friends today, friends that will be missed more than you can know."

He spoke of the hundreds of his colleagues, both military and scientific, who had died in the attack. He spoke of Admirals Cochrane and Takano, of Captain Bhade, and of all their brave sailors and pilots who had fought till the end. He spoke of Dr. Hauptman and the inconceivably brave Captain Cashman who had chosen to stay with her as he jettisoned them both off into space.

And he spoke of his friend, one the first of his allies in this long, bloody war. A man they still had not been able to find. A man that his people on site at Rolas searched for even now in the rubble that had been man's first SpacePort. A man whose loss Neal was going to have to come to terms with over the next days and weeks as they lost hope of ever finding his remains in the bloody stump that was the once mighty SpacePort.

A man whose wife was, even now, exacting cold revenge on the Russian forces still left alive in Western Ukraine, neutering the once mighty Russian Army one battalion at a time with her scalpel-like Spezialist forces.

"Monsieur President, I think it is important to stress that I speak to you now not to offer apologies or explanations, that time has passed. I speak to you now from the base formerly known as Rolas Base, from now on to be referred to as TASC District One. I speak to you now from the base I fully intend to rebuild. In fact, I have already initiated plans for that work, including the production of the machines I will need, to be built at TASC District Two."

"District Two?" the Frenchman asked, still trying to process what Neal was saying.

"Yes, Mr. President, TASC District Two, formerly Deception Island, a small, desolate place in the South Seas, but the site of the until-now secret development of my first full-sized Resonance Dome, the source of the craft you have no doubt been hearing about from your intelligence services. The craft that finally dispatched the Russian and Chinese air force that attacked SpacePort One."

"Dr. Danielson, I hate to correct you once more," said the French leader, as his counterparts had earlier, "but you speak of *your* Resonance Dome, and *your* forces. Now more than ever, I must insist that you recognize that these are forces that are on loan to you, and given the events of the last few days, that trust in you is going to need to be rebuilt if you hope to continue to enjoy the support of France and her allies."

"Your point is well taken, Mr. President, but once again, I am afraid you are not listening to me. I speak to you now not from a position of leadership over a taskforce, but as the leader of an independent military body. As of this moment, I am declaring the Terrestrial Allied Space Command as a state unto itself. A nationalized state, with, for now, only ninety citizens, though more are swearing allegiance as we speak. At its head: myself, Ayala Zubaideh, and Madeline Cavanagh. Among our generals are Jack Toranssen, Quavoce Mantil, and John Hunt. Among our citizens, well, you need only concern yourself with one: Banu Mantil."

The Frenchman was silent, profoundly silent, and with no small amount of relish Neal went on, "I speak to you now as the appointed representative of that state, and inform you that your support, while not required, will be asked for. But your interference in any matter that we deem of importance will *not be tolerated.*

"Mr. President, as of today I represent a small but incredibly powerful military body. A military that can reach anyone, anywhere. A military that recently summarily executed the illegitimate leader of Russia for crimes against humanity."

The Frenchman blurted, "You did what! That was you? We had assumed, no, we had hoped, that the death of Svidrigaïlov had been the work of internal forces, retribution for his defeat in Hungary. But it was you! This will not stand, Dr. Danielson, we will be speaking with our representatives at the Hague, we will …"

"No, Mr. President, you will not!" Neal shouted, raising his voice for the first and last time in the meeting. "Whether you appreciate it or not, I am engaged in the most important project in human history. A project so vital that any act against it is an act of the vilest treason, and as of this very moment I am here to tell you that such acts will not be tolerated.

Not anymore, not from anyone, not even you, am I making myself clear? I am here to tell you that TASC will defend itself and its mission, with lethal force if necessary, against any and all threats. Do you understand me, Mr. President?"

The Frenchman was silent, no doubt quite stunned. Good, thought Neal.

So Neal went on, reinstating his sheen of calm like a shield over his barely contained wrath, "And let me also take this opportunity to tell you that TASC is officially declaring independent oversight over not only District One here on Rolas, and District Two on the island of Deception. We are also declaring TASC District Three in the mountains of Japan. My representative there, Ms. Cavanagh, and her liaison Mr. Matsuoka, have already begun negotiations for the annexation of that land with the Japanese government, in return for concessions in the *Fourth* TASC District."

Neal took a breath. This was the fourth time he had said these words, or ones to their effect, and it was equal parts terrifying and liberating to do so. "TASC District Four, over which we are also claiming unlimited and exclusive sovereignty as of this moment, represents the only one of our four districts that is not currently claimed by anyone else, and yet I am sure it will also be the most hotly contested. TASC District Four represents that place we must, by rite of our mission, have unquestioned access and domain over.

"As of today, Mr. President, we claim sovereignty over space. With a unique ability to defend it, and, once the Space Elevator is rebuilt, unparalleled access to it, I am here to tell you now that any country wishing to maintain a presence of any kind outside of Earth's atmosphere is going to have to actively participate in and contribute to our work. I come to you today not to ask for your permission to move forward, the days of me having to negotiate for the right to save humanity are through. I come here today to *offer* permission, Mr. President. Permission to continue to use your communications satellites. Permission to continue to have access to GPS and other data sources, and permission to use the new SpacePort we will build here and the others we have planned around the equator to maintain those systems."

Neal went silent to allow the Frenchman to respond, and to object, as Neal knew he must.

After a moment the president did not disappoint, "Neal … Doctor … it is clear to me that you have lost your grip on reality. I will not negotiate with you over such things. You have gone too far. This is madness. We all appreciate the importance of what you are doing but you have crossed the line. Your team, if it wishes to continue to exist, will have to work within the agreed upon terms and conditions, and operate with international law! And whatever happens, your days of running, or even participating in this effort are through, Dr. Danielson. France will not negotiate with terrorists! Hear me now when I say you will be held accountable for this."

Neal smiled coldly, then spoke with the clear French perfection his link with Minnie allowed him to, "Mr. President, I will ignore your posturing and threats, mostly out of respect for our past work together, but also because I no longer care whether you agree with me or not. You have been informed of our terms. Your state department, along with all other members of the UN, will be receiving the details of our new Independent Charter shortly. You can cooperate, or you can not. You can participate, or you can not. You can keep your nation's technological place in the twenty-first century, or you can watch your economy fail as you compete with nations that still have access to satellite communications, and to the advanced technologies we will continue to provide to our allies.

"The choice is yours, Mr. President. I hope you will take the time to consider it very carefully. But whatever you decide, be under no illusions. *Any* incursion into *any* of the districts detailed in our charter, *any* attack on our citizens, their families, or our ships, both naval or in space, will be met with the deadliest of force. As will any actions, either military or economic, that are taken against nations that choose to ally with us.

"We will build Earth's defenses, Mr. President. We will drag humanity into a new era of technological capability whether you want us to or not. I hope you will join us, but that, my friend, is up to you. Ask yourself this, though: if you refuse us, we will be forced to approach your opponents in the French leadership. And what, do you think, will the French people do when your rivals come bearing all the gifts we can offer?"

And with that he closed the line, the time for diplomacy was done. His next call would be to the US president, a man who had tempered his initial pride somewhat since their first meeting, but who, unfortunately, had ever less to offer Neal's cause. So Neal would offer him something he could not refuse: protection. A chance to stop spending on his nation's military, a force that was soon to be obsolete anyway. A chance to bring his troops home and repurpose them to the job of rebuilding their nation.

Neal would ask for two things in return. Firstly, the gifting, not loaning, of two of the US's once mighty aircraft carriers to form the hub of his rebuilding at District One and his growing operations at District Two. And the second thing: the willing release of Jack Toranssen, Jennifer Falster, and the host of other American pilots, commandoes, seals, and scientists that were even now being invited to join his growing city-state.

The call would, surprisingly, be the easiest he would have that morning, and Neal would be even more surprised, and happy even, when Jim Hacker asked to be among those new citizens. Though he spoke of his new state as foregone conclusion, he would need the help of experienced administrators and governors in order to make it viable.

- - -

Once the most important calls were finished, Neal changed his focus once more. He was tired and beaten, but also newly invigorated by his mission. But he had one more important piece of housecleaning to do.

Neal: '¿minnie, have we received news from quavoce and jennifer?'

Minnie: <they are closing in now, neal, and banu is in position.>

If any of his potential allies needed further demonstration of his resolve, they were about to get it.

Chapter 48: A Bull in China

The fleet was small, almost invisible. Three Slinks silently penetrating the night sky over Siberia, then down over Novosibirsk. Tracking all the way, following a signal.

The call had been simple. A request to talk. Not face-to-face but via subspace. Quavoce and the final Mobiliei Agent, talking in the ether.

It was a long and bitter conversation.

Pei Leong-Lam: 'quavoce, i still do not see what the point of this call is. you are a traitor, pure and simple. certainly you have had some success but only because you managed to hide the resonance dome from us. you cannot think you will be able hide it much longer. eventually i will get to it. just like i will get to your *new moon one, when it returns.*'

Quavoce: 'pei, my friend …'

Pei: 'i am not your friend, quavoce.'

Quavoce: 'no. no, you are not, pei. no one could be my friend who would support such a genocidal mission as yours.'

Pei: 'oh please, quavoce, save you rhetoric for the plebs. you will find no converts here. these humans and their petty struggles. they have all but ruined this planet. we will be doing earth a favor by eradicating this infestation.'

Quavoce: '¿and we did any better with mobilius, pei? ¿are we such saints that we can pronounce judgment on these people?'

Pei: 'do not think you can bandy logic here, quavoce. this is not judgment. this is conquest. pure and simple. and it needs no further explanation than that. they have something we need. they will not give it to us and we cannot take it without them dying. so they must die. it is not pretty, i grant you, but nor is it difficult to understand if you are honest with yourself. ¿when did you become so soft?'

They had been speaking for nearly two hours, but now, in another part of his mind, Quavoce felt another voice.

Jennifer Falster at Quavoce: 'the signal has reached its terminus, sir. it is beijing, as we suspected. the headquarters of the politburo standing committee. he must have taken at least wu jiabao hostage, sir. possibly others.'

Quavoce at Cpt. Falster and Minnie: 'thank you, jennifer. please deploy your troops in a cordon and stand by. minnie, let neal and banu know, please, if you haven't already.'

She pinged a confirmation and Quavoce returned to his conversation with Pei.

Quavoce: 'you call me soft, pei. soft is an interesting word. and one we often misuse. following difficult orders can be hard, but refusing to follow orders you know to be wrong can be harder still.'

Pei: '¿and is that how you justify this, quavoce? that you are a big, brave, boy for refusing to follow your orders, for betraying your own people to fight for another.'

Quavoce: 'no pei. as another, better man once said to me, i do not need to justify standing against genocide, pei, you need to justify committing it. and you have not, pei, not by a long shot. this is a war of greed, not of the mobiliei race as a whole, but of its leaders. and john and i are going to try and stop that, not for the humans, but for the sake of all mobiliei …'

Pei: 'quavoce, do not pretend that …'

Quavoce: 'just shut up and listen, pei. you do not have much time left. we know where you are. we are coming for you even now. do not think you can run. you have nowhere to hide now. you are alone. we have advanced troops surrounding your position …'

Pei went to scoff, but Quavoce went on.

Quavoce: 'they are not there to fight you, pei. just to track you. the fighting will be left to a little girl. a little girl piloting a skalm, a fully functional skalm, inbound on your position as we speak.'

Pei did not let it go through the wires but he flinched at the word. He had seen the blurred images circulating the world's military intelligence networks. There had been attempts to photograph the shadow as it flew over South America. He had known what it might mean and he had feared it, but he had not believed it. He tried not to even now.

Quavoce: '¿not so confident now, pei? yes, my former friend, this is the skalm that killed agent kovalenko. and he was in a fusion fighter of his own. you are not. you are in the politburo standing committee headquarters in beijing's government district. so i give you this simple ultimatum: surrender now or be obliterated.'

Pei: 'i care not for this machine body, you fool! and anyway, you would not dare come at me here. you would have to kill half the chinese leadership to do it. are you willing to do that! are you!'

Quavoce: 'yes, pei. at this point, we are. they have been nothing but a hindrance anyway, and while you cannot know yet, the game has changed. you and Mikhail have forced our hand, pei. you have forced us to break from our political allies and stand alone. whatever you do, the chinese leadership that has sheltered and abetted you will answer for their crimes, we will see to that. so it really just comes down to this: will you send them to jail or to hell; we do not care which.'

Pei looked around. He wanted to believe that they did not have the courage to do it, but knew that he would be a fool to assume they were incapable of such things after what he and Mikhail had done to the SpacePort and its defenders. He thought of running, of leaving this place. But as he considered this option, he knew he did not have anywhere left to run. He was the last of his ilk. To think he could make much of a difference if he gave up his position here, at the heart of the most populace country on earth, to think that would be folly.

If he could even escape.

A Skalm was a fearsome thing to have chasing you. A lion hunting a mouse, and even if he could scurry beneath some rock, the troopers Quavoce had told him were out there would eventually find him. No, his only hope lay in staying his execution a while longer. His only hope lay in using his still powerful influence over the Chinese government and military to call what he hoped was a bluff.

The Chinese Politburo Standing Committee Chairman, effectively the most powerful man in China, and in some ways, the world, was weeping at Pei's side. He was a phenomenally clever man. A man who had achieved his high post through wit, dedication, and hard work, combined with an unholy dedication, both to his own success and to the party. His reputation as such had carried him through the last few months. It was a reputation that had kept the rest of the committee loyal despite a series of devastating foreign policy decisions during that time.

"Chairman," said Pei out loud to the Chinese man, his voice thick with disdain, "you will alert your military. Your nation is under attack. Your borders and airspace have been violated. You will send notice to the Americans and Europeans that they must withdraw or face nuclear reprisal. You will do it now!"

To emphasize his point, Pei sent a signal to the device by which he controlled the poor man. Embedded in the Chinese leader's back, a small, clawed machine twitched at its master's bequest, pulling and tearing at the man's flesh in the most terrible ways. The chairman cried out as he had so many times as his wounds bled into the dressings that covered them. The only thing that had stopped his permanently open lesions from festering was the synthetic antigen Madeline had created and given the world. An antigen that even now coursed through the powerful politician's blood keeping his wounds healthy so the torture could continue. The irony was not lost on Pei.

"Yes, Pei. Of course." said the politician as he moved toward his phone.

Pei: '¿did you hear that, quavoce? even now the chinese leader is activating his military and his nuclear arsenal. even *you* would not risk nuclear war. withdraw your troops. call off the skalm. i will not ask again.'

Quavoce did not reply immediately. Far away, Neal sighed. He had hoped to avoid it, but he feared they could not wait any longer. They could not let the Chinese leader complete that call. Ayala, also listening, was not so reluctant.

Ayala: 'neal, order it. do it now. they have declared war on us and committed an atrocity. they must pay.'

Her anger and thirst for retribution was terrible. They had broken something deep within her when they had killed the man she loved. Her capacity for mercy had died with Barrett. Neal asked once more.

Neal: '¿quavoce, can he be turned? ¿is there any hope of a peaceful end to this?'

Quavoce: 'i cannot be certain of such things, neal. but if you are asking for my opinion, then the answer is no. i fear there is only one solution here.'

Minnie: <banu is ten seconds out. ¿is she cleared to attack?>

There was a pause, and then ...

Neal: 'she is.'

- - -

A Skalm.

A crossed wing built as one whole in order to withstand the forces it was trying to contain. It did not fly into Beijing, it came down upon it. Viewing the city from directly above, it descended on a tall, luxurious office building. The center of the single political party in the façade that was the Chinese democratic system.

Banu did not go for precision. The order was simple. The target was somewhere inside that building. Triangulating the chain of subspace relays that had been placed between here and Moscow had led, inexorably, to this place.

Banu could make out in her infinitely precise view of the ground the tiny black specs that were the three Slinks, poised on rooftops around the main government complex. Informed as she was of the locations of the Spezialists Ayala had sent, Banu could also overlay their stealthy presence as they fanned out around her quarry. But they would not be needed.

At the center of that circle was the building. The target was in the building. The target was the building.

0.03

0.02

0.01

She ejected her mighty engines' power, focusing it all downward into five stellar lances as she descended at stupendous speed toward the ground. The inhabitants of the capital spun in shock as the white beams pierced the edifice, seemingly driven into to it by the star suddenly plummeting from the sky.

Under the merciless beams the huge building instantly began folding in on itself, falling and crumbling into the epicenter of the attack. Inside, the Chinese chairman was only just bringing the headset of his phone to his ear, and would not even know what hit him before he was vaporized. Pei, however, would experience a split second of regret as he realized his gamble had failed. Just a split second before his world turned white, then black.

And in an instant, the last of the Agents were gone, along with the politburo's headquarters, a hundred lives, and the last semblance of the sanctity of Earth's once sovereign nations.

At the last possible moment, Banu spun the Skalm on its axis, flipping it in a flash and instantly putting all her might now into her thrusters, halting her tumultuous descent with a scream of her fusion lungs, her white owl's wings brushing the walls of the barn as she powered her ship backward, up and away once more.

China's vast and advanced military was not without reaction. A series of missiles had been dispatched to intercept the Skalm and the first were almost upon it now. But the protocols and response times of the massive military machine that had once been home to a hopeful and indeed successful Agent Pei Leong-Lam were simply not designed to account for the severity and speed of the Skalm's attack, and the missiles, fast as they were, were now but spears thrown after a departing god.

As they came striking in, the Skalm was reversing her fall with a downward thrust that beggared belief. The power of the engines' mighty plumes as the Skalm all but touched the ground turned the rubble of the building she had just destroyed into nothing but a wide smoldering crater, a wound at the very heart of China's capital and a testament for any and all watching world leaders to the folly of standing against Neal's new nation-state.

With the lair of the last Agent obliterated, the Skalm surged skyward as quickly as it arrived, the swarm of Chinese missiles accelerating up after it in a brash but futile attempt to smite it. Banu did not even bother to swat at the little pests. Her fusion rockets blared like stars as she surged up, up and back out of the atmosphere.

She was returning to orbit. The Skalm was far happier in the vacuum of space anyway. She was returning to her perch, high in the eaves of Earth's skies, there to patiently wait, ready to descend on any prey foolish enough to cross her or her friends again.

Epilogue

Earth's mightiest achievements burn. SpacePort One is razed to the ground, reduced to a massive pile of dirt and bone. But it will not be cleared. It will be a foundation. A foundation for a new SpacePort. Built to the same specifications as the first, but defended now with the full merciless might that is TASC. At the head of that defense is soon-to-be General Jack Toranssen, leading TASC's military forces in Barrett Milton's stead.

At his side is Ayala. A general she is not. But she is one of Jack and Neal's greatest weapons, second only to Banu and her Skalm. As Ayala informs her erstwhile comrades within the world's intelligence organizations of TASC's full intent and commitment, few doubt her resolve. They will strategize ways to circumvent her and TASC as a whole. They will look for weaknesses, ways to help their respective governments regain control of the rogue group, but for now they will correctly advise that to resist them by force would be tantamount to suicide.

In the wake of the attack in Beijing, the world's leaders will listen.

But while open acts of aggression will be hard to find, willing allies will be just as few and far between. With the help of Jim Hacker, America will be the first to sign a treaty with Neal, though only out of necessity. Brazil will follow, having seen the full might of the Skalm up close, and as the conquered nations of Russia's fledgling empire are freed, they will also answer the call in droves.

Europe will eventually follow, reluctantly. First in drabs, then as a whole, refusing to be left out of the flow of technological marvels coming out of Districts Two and Three.

They will bicker. They will complain. But none will be foolish enough to suggest trying to stand against Neal and his growing nation of followers. For individually, the brave and the brilliant will flock to his banner, drawn by curiosity, valor, or greed. They will be vetted. And they will be watched by Minnie and her more elusive cousin Mynd as the two Artificial Minds help Neal and his team manage the ever-greater enterprise.

Meanwhile, Birgit Hauptman and Rob Cashman will continue to fall away from Earth, entering a wild and doomed orbit of the sun, a new, if temporary celestial body. They will work hard every day. Birgit on her many experiments, Rob on maintaining the station, using the many robotic devices in its complement to mount the lasers it will need both to communicate with Earth and to fend off its fellow stellar debris. They have little hope of getting home on their own, but their part in the coming war is far from over.

Among Neal's inner circle there will be talk of going after them and maybe they will be able to, one day. But for now the only ships capable of chasing them down are tasked with vastly more important missions.

New Moon One is latching on to Asteroid 1979 va, and even now the telescopes of Earth can see the huge rock being saddled and broken. They will start home soon, bringing with them two million tons of iron, oxygen, hydrogen, gold, platinum, and a host of other materials, both exotic and inert.

The other ship that might retrieve the lost Terminus is the Skalm. But it cannot be sent for a wholly different reason. It is Neal's guarantee. His promise to the world: cross us and suffer. Help us and behold: this is what we can do. We will build Earth such wonders as will defy imagination. And we will defend her against the coming Armada.

But Neal's confidence is only a show. As he contemplates the marvel that is the Skalm and its nation-killing power, he thinks of the time and investment it took to construct just one of the mighty ships. He thinks of the state of his world, and the toll this war has already taken. Then he looks skyward and contemplates the thousand Skalms that he knows are coming for us even now, and as he stares into the blackness he trembles with fear.

Look for the third and final chapter in The Fear Saga: *Fear the Future*, coming in November 2014.

I hope you enjoyed *Fear the Survivors*, and would love to hear from you. To join the conversation or sign up to receive updates on The Fear Saga, and other upcoming novels, you can find me on Facebook, post a question for me on Goodreads, or just send me an email at TheFearSaga@gmail.com.

In a sea of new authors and large publishing houses, getting your work discovered is ever harder. Reviews on Amazon are hugely important, especially to independent authors. If you have enjoyed the series so far, I really hope you'll help spread the word.

Thank you, and see you in November,
-Stephen Moss

Made in the USA
Columbia, SC
12 May 2020